The Whale Isles

Komokome   Chemish

North
Enw...
Sou...
En...

Bereswek

Ailernots

The North Reach

Ferrins

The Kargad Lands

The Andrades

The North Teeth

Orandrad

Hur-
at-Hur

Nesretth

The Jaws

The S. Teeth   Andrad

Oranéa

...mouth   Perregal

Gar...ilirion

Gont   Gont Port

Kameber   South
Port

Spevy

Atnini

Ebéa

Awabath

Atuan

Barnisk

Tombs

Törheven

Karego-At

Reyman
K. Mts

Eskel

Onn

The
Torikles

B. Great
Port

Kembermouth

Eskel

The Hands

Way

Felkway

Shelieth

Vemish   Sattins

Straits

Waymarsh

Mishport   Yor

Otokne

Perilane

Venway

Outer
Innran

The East Reach

Sneg

The Closed Sea

Bars of Uny

Tsmay

Far
Toly

Tok

Iffish

Koppish

Korp

Uny

Holp

Insmer

Namien

Kopp

Apsa

Rola-
meny

Soders

The
Sellets

Misk

Dunnel

Gale

Pelimer

Wasny
Shoals

Gosk

Kornay

The Great South Shoals

Isle of the
Ear

Astowell

Ursula K. Le Guin

Ursula K. Le Guin

TALES FROM
Earthsea

HARCOURT, INC.

New York   San Diego   London

www.harcourt.com

"Darkrose and Diamond" first appeared in *The Magazine of Fantasy and Science Fiction*.
Copyright © 1999 by Ursula K. Le Guin. "Dragonfly" first appeared in *Legends*.
Copyright © 1997 by Ursula K. Le Guin.

Library of Congress Cataloging-in-Publication Data
Le Guin, Ursula K., 1929–
Tales from Earthsea/Ursula K. Le Guin.—1st ed.
p.   cm.
Contents: The finder—Darkrose and Diamond—The bones of the earth—
On the high marsh—Dragonfly—A description of Earthsea.
Summary: Explores further the magical world of Earthsea through five tales
of events which occur before or after the time of the original novels, as well
as an essay on the people, languages, history and magic of the place.
ISBN 0-15-100561-3
1. Fantasy fiction, American. [1. Fantasy. 2. Short stories.]   I. Title.
PZ7.L5215 Tal 2001
[Fic]—dc21   2001016554

Designed by Linda Lockowitz
Text set in Adobe Jenson

First edition

A C E G I K J H F D B

Printed in the United States of America

Contents

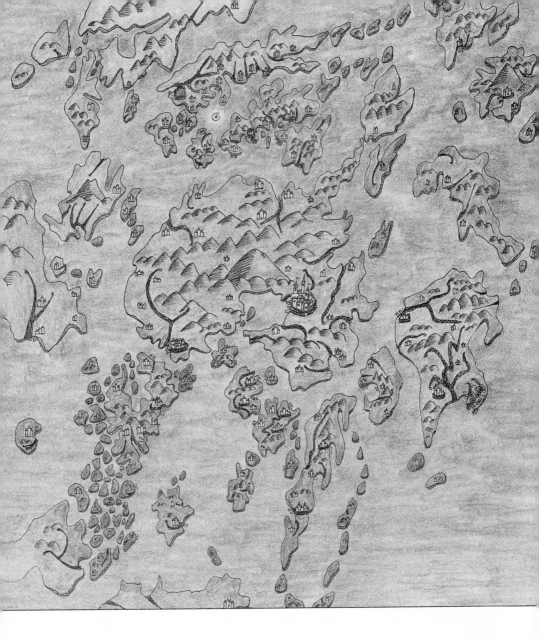

THE INNER LANDS OF THE ARCHIPELAGO
An eighth-century map from the Isle of Ark

This is a teaching map, not a sailing chart, as the proportions of the
islands are exaggerated, though their relative positions and distances
are fairly accurate. There is no writing of any kind on the map. The
lost island of Soléa is shown by a spiral.

Foreword

AT THE END OF the fourth book of Earthsea, *Tehanu*, the story had arrived at what I felt to be *now*. And, just as in the now of the so-called real world, I didn't know what would happen next. I could guess, foretell, fear, hope, but I didn't know.

Unable to continue Tehanu's story (because it hadn't happened yet) and foolishly assuming that the story of Ged and Tenar had reached its happily-ever-after, I gave the book a subtitle: "The Last Book of Earthsea."

O foolish writer. *Now* moves. Even in storytime, dreamtime, once-upon-a time, *now* isn't *then*.

Seven or eight years after *Tehanu* was published, I was asked to write a story set in Earthsea. A mere glimpse at the place told me that things had been happening there while I wasn't looking. It was high time to go back and find out what was going on *now*.

I also wanted information on various things that had happened back *then*, before Ged and Tenar were born. A good deal about Earthsea, about wizards, about Roke Island, about dragons, had begun to puzzle me. In order to understand current events, I needed to do some historical research, to spend some time in the Archives of the Archipelago.

The way one does research into nonexistent history is to tell the story and find out what happened. I believe this isn't very different from what historians of the so-called real world do. Even if we are present at some historic event, do we comprehend it—can we even remember it—until we can tell it as a story? And for events in times or places outside our own experience, we have nothing to go on but the stories other people tell us. Past events exist, after all, only in memory, which is a form of imagination. The event is real *now*, but once it's *then*, its continuing reality is entirely up to us, dependent on our energy and honesty. If we let it drop from memory, only imagination can restore the least glimmer of it. If we lie about the past, forcing it to tell a story we want it to tell, to mean what we want it to mean, it loses its reality, becomes a fake. To bring the past along with us through time in the hold-alls of myth and history is a heavy undertaking; but as Lao Tzu says, wise people march along with the baggage wagons.

When you construct or reconstruct a world that never existed, a wholly fictional history, the research is of a somewhat different order, but the basic impulse and techniques are much the same. You look at what happens and try to see why it happens, you listen to what the people there tell you and watch what they do, you think about it seriously, and you try to tell it honestly, so that the story will have weight and make sense.

The five tales in this book explore or extend the world established by the first four Earthsea novels. Each is a story in its own right, but they will profit by being read after, not before, the novels.

"The Finder" takes place about three hundred years before the time of the novels, in a dark and troubled time; its story casts light on how some of the customs and institutions of the Archipelago came to be. "The Bones of the Earth" is about the wizards who taught the wizard who first taught Ged, and shows that it takes more than one mage to stop an earthquake. "Darkrose and Diamond" might take place at any time during the last couple of hundred years in Earthsea; after all, a love story can happen at any time, anywhere. "On the High Marsh" is a story from the brief but eventful six years that Ged was Archmage of Earthsea. And the last story, "Dragonfly," which takes place a few years after the end of *Tehanu*, is the bridge between that book and the next one, *The Other Wind* (to be published soon). A dragon bridge.

So that my mind could move about among the years and centuries wihout getting things all out of order, and to keep contradictions and discrepancies at a minimum while I was writing these stories, I became (somewhat) more systematic and methodical, and put my knowledge of the peoples and their history together into "A Description of Earthsea." Its function is like that of the first big map I drew of all the Archipelago and the Reaches, when I began to work on *A Wizard of Earthsea* over thirty years ago: I needed to know where things are, and how to get from here to there—in time as well as in space.

Because this kind of fictional fact, like maps of imaginary realms, is of real interest to some readers, I include the description after the stories. I also redrew the geographical maps for this book, and while doing so, happily discovered a very old one in the Archives in Havnor.

In the years since I began to write about Earthsea I've changed, of course, and so have the people who read the books. All times are changing times, but ours is one of massive, rapid moral and mental transformation. Archetypes turn into millstones, large simplicities get complicated, chaos becomes elegant, and what everybody knows is true turns out to be what some people used to think.

It's unsettling. For all our delight in the impermanent, the entrancing flicker of electronics, we also long for the unalterable.

We cherish the old stories for their changelessness. Arthur dreams eternally in Avalon. Bilbo can go "there and back again," and "there" is always the beloved familiar Shire. Don Quixote sets out forever to kill a windmill . . . So people turn to the realms of fantasy for stability, ancient truths, immutable simplicities.

And the mills of capitalism provide them. Supply meets demand. Fantasy becomes a commodity, an industry.

Commodified fantasy takes no risks: it invents nothing, but imitates and trivialises. It proceeds by depriving the old stories of their intellectual and ethical complexity, turning their action to violence, their actors to dolls, and their truth- telling to sentimental platitude. Heroes brandish their swords, lasers, wands, as mechanically as combine harvesters, reaping profits. Profoundly disturbing moral choices are sanitized, made cute, made safe. The passionately conceived ideas of the great story-tellers are copied, stereotyped, reduced to toys, molded in bright-colored plastic, advertised, sold, broken, junked, replaceable, interchangeable.

What the commodifiers of fantasy count on and exploit is the insuperable imagination of the reader, child or adult, which gives even these dead things life—of a sort, for a while.

Imagination like all living things lives *now*, and it lives with, from, on true change. Like all we do and have, it can be co-opted and degraded; but it survives commercial and didactic exploitation. The land outlasts the empires. The conquerors may leave desert where there was forest and meadow, but the rain will fall, the rivers will run to the sea. The unstable, mutable, untruthful realms of Once-upon-a-time are as much a part of human history and thought as the nations in our kaleidoscopic atlases, and some are more enduring.

We have inhabited both the actual and the imaginary realms for a long time. But we don't live in either place the way our parents or ancestors did. Enchantment alters with age, and with the age.

We know a dozen different Arthurs now, all of them true. The Shire changed irrevocably even in Bilbo's lifetime. Don Quixote went riding out to Argentina and met Jorge Luis Borges there. *Plus c'est la même chose, plus ça change.*

It's been a joy to me to go back to Earthsea and find it still there, entirely familiar, and yet changed and still changing. What I thought was going to happen isn't what's happening, people aren't who—or what—I thought they were, and I lose my way on islands I thought I knew by heart.

So these are reports of my explorations and discoveries: tales from Earthsea for those who have liked or think they might like the place, and who are willing to accept these hypotheses:

things change:

authors and wizards are not always to be trusted:

nobody can explain a dragon.

TALES FROM
Earthsea

The Finder

I. In the Dark Time

THIS IS THE FIRST PAGE of the *Book of the Dark*, written some six hundred years ago in Berila, on Enlad:

"After Elfarran and Morred perished and the Isle of Soléa sank beneath the sea, the Council of the Wise governed for the child Serriadh until he took the throne. His reign was bright but brief. The kings who followed him in Enlad were seven, and their realm increased in peace and wealth. Then the dragons came to raid among the western lands, and wizards went out in vain against them. King Akambar moved the court from Berila in Enlad to the City of Havnor, whence he sent out his fleet against invaders from the Kargad Lands and drove them back into the East. But still they sent raiding ships even as far as the Inmost Sea. Of the fourteen Kings of Havnor the last was Maharion, who made peace both with the dragons and the Kargs, but at great cost. And after the Ring of the Runes was broken, and Erreth-Akbe died with the great dragon, and Maharion the Brave was killed by treachery, it seemed that no good thing happened in the Archipelago.

"Many claimed Maharion's throne, but none could keep it, and the quarrels of the claimants divided all loyalties. No commonwealth was left and no justice, only the will of the wealthy. Men of noble houses, merchants, and pirates, any who could hire soldiers and wizards called himself a lord, claiming lands and cities as his property. The warlords made those they conquered slaves, and those they hired were in truth slaves, having only their masters to safeguard them from rival warlords seizing the lands, and sea-pirates raiding the ports, and bands and hordes of lawless, miserable men dispossessed of their living, driven by hunger to raid and rob."

The *Book of the Dark*, written late in the time it tells of, is a compilation of self-contradictory histories, partial biographies, and garbled legends. But it's the best of the records that survived the dark years. Wanting praise, not history, the warlords burnt the books in which the poor and powerless might learn what power is.

But when the lore-books of a wizard came into a warlord's hands he was likely to treat them with caution, locking them away to keep them harmless or giving them to a wizard in his hire to do with as he wished. In the margins of the spells and word lists and in the endpapers of these books of lore a wizard or his prentice might record a plague, a famine, a raid, a change of masters, along with the spells worked in such events and their success or unsuccess. Such random records reveal a clear moment here and there, though all between those moments is darkness. They are like glimpses of a lighted ship far out at sea, in darkness, in the rain.

And there are songs, old lays and ballads from small islands and from the quiet uplands of Havnor, that tell the story of those years.

Havnor Great Port is the city at the heart of the world, white-towered above its bay; on the tallest tower the sword of Erreth-Akbe catches the first and last of daylight. Through that city passes all the trade and commerce and learning and craft of Earthsea, a wealth not hoarded. There the King sits, having returned after the healing of the Ring, in sign of healing. And in that city, in these latter days, men and women of the islands speak with dragons, in sign of change.

But Havnor is also the Great Isle, a broad, rich land; and in the villages inland from the port, the farmlands of the slopes of Mount Onn, nothing ever changes much. There a song worth singing is likely to be sung again. There old men at the tavern talk of Morred as if they had known him when they too were young and heroes. There girls walking out to fetch the cows home tell stories of the women of the Hand, who are forgotten everywhere else in the world, even on Roke, but remembered among those silent, sunlit roads and fields and in the kitchens by the hearths where housewives work and talk.

In the time of the kings, mages gathered in the court of Enlad and later in the court of Havnor to counsel the king and take counsel together, using their arts to pursue goals they agreed were good. But in the dark years, wizards sold their skills to the highest bidder, pitting their powers one against the other in duels and combats of sorcery, careless of the evils they did, or worse than careless. Plagues and famines, the failure of springs of water, summers with no rain and years with no summer, the birth of sickly and monstrous young to sheep and cattle, the birth of sickly and monstrous children to the people of the isles—all these things were charged to the practices of wizards and witches, and all too often rightly so.

So it became dangerous to practice sorcery, except under the protection of a strong warlord; and even then, if a wizard met up with one whose powers were greater than his own, he might be destroyed. And if a wizard let down his guard among the common folk, they too might destroy him if they could, seeing him as the source of the worst evils they suffered, a malign being. In those years, in the minds of most people, all magic was black.

It was then that village sorcery, and above all women's witchery, came into the ill repute that has clung to it since. Witches paid dearly for practicing the arts they thought of as their own. The care of pregnant beasts and women, birthing, teaching the songs and rites, the fertility and order of field and garden, the building and care of the house and its furniture, the mining of ores and metals—these great things had always been in the charge of women. A rich lore of spells and charms to ensure the good outcome of such undertakings was shared among the witches. But when things went wrong at the birth, or in the field, that would be the witches' fault. And things went wrong more often than right, with the wizards warring, using poisons and curses recklessly to gain immediate advantage without thought for what followed after. They brought drought and storm, blights and fires and sicknesses across the land, and the village witch was punished for them. She didn't know why her charm of healing caused the wound to gangrene, why the child she brought into the world was imbecile, why her blessing seemed to burn the seed in the furrows and blight the apple on the tree. But for these ills, somebody had to be to blame: and the witch or sorcerer was there, right there in the village or the town, not off in the warlord's castle or fort, not protected by armed men and spells of defense. Sorcerers and witches were drowned in the poisoned wells, burned in the withered fields, buried alive to make the dead earth rich again.

So the practice of their lore and the teaching of it had become perilous. Those who undertook it were often those already out-cast, crippled, deranged, without family, old—women and men who had little to lose. The wise man and wise woman, trusted and held in reverence, gave way to the stock figures of the shuffling, impotent village sorcerer with his trickeries, the hag-witch with her potions used in aid of lust, jealousy, and malice. And a child's gift for magic became a thing to dread and hide.

This is a tale of those times. Some of it is taken from the *Book of the Dark*, and some comes from Havnor, from the upland farms of Onn and the woodlands of Faliern. A story may be pieced together from such scraps and fragments, and though it will be an airy quilt, half made of hearsay and half of guesswork, yet it may be true enough. It's a tale of the Founding of Roke, and if the Masters of Roke say it didn't happen so, let them tell us how it happened otherwise. For a cloud hangs over the time when Roke first became the Isle of the Wise, and it may be that the wise men put it there.

II. Otter

There was an otter in our brook
That every mortal semblance took,
Could any spell of magic make,
And speak the tongues of man and drake.
So runs the water away, away,
So runs the water away.

OTTER WAS THE SON of a boatwright who worked in the shipyards of Havnor Great Port. His mother gave him his country name; she was a farm woman from Endlane village, around northwest of

Mount Onn. She had come to the city seeking work, as many came. Decent folk in a decent trade in troubled times, the boatwright and his family were anxious not to come to notice lest they come to grief. And so, when it became clear that the boy had a gift of magery, his father tried to beat it out of him.

"You might as well beat a cloud for raining," said Otter's mother.

"Take care you don't beat evil into him," said his aunt.

"Take care he doesn't turn your belt on you with a spell!" said his uncle.

But the boy played no tricks against his father. He took his beatings in silence and learned to hide his gift.

It didn't seem to him to amount to much. It was such an easy matter to him to make a silvery light shine in a dark room, or find a lost pin by thinking about it, or true up a warped joint by running his hands over the wood and talking to it, that he couldn't see why they made a fuss over such things. But his father raged at him for his "shortcuts," even struck him once on the mouth when he was talking to the work, and insisted that he do his carpentry with tools, in silence.

His mother tried to explain. "It's as if you'd found some great jewel," she said, "and what's one of us to do with a diamond but hide it? Anybody rich enough to buy it from you is strong enough to kill you for it. Keep it hid. And keep away from great people and their crafty men!"

"Crafty men" is what they called wizards in those days.

One of the gifts of power is to know power. Wizard knows wizard, unless the concealment is very skillful. And the boy had no skills at all except in boat-building, of which he was a promising scholar by the age of twelve. About that time the midwife who had helped his mother at his birth came by and said to his parents, "Let Otter come to me in the evenings after work. He should learn the songs and be prepared for his naming day."

That was all right, for she had done the same for Otter's elder sister, and so his parents sent him to her in the evenings. But she taught Otter more than the song of the Creation. She knew his gift. She and some men and women like her, people of no fame and some of questionable reputation, had all in some degree that gift; and they shared, in secret, what lore and craft they had. "A gift untaught is a ship unguided," they said to Otter, and they taught him all they knew. It wasn't much, but there were some beginnings of the great arts in it; and though he felt uneasy at deceiving his parents, he couldn't resist this knowledge, and the kindness and praise of his poor teachers. "It will do you no harm if you never use it for harm," they told him, and that was easy for him to promise them.

At the stream Serrenen, where it runs within the north wall of the city, the midwife gave Otter his true name, by which he is remembered in islands far from Havnor.

Among these people was an old man whom they called, among themselves, the Changer. He showed Otter a few spells of illusion; and when the boy was fifteen or so, the old man took him out into the fields by Serrenen to show him the one spell of true change he knew. "First let's see you turn that bush into the seeming of a tree," he said, and promptly Otter did so. Illusion came so easy to the boy that the old man took alarm. Otter had to beg and wheedle him for any further teaching and finally to promise him, swearing on his own true and secret name, that if he learned the Changer's great spell he would never use it but to save a life, his own or another's.

Then the old man taught it to him. But it wasn't much use, Otter thought, since he had to hide it.

What he learned working with his father and uncle in the shipyard he could use, at least; and he was becoming a good craftsman, even his father would admit that.

Losen, a sea-pirate who called himself King of the Inmost Sea, was then the chief warlord in the city and all the east and south of Havnor. Exacting tribute from that rich domain, he spent it to increase his soldiery and the fleets he sent out to take slaves and plunder from other lands. As Otter's uncle said, he kept the shipwrights busy. They were grateful to have work in a time when men seeking work found only beggary, and rats ran in the courts of Maharion. They did an honest job, Otter's father said, and what the work was used for was none of their concern.

But the other learning he had been given had made Otter touchy in these matters, delicate of conscience. The big galley they were building now would be rowed to war by Losen's slaves and would bring back slaves as cargo. It galled him to think of the good ship in that vicious usage. "Why can't we build fishing boats, the way we used to?" he asked, and his father said, "Because the fishermen can't pay us."

"Can't pay us as well as Losen does. But we could live," Otter argued.

"You think I can turn the King's order down? You want to see me sent to row with the slaves in the galley we're building? Use your head, boy!"

So Otter worked along with them with a clear head and an angry heart. They were in a trap. What's the use of a gift of power, he thought, if not to get out of a trap?

His conscience as a craftsman would not let him fault the carpentry of the ship in any way; but his conscience as a wizard told him he could put a hex on her, a curse woven right into her beams and hull. Surely that was using the secret art to a good end? For harm, yes, but only to harm the harmful. He did not talk to his teachers about it. If he was doing wrong, it was none of their fault and they would know nothing about it. He thought about it for a long time, working out how to do it, making the spell very carefully. It was the reversal of a finding charm: a losing charm, he called it to himself. The ship would float, and handle well, and steer, but she would never steer quite true.

It was the best he could do in protest against the misuse of good work and a good ship. He was pleased with himself. When the ship was launched (and all seemed well with her, for her fault would not show up until she was out on the open sea) he could not keep from his teachers what he had done, the little circle of old men and midwives, the young hunchback who could speak with the dead, the blind girl who knew the names of things. He told them his trick, and the blind girl laughed, but the old people said, "Look out. Take care. Keep hidden."

In Losen's service was a man who called himself Hound, because, as he said, he had a nose for witchery. His employment was to sniff Losen's food and drink and garments and women, anything that might be used by enemy wizards against him; and also to inspect his warships. A ship is a fragile thing in a dangerous element, vulnerable to spells and hexes. As soon as Hound came aboard the new galley he scented something. "Well, well," he said, "who's this?" He walked to the helm and put his hand on it. "This is clever," he said. "But who is it? A newcomer, I think." He sniffed appreciatively. "Very clever," he said.

They came to the house in Boatwright Street after dark. They kicked the door in, and Hound, standing among the armed and armored men, said, "Him. Let the others be." And to Otter he said, "Don't move," in a low, amicable voice. He sensed great power in the young man, enough that he was a little afraid of him. But

Otter's distress was too great and his training too slight for him to think of using magic to free himself or stop the men's brutality. He flung himself at them and fought them like an animal till they knocked him on the head. They broke Otter's father's jaw and beat his aunt and mother senseless to teach them not to bring up crafty men. Then they carried Otter away.

Not a door opened in the narrow street. Nobody looked out to see what the noise was. Not till long after the men were gone did some neighbors creep out to comfort Otter's people as best they could. "Oh, it's a curse, a curse, this wizardry!" they said.

Hound told his master that they had the hexer in a safe place, and Losen said, "Who was he working for?"

"He worked in your shipyard, your highness." Losen liked to be called by kingly titles.

"Who hired him to hex the ship, fool?"

"It seems it was his own idea, your majesty."

"Why? What was he going to get out of it?"

Hound shrugged. He didn't choose to tell Losen that people hated him disinterestedly.

"He's crafty, you say. Can you use him?"

"I can try, your highness."

"Tame him or bury him," said Losen, and turned to more important matters.

Otter's humble teachers had taught him pride. They had trained into him a deep contempt for wizards who worked for such men as Losen, letting fear or greed pervert magic to evil ends. Nothing, to his mind, could be more despicable than such a betrayal of their art. So it troubled him that he couldn't despise Hound.

He had been stowed in a storeroom of one of the old palaces that Losen had appropriated. It had no window, its door was cross-grained oak barred with iron, and spells had been laid on that door that would have kept a far more experienced wizard captive. There were men of great skill and power in Losen's pay.

Hound did not consider himself to be one of them. "All I have is a nose," he said. He came daily to see that Otter was recovering from his concussion and dislocated shoulder, and to talk with him. He was, as far as Otter could see, well-meaning and honest. "If you won't work for us they'll kill you," he said. "Losen can't have fellows like you on the loose. You'd better hire on while he'll take you."

"I can't."

Otter stated it as an unfortunate fact, not as a moral assertion. Hound looked at him with appreciation. Living with the pirate king, he was sick of boasts and threats, of boasters and threateners.

"What are you strongest in?"

Otter was reluctant to answer. He had to like Hound, but didn't have to trust him. "Shape-changing," he mumbled at last.

"Shape-taking?"

"No. Just tricks. Turn a leaf to a gold piece. Seemingly."

In those days they had no fixed names for the various kinds and arts of magic, nor were the connections among those arts clear. There was—as the wise men of Roke would say later—no science in what they knew. But Hound knew pretty surely that his prisoner was concealing his talents.

"Can't change your own form, even seemingly?"

Otter shrugged.

It was hard for him to lie. He thought he was awkward at it because he had no practice. Hound knew better. He knew that magic itself resists untruth. Conjuring, sleight of hand, and false commerce with the dead are counterfeits of magic, glass to the diamond, brass to the gold. They are fraud, and lies flourish in that soil. But the art of magic, though it may be used for false ends, deals with what is real, and the words it works with are the true words. So true wizards find it hard to lie about their art. In their heart they know that their lie, spoken, may change the world.

Hound was sorry for him. "You know, if it was Gelluk questioning you, he'd have everything you know out of you just with a word or two, and your wits with it. I've seen what old Whiteface leaves behind when he asks questions. Listen, can you work with the wind at all?"

Otter hesitated and said, "Yes."

"D'you have a bag?"

Weatherworkers used to carry a leather sack in which they said they kept the winds, untying it to let a fair wind loose or to capture a contrary one. Maybe it was only for show, but every weatherworker had a bag, a great long sack or a little pouch.

"At home," Otter said. It wasn't a lie. He did have a pouch at home. He kept his fine-work tools and his bubble level in it. And he wasn't altogether lying about the wind. Several times he had managed to bring a bit of magewind into the sail of a boat, though he had no idea how to combat or control a storm, as a ship's weatherworker must do. But he thought he'd rather drown in a gale than be murdered in this hole.

"But you wouldn't be willing to use that skill in the King's service?"

"There is no king in Earthsea," the young man said, stern and righteous.

"In my master's service, then," Hound amended, patient.

"No," Otter said, and hesitated. He felt he owed this man an explanation. "See, it's not so much won't as can't. I thought of making plugs in the planking of that galley, near the keel—you know what I mean by plugs? They'd work out as the timbers work when she gets in a heavy sea." Hound nodded. "But I couldn't do it. I'm a shipbuilder. I can't build a ship to sink. With the men aboard her. My hands wouldn't do it. So I did what I could. I made her go her own way. Not his way."

Hound smiled. "They haven't undone what you did yet, either," he said. "Old Whiteface was crawling all over her yesterday, growling and muttering. Ordered the helm replaced." He meant Losen's chief mage, a pale man from the North named Gelluk, who was much feared in Havnor.

"That won't do it."

"Could you undo the spell you put on her?"

A flicker of complacency showed in Otter's tired, battered young face. "No," he said. "I don't think anybody can."

"Too bad. You might have used that to bargain with."

Otter said nothing.

"A nose, now, is a useful thing, a salable thing," Hound went on. "Not that I'm looking for competition. But a finder can always find work, as they say... You ever been in a mine?"

The guesswork of a wizard is close to knowledge, though he may not know what it is he knows. The first sign of Otter's gift, when he was two or three years old, was his ability to go straight to anything lost, a dropped nail, a mislaid tool, as soon as he understood the word for it. And as a boy one of his dearest pleasures had been to go alone out into the countryside and wander along the lanes or over the hills, feeling through the soles of his bare feet and throughout his body the veins of water underground, the lodes and knots of ore, the lay and interfolding of the kinds of rock and earth. It was as if he walked in a great building, seeing its passages and rooms, the descents to airy caverns, the glimmer of branched silver in the walls; and as he went on, it was as if his body became the body of earth, and he knew its arteries and organs and muscles as his own. This power had been a delight to him as a boy. He had never sought any use for it. It had been his secret.

He did not answer Hound's question.

"What's below us?" Hound pointed to the floor, paved with rough slate flags.

Otter was silent a while. Then he said in a low voice, "Clay, and gravel, and under that the rock that bears garnets. All under this part of the city is that rock. I don't know the names."

"You can learn 'em."

"I know how to build boats, how to sail boats."

"You'll do better away from the ships, all the fighting and raiding. The King's working the old mines at Samory, round the mountain. There you'd be out of his way. Work for him you must, if you want to stay alive. I'll see that you're sent there. If you'll go."

After a little silence Otter said, "Thanks." And he looked up at Hound, one brief, questioning, judging glance.

Hound had taken him, had stood and seen his people beaten senseless, had not stopped the beating. Yet he spoke as a friend. Why? said Otter's look. Hound answered it.

"Crafty men need to stick together," he said. "Men who have no art at all, nothing but wealth—they pit us one against the other, for their gain not ours. We sell 'em our power. Why do we? If we went our own way together, we'd do better, maybe."

Hound meant well in sending the young man to Samory, but he did not understand the quality of Otter's will. Nor did Otter himself. He was too used to obeying others to see that in fact he had always followed his own bent, and too young to believe that anything he did could kill him.

He planned, as soon as they took him out of his cell, to use the old Changer's spell of self-transformation and so escape. Surely his life was in danger, and it would be all right to use the spell? Only he couldn't decide what to turn himself into—a bird, or a wisp of smoke, what would be safest? But while he was thinking about it, Losen's men, used to wizard's tricks, drugged his food and he ceased to think of anything at all. They dumped him into a mule-cart like a sack of oats. When he showed signs of reviving during the journey, one of them bashed him on the head, remarking that he wanted to make sure he got his rest.

When he came to himself, sick and weak from the poison and with an aching skull, he was in a room with brick walls and bricked-up windows. The door had no bars and no visible lock. But when he tried to get to his feet he felt bonds of sorcery holding his body and mind, resilient, clinging, tightening as he moved. He could stand, but could not take a step towards the door. He could not even reach his hand out. It was a horrible sensation, as if his muscles were not his own. He sat down again and tried to hold still. The spellbonds around his chest kept him from breathing deeply, and his mind felt stifled too, as if his thoughts were crowded into a space too small for them.

After a long time the door opened and several men came in. He could do nothing against them as they gagged him and bound his arms behind him. "Now you won't weave charms nor speak spells, young 'un," said a broad, strong man with a furrowed face, "but you can nod your head well enough, right? They sent you here as a dowser. If you're a good dowser you'll feed well and sleep easy. Cinnabar, that's what you're to nod for. The King's wizard says it's still here somewhere about these old mines. And he wants it. So it's best for us that we find it. Now I'll walk you out. It's like I'm the water finder and you're my wand, see? You lead on. And if you want to go this way or that way you dip your head, so. And when you know there's ore underfoot, you stamp on the place, so. Now that's the bargain, right? And if you play fair I will."

He waited for Otter to nod, but Otter stood motionless.

"Sulk away," the man said. "If you don't like this work, there's always the roaster."

The man, whom the others called Licky, led him out into a hot, bright morning that dazzled his eyes. Leaving his cell he had felt the spellbonds loosen and fall away, but there were other spells woven about other buildings of the place, especially around a tall stone tower, filling the air with sticky lines of resistance and repulsion. If he tried to push forward into them his face and belly stung with jabs of agony, so that he looked at his body in horror for the wound; but there was no wound. Gagged and bound, without his voice and hands to work magic, he could do nothing against these spells. Licky had tied one end of a braided leather cord around his neck and held the other end, following him. He let Otter walk into a couple of the spells, and after that Otter avoided them. Where they were was plain enough: the dusty pathways bent to miss them.

Leashed like a dog, he walked along, sullen and shivering with sickness and rage. He stared around him, seeing the stone tower, stacks of wood by its wide doorway, rusty wheels and machines by a pit, great heaps of gravel and clay. Turning his sore head made him dizzy.

"If you're a dowser, better dowse," said Licky, coming up alongside him and looking sidelong into his face. "And if you're not, you'd better dowse all the same. That way you'll stay above ground longer."

A man came out of the stone tower. He passed them, walking hurriedly with a queer shambling gait, staring straight ahead. His chin shone and his chest was wet with spittle leaking from his lips.

"That's the roaster tower," said Licky. "Where they cook the cinnabar to get the metal from it. Roasters die in a year or two. Where to, dowser?"

After a bit Otter nodded left, away from the grey stone tower. They walked on towards a long, treeless valley, past grass-grown dumps and tailings.

"All under here's worked out long since," Licky said. And Otter had begun to be aware of the strange country under his feet: empty shafts and rooms of dark air in the dark earth, a vertical labyrinth, the deepest pits filled with unmoving water. "Never was much silver, and the watermetal's long gone. Listen, young 'un, do you even know what cinnabar is?"

Otter shook his head.

"I'll show you some. That's what Gelluk's after. The ore of watermetal. Watermetal eats all the other metals, even gold, see. So he calls it the King. If you find him his King, he'll treat you well. He's often here. Come on, I'll show you. Dog can't track till he's had the scent."

Licky took him down into the mines to show him the gangues, the kinds of earth the ore was likely to occur in. A few miners were working at the end of a long level.

Because they were smaller than men and could move more easily in narrow places, or because they were at home with the earth, or most likely because it was the custom, women had always worked the mines of Earthsea. These miners were free women, not slaves like the workers in the roaster tower. Gelluk had made him foreman over the miners, Licky said, but he did no work in the mine; the miners forbade it, earnestly believing it was the worst of bad luck for a man to pick up a shovel or shore a timber. "Suits me," Licky said.

A shock-haired, bright-eyed woman with a candle bound to her forehead set down her pick to show Otter a little cinnabar in a bucket, brownish red clots and crumbs. Shadows leapt across the earth face at which the miners worked. Old timbers creaked, dirt sifted down. Though the air ran cool through the darkness, the drifts and levels were so low and narrow the miners had to stoop and squeeze their way. In places the ceilings had collapsed. Ladders were shaky. The mine was a terrifying place; yet Otter felt a sense of shelter in it. He was half sorry to go back up into the burning day.

Licky did not take him into the roaster tower, but back to the barracks. From a locked room he brought out a small, soft, thick, leather bag that weighed heavy in his hands. He opened it to show Otter the little pool of dusty brilliance lying in it. When he closed the bag the metal moved in it, bulging, pressing, like an animal trying to get free.

"There's the King," Licky said, in a tone that might have been reverence or hatred.

Though not a sorcerer, Licky was a much more formidable man than Hound. Yet like Hound he was brutal not cruel. He demanded obedience, but nothing else. Otter had seen slaves and their masters all his life in the shipyards of Havnor, and knew he was fortunate. At least in daylight, when Licky was his master.

He could eat only in the cell, where they took his gag off. Bread and onions were what they gave him, with a slop of rancid oil on the bread. Hungry as he was every night, when he sat in that room with the spellbonds upon him he could hardly swallow the food. It tasted of metal, of ash. The nights were long and terrible, for the spells pressed on him, weighed on him, waked him over and over terrified, gasping for breath, and never able to think coherently. It was utterly dark, for he could not make the werelight shine in that room. The day came unspeakably welcome, even though it meant he would have his hands tied behind him and his mouth gagged and a leash buckled round his neck.

Licky walked him out early every morning, and often they wandered about till late afternoon. Licky was silent and patient.

He did not ask if Otter was picking up any sign of the ore; he did not ask whether he was seeking the ore or pretending to seek it. Otter himself could not have answered the question. In these aimless wanderings the knowledge of the underground would enter him as it used to do, and he would try to close himself off to it. "I will not work in the service of evil!" he told himself. Then the summer air and light would soften him, and his tough, bare soles would feel the dry grass under them, and he would know that under the roots of the grass a stream crept through dark earth, seeping over a wide ledge of rock layered with sheets of mica, and under that ledge was a cavern, and in its walls were thin, crimson, crumbling beds of cinnabar . . . He made no sign. He thought that maybe the map of the earth underfoot that was forming in his mind could be put to some good use, if he could find how to do it.

But after ten days or so, Licky said, "Master Gelluk's coming here. If there's no ore for him, he'll likely find another dowser."

Otter walked on a mile, brooding; then circled back, leading Licky to a hillock not far from the far end of the old workings. There he nodded downward and stamped his foot.

Back in the cell room, when Licky had unleashed him and untied his gag, he said, "There's some ore there. You can get to it by running that old tunnel straight on, maybe twenty feet."

"A good bit of it?"

Otter shrugged.

"Just enough to keep going on, eh?"

Otter said nothing.

"Suits me," said Licky.

Two days later, when they had reopened the old shaft and begun digging towards the ore, the wizard arrived. Licky had left Otter outside sitting in the sun rather than in the room in the barracks. Otter was grateful to him. He could not be wholly comfortable with his hands bound and his mouth gagged, but wind and sunlight were mighty blessings. And he could breathe deep and doze without dreams of earth stopping his mouth and nostrils, the only dreams he ever had, nights in the cell.

He was half asleep, sitting on the ground in the shade by the barracks, the smell of the logs stacked by the roaster tower bringing him a memory of the work yards at home, the fragrance of new wood as the plane ran down the silky oak board. Some noise or movement roused him. He looked up and saw the wizard standing before him, looming above him.

Gelluk wore fantastic clothes, as many of his kind did in those days. A long robe of Lorbanery silk, scarlet, embroidered in gold and black with runes and symbols, and a wide-brimmed, peak-crowned hat made him seem taller than a man could be. Otter did not need to see his clothes to know him. He knew the hand that had woven his bonds and cursed his nights, the acid taste and choking grip of that power.

"I think I've found my little finder," said Gelluk. His voice was deep and soft, like the notes of a viol. "Sleeping in the sunshine, like one whose work has been well done. So you've sent them digging for the Red Mother, have you? Did you know the Red Mother before you came here? Are you a courtier of the King? Here, now, there's no need for ropes and knots." Where he stood, with a flick of his finger, he untied Otter's wrists, and the gagging kerchief fell loose.

"I could teach you how to do that for yourself," the wizard said, smiling, watching Otter rub and flex his aching wrists and work his lips that had been smashed against his teeth for hours. "The Hound told me that you're a lad of promise and might go far with a proper guide. If you'd like to visit the Court of the King, I can take you there. But maybe you don't know the King I'm talking of?"

Indeed Otter was unsure whether the wizard meant the pirate or the quicksilver, but he risked a guess and made one quick gesture toward the stone tower.

The wizard's eyes narrowed and his smile broadened.

"Do you know his name?"

"The watermetal," Otter said.

"So the vulgar call it, or quicksilver, or the water of weight. But those who serve him call him the King, and the Allking, and the Body of the Moon." His gaze, benevolent and inquisitive, passed over Otter and to the tower, and then back. His face was large and long, whiter than any face Otter had seen, with bluish eyes. Grey and black hairs curled here and there on his chin and cheeks. His calm, open smile showed small teeth, several of them missing. "Those who have learned to see truly can see him as he is, the lord of all substances. The root of power lies in him. Do you know what we call him in the secrecy of his palace?"

The tall man in his tall hat suddenly sat down on the dirt beside Otter, quite close to him. His breath smelled earthy. His light eyes gazed directly into Otter's eyes. "Would you like to know? You can know anything you like. I need have no secrets from you. Nor you from me," and he laughed, not threateningly, but with pleasure. He gazed at Otter again, his large, white face smooth and thoughtful. "Powers you have, yes, all kinds of little traits and tricks. A clever lad. But not too clever; that's good. Not too clever to learn, like some . . . I'll teach you, if you like. Do you like learning? Do you like knowledge? Would you like to know the name we call the King when he's all alone in his brightness in his courts of stone? His name is Turres. Do you know that name? It's a word in the language of the Allking. His own name in his own language. In our base tongue we would say Semen." He smiled again and patted Otter's hand. "For he is the seed and fructifier. The seed and source of might and right. You'll see. You'll see. Come along! Come along! Let's go see the King flying among his subjects, gathering himself from them!" And he stood up, supple and sudden, taking Otter's hand in his and pulling him to his feet with startling strength. He was laughing with excitement.

Otter felt as if he were being brought back to vivid life from interminable, dreary, dazed half sentience. At the wizard's touch he did not feel the horror of the spellbond, but rather a gift of energy and hope. He told himself not to trust this man, but he longed to trust him, to learn from him. Gelluk was powerful, masterful, strange, yet he had set him free. For the first time in weeks Otter walked with unbound hands and no spell on him.

"This way, this way," Gelluk murmured. "No harm will come to you." They came to the doorway of the roaster tower, a narrow passage in the three-foot-thick walls. He took Otter's arm, for the young man hesitated.

Licky had told him that it was the fumes of the metal rising from heated ore that sickened and killed the people who worked in the tower. Otter had never entered it nor seen Licky enter it. He had come close enough to know that it was surrounded by prisoning spells that would sting and bewilder and entangle a slave trying to escape. Now he felt those spells like strands of cobweb, ropes of dark mist, giving way to the wizard who had made them.

"Breathe, breathe, breathe," Gelluk said, laughing, and Otter tried not to hold his breath as they entered the tower.

The roasting pit took up the center of a huge domed chamber. Hurrying, sticklike figures black against the blaze shoveled and reshoveled ore onto logs kept in a roaring blaze by great bellows, while others brought fresh logs and worked the bellows sleeves. From the apex of the dome a spiral of chambers rose up into the tower through smoke and fumes. In those chambers,

Licky had told him, the vapor of the quicksilver was trapped and condensed, reheated and recondensed, till in the topmost vault the pure metal ran down into a stone trough or bowl—only a drop or two a day, he said, from the low-grade ores they were roasting now.

"Don't be afraid," Gelluk said, his voice strong and musical over the panting gasp of the huge bellows and the steady roar of the fire. "Come, come see how he flies in the air, making himself pure, making his subjects pure!" He drew Otter to the edge of the roasting pit. His eyes shone in the flare and dazzle of the flames. "Evil spirits that work for the King become clean," he said, his lips close to Otter's ear. "As they slaver, the dross and stains flow out of them. Illness and impurities fester and run free from their sores. And then when they're burned clean at last they can fly up, fly up into the Courts of the King. Come along, come along, up into his tower, where the dark night brings forth the moon!"

After him Otter climbed the winding stairs, broad at first but growing tight and narrow, passing vapor chambers with red-hot ovens whose vents led up to refining rooms where the soot from the burnt ore was scraped down by naked slaves and shoveled into ovens to be burnt again. They came to the topmost room. Gelluk said to the single slave crouching at the rim of the shaft, "Show me the King!"

The slave, short and thin, hairless, with running sores on his hands and arms, uncapped a stone cup by the rim of the condensing shaft. Gelluk peered in, eager as a child. "So tiny," he murmured. "So young. The tiny Prince, the baby Lord, Lord Turres. Seed of the world! Soul-jewel!"

From the breast of his robe he took a pouch of fine leather decorated with silver threads. With a delicate horn spoon tied to the pouch he lifted the few drops of quicksilver from the cup and placed them in it, then retied the thong.

The slave stood by, motionless. All the people who worked in the heat and fumes of the roaster tower were naked or wore only breechclout and moccasins. Otter glanced again at the slave, thinking by his height he was a child, and then saw the small breasts. It was a woman. She was bald. Her joints were swollen knobs in her bone-thin limbs. She looked up once at Otter, moving her eyes only. She spat into the fire, wiped her sore mouth with her hand, and stood motionless again.

"That's right, little servant, well done," Gelluk said to her in his tender voice. "Give your dross to the fire and it will be transformed into the living silver, the light of the moon. Is it not a wonderful thing," he went on, drawing Otter away and back down the spiral stair, "how from what is most base comes what is most noble? That is a great principle of the art! From the vile Red Mother is born the Allking. From the spittle of a dying slave is made the silver Seed of Power."

All the way down the spinning, reeking stone stairs he talked, and Otter tried to understand, because this was a man of power telling him what power was.

But when they came out into the daylight again his head kept on spinning in the dark, and after a few steps he doubled over and vomited on the ground.

Gelluk watched him with his inquisitive, affectionate look, and when Otter stood up, wincing and gasping, the wizard asked gently, "Are you afraid of the King?"

Otter nodded.

"If you share his power he won't harm you. To fear a power, to fight a power, is very dangerous. To love power and to share it is the royal way. Look. Watch what I do." Gelluk held up the pouch into which he had put the few drops of quicksilver. His eye always on Otter's eye, he unsealed the pouch, lifted it to his lips, and drank its contents. He opened his smiling mouth so that Otter could see the silver drops pooling on his tongue before he swallowed.

"Now the King is in my body, the noble guest of my house. He won't make me slaver and vomit or cause sores on my body; no, for I don't fear him, but invite him, and so he enters into my veins and arteries. No harm comes to me. My blood runs silver. I see things unknown to other men. I share the secrets of the King. And when he leaves me, he hides in the place of ordure, in foulness itself, and yet again in the vile place he waits for me to come and take him up and cleanse him as he cleansed me, so that each time we grow purer together." The wizard took Otter's arm and walked along with him. He said, smiling and confidential, "I am one who shits moonlight. You will not know another such. And more than that, more than that, the King enters into my seed. He is my semen. I am Turres and he is me..."

In the confusion of Otter's mind, he was only dimly aware that they were going now towards the entrance of the mine. They went underground. The passages of the mine were a dark maze like the wizard's words. Otter stumbled on, trying to understand. He saw the slave in the tower, the woman who had looked at him. He saw her eyes.

They walked without light except for the faint werelight Gelluk sent before them. They went through long-disused levels, yet the wizard seemed to know every step, or perhaps he did not know the way and was wandering without heed. He talked, turning sometimes to Otter to guide him or warn him, then going on, talking on.

They came to where the miners were extending the old tunnel. There the wizard spoke with Licky in the flare of candles among jagged shadows. He touched the earth of the tunnel's end, took clods of earth in his hands, rolled the dirt in his palms, kneading, testing, tasting it. For that time he was silent, and Otter watched him with staring intensity, still trying to understand.

Licky came back to the barracks with them. Gelluk bade Otter goodnight in his soft voice. Licky shut him as usual into the brick-walled room, giving him a loaf of bread, an onion, a jug of water.

Otter crouched as always in the uneasy oppression of the spellbond. He drank thirstily. The sharp earthy taste of the onion was good, and he ate it all.

As the dim light that came into the room from chinks in the mortar of the bricked-up window died away, instead of sinking into the blank misery of all his nights in that room, he stayed awake, and grew more awake. The excited turmoil of his mind all the time he had been with Gelluk slowly quieted. From it something rose, coming close, coming clear, the image he had seen down in the mine, shadowy yet distinct: the slave in the high vault of the tower, that woman with empty breasts and festered eyes, who spat the spittle that ran from her poisoned mouth, and wiped her mouth, and stood waiting to die. She had looked at him.

He saw her now more clearly than he had seen her in the tower. He saw her more clearly than he had ever seen anyone. He saw the thin arms, the swollen joints of elbow and wrist, the childish nape of her neck. It was as if she was with him in the room. It was as if she was in him, as if she was him. She looked at him. He saw her look at him. He saw himself through her eyes.

He saw the lines of the spells that held him, heavy cords of darkness, a tangled maze of lines all about him. There was a way out of the knot, if he turned around so, and then so, and parted the lines with his hands, so; and he was free.

He could not see the woman any more. He was alone in the room, standing free.

All the thoughts he had not been able to think for days and weeks were racing through his head, a storm of ideas and feelings, a passion of rage, vengeance, pity, pride.

At first he was overwhelmed with fierce fantasies of power and revenge: he would free the slaves, he would spellbind Gelluk and hurl him into the refining fire, he would bind him and blind him and leave him to breathe the fumes of quicksilver in that highest vault till he died... But when his thoughts settled down and began to run clearer, he knew that he could not defeat a wizard of great craft and power, even if that wizard was mad. If he had any hope it was to play on his madness, and lead the wizard to defeat himself.

He pondered. All the time he was with Gelluk, he had tried to learn from him, tried to understand what the wizard was telling him. Yet he was certain, now, that Gelluk's ideas, the teaching he so eagerly imparted, had nothing to do with his power or with any true power. Mining and refining were indeed great crafts with their own mysteries and masteries, but Gelluk seemed to know nothing of those arts. His talk of the Allking and the Red Mother was mere words. And not the right words. But how did Otter know that?

In all his flood of talk the only word Gelluk had spoken in the Old Tongue, the language of which wizards' spells were made, was the word *turres*. He had said it meant semen. Otter's own gift of magery had recognised that meaning as the true one. Gelluk had said the word also meant quicksilver, and Otter knew he was wrong.

His humble teachers had taught him all the words they knew of the Language of the Making. Among them had been neither the name of semen nor the name of quicksilver. But his lips parted, his tongue moved. "*Ayezur,*" he said.

His voice was the voice of the slave in the stone tower. It was she who knew the true name of quicksilver and spoke it through him.

Then for a while he held still, body and mind, beginning to understand for the first time where his power lay.

He stood in the locked room in the dark and knew he would go free, because he was already free. A storm of praise ran through him.

After a while, deliberately, he re-entered the trap of spell-bonds, went back to his old place, sat down on the pallet, and went on thinking. The prisoning spell was still there, yet it had no power over him now. He could walk into it and out of it as if it were mere lines painted on the floor. Gratitude for this freedom beat in him as steady as his heartbeat.

He thought what he must do, and how he must do it. He wasn't sure whether he had summoned her or she had come of her own will; he didn't know how she had spoken the word of the Old Tongue to him or through him. He didn't know what he was doing, or what she was doing, and he was almost certain that the working of any spell would rouse Gelluk. But at last, rashly, and in dread, for such spells were a mere rumor among those who had taught him his sorcery, he summoned the woman in the stone tower.

He brought her into his mind and saw her as he had seen her, there, in that room, and called out to her; and she came.

Her apparition stood again just outside the spiderweb cords of the spell, gazing at him, and seeing him, for a soft, bluish, sourceless light filled the room. Her sore, raw lips quivered but she did not speak.

He spoke, giving her his true name: "I am Medra."

"I am Anieb," she whispered.

"How can we get free?"

"His name."

"Even if I knew it ... When I'm with him I can't speak."

"If I was with you, I could use it."

"I can't call you."

"But I can come," she said.

She looked round, and he looked up. Both knew that Gelluk had sensed something, had wakened. Otter felt the bonds close and tighten, and the old shadow fall.

"I will come, Medra," she said. She held out her thin hand in a fist, then opened it palm up as if offering him something. Then she was gone.

The light went with her. He was alone in the dark. The cold grip of the spells took him by the throat and choked him, bound his hands, pressed on his lungs. He crouched, gasping. He could not think; he could not remember. "Stay with me," he said, and did not know who he spoke to. He was frightened, and did not know what he was frightened of. The wizard, the power, the spell ... It was all darkness. But in his body, not in his mind, burned a knowledge he could not name any more, a certainty that was like a tiny lamp held in his hands in a maze of caverns underground. He kept his eyes on that seed of light.

Weary, evil dreams of suffocation came to him, but took no hold on him. He breathed deep. He slept at last. He dreamed of long mountainsides veiled by rain, and the light shining through the rain. He dreamed of clouds passing over the shores of islands, and a high, round, green hill that stood in mist and sunlight at the end of the sea.

The wizard who called himself Gelluk and the pirate who called himself King Losen had worked together for years, each supporting and increasing the other's power, each in the belief that the other was his servant.

Gelluk was sure that without him Losen's rubbishy kingdom

would soon collapse and some enemy mage would rub out its king with half a spell. But he let Losen act the master. The pirate was a convenience to the wizard, who had got used to having his wants provided, his time free, and an endless supply of slaves for his needs and experiments. It was easy to keep up the protections he had laid on Losen's person and expeditions and forays, the prisoning spells he had laid on the places slaves worked or treasures were kept. Making those spells had been a different matter, a long hard work. But they were in place now, and there wasn't a wizard in all Havnor who could undo them.

Gelluk had never met a man he feared. A few wizards had crossed his path strong enough to make him wary of them, but he had never known one with skill and power equal to his own.

Of late, entering always deeper into the mysteries of a certain lore-book brought back from the Isle of Way by one of Losen's raiders, Gelluk had become indifferent to most of the arts he had learned or had discovered for himself. The book convinced him that all of them were only shadows or hints of a greater mastery. As one true element controlled all substances, one true knowledge contained all others. Approaching ever closer to that mastery, he understood that the crafts of wizards were as crude and false as Losen's title and rule. When he was one with the true element, he would be the one true king. Alone among men he would speak the words of making and unmaking. He would have dragons for his dogs.

In the young dowser he recognised a power, untaught and inept, which he could use. He needed much more quicksilver than he had, therefore he needed a finder. Finding was a base skill. Gelluk had never practiced it, but he could see that the young fellow had the gift. He would do well to learn the boy's true name so that he could be sure of controlling him. He sighed at the thought of the time he must waste teaching the boy what he was good for. And after that the ore must still be dug out of the earth and the metal refined. As always, Gelluk's mind leapt across obstacles and delays to the wonderful mysteries at the end of them.

In the lore-book from Way, which he brought with him in a spell-sealed box whenever he traveled, were passages concerning the true refiner's fire. Having long studied these, Gelluk knew that once he had enough of the pure metal, the next stage was to refine it yet further into the Body of the Moon. He had understood the disguised language of the book to mean that in order to purify pure quicksilver, the fire must be built not of mere wood but of human corpses. Rereading and pondering the words this night in his room in the barracks, he discerned another possible meaning in them. There was always another meaning in the words of this lore. Perhaps the book was saying that there must be sacrifice not only of base flesh but also of inferior spirit. The great fire in the tower should burn not dead bodies but living ones. Living and conscious. Purity from foulness: bliss from pain. It was all part of the great principle, perfectly clear once seen. He was sure he was right, had at last understood the technique. But he must not hurry, he must be patient, must make certain. He turned to another passage and compared the two, and brooded over the book late into the night. Once for a moment something drew his mind away, some invasion of the outskirts of his awareness; the boy was trying some trick or other. Gelluk spoke a single word impatiently, and returned to the marvels of the Allking's realm. He never noticed that his prisoner's dreams had escaped him.

Next day he had Licky send him the boy. He looked forward to seeing him, to being kind to him, teaching him, petting him a bit as he had done yesterday. He sat down with him in the sun. Gelluk was fond of children and animals. He liked all beautiful things. It was pleasant to have a young creature about. Otter's

uncomprehending awe was endearing, as was his uncompre-
hended strength. Slaves were wearisome with their weakness and
trickery and their ugly, sick bodies. Of course Otter was his slave,
but the boy need not know it. They could be teacher and prentice. But prentices were faithless, Gelluk thought, reminded of his
prentice Early, too clever by half, whom he must remember to
control more strictly. Father and son, that's what he and Otter
could be. He would have the boy call him Father. He recalled that
he had intended to find out his true name. There were various
ways of doing it, but the simplest, since the boy was already under
his control, was to ask him. "What is your name?" he said, watching Otter intently.

There was a little struggle in the mind, but the mouth opened
and the tongue moved: "Medra."

"Very good, very good, Medra," said the wizard. "You may call
me Father."

"You must find the Red Mother," he said, the day after that. They
were sitting side by side again outside the barracks. The autumn
sun was warm. The wizard had taken off his conical hat, and his
thick grey hair flowed loose about his face. "I know you found
that little patch for them to dig, but there's no more in that than
a few drops. It's scarcely worth burning for so little. If you are to
help me, and if I am to teach you, you must try a little harder. I
think you know how." He smiled at Otter. "Don't you?"

Otter nodded.

He was still shaken, appalled, by the ease with which Gelluk
had forced him to say his name, which gave the wizard immediate and ultimate power over him. Now he had no hope of resist-
ing Gelluk in any way. That night he had been in utter despair.
But then Anieb had come into his mind: come of her own will, by

her own means. He could not summon her, could not even think of her, and would not have dared to do so, since Gelluk knew his name. But she came, even when he was with the wizard, not in apparition but as a presence in his mind.

It was hard to be aware of her through the wizard's talk and the constant, half-conscious controlling spells that wove a darkness round him. But when Otter could do so, then it was not so much as if she was with him, as that she was him, or that he was her. He saw through her eyes. Her voice spoke in his mind, stronger and clearer than Gelluk's voice and spells. Through her eyes and mind he could see, and think. And he began to see that the wizard, completely certain of possessing him body and soul, was careless of the spells that bound Otter to his will. A bond is a connection. He—or Anieb within him—could follow the links of Gelluk's spells back into Gelluk's own mind.

Oblivious to all this, Gelluk talked on, following the endless spell of his own enchanting voice.

"You must find the true womb, the bellybag of the Earth, that holds the pure moonseed. Did you know that the Moon is the Earth's father? Yes, yes; and he lay with her, as is the father's right. He quickened her base clay with the true seed. But she will not give birth to the King. She is strong in her fear and wilful in her vileness. She holds him back and hides him deep, fearing to give birth to her master. That is why, to give him birth, she must be burned alive."

Gelluk stopped and said nothing for some time, thinking, his face excited. Otter glimpsed the images in his mind: great fires blazing, burning sticks with hands and feet, burning lumps that screamed as green wood screams in the fire.

"Yes," Gelluk said, his deep voice soft and dreamy, "she must be burned alive. And then, only then, he will spring forth, shining!

Oh, it's time, and past time. We must deliver the King. We must find the great lode. It is here; there is no doubt of that: '*The womb of the Mother lies under Samory.*'"

Again he paused. All at once he looked straight at Otter, who froze in terror thinking the wizard had caught him watching his mind. Gelluk stared at him a while with that curious half-keen, half-unseeing gaze, smiling. "Little Medra!" he said, as if just discovering he was there. He patted Otter's shoulder. "I know you have the gift of finding what's hidden. Quite a great gift, were it suitably trained. Have no fear, my son. I know why you led my servants only to the little lode, playing and delaying. But now that I've come, you serve me, and have nothing to be afraid of. And there's no use trying to conceal anything from me, is there? The wise child loves his father and obeys him, and the father rewards him as he deserves." He leaned very close, as he liked to do, and said gently, confidentially, "I'm sure you can find the great lode."

"I know where it is," Anieb said.

Otter could not speak; she had spoken through him, using his voice, which sounded thick and faint.

Very few people ever spoke to Gelluk unless he compelled them to. The spells by which he silenced, weakened, and controlled all who approached him were so habitual to him that he gave them no thought. He was used to being listened to, not to listening. Serene in his strength and obsessed with his ideas, he had no thought beyond them. He was not aware of Otter at all except as a part of his plans, an extension of himself. "Yes, yes, you will," he said, and smiled again.

But Otter was intensely aware of Gelluk, both physically and as a presence of immense controlling power; and it seemed to him that Anieb's speaking had taken away that much of Gelluk's power over him, gaining him a place to stand, a foothold. Even with Gelluk so close to him, fearfully close, he managed to speak.

"I will take you there," he said, stiffly, laboriously.

Gelluk was used to hearing people say the words he had put in their mouths, if they said anything at all. These were words he wanted but had not expected to hear. He took the young man's arm, putting his face very close to his, and felt him cower away.

"How clever you are," he said. "Have you found better ore than that patch you found first? Worth the digging and the roasting?"

"It is the lode," the young man said.

The slow stiff words carried great weight.

"The great lode?" Gelluk looked straight at him, their faces not a hand's breadth apart. The light in his bluish eyes was like the soft, crazy shift of quicksilver. "The womb?"

"Only the Master can go there."

"What Master?"

"The Master of the House. The King."

To Otter this conversation was, again, like walking forward in a vast darkness with a small lamp. Anieb's understanding was that lamp. Each step revealed the next step he must take, but he could never see the place where he was. He did not know what was coming next, and did not understand what he saw. But he saw it, and went forward, word by word.

"How do you know of that House?"

"I saw it."

"Where? Near here?"

Otter nodded.

"Is it in the earth?"

Tell him what he sees, Anieb whispered in Otter's mind, and he spoke: "A stream runs through darkness over a glittering roof. Under the roof is the House of the King. The roof stands high above the floor, on high pillars. The floor is red. All the pillars are red. On them are shining runes."

Gelluk caught his breath. Presently he said, very softly, "Can you read the runes?"

"I cannot read them." Otter's voice was toneless. "I cannot go there. No one can enter there in the body but only the King. Only he can read what is written."

Gelluk's white face had gone whiter; his jaw trembled a little. He stood up, suddenly, as he always did. "Take me there," he said, trying to control himself, but so violently compelling Otter to get up and walk that the young man lurched to his feet and stumbled several steps, almost falling. Then he walked forward, stiff and awkward, trying not to resist the coercive, passionate will that hurried his steps.

Gelluk pressed close beside him, often taking his arm. "This way," he said several times. "Yes, yes! This is the way." Yet he was following Otter. His touch and his spells pushed him, rushed him, but in the direction Otter chose to go.

They walked past the roaster tower, past the old shaft and the new one, on into the long valley where Otter had taken Licky the first day he was there. It was late autumn now. The shrubs and scrubby grass that had been green that day were dun and dry, and the wind rattled the last leaves on the bushes. To their left a little stream ran low among willow thickets. Mild sunlight and long shadows streaked the hillsides.

Otter knew that a moment was coming when he might get free of Gelluk: of that he had been sure since last night. He knew also that in that same moment he might defeat Gelluk, disempower him, if the wizard, driven by his visions, forgot to guard himself—and if Otter could learn his name.

The wizard's spells still bound their minds together. Otter pressed rashly forward into Gelluk's mind, seeking his true name. But he did not know where to look or how to look. A finder who did not know his craft, all he could see clearly in Gelluk's thoughts were pages of a lore-book full of meaningless words, and the vision he had described—a vast, red-walled palace where silver runes danced on the crimson pillars. But Otter could not read the book or the runes. He had never learned to read.

All this time he and Gelluk were going on farther from the tower, away from Anieb, whose presence sometimes weakened and faded. Otter dared not try to summon her.

Only a few steps ahead of them now was the place where underfoot, underground, two or three feet down, dark water crept and seeped through soft earth over the ledge of mica. Under that opened the hollow cavern and the lode of cinnabar.

Gelluk was almost wholly absorbed in his own vision, but since Otter's mind and his were connected, he saw something of what Otter saw. He stopped, gripping Otter's arm. His hand shook with eagerness.

Otter pointed at the low slope that rose before them. "The King's House is there," he said. Gelluk's attention turned entirely away from him then, fixed on the hillside and the vision he saw within it. Then Otter could call to Anieb. At once she came into his mind and being, and was there with him.

Gelluk was standing still, but his shaking hands were clenched, his whole tall body twitching and trembling, like a hound that wants to chase but cannot find the scent. He was at a loss. There was the hillside with its grass and bushes in the last of the sunlight, but there was no entrance. Grass growing out of gravelly dirt; the seamless earth.

Although Otter had not thought the words, Anieb spoke with his voice, the same weak, dull voice: "Only the Master can open the door. Only the King has the key."

"The key," Gelluk said.

Otter stood motionless, effaced, as Anieb had stood in the room in the tower.

"The key," Gelluk repeated, urgent.

"The key is the King's name."

That was a leap in the darkness. Which of them had said it?

Gelluk stood tense and trembling, still at a loss. "Turres," he said, after a time, almost in a whisper.

The wind blew in the dry grass.

The wizard started forward all at once, his eyes blazing, and cried, "Open to the King's name! I am Tinaral!" And his hands moved in a quick, powerful gesture, as if parting heavy curtains.

The hillside in front of him trembled, writhed, and opened. A gash in it deepened, widened. Water sprang up out of it and ran across the wizard's feet.

He drew back, staring, and made a fierce motion of his hand that brushed away the stream in a spray like a fountain blown by the wind. The gash in the earth grew deeper, revealing the ledge of mica. With a sharp rending crack the glittering stone split apart. Under it was darkness.

The wizard stepped forward. "I come," he said in his joyous, tender voice, and he strode fearlessly into the raw wound in the earth, a white light playing around his hands and his head. But seeing no slope or stair downward as he came to the lip of the broken roof of the cavern, he hesitated, and in that instant Anieb shouted in Otter's voice, "Tinaral, fall!"

Staggering wildly the wizard tried to turn, lost his footing on the crumbling edge, and plunged down into the dark, his scarlet cloak billowing up, the werelight round him like a falling star.

"Close!" Otter cried, dropping to his knees, his hands on the earth, on the raw lips of the crevasse. "Close, Mother! Be healed, be whole!" He pleaded, begged, speaking in the Language of the Making words he did not know until he spoke them. "Mother, be whole!" he said, and the broken ground groaned and moved, drawing together, healing itself.

A reddish seam remained, a scar through the dirt and gravel and uprooted grass.

The wind rattled the dry leaves on the scrub-oak bushes. The sun was behind the hill, and clouds were coming over in a low, grey mass.

Otter crouched there at the foot of the hillslope, alone.

The clouds darkened. Rain passed through the little valley, falling on the dirt and the grass. Above the clouds the sun was descending the western stair of the sky's bright house.

Otter sat up at last. He was wet, cold, bewildered. Why was he here?

He had lost something and had to find it. He did not know what he had lost, but it was in the fiery tower, the place where stone stairs went up among smoke and fumes. He had to go there. He got to his feet and shuffled, lame and unsteady, back down the valley.

He had no thought of hiding or protecting himself. Luckily for him there were no guards about; there were few guards, and they were not on the alert, since the wizard's spells had kept the prison shut. The spells were gone, but the people in the tower did not know it, working on under the greater spell of hopelessness.

Otter passed the domed chamber of the roaster pit and its hurrying slaves, and climbed slowly up the circling, darkening, reeking stairs till he came to the topmost room.

She was there, the sick woman who could heal him, the poor woman who held the treasure, the stranger who was himself.

He stood silent in the doorway. She sat on the stone floor near the crucible, her thin body greyish and dark like the stones. Her chin and breasts were shiny with the spittle that ran from her mouth. He thought of the spring of water that had run from the broken earth.

"Medra," she said. Her sore mouth could not speak clearly. He knelt down and took her hands, looking into her face.

"Anieb," he whispered, "come with me."

"I want to go home," she said.

He helped her stand. He made no spell to protect or hide them. His strength had been used up. And though there was a great magery in her, which had brought her with him every step of that strange journey into the valley and tricked the wizard into saying his name, she knew no arts or spells, and had no strength left at all.

Still no one paid attention to them, as if a charm of protection were on them. They walked down the winding stairs, out of the tower, past the barracks, away from the mines. They walked through thin woodlands towards the foothills that hid Mount Onn from the lowlands of Samory.

Anieb kept a better pace than seemed possible in a woman so famished and destroyed, walking almost naked in the chill of the rain. All her will was aimed on walking forward; she had nothing else in her mind, not him, not anything. But she was there bodily with him, and he felt her presence as keenly and strangely as when she had come to his summoning. The rain ran down her naked head and body. He made her stop to put on his shirt. He was ashamed of it, for it was filthy, he having worn it all these weeks. She let him pull it over her head and then walked right on. She could not go quickly, but she went steadily, her eyes fixed on the faint cart track they followed, till the night came early under the rain clouds, and they could not see where to set their feet.

"Make the light," she said. Her voice was a whimper, plaintive. "Can't you make the light?"

"I don't know," he said, but he tried to bring the werelight round them, and after a while the ground glimmered faintly before their feet.

"We should find shelter and rest," he said.

"I can't stop," she said, and started to walk again.

"You can't walk all night."

"If I lie down I won't get up. I want to see the Mountain."

Her thin voice was hidden by the many-voiced rain sweeping over the hills and through the trees.

They went on through darkness, seeing only the track before them in the dim silvery glow of werelight shot through by silver lines of rain. When she stumbled he caught her arm. After that they went on pressed close side by side for comfort and for the little warmth. They walked slower, and yet slower, but they walked on. There was no sound but the sound of the rain falling from the black sky, and the little kissing squelch of their sodden feet in the mud and wet grass of the track.

"Look," she said, halting. "Medra, look."

He had been walking almost asleep. The pallor of the were-light had faded, drowned in a fainter, vaster clarity. Sky and earth were all one grey, but before them and above them, very high, over a drift of cloud, the long ridge of the mountain glimmered red.

"There," Anieb said. She pointed at the mountain and smiled. She looked at her companion, then slowly down at the ground. She sank down kneeling. He knelt with her, tried to support her, but she slid down in his arms. He tried to keep her head at least from the mud of the track. Her limbs and face twitched, her teeth chattered. He held her close against him, trying to warm her.

"The women," she whispered, "the hand. Ask them. In the village. I did see the Mountain."

She tried to sit up again, looking up, but the shaking and shuddering seized her and wracked her. She began to gasp for breath. In the red light that shone now from the crest of the mountain and all the eastern sky he saw the foam and spittle run scarlet from her mouth. Sometimes she clutched at him, but she did not speak again. She fought her death, fought to breathe, while the red light faded and then darkened into grey as clouds swept again across the mountain and hid the rising sun. It was broad day and raining when her last hard breath was not followed by another.

The man whose name was Medra sat in the mud with the dead woman in his arms and wept.

A carter walking at his mule's head with a load of oakwood came upon them and took them both to Woodedge. He could not make the young man let go of the dead woman. Weak and shaky as he was, he would not set his burden down on the load, but clambered into the cart holding her, and held her all the miles to Woodedge. All he said was "She saved me," and the carter asked no questions.

"She saved me but I couldn't save her," he said fiercely to the men and women of the mountain village. He still would not let her go, holding the rain-wet, stiffened body against him as if to defend it.

Very slowly they made him understand that one of the women was Anieb's mother, and that he should give Anieb to her to hold. He did so at last, watching to see if she was gentle with his friend and would protect her. Then he followed another woman meekly enough. He put on dry clothing she gave him to put on, and ate a little food she gave him to eat, and lay down on the pallet she led him to, and sobbed in weariness, and slept.

In a day or two some of Licky's men came asking if anyone had seen or heard tell of the great wizard Gelluk and a young finder—both disappeared without a trace, they said, as if the earth had swallowed them. Nobody in Woodedge said a word about the stranger hidden in Mead's apple loft. They kept him safe. Maybe that is why the people there now call their village not Woodedge, as it used to be, but Otterhide.

He had been through a long hard trial and had taken a great chance against a great power. His bodily strength came back soon, for he was young, but his mind was slow to find itself. He had lost something, lost it forever, lost it as he found it.

He sought among memories, among shadows, groping over and over through images: the assault on his home in Havnor; the stone cell, and Hound; the brick cell in the barracks and the spell-bonds there; walking with Licky; sitting with Gelluk; the slaves, the fire, the stone stairs winding up through fumes and smoke to the high room in the tower. He had to regain it all, to go through it all, searching. Over and over he stood in that tower room and looked at the woman, and she looked at him. Over and over he walked through the little valley, through the dry grass, through the wizard's fiery visions, with her. Over and over he saw the wizard fall, saw the earth close. He saw the red ridge of the mountain in the dawn. Anieb died while he held her, her ruined face against his arm. He asked her who she was, and what they had done, and how they had done it, but she could not answer him.

Her mother Ayo and her mother's sister Mead were wise women. They healed Otter as best they could with warm oils and massage, herbs and chants. They talked to him and listened when he talked. Neither of them had any doubt but that he was a man of great power. He denied this. "I could have done nothing without your daughter," he said.

"What did she do?" Ayo asked, softly.

He told her, as well as he could. "We were strangers. Yet she gave me her name," he said. "And I gave her mine." He spoke haltingly, with long pauses. "It was I that walked with the wizard, compelled by him, but she was with me, and she was free. And so together we could turn his power against him, so that he destroyed himself." He thought for a long time, and said, "She gave me her power."

"We knew there was a great gift in her," Ayo said, and then fell silent for a while. "We didn't know how to teach her. There are no teachers left on the mountain. King Losen's wizards destroy the sorcerers and witches. There's no one to turn to."

"Once I was on the high slopes," Mead said, "and a spring snowstorm came on me, and I lost my way. She came there. She came to me, not in the body, and guided me to the track. She was only twelve then."

"She walked with the dead, sometimes," Ayo said very low. "In the forest, down towards Faliern. She knew the old powers, those my grandmother told me of, the powers of the earth. They were strong there, she said."

"But she was only a girl like the others, too," Mead said, and hid her face. "A good girl," she whispered.

After a while Ayo said, "She went down to Firn with some of the young folk. To buy fleece from the shepherds there. A year ago last spring. That wizard they spoke of came there, casting spells. Taking slaves."

Then they were all silent.

Ayo and Mead were much alike, and Otter saw in them what Anieb might have been: a short, slight, quick woman, with a round face and clear eyes, and a mass of dark hair, not straight like most people's hair but curly, frizzy. Many people in the west of Havnor had hair like that.

But Anieb had been bald, like all the slaves in the roaster tower.

Her use-name had been Flag, the blue iris of the springs. Her mother and aunt called her Flag when they spoke of her.

"Whatever I am, whatever I can do, it's not enough," he said.

"It's never enough," Mead said. "And what can anyone do alone?"

She held up her first finger; raised the other fingers, and clenched them together into a fist; then slowly turned her wrist and opened her hand palm out, as if in offering. He had seen Anieb make that gesture. It was not a spell, he thought, watching intently, but a sign. Ayo was watching him.

"It is a secret," she said.

"Can I know the secret?" he asked after a while.

"You already know it. You gave it to Flag. She gave it to you. Trust."

"Trust," the young man said. "Yes. But against— Against them?— Gelluk's gone. Maybe Losen will fall now. Will it make any difference? Will the slaves go free? Will beggars eat? Will justice be done? I think there's an evil in us, in humankind. Trust denies it. Leaps across it. Leaps the chasm. But it's there. And everything we do finally serves evil, because that's what we are. Greed and cruelty. I look at the world, at the forests and the mountain here, the sky, and it's all right, as it should be. But we aren't. People aren't. We're wrong. We do wrong. No animal does wrong. How could they? But we can, and we do. And we never stop."

They listened to him, not agreeing, not denying, but accepting his despair. His words went into their listening silence, and rested there for days, and came back to him changed.

"We can't do anything without each other," he said. "But it's the greedy ones, the cruel ones who hold together and strengthen each other. And those who won't join them stand each alone." The image of Anieb as he had first seen her, a dying woman standing alone in the tower room, was always with him. "Real power goes to waste. Every wizard uses his arts against the others, serving the men of greed. What good can any art be used that way? It's wasted. It goes wrong, or it's thrown away. Like slaves' lives. Nobody can be free alone. Not even a mage. All of them working their magic in prison cells, to gain nothing. There's no way to use power for good."

Ayo closed her hand and opened it palm up, a fleeting sketch of a gesture, of a sign.

A man came up the mountain to Woodedge, a charcoal burner from Firn. "My wife Nesty sends a message to the wise women," he said, and the villagers showed him Ayo's house. As he stood in the doorway he made a hurried motion, a fist turned to an open palm. "Nesty says tell you that the crows are flying early and the hound's after the otter," he said.

Otter, sitting by the fire shelling walnuts, held still. Mead thanked the messenger and brought him in for a cup of water and a handful of shelled nuts. She and Ayo chatted with him about his wife. When he had gone she turned to Otter.

"The Hound serves Losen," he said. "I'll go today."

Mead looked at her sister. "Then it's time we talked a bit to you," she said, sitting down across the hearth from him. Ayo stood by the table, silent. A good fire burned in the hearth. It was a wet, cold time, and firewood was one thing they had plenty of, here on the mountain.

"There's people all over these parts, and maybe beyond, who think, as you said, that nobody can be wise alone. So these people try to hold to each other. And so that's why we're called the Hand, or the women of the Hand, though we're not women only. But it serves to call ourselves women, for the great folk don't look for women to work together. Or to have thoughts about such things as rule or misrule. Or to have any powers."

"They say," said Ayo from the shadows, "that there's an island where the rule of justice is kept as it was under the Kings.

Morred's Isle, they call it. But it's not Enlad of the Kings, nor Éa. It's south, not north of Havnor, they say. There they say the women of the Hand have kept the old arts. And they teach them, not keeping them secret each to himself, as the wizards do."

"Maybe with such teaching you could teach the wizards a lesson," Mead said.

"Maybe you can find that island," said Ayo.

Otter looked from one to the other. Clearly they had told him their own greatest secret and their hope.

"Morred's Isle," he said.

"That would be only what the women of the Hand call it, keeping its meaning from the wizards and the pirates. To them no doubt it would bear some other name."

"It would be a terrible long way," said Mead.

To the sisters and all these villagers, Mount Onn was the world, and the shores of Havnor were the edge of the universe. Beyond that was only rumor and dream.

"You'll come to the sea, going south, they say," said Ayo.

"He knows that, sister," Mead told her. "Didn't he tell us he was a ship carpenter? But it's a terrible long way down to the sea, surely. With this wizard on your scent, how are you to go there?"

"By the grace of water, that carries no scent," Otter said, standing up. A litter of walnut shells fell from his lap, and he took the hearth broom and swept them into the ashes. "I'd better go."

"There's bread," Ayo said, and Mead hurried to pack hard bread and hard cheese and walnuts into a pouch made of a sheep's stomach. They were very poor people. They gave him what they had. So Anieb had done.

"My mother was born in Endlane, round by Faliern Forest," Otter said. "Do you know that town? She's called Rose, Rowan's daughter."

"The carters go down to Endlane, summers."

"If somebody could talk to her people there, they'd get word to her. Her brother, Littleash, used to come to the city every year or two."

They nodded.

"If she knew I was alive," he said.

Anieb's mother nodded. "She'll hear it."

"Go on now," said Mead.

"Go with the water," said Ayo.

He embraced them, and they him, and he left the house.

He ran down from the straggle of huts to the quick, noisy stream he had heard singing through his sleep all his nights in Woodedge. He prayed to it. "Take me and save me," he asked it. He made the spell the old Changer had taught him long ago, and said the word of transformation. Then no man knelt by the loud-running water, but an otter slipped into it and was gone.

III. Tern

There was a wise man on our hill
Who found his way to work his will.
He changed his shape, he changed his name,
But ever the other will be the same.
    So runs the water away, away,
    So runs the water away.

ONE WINTER AFTERNOON on the shore of the Onneva River where it fingers out into the north bight of the Great Bay of Havnor, a man stood up on the muddy sand: a man poorly dressed and poorly shod, a thin brown man with dark eyes and hair so fine and thick it shed the rain. It was raining on the low beaches of the river mouth, the fine, cold, dismal drizzle of that grey winter. His clothes were soaked. He hunched his shoulders, turned about, and set off towards a wisp of chimney smoke he saw far down the shore. Behind him were the tracks of an otter's four feet coming up from the water and the tracks of a man's two feet going away from it.

Where he went then, the songs don't tell. They say only that he wandered, "he wandered long from land to land." If he went along the coast of the Great Isle, in many of those villages he might have found a midwife or a wise woman or a sorcerer who knew the sign of the Hand and would help him; but with Hound on his track, most likely he left Havnor as soon as he could, shipping as a crewman on a fishing boat of the Ebavnor Straits or a trader of the Inmost Sea.

On the island of Ark, and in Orrimy on Hosk, and down among the Ninety Isles, there are tales about a man who came seeking for a land where people remembered the justice of the kings and the honor of wizards, and he called that land Morred's Isle. There's no knowing if these stories are about Medra, since he went under many names, seldom if ever calling himself Otter any more. Gelluk's fall had not brought Losen down. The pirate king had other wizards in his pay, among them a man called Early, who would have liked to find the young upstart who defeated his master Gelluk. And Early had a good chance of tracing him. Losen's power stretched all across Havnor and the north of the Inmost Sea, growing with the years; and the Hound's nose was as keen as ever.

Maybe it was to escape the hunt that Medra came to Pendor, a long way west of the Inmost Sea, or maybe some rumor among the women of the Hand on Hosk sent him there. Pendor was a rich island, then, before the dragon Yevaud despoiled it. Wherever Medra had gone until then, he had found the lands like Havnor or worse, sunk in warfare, raids, and piracy, the fields full of weeds, the towns full of thieves. Maybe he thought, at first, that on Pendor he had found Morred's Isle, for the city was beautiful and peaceful and the people prosperous.

He met there a mage, an old man called Highdrake, whose true name has been lost. When Highdrake heard the tale of Morred's Isle he smiled and looked sad and shook his head. "Not here," he said. "Not this. The Lords of Pendor are good men. They remember the kings. They don't seek war or plunder. But they send their sons west dragon hunting. In sport. As if the dragons of the West Reach were ducks or geese for the killing! No good will come of that."

Highdrake took Medra as his student, gratefully. "I was taught my art by a mage who gave me freely all he knew, but I never found anybody to give that knowledge to, until you came," he told Medra. "The young men come to me and they say, 'What good is it? Can you find gold?' they say. 'Can you teach me how to make stones into diamonds? Can you give me a sword that will kill a dragon? What's the use of talking about the balance of things? There's no profit in it,' they say. No profit!" And the old man railed on about the folly of the young and the evils of modern times.

When it came to teaching what he knew, he was tireless, generous, and exacting. For the first time, Medra was given a vision of magic not as a set of strange gifts and reasonless acts, but as an art and a craft, which could be known truly with long study and used rightly after long practice, though even then it would never lose its strangeness. Highdrake's mastery of spells and sorcery was not much greater than his pupil's, but he had clear in his mind the idea of something very much greater, the wholeness of knowledge. And that made him a mage.

Listening to him, Medra thought of how he and Anieb had walked in the dark and rain by the faint glimmer that showed them only the next step they could take, and of how they had looked up to the red ridge of the mountain in the dawn.

"Every spell depends on every other spell," said Highdrake. "Every motion of a single leaf moves every leaf of every tree on every isle of Earthsea! There is a pattern. That's what you must look for and look to. Nothing goes right but as part of the pattern. Only in it is freedom."

Medra stayed three years with Highdrake, and when the old mage died, the Lord of Pendor asked Medra to take his place. Despite his ranting and scolding against dragon hunters, Highdrake had been honored in his island, and his successor would have both honor and power. Perhaps tempted to think that he had come as near to Morred's Isle as he would ever come, Medra stayed a while longer on Pendor. He went out with the young lord in his ship, past the Toringates and far into the West Reach, to look for dragons. There was a great longing in his heart to see a dragon. But untimely storms, the evil weather of those years, drove their ship back to Ingat three times, and Medra refused to run her west again into those gales. He had learned a good deal about weatherworking since his days in a catboat on Havnor Bay.

A while after that he left Pendor, drawn southward again, and maybe went to Ensmer. In one guise or another he came at last to Geath in the Ninety Isles.

There they fished for whales, as they still do. That was a trade he wanted no part of. Their ships stank and their town stank. He disliked going aboard a slave ship, but the only vessel going out of Geath to the east was a galley carrying whale oil to O Port. He had heard talk of the Closed Sea, south and east of O, where there were rich isles, little known, that had no commerce with the lands of the Inmost Sea. What he sought might be there. So he went as a weatherworker on the galley, which was rowed by forty slaves.

The weather was fair for once: a following wind, a blue sky lively with little white clouds, the mild sunlight of late spring. They made good way from Geath. Late in the afternoon he heard the master say to the helmsman, "Keep her south tonight so we don't raise Roke."

He had not heard of that island, and asked, "What's there?"

"Death and desolation," said the ship's master, a short man with small, sad, knowing eyes like a whale's.

"War?"

"Years back. Plague, black sorcery. The waters all round it are cursed."

"Worms," said the helmsman, the master's brother. "Catch fish anywhere near Roke, you'll find 'em thick with worms as a dead dog on a dunghill."

"Do people still live there?" Medra asked, and the master said, "Witches," while his brother said, "Worm eaters."

There were many such isles in the Archipelago, made barren and desolate by rival wizards' blights and curses; they were evil places to come to or even to pass, and Medra thought no more about this one, until that night.

Sleeping out on deck with the starlight on his face, he had a simple, vivid dream: it was daylight, clouds racing across a bright sky, and across the sea he saw the sunlit curve of a high green hill. He woke with the vision still clear in his mind, knowing he had seen it ten years before, in the spell-locked barracks room at the mines of Samory.

He sat up. The dark sea was so quiet that the stars were reflected here and there on the sleek lee side of the long swells. Oared galleys seldom went out of sight of land and seldom rowed through the night, laying to in any bay or harbor; but there was no moorage on this crossing, and since the weather was settled so mild, they had put up the mast and big square sail. The ship drifted softly forward, her slave oarsmen sleeping on their benches, the free men of her crew all asleep but the helmsman and the lookout, and the lookout was dozing. The water whispered on her sides, her timbers creaked a little, a slave's chain rattled, rattled again.

"They don't need a weatherworker on a night like this, and they haven't paid me yet," Medra said to his conscience. He had waked from his dream with the name Roke in his mind. Why had he never heard of the isle or seen it on a chart? It might be accursed and deserted as they said, but wouldn't it be set down on the charts?

"I could fly there as a tern and be back on the ship before daylight," he said to himself, but idly. He was bound for O Port. Ruined lands were all too common. No need to fly to seek them. He made himself comfortable in his coil of cable and watched the stars. Looking west, he saw the four bright stars of the Forge, low over the sea. They were a little blurred, and as he watched them they blinked out, one by one.

The faintest little sighing tremor ran over the slow, smooth swells.

"Master," Medra said, afoot, "wake up."

"What now?"

"A witchwind coming. Following. Get the sail down."

No wind stirred. The air was soft, the big sail hung slack. Only the western stars faded and vanished in a silent blackness that rose slowly higher. The master looked at that. "Witchwind, you say?" he asked, reluctant.

Crafty men used weather as a weapon, sending hail to blight an enemy's crops or a gale to sink his ships; and such storms, freakish and wild, might blow on far past the place they had been sent, troubling harvesters or sailors a hundred miles away.

"Get the sail down," Medra said, peremptory. The master

yawned and cursed and began to shout commands. The crewmen got up slowly and slowly began to take the awkward sail in, and the oarmaster, after asking several questions of the master and Medra, began to roar at the slaves and stride among them rousing them right and left with his knotted rope. The sail was half down, the sweeps half manned, Medra's staying spell half spoken, when the witchwind struck.

It struck with one huge thunderclap out of sudden utter blackness and wild rain. The ship pitched like a horse rearing and then rolled so hard and far that the mast broke loose from its footing, though the stays held. The sail struck the water, filled, and pulled the galley right over, the great sweeps sliding in their oarlocks, the chained slaves struggling and shouting on their benches, barrels of oil breaking loose and thundering over one an-other—pulled her over and held her over, the deck vertical to the sea, till a huge storm wave struck and swamped her and she sank. All the shouting and screaming of men's voices was suddenly silent. There was no noise but the roar of the rain on the sea, less-ening as the freak wind passed on eastward. Through it one white seabird beat its wings up from the black water and flew, frail and desperate, to the north.

Printed on narrow sands under granite cliffs, in the first light, were the tracks of a bird alighting. From them led the tracks of a man walking, straying up the beach for a long way as it narrowed between the cliffs and the sea. Then the tracks ceased.

Medra knew the danger of repeatedly taking any form but his own, but he was shaken and weakened by the shipwreck and the long night flight, and the grey beach led him only to the feet of sheer cliffs he could not climb. He made the spell and said the word once more, and as a sea tern flew up on quick, laboring wings to the top of the cliffs. Then, possessed by flight, he flew on over a shadowy sunrise land. Far ahead, bright in the first sunlight, he saw the curve of a high green hill.

To it he flew, and on it landed, and as he touched the earth he was a man again.

He stood there for a while, bewildered. It seemed to him that it was not by his own act or decision that he had taken his own form, but that in touching this ground, this hill, he had become himself. A magic greater than his own prevailed here.

He looked about, curious and wary. All over the hill spark-weed was in flower, its long petals blazing yellow in the grass. Children on Havnor knew that flower. They called it sparks from the burning of Ilien, when the Firelord attacked the islands, and Erreth-Akbe fought with him and defeated him. Tales and songs of the heroes rose up in Medra's memory as he stood there: Erreth-Akbe and the heroes before him, the Eagle Queen, Heru, Akambar who drove the Kargs into the east, and Serriadh the peacemaker, and Elfarran of Soléa, and Morred, the White En-chanter, the beloved king. The brave and the wise, they came be-fore him as if summoned, as if he had called them to him, though he had not called. He saw them. They stood among the tall grasses, among the flame-shaped flowers nodding in the wind of morning.

Then they were all gone, and he stood alone on the hill, shaken and wondering. "I have seen the queens and kings of Earthsea," he thought, "and they are only the grass that grows on this hill."

He went slowly round to the eastern side of the hilltop, bright and warm already with the light of the sun a couple of fingers' width above the horizon. Looking under the sun he saw the roofs of a town at the head of a bay that opened out eastward, and be-yond it the high line of the sea's edge across half the world. Turn-ing west he saw fields and pastures and roads. To the north were long green hills. In a fold of land southward a grove of tall trees drew his gaze and held it. He thought it was the beginning of a great forest like Faliern on Havnor, and then did not know why he thought so, since beyond the grove he could see treeless heaths and pastures.

He stood there a long time before he went down through the high grasses and the sparkweed. At the foot of the hill he came into a lane. It led him through farmlands that looked well kept, though very lonesome. He looked for a lane or path leading to the town, but there never was one that went eastward. Not a soul was in the fields, some of which were newly ploughed. No dog barked as he went by. Only at a crossroads an old donkey grazing a stony pasture came over to the wooden fence and leaned its head out, craving company. Medra stopped to stroke the grey-brown, bony face. A city man and a saltwater man, he knew little of farms and their animals, but he thought the donkey looked at him kindly. "Where am I, donkey?" he said to it. "How do I get to the town I saw?"

The donkey leaned its head hard against his hand so that he would go on scratching the place just above its eyes and below its ears. When he did so, it flicked its long right ear. So when he parted from the donkey he took the right hand of the crossroad, though it looked as if it would lead back to the hill; and soon enough he came among houses, and then onto a street that brought him down at last into the town at the head of the bay.

It was as strangely quiet as the farmlands. Not a voice, not a face. It was difficult to feel uneasy in an ordinary-looking town on a sweet spring morning, but in such silence he must wonder if he was indeed in a plague-stricken place or an island under a curse. He went on. Between a house and an old plum tree was a wash line, the clothes pinned on it flapping in the sunny breeze. A cat came round the corner of a garden, no abandoned starveling but a white-pawed, well-whiskered, prosperous cat. And at last, coming down the steep little street, which here was cobbled, he heard voices.

He stopped to listen, and heard nothing.

He went on to the the foot of the street. It opened into a small market square. People were gathered there, not many of them. They were not buying or selling. There were no booths or stalls set up. They were waiting for him.

Ever since he had walked on the green hill above the town and had seen the bright shadows in the grass, his heart had been easy. He was expectant, full of a sense of great strangeness, but not frightened. He stood still and looked at the people who came to meet him.

Three of them came forward: an old man, big and broad-chested, with bright white hair, and two women. Wizard knows wizard, and Medra knew they were women of power.

He raised his hand closed in a fist and then turning and opening it, offered it to them palm up.

"Ah," said one of the women, the taller of the two, and she laughed. But she did not answer the gesture.

"Tell us who you are," the white-haired man said, courteously enough, but without greeting or welcome. "Tell us how you came here."

"I was born in Havnor and trained as a shipwright and a sorcerer. I was on a ship bound from Geath to O Port. I was spared alone from drowning, last night, when a witchwind struck." He was silent then. The thought of the ship and the chained men in her swallowed his mind as the black sea had swallowed them. He gasped, as if coming up from drowning.

"How did you come here?"

"As . . . as a bird, a tern. Is this Roke Island?"

"You changed yourself?"

He nodded.

"Whom do you serve?" asked the shorter and younger of the women, speaking for the first time. She had a keen, hard face, with long black brows.

"I have no master."

"What was your errand in O Port?"

"In Havnor, years ago, I was in servitude. Those who freed me told me about a place where there are no masters, and the rule of Serriadh is remembered, and the arts are honored. I have been looking for that place, that island, seven years."

"Who told you about it?"

"Women of the Hand."

"Anyone can make a fist and show a palm," said the tall woman, pleasantly. "But not everyone can fly to Roke. Or swim, or sail, or come in any way at all. So we must ask what brought you here."

Medra did not answer at once. "Chance," he said at last, "favoring long desire. Not art. Not knowledge. I think I've come to the place I sought, but I don't know. I think you may be the people they told me of, but I don't know. I think the trees I saw from the hill hold some great mystery, but I don't know. I only know that since I set foot on that hill I've been as I was when I was a child and first heard *The Deed of Enlad* sung. I am lost among wonders."

The white-haired man looked at the two women. Other people had come forward, and there was some quiet talk among them.

"If you stayed here, what would you do?" the black-browed woman asked him.

"I can build boats, or mend them, and sail them. I can find, above and under ground. I can work weather, if you have any need of that. And I'll learn the art from any who will teach me."

"What do you want to learn?" asked the taller woman in her mild voice.

Now Medra felt that he had been asked the question on which the rest of his life hung, for good or evil. Again he stood silent a while. He started to speak, and didn't speak, and finally spoke. "I could not save one, not one, not the one who saved me," he said. "Nothing I know could have set her free. I know nothing. If you know how to be free, I beg you, teach me!"

"Free!" said the tall woman, and her voice cracked like a whip. Then she looked at her companions, and after a while she smiled a little. Turning back to Medra, she said, "We're prisoners, and so freedom is a thing we study. You came here through the walls of our prison. Seeking freedom, you say. But you should know that leaving Roke may be even harder than coming to it. Prison within prison, and some of it we have built ourselves." She looked at the others. "What do you say?" she asked them.

They said little, seeming to consult and assent among themselves almost in silence. At last the shorter woman looked with her fierce eyes at Medra. "Stay if you will," she said.

"I will."

"What will you have us call you?"

"Tern," he said; and so he was called.

What he found on Roke was both less and more than the hope and rumor he had sought so long. Roke Island was, they told him, the heart of Earthsea. The first land Segoy raised from the waters in the beginning of time was bright Éa of the northern sea, and the second was Roke. That green hill, Roke Knoll, was founded deeper than all the islands. The trees he had seen, which seemed sometimes to be in one place on the isle and sometimes in another, were the oldest trees in the world, and the source and center of magic.

"If the Grove were cut, all wizardry would fail. The roots of those trees are the roots of knowledge. The patterns the shadows of their leaves make in the sunlight write the words Segoy spoke in the Making."

So said Ember, his fierce, black-browed teacher.

All the teachers of the art magic on Roke were women. There were no men of power, few men at all, on the island.

Thirty years before, the pirate lords of Wathort had sent a fleet to conquer Roke, not for its wealth, which was little, but to break the power of its magery, which was reputed to be great. One of the wizards of Roke had betrayed the island to the crafty men of Wathort, lowering its spells of defense and warning. Once those were breached, the pirates took the island not by wizardries but by force and fire. Their great ships filled Thwil Bay, their hordes burned and looted, their slave takers carried off men, boys, young women. Little children and the old they slaughtered. They fired every house and field they came to. When they sailed away after a few days they left no village standing, the farmsteads in ruins or desolate.

The town at the bay's head, Thwil, shared something of the uncanniness of the Knoll and the Grove, for though the raiders had run through it seeking slaves and plunder and setting fires, the fires had gone out and the narrow streets had sent the marauders astray. Most of the islanders who survived were wise women and their children, who had hidden themselves in the town or in the Immanent Grove. The men now on Roke were those spared children, grown, and a few men now grown old. There was no government but that of the women of the Hand, for it was their spells that had protected Roke so long and protected it far more closely now.

They had little trust in men. A man had betrayed them. Men had attacked them. It was men's ambitions, they said, that had perverted all the arts to ends of gain. "We do not deal with their governments," said tall Veil in her mild voice.

And yet Ember said to Medra, "We were our own undoing."

Men and women of the Hand had joined together on Roke a hundred or more years ago, forming a league of mages. Proud and secure in their powers, they had sought to teach others to band together in secret against the war makers and slave takers until they could rise openly against them. Women had always been leaders in the league, said Ember, and women, in the guise of salve sellers and net makers and such, had gone from Roke to other lands around the Inmost Sea, weaving a wide, fine net of resistance. Even now there were strands and knots of that net left. Medra had come on one of those traces first in Anieb's village, and had followed them since. But they had not led him here. Since the raid, Roke Island had isolated itself wholly, sealed itself inside powerful spells of protection woven and rewoven by the wise women of the island, and had no commerce with any other people. "We can't save them," Ember said. "We couldn't save ourselves."

Veil, with her gentle voice and smile, was implacable. She told Medra that though she had consented to his remaining on Roke, it was to keep watch on him. "You broke through our defenses once," she said. "All that you say of yourself may be true, and may not. What can you tell me that would make me trust you?"

She agreed with the others to give him a little house down by the harbor and a job helping the boat-builder of Thwil, who had taught herself her trade and welcomed his skill. Veil put no difficulties in his path and always greeted him kindly. But she had said, "What can you tell me that would make me trust you?" and he had no answer for her.

Ember usually scowled when he greeted her. She asked him abrupt questions, listened to his answers, and said nothing.

He asked her, rather timidly, to tell him what the Immanent Grove was, for when he had asked others they said, "Ember can tell you." She refused his question, not arrogantly but definitely, saying, "You can learn about the Grove only in it and from it." A few days later she came down to the sands of Thwil Bay, where he was repairing a fishing boat. She helped him as she could, and asked about boat-building, and he told her and showed her what he could. It was a peaceful afternoon, but after it she went off in her abrupt way. He felt some awe of her; she was incalculable. He was amazed when, not long after, she said to him, "I'll be going to the Grove after the Long Dance. Come if you like."

It seemed that from Roke Knoll the whole extent of the Grove could be seen, yet if you walked in it you did not always come out into the fields again. You walked on under the trees. In the inner Grove they were all of one kind, which grew nowhere else, yet had no name in Hardic but "tree." In the Old Speech, Ember said, each of those trees had its own name. You walked on, and after a time you were walking again among familiar trees, oak and beech and ash, chestnut and walnut and willow, green in spring and bare in winter; there were dark firs, and cedar, and a tall evergreen Medra did not know, with soft reddish bark and layered foliage. You walked on, and the way through the trees was never twice the same. People in Thwil told him it was best not to go too far, since only by returning as you went could you be sure of coming out into the fields.

"How far does the forest go?" Medra asked, and Ember said, "As far as the mind goes."

The leaves of the trees spoke, she said, and the shadows could be read. "I am learning to read them," she said.

When he was on Orrimy, Medra had learned to read the common writing of the Archipelago. Later, Highdrake of Pendor had taught him some of the runes of power. That was known lore. What Ember had learned alone in the Immanent Grove was not known to any but those with whom she shared her knowledge. She lived all summer under the eaves of the Grove, having no more than a box to keep the mice and wood rats from her small store of food, a shelter of branches, and a cook fire near a stream that came out of the woods to join the little river running down to the bay.

Medra camped nearby. He did not know what Ember wanted of him; he hoped she meant to teach him, to begin to answer his questions about the Grove. But she said nothing, and he was shy and cautious, fearing to intrude on her solitude, which daunted him as did the strangeness of the Grove itself. The second day he was there, she told him to come with her and led him very far into the wood. They walked for hours in silence. In the summer midday the woods were silent. No bird sang. The leaves did not stir. The aisles of the trees were endlessly different and all the same. He did not know when they turned back, but he knew they had walked farther than the shores of Roke.

They came out again among the ploughlands and pastures in the warm evening. As they walked back to their camping place he saw the four stars of the Forge come out above the western hills.

Ember parted from him with only a "Good night."

The next day she said, "I'm going to sit under the trees." Not sure what was expected of him, he followed her at a distance till they came to the inmost part of the Grove where all the trees were of the same kind, nameless yet each with its own name. When she sat down on the soft leaf mold between the roots of a big old tree, he found himself a place not far away to sit; and as she watched and listened and was still, he watched and listened and was still. So they did for several days. Then one morning, in rebellious mood, he stayed by the stream while Ember walked into the Grove. She did not look back.

Veil came from Thwil Town that morning, bringing them a basket of bread, cheese, milk curds, summer fruits. "What have you learned?" she asked Medra in her cool, gentle way, and he answered, "That I'm a fool."

"Why so, Tern?"

"A fool could sit under the trees forever and grow no wiser."

The tall woman smiled a little. "My sister has never taught a man before," she said. She glanced at him, and gazed away, over the summery fields. "She's never looked at a man before," she said.

Medra stood silent. His face felt hot. He looked down. "I thought," he said, and stopped.

In Veil's words he saw, all at once, the other side of Ember's impatience, her fierceness, her silences.

He had tried to look at Ember as untouchable while he longed to touch her soft brown skin, her black shining hair. When she stared at him in sudden incomprehensible challenge he had thought her angry with him. He feared to insult, to offend her. What did she fear? His desire? Her own?— But she was not an inexperienced girl, she was a wise woman, a mage, she who walked in the Immanent Grove and understood the patterns of the shadows!

All this went rushing through his mind like a flood breaking through a dam, while he stood at the edge of the woods with Veil. "I thought mages kept themselves apart," he said at last. "Highdrake said that to make love is to unmake power."

"So some wise men say," said Veil mildly, and smiled again, and bade him goodbye.

He spent the whole afternoon in confusion, angry. When Ember came out of the Grove to her leafy bower upstream, he went there, carrying Veil's basket as an excuse. "May I talk to you?" he said.

She nodded shortly, frowning her black brows.

He said nothing. She squatted down to find out what was in the basket. "Peaches!" she said, and smiled.

"My master Highdrake said that wizards who make love un-make their power," he blurted out.

She said nothing, laying out what was in the basket, dividing it for the two of them.

"Do you think that's true?" he asked.

She shrugged. "No," she said.

He stood tongue-tied. After a while she looked up at him. "No," she said in a soft, quiet voice, "I don't think it's true. I think all the true powers, all the old powers, at root are one."

He still stood there, and she said, "Look at the peaches! They're all ripe. We'll have to eat them right away."

"If I told you my name," he said, "my true name—"

"I'd tell you mine," she said. "If that . . . if that's how we should begin."

They began, however, with the peaches.

They were both shy. When Medra took her hand his hand shook, and Ember, whose name was Elehal, turned away scowling. Then she touched his hand very lightly. When he stroked the sleek black flow of her hair she seemed only to endure his touch, and he stopped. When he tried to embrace her she was stiff, rejecting him. Then she turned and, fierce, hasty, awkward, seized him in her arms. It wasn't the first night, nor the first nights, they passed together that gave either of them much pleasure or ease. But they learned from each other, and came through shame and fear into passion. Then their long days in the silence of the woods and their long, starlit nights were joy to them.

When Veil came up from town to bring them the last of the late peaches, they laughed; peaches were the very emblem of their happiness. They tried to make her stay and eat supper with them, but she wouldn't. "Stay here while you can," she said.

The summer ended too soon that year. Rain came early; snow fell in autumn even as far south as Roke. Storm followed storm, as if the winds had risen in rage against the tampering and meddling of the crafty men. Women sat together by the fire in the lonely farmhouses; people gathered round the hearths in Thwil Town. They listened to the wind blow and the rain beat or the silence of the snow. Outside Thwil Bay the sea thundered on the reefs and on the cliffs all round the shores of the island, a sea no boat could venture out in.

What they had they shared. In that it was indeed Morred's Isle. Nobody on Roke starved or went unhoused, though nobody had much more than they needed. Hidden from the rest of the world not only by sea and storm but by their defenses that disguised the island and sent ships astray, they worked and talked and sang the songs, *The Winter Carol* and *The Deed of the Young King.* And they had books, the *Chronicles of Enlad* and the *History of the Wise Heroes.* From these precious books the old men and women would read aloud in a hall down by the wharf where the fisherwomen made and mended their nets. There was a hearth there, and they would light the fire. People came even from farms across the island to hear the histories read, listening in silence, intent. "Our souls are hungry," Ember said.

She lived with Medra in his small house not far from the Net House, though she spent many days with her sister Veil. Ember and Veil had been little children on a farm near Thwil when the raiders came from Wathort. Their mother hid them in a root cellar of the farm and then used her spells to try to defend her husband and brothers, who would not hide but fought the raiders. They were butchered with their cattle. The house and barns were burnt. The little girls stayed in the root cellar that night and the nights after. Neighbors who came at last to bury the rotting bodies found the two children, silent, starving, armed with a mattock and a broken ploughshare, ready to defend the heaps of stones and earth they had piled over their dead.

Medra knew only a hint of this story from Ember. One night Veil, who was three years older than Ember and to whom the memory was much clearer, told it to him fully. Ember sat with them, listening in silence.

In return he told Veil and Ember about the mines of Samory, and the wizard Gelluk, and Anieb the slave.

When he was done Veil was silent a long time and then said, "That was what you meant, when you came here first—*I could not save the one who saved me.*"

"And you asked me, *What can you tell me that could make me trust you?*"

"You have told me," Veil said.

Medra took her hand and put his forehead against it. Telling his story he had kept back tears. He could not do so now.

"She gave me freedom," he said. "And I still feel that all I do is done through her and for her. No, not for her. We can do nothing for the dead. But for . . ."

"For us," said Ember. "For us who live, in hiding, neither killed nor killing. The dead are dead. The great and mighty go their way unchecked. All the hope left in the world is in the people of no account."

"Must we hide forever?"

"Spoken like a man," said Veil with her gentle, wounded smile.

"Yes," said Ember. "We must hide, and forever if need be. Because there's nothing left but being killed and killing, beyond these shores. You say it, and I believe it."

"But you can't hide true power," Medra said. "Not for long. It dies in hiding, unshared."

"Magic won't die on Roke," said Veil. "*On Roke all spells are strong.* So said Ath himself. And you have walked under the trees . . . Our job must be to keep that strength. Hide it, yes. Hoard it, as a young dragon hoards up its fire. And share it. But only here. Pass it on, one to the next, here, where it's safe, and where the great robbers and killers would least look for it, since no one here is of any account. And one day the dragon will come into its strength. If it takes a thousand years . . ."

"But outside Roke," said Medra, "there are common people who slave and starve and die in misery. Must they do so for a thousand years with no hope?"

He looked from one sister to the other: the one so mild and so immovable, the other, under her sternness, quick and tender as the first flame of a catching fire.

"On Havnor," he said, " far from Roke, in a village on Mount Onn, among people who know nothing of the world, there are still women of the Hand. That net hasn't broken after so many years. How was it woven?"

"Craftily," said Ember.

"And cast wide!" He looked from one to the other again. "I wasn't well taught, in the City of Havnor," he said. "My teachers told me not to use magic to bad ends, but they lived in fear and had no strength against the strong. They gave me all they had to give, but it was little. It was by mere luck I didn't go wrong. And by Anieb's gift of strength to me. But for her I'd be Gelluk's servant now. Yet she herself was untaught, and so enslaved. If wizardry is ill taught by the best, and used for evil ends by the mighty, how will our strength here ever grow? What will the young dragon feed on?"

"This is the center," said Veil. "We must keep to the center. And wait."

"We must give what we have to give," said Medra. "If all but us are slaves, what's our freedom worth?"

"The true art prevails over the false. The pattern will hold," Ember said, frowning. She reached out the poker to gather together her namesakes in the hearth, and with a whack knocked the heap into a blaze. "That I know. But our lives are short, and the pattern's very long. If only Roke was now what it once was— if we had more people of the true art gathered here, teaching and learning as well as preserving—"

"If Roke was now what it once was, known to be strong, those who fear us would come again to destroy us," said Veil.

"The solution lies in secrecy," said Medra. "But so does the problem."

"Our problem is with men," Veil said, "if you'll forgive me, dear brother. Men are of more account to other men than women and children are. We might have fifty witches here and they'll pay little heed. But if they knew we had five men of power, they'd seek to destroy us again."

"So though there were men among us we were the *women* of the Hand," said Ember.

"You still are," Medra said. "Anieb was one of you. She and you and all of us live in the same prison."

"What can we do?" said Veil.

"Learn our strength!" said Medra.

"A school," Ember said. "Where the wise might come to learn from one another, to study the pattern . . . The Grove would shelter us."

"The lords of war despise scholars and schoolmasters," said Medra.

"I think they fear them too," said Veil.

So they talked, that long winter, and others talked with them. Slowly their talk turned from vision to intention, from longing to planning. Veil was always cautious, warning of dangers. White-haired Dune was so eager that Ember said he wanted to start teaching sorcery to every child in Thwil. Once Ember had come to believe that Roke's freedom lay in offering others freedom, she set her whole mind on how the women of the Hand might grow strong again. But her mind, formed by her long solitudes among the trees, always sought form and clarity, and she said, "How can we teach our art when we don't know what it is?"

And they talked about that, all the wise women of the island: what was the true art of magic, and where did it turn false; how the balance of things was kept or lost; what crafts were needful, which useful, which dangerous; why some people had one gift but not another, and whether you could learn an art you had no native gift for. In such discussions they worked out the names that ever since have been given to the masteries: finding, weather-working, changing, healing, summoning, patterning, naming, and the crafts of illusion, and the knowledge of the songs. Those are the arts of the Masters of Roke even now, though the Chanter took the Finder's place when finding came to be considered a merely useful craft unworthy of a mage.

And it was in these discussions that the school on Roke began.

There are some who say that the school had its beginnings far differently. They say that Roke used to be ruled by a woman called the Dark Woman, who was in league with the Old Powers of the earth. They say she lived in a cave under Roke Knoll, never coming into the daylight, but weaving vast spells over land and sea that compelled men to her evil will, until the first Archmage came to Roke, unsealed and entered the cave, defeated the Dark Woman, and took her place.

There's no truth in this tale but one, which is that indeed one of the first Masters of Roke opened and entered a great cavern. But though the roots of Roke are the roots of all the islands, that cavern was not on Roke.

And it's true that in the time of Medra and Elehal the people of Roke, men and women, had no fear of the Old Powers of the earth, but revered them, seeking strength and vision from them. That changed with the years.

Spring came late again that year, cold and stormy. Medra set to boat-building. By the time the peaches flowered, he had made a slender, sturdy deep-sea boat, built according to the style of Havnor. He called her *Hopeful*. Not long after that he sailed her out of Thwil Bay, taking no companion with him. "Look for me at the end of summer," he said to Ember.

"I'll be in the Grove," she said. "And my heart with you, my dark otter, my white tern, my love, Medra."

"And mine with you, my ember of fire, my flowering tree, my love, Elehal."

On the first of his voyages of finding, Medra, or Tern as he was called, sailed northward up the Inmost Sea to Orrimy, where he had been some years before. There were people of the Hand there whom he trusted. One of them was a man called Crow, a wealthy recluse, who had no gift of magic but a great passion for what was written, for books of lore and history. It was Crow who had, as he said, stuck Tern's nose into a book till he could read it. "Illiterate wizards are the curse of Earthsea!" he cried. "Ignorant power is a bane!" Crow was a strange man, wilful, arrogant, obstinate, and, in defense of his passion, brave. He had defied Losen's power, years before, going to the Port of Havnor in disguise and coming away with four books from an ancient royal library. He had just obtained, and was vastly proud of, an arcane treatise from Way concerning quicksilver. "Got that from under Losen's nose too," he said to Tern. "Come have a look at it! It belonged to a famous wizard."

"Tinaral," said Tern. "I knew him."

"Book's trash, is it?" said Crow, who was quick to pick up signals if they had to do with books.

"I don't know. I'm after bigger prey."

Crow cocked his head.

"The Book of Names."

"Lost with Ath when he went into the west," Crow said.

"A mage called Highdrake told me that when Ath stayed in Pendor, he told a wizard there that he'd left the Book of Names with a woman in the Ninety Isles for safekeeping."

"A woman! For safekeeping! In the Ninety Isles! Was he mad?"

Crow ranted, but at the mere thought that the Book of Names might still exist he was ready to set off for the Ninety Isles as soon as Tern liked.

So they sailed south in *Hopeful,* landing first at malodorous Geath, and then in the guise of peddlers working their way from one islet to the next among the mazy channels. Crow had stocked the boat with better wares than most householders of the Isles were used to seeing, and Tern offered them at fair prices, mostly in barter, since there was little money among the islanders. Their popularity ran ahead of them. It was known that they would trade for books, if the books were old and uncanny. But in the Isles all books were old and all uncanny, what there was of them.

Crow was delighted to get a water-stained bestiary from the time of Akambar in return for five silver buttons, a pearl-hilted knife, and a square of Lorbanery silk. He sat in *Hopeful* and crooned over the antique descriptions of harikki and otak and icebear. But Tern went ashore on every isle, showing his wares in the kitchens of the housewives and the sleepy taverns where the old men sat. Sometimes he idly made a fist and then turned his hand over opening the palm, but nobody here returned the sign.

"Books?" said a rush plaiter on North Sudidi. "Like that there?" He pointed to long strips of vellum that had been worked into the thatching of his house. "They good for something else?" Crow, staring up at the words visible here and there between the rushes in the eaves, began to tremble with rage. Tern hurried him back to the boat before he exploded.

"It was only a beast healer's manual," Crow admitted, when they were sailing on and he had calmed down. "'Spavined,' I saw, and something about ewes' udders. But the ignorance! the brute ignorance! To roof his house with it!"

"And it was useful knowledge," Tern said. "How can people be anything but ignorant when knowledge isn't saved, isn't taught? If books could be brought together in one place..."

"Like the Library of the Kings," said Crow, dreaming of lost glories.

"Or your library," said Tern, who had become a subtler man than he used to be.

"Fragments," Crow said, dismissing his life's work. "Remnants!"

"Beginnings," said Tern.

Crow only sighed.

"I think we might go south again," Tern said, steering for the open channel. "Towards Pody."

"You have a gift for the business," Crow said. "You know where to look. Went straight to that bestiary in the barn loft... But there's nothing much to look for here. Nothing of importance. Ath wouldn't have left the greatest of all the lore-books among boors who'd make thatch of it! Take us to Pody if you like. And then back to Orrimy. I've had about enough."

"And we're out of buttons," Tern said. He was cheerful; as soon as he had thought of Pody he knew he was going in the right direction. "Perhaps I can find some along the way," he said. "It's my gift, you know."

Neither of them had been on Pody. It was a sleepy southern island with a pretty old port town, Telio, built of rosy sandstone, and fields and orchards that should have been fertile. But the

lords of Wathort had ruled it for a century, taxing and slave taking and wearing the land and people down. The sunny streets of
Telio were sad and dirty. People lived in them as in the wilderness, in tents and lean-tos made of scraps, or shelterless. "Oh, this
won't do," Crow said, disgusted, avoiding a pile of human excre-
ment. "These creatures don't have books, Tern!"

"Wait, wait," his companion said. "Give me a day."

"It's dangerous," Crow said, "it's pointless," but he made no further objection. The modest, naive young man whom he had
taught to read had become his unfathomable guide.

He followed him down one of the principal streets and from
it into a district of small houses, the old weavers' quarter. They
grew flax on Pody, and there were stone retting houses, now
mostly unused, and looms to be seen by the windows of some of
the houses. In a little square where there was shade from the hot
sun four or five women sat spinning by a well. Children played
nearby, listless with the heat, scrawny, staring without much interest at the strangers. Tern had walked there unhesitating, as if
he knew where he was going. Now he stopped and greeted the
women.

"Oh, pretty man," said one of them with a smile, "don't even
show us what you have in your pack there, for I haven't a penny of
copper or ivory, nor seen one for a month."

"You might have a bit of linen, though, mistress? woven, or
thread? Linen of Pody is the best—so I've heard as far as Havnor.
And I can tell the quality of what you're spinning. A beautiful
thread it is." Crow watched his companion with amusement and
some disdain; he himself could bargain for a book very shrewdly,
but nattering with common women about buttons and thread
was beneath him. "Let me just open this up," Tern was saying as
he spread his pack out on the cobbles, and the women and the
dirty, timid children drew closer to see the wonders he would

show them. "Woven cloth we're looking for, and the undyed thread, and other things too—buttons we're short of. If you had any of horn or bone, maybe? I'd trade one of these little velvet caps here for three or four buttons. Or one of these rolls of ribbon; look at the color of it. Beautiful with your hair, mistress! Or paper, or books. Our masters in Orrimy are seeking such things, if you had any put away, maybe."

"Oh, you are a pretty man," said the woman who had spoken first, laughing, as he held the red ribbon up to her black braid. "And I wish I had something for you!"

"I won't be so bold as to ask for a kiss," said Medra, "but an open hand, maybe?"

He made the sign; she looked at him for a moment. "That's easy," she said softly, and made the sign in return, "but not always safe, among strangers."

He went on showing his wares and joking with the women and children. Nobody bought anything. They gazed at the trinkets as if they were treasures. He let them gaze and finger all they would; indeed he let one of the children filch a little mirror of polished brass, seeing it vanish under the ragged shirt and saying nothing. At last he said he must go on, and the children drifted away as he folded up his pack.

"I have a neighbor," said the black-braided woman, "who might have some paper, if you're after that."

"Written on?" said Crow, who had been sitting on the well coping, bored. "Marks on it?"

She looked him up and down. "Marks on it, sir," she said. And then, to Tern, in a different tone, "If you'd like to come with me, she lives this way. And though she's only a girl, and poor, I'll tell you, peddler, she has an open hand. Though perhaps not all of us do."

"Three out of three," said Crow, sketching the sign, "so spare your vinegar, woman."

"Oh, it's you who have it to spare, sir. We're poor folk here. And ignorant," she said, with a flash of her eyes, and led on.

She brought them to a house at the end of a lane. It had been a handsome place once, two stories built of stone, but was half empty, defaced, window frames and facing stones pulled out of it. They crossed a courtyard with a well in it. She knocked at a side door, and a girl opened it.

"Ach, it's a witch's den," Crow said, at the whiff of herbs and aromatic smoke, and he stepped back.

"Healers," their guide said. "Is she ill again, Dory?"

The girl nodded, looking at Tern, then at Crow. She was thirteen or fourteen, heavyset though thin, with a sullen, steady gaze.

"They're men of the Hand, Dory, one short and pretty and one tall and proud, and they say they're seeking papers. I know you had some once, though you may not now. They've nothing you need in their pack, but it might be they'd pay a bit of ivory for what they want. Is it so?" She turned her bright eyes on Tern, and he nodded.

"She's very sick, Rush," the girl said. She looked again at Tern. "You're not a healer?" It was an accusation.

"No."

"She is," said Rush. "Like her mother and her mother's mother. Let us in, Dory, or me at least, to speak to her." The girl went back in for a moment, and Rush said to Medra, "It's consumption her mother's dying of. No healer could cure her. But she could heal the scrofula, and touch for pain. A wonder she was, and Dory bade fair to follow her."

The girl motioned them to come in. Crow chose to wait outside. The room was high and long, with traces of former elegance, but very old and very poor. Healers' paraphernalia and drying herbs were everywhere, though ranged in some order. Near the fine stone fireplace, where a tiny wisp of sweet herbs burned, was a bedstead. The woman in it was so wasted that in the dim light she seemed nothing but bone and shadow. As Tern came close she tried to sit up and to speak. Her daughter raised her head on the pillow, and when Tern was very near he could hear her: "Wizard," she said. "Not by chance."

A woman of power, she knew what he was. Had she called him there?

"I'm a finder," he said. "And a seeker."

"Can you teach her?"

"I can take her to those who can."

"Do it."

"I will."

She laid her head back and closed her eyes.

Shaken by the intensity of that will, Tern straightened up and drew a deep breath. He looked round at the girl, Dory. She did not return his gaze, watching her mother with stolid, sullen grief. Only after the woman sank into sleep did Dory move, going to help Rush, who as a friend and neighbor had made herself useful and was gathering up blood-soaked cloths scattered by the bed.

"She bled again just now, and I couldn't stop it," Dory said. Tears ran out of her eyes and down her cheeks. Her face hardly changed.

"Oh child, oh lamb," said Rush, taking her into her embrace; but though she hugged Rush, Dory did not bend.

"She's going there, to the wall, and I can't go with her," she said. "She's going alone and I can't go with her— Can't you go there?" She broke away from Rush, looking again at Tern. "You can go there!"

"No," he said. "I don't know the way."

Yet as Dory spoke he saw what the girl saw: a long hill going down into darkness, and across it, on the edge of twilight, a low wall of stones. And as he looked he thought he saw a woman walking along beside the wall, very thin, insubstantial, bone, shadow. But she was not the dying woman in the bed. She was Anieb.

Then that was gone and he stood facing the witch-girl. Her look of accusation slowly changed. She put her face in her hands.

"We have to let them go," he said.

She said, "I know."

Rush glanced from one to the other with her keen, bright eyes. "Not only a handy man," she said, "but a crafty man. Well, you're not the first."

He looked his question.

"This is called Ath's House," she said.

"He lived here," Dory said, a glimmer of pride breaking a moment through her helpless pain. "The Mage Ath. Long ago. Before he went into the west. All my foremothers were wise women. He stayed here. With them."

"Give me a basin," Rush said. "I'll get water to soak these."

"I'll get the water," Tern said. He took the basin and went out to the courtyard, to the well. Just as before, Crow was sitting on the coping, bored and restless.

"Why are we wasting time here?" he demanded, as Tern let the bucket down into the well. "Are you fetching and carrying for witches now?"

"Yes," Tern said, "and I will till she dies. And then I'll take her daughter to Roke. And if you want to read the Book of Names, you can come with us."

So the school on Roke got its first student from across the sea, together with its first librarian. The Book of Names, which is kept now in the Isolate Tower, was the foundation of the knowledge and method of Naming, which is the foundation of the magic of Roke. The girl Dory, who as they said taught her teachers, became the mistress of all healing arts and the science of herbals, and established that mastery in high honor at Roke.

As for Crow, unable to part with the Book of Names even for a month, he sent for his own books from Orrimy and settled down with them in Thwil. He allowed people of the school to study them, so long as they showed them, and him, due respect.

So the pattern of the years was set for Tern. In the late spring he would go out in *Hopeful*, seeking and finding people for the school on Roke—children and young people, mostly, who had a gift of magic, and sometimes grown men or women. Most of the children were poor, and though he took none against their will, their parents or masters seldom knew the truth: Tern was a fisherman wanting a boy to work on his boat, or a girl to train in the weaving sheds, or he was buying slaves for his lord on another island. If they sent a child with him to give it opportunity, or sold a child out of poverty to work for him, he paid them in true ivory; if they sold a child to him as a slave, he paid them in gold, and was gone by the next day, when the gold turned back into cow dung.

He traveled far in the Archipelago, even out into the East Reach. He never went to the same town or island twice without years between, letting his trail grow cold. Even so he began to be spoken of. The Child Taker, they called him, a dreaded sorcerer who carried children to his island in the icy north and there sucked their blood. In villages on Way and Felkway they still tell children about the Child Taker, as an encouragement to distrust strangers.

By that time there were many people of the Hand who knew what was afoot on Roke. Young people came there sent by them. Men and women came to be taught and to teach. Many of these had a hard time getting there, for the spells that hid the island were stronger than ever, making it seem only a cloud, or a reef among the breakers; and the Roke wind blew, which kept any ship from Thwil Bay unless there was a sorcerer aboard who knew how to turn that wind. Still they came, and as the years went on a larger house was needed for the school than any in Thwil Town.

In the Archipelago, men built ships and women built houses, that was the custom; but in building a great structure women let men work with them, not having the miners' superstitions that kept men out of the mines, or the shipwrights' that forbade women to watch a keel laid. So both men and women of great power raised the Great House on Roke. Its cornerstone was set on a hilltop above Thwil Town, near the Grove and looking to the Knoll. Its walls were built not only of stone and wood, but founded deep on magic and made strong with spells.

Standing on that hill, Medra had said, "There is a vein of water, just under where I stand, that will not go dry." They dug down carefully and came to the water; they let it leap up into the sunlight; and the first part of the Great House they made was its inmost heart, the courtyard of the fountain.

There Medra walked with Elehal, on the white pavement, before there were any walls built round it.

She had planted a young rowan from the Grove beside the fountain. They came to be sure it was thriving. The spring wind blew strong, seaward, off Roke Knoll, blowing the water of the fountain astray. Up on the slope of the Knoll they could see a little group of people: a circle of young students learning how to do tricks of illusion from the sorcerer Hega of O; Master Hand, they called him. The sparkweed, past flowering, cast its ashes on the wind. There were streaks of grey in Ember's hair.

"Off you go, then," she said, "and leave us to settle this matter of the Rule." Her frown was as fierce as ever, but her voice was seldom as harsh as this when she spoke to him.

"I'll stay if you want, Elehal."

"I do want you to stay. But don't stay! You're a finder, you have to go find. It's only that agreeing on the Way—or the Rule, Waris wants us to call it—is twice the work of building the House. And causes ten times the quarrels. I wish I could get away from it! I wish I could just walk with you, like this...And I wish you wouldn't go north."

"Why do we quarrel?" he said rather despondently.

"Because there are more of us! Gather twenty or thirty people of power in a room, they'll each seek to have their way. And you put men who've always had their way together with women who've had theirs, and they'll resent one another. And then, too, there are some true and real divisions among us, Medra. They must be settled, and they can't be settled easily. Though a little goodwill would go a long way."

"Is it Waris?"

"Waris and several other men. And they *are* men, and they make that important beyond anything else. To them, the Old Powers are abominable. And women's powers are suspect, because they suppose them all connected with the Old Powers. As if those Powers were to be controlled or used by any mortal soul! But they put men where we put the world. And so they hold that a true wizard must be a man. And celibate."

"Ah, that," Medra said, rueful.

"That indeed. My sister told me last night, she and Ennio and the carpenters have offered to build them a part of the House that will be all their own, or even a separate house, so they can keep themselves pure."

"Pure?"

"It's not my word, it's Waris's. But they've refused. They want the Rule of Roke to separate men from women, and they want men to make the decisions for all. Now what compromise can we make with them? Why did they come here, if they won't work with us?"

"We should send away the men who won't."

"Away? In anger? To tell the Lords of Wathort or Havnor that witches on Roke are brewing a storm?"

"I forget—I always forget," he said, downcast again. "I forget the walls of the prison. I'm not such a fool when I'm outside them . . . When I'm here I can't believe it is a prison. But outside, without you, I remember . . . I don't want to go, but I have to go. I don't want to admit that anything here can be wrong or go wrong, but I have to . . . I'll go this time, and I will go north, Elehal. But when I come back I'll stay. What I need to find I'll find here. Haven't I found it already?"

"No," she said, "only me . . . But there's a great deal of seeking and finding to be done in the Grove. Enough to keep even you from being restless. Why north?"

"To reach out the Hand to Enlad and Éa. I've never gone there. We know nothing about their wizardries. *Enlad of the Kings, and bright Éa, eldest of isles!* Surely we'll find allies there."

"But Havnor lies between us," she said.

"I won't sail my boat across Havnor, dear love. I plan to go around it. By water." He could always make her laugh; he was the only one who could. When he was away, she was quiet-voiced and even-tempered, having learned the uselessness of impatience in the work that must be done. Sometimes she still scowled, sometimes she smiled, but she did not laugh. When she could, she went to the Grove alone, as she had always done. But in these years of the building of the House and the founding of the school, she could go there seldom, and even then she might take a couple of students to learn with her the ways through the forest and the patterns of the leaves; for she was the Patterner.

Tern left late that year on his journey. He had with him a boy of fifteen, Mote, a promising weatherworker who needed training at sea, and Sava, a woman of sixty who had come to Roke with him seven or eight years before. Sava had been one of the women of the Hand on the isle of Ark. Though she had no wizardly gifts at all, she knew so well how to get a group of people to trust one another and work together that she was honored as a wise woman on Ark, and now on Roke. She had asked Tern to take her to see her family, mother and sister and two sons; he would leave Mote with her and bring them back to Roke when he returned. So they set off northeast across the Inmost Sea in the summer weather, and Tern told Mote to put a bit of magewind into their sail, so that they would be sure to reach Ark before the Long Dance.

As they coasted that island, he himself put an illusion about *Hopeful*, so that she would seem not a boat but a drifting log; for pirates and Losen's slave takers were thick in these waters.

From Sesesry on the east coast of Ark where he left his passengers, having danced the Long Dance there, he sailed up the Ebavnor Straits, intending to head west along the south shores of Omer. He kept the illusion spell about his boat. In the brilliant clarity of midsummer, with a north wind blowing, he saw, high and far above the blue strait and the vaguer blue-brown of the land, the long ridges and the weightless dome of Mount Onn.

Look, Medra. Look!

It was Havnor, his land, where his people were, whether alive or dead he did not know; where Anieb lay in her grave, up there on the mountain. He had never been back, never come this close. It had been how long? Sixteen years, seventeen years. Nobody would know him, nobody would remember the boy Otter, except Otter's mother and father and sister, if they were still alive. And surely there were people of the Hand in the Great Port. Though he had not known of them as a boy, he should know them now.

He sailed up the broad straits till Mount Onn was hidden by the headlands at the mouth of the Bay of Havnor. He would not see it again unless he went through that narrow passage. Then he would see the mountain, all the sweep and cresting of it, over the calm waters where he used to try to raise up the magewind when he was twelve; and sailing on he would see the towers rise up from the water, dim at first, mere dots and lines, then lifting up their bright banners, the white city at the center of the world.

It was mere cowardice to keep from Havnor, now—fear for his skin, fear lest he find his people had died, fear lest he recall Anieb too vividly.

For there had been times when he felt that, as he had summoned her living, so dead she might summon him. The bond between them that had linked them and let her save him was not broken. Many times she had come into his dreams, standing silent as she stood when he first saw her in the reeking tower at Samory. And he had seen her, years ago, in the vision of the dying healer in Telio, in the twilight, beside the wall of stones.

He knew now, from Elehal and others on Roke, what that wall was. It lay between the living and the dead. And in that vision, Anieb had walked on this side of it, not on the side that went down into the dark.

Did he fear her, who had freed him?

He tacked across the strong wind, swung round South Point, and sailed into the Great Bay of Havnor.

Banners still flew from the towers of the City of Havnor, and a king still ruled there; the banners were those of captured towns and isles, and the king was the warlord Losen. Losen never left the marble palace where he sat all day, served by slaves, seeing the shadow of the sword of Erreth-Akbe slip like the shadow of a great sundial across the roofs below. He gave orders, and the slaves said, "It is done, your majesty." He held audiences, and old men came and said, "We obey, your majesty." He summoned his wizards, and the mage Early came, bowing low. "Make me walk!" Losen shouted, beating his paralysed legs with his weak hands.

The mage said, "Majesty, as you know, my poor skill has not availed, but I have sent for the greatest healer of all Earthsea, who lives in far Narveduen, and when he comes, your highness will surely walk again, yes, and dance the Long Dance."

Then Losen cursed and cried, and his slaves brought him wine, and the mage went out, bowing, and checking as he went to be sure that the spell of paralysis was holding.

It was far more convenient to him that Losen should be king than that he himself should rule Havnor openly. Men of arms didn't trust men of craft and didn't like to serve them. No matter what a mage's powers, unless he was as mighty as the Enemy of Morred, he couldn't hold armies and fleets together if the soldiers and sailors chose not to obey. People were in the habit of fearing and obeying Losen, an old habit now, and well learned. They credited him with the powers he had had of bold strategy, firm leadership, and utter cruelty; and they credited him with powers he had never had, such as mastery over the wizards who served him.

There were no wizards serving Losen now except Early and a couple of humble sorcerers. Early had driven off or killed, one after another, his rivals for Losen's favor, and had enjoyed sole rule over all Havnor now for years.

When he was Gelluk's prentice and assistant, he had encouraged his master in the study of the lore of Way, finding himself free while Gelluk was off doting on his quicksilver. But Gelluk's abrupt fate had shaken him. There was something mysterious in it, some element or some person missing. Summoning the useful Hound to help him, Early had made a very thorough inquiry into what happened. Where Gelluk was, of course, was no mystery. Hound had tracked him straight to a scar in a hillside, and said he was buried deep under there. Early had no wish to exhume him. But the boy who had been with him, Hound could not track: could not say whether he was under that hill with Gelluk, or had got clean away. He had left no spell traces as the mage did, said Hound, and it had rained very hard all the night after, and when Hound thought he had found the boy's tracks, they were a woman's; and she was dead.

Early did not punish Hound for his failure, but he remembered it. He was not used to failures and did not like them. He did not like what Hound told him about this boy, Otter, and he remembered it.

The desire for power feeds off itself, growing as it devours. Early suffered from hunger. He starved. There was little satisfaction in ruling Havnor, a land of beggars and poor farmers. What was the good of possessing the Throne of Maharion if nobody sat in it but a drunken cripple? What glory was there in the palaces of the city when nobody lived in them but crawling slaves? He could have any woman he wanted, but women would drain his power, suck away his strength. He wanted no woman near him. He craved an enemy: an opponent worth destroying.

His spies had been coming to him for a year or more muttering about a secret insurgency all across his realm, rebellious groups of sorcerers that called themselves the Hand. Eager to find his enemy, he had one such group investigated. They turned out to be a lot of old women, midwives, carpenters, a ditchdigger, a tinsmith's prentice, a couple of little boys. Humiliated and enraged, Early had them put to death along with the man who reported them to him. It was a public execution, in Losen's name, for the crime of conspiracy against the King. There had perhaps not been enough of that kind of intimidation lately. But it went against his grain. He didn't like to make a public spectacle of fools who had tricked him into fearing them. He would rather have dealt with them in his own way, in his own time. To be nourishing, fear must be immediate; he needed to see people afraid of him, hear their terror, smell it, taste it. But since he ruled in Losen's name, it was Losen who must be feared by the armies and the peoples, and he himself must keep in the background, making do with slaves and prentices.

Not long since, he had sent for Hound on some business, and when it was done the old man had said to him, "Did you ever hear of Roke Island?"

"South and west of Kamery. The Lord of Wathort's owned it for forty or fifty years."

Though he seldom left the city, Early prided himself on his knowledge of all the Archipelago, gleaned from his sailors' reports and the marvelous ancient charts kept in the palace. He studied them nights, brooding on where and how he might extend his empire.

Hound nodded, as if its location was all that had interested him in Roke.

"Well?"

"One of the old women you had tortured before they burned the lot, you know? Well, the fellow who did it told me. She talked about her son on Roke. Calling out to him to come, you know. But like as if he had the power to."

"Well?"

"Seemed odd. Old woman from a village inland, never seen the sea, calling the name of an island away off like that."

"The son was a fisherman who talked about his travels."

Early waved his hand. Hound sniffed, nodded, and left.

Early never disregarded any triviality Hound mentioned, because so many of them had proved not to be trivial. He disliked the old man for that, and because he was unshakable. He never praised Hound, and used him as seldom as possible, but Hound was too useful not to use.

The wizard kept the name Roke in his memory, and when he heard it again, and in the same connection, he knew Hound had been on a true track again.

Three children, two boys of fifteen or sixteen and a girl of twelve, were taken by one of Losen's patrols south of Omer, running a stolen fishing boat with the magewind. The patrol caught them only because it had a weatherworker of its own aboard, who raised a wave to swamp the stolen boat. Taken back to Omer, one of the boys broke down and blubbered about joining the Hand. Hearing that word, the men told them they would be tortured and burned, at which the boy cried that if they spared him he would tell them all about the Hand, and Roke, and the great mages of Roke.

"Bring them here," Early said to the messenger.

"The girl flew away, lord," the man said unwillingly.

"Flew away?"

"She took bird form. Osprey, they said. Didn't expect that from a girl so young. Gone before they knew it."

"Bring the boys, then," Early said with deadly patience.

They brought him one boy. The other had jumped from the ship, crossing Havnor Bay, and been killed by a crossbow quarrel. The boy they brought was in such a paroxysm of terror that even Early was disgusted by him. How could he frighten a creature already blind and beshatten with fear? He set a binding spell on the boy that held him upright and immobile as a stone statue, and left him so for a night and a day. Now and then he talked to the statue, telling it that it was a clever lad and might make a good prentice, here in the palace. Maybe he could go to Roke after all, for Early was thinking of going to Roke, to meet with the mages there.

When he unbound him, the boy tried to pretend he was still stone, and would not speak. Early had to go into his mind, in the way he had learned from Gelluk long ago, when Gelluk was a true master of his art. He found out what he could. Then the boy was no good for anything and had to be disposed of. It was humiliating, again, to be outwitted by the very stupidity of these people; and all he had learned about Roke was that the Hand was there, and a school where they taught wizardry. And he had learned a man's name.

The idea of a school for wizards made him laugh. A school for wild boars, he thought, a college for dragons! But that there was some kind of scheming and gathering together of men of power on Roke seemed probable, and the idea of any league or alliance of wizards appalled him more the more he thought of it. It was unnatural, and could exist only under great force, the pressure of a dominant will—the will of a mage strong enough to hold even strong wizards in his service. There was the enemy he wanted!

Hound was down at the door, they said. Early sent for him to come up. "Who's Tern?" he asked as soon as he saw the old man.

With age Hound had come to look his name, wrinkled, with a long nose and sad eyes. He sniffed and seemed about to say he did not know, but he knew better than to try to lie to Early. He sighed. "Otter," he said. "Him that killed old Whiteface."

"Where's he hiding?"

"Not hiding at all. Went about the city, talking to people. Went to see his mother in Endlane, round the mountain. He's there now."

"You should have told me at once," Early said.

"Didn't know you were after him. I've been after him a long time. He fooled me." Hound spoke without rancor.

"He tricked and killed a great mage, my master. He's dangerous. I want vengeance. Who did he talk to here? I want them. Then I'll see to him."

"Some old women down by the docks. An old sorcerer. His sister."

"Get them here. Take my men."

Hound sniffed, sighed, nodded.

There was not much to be got from the people his men brought to him. The same thing again: they belonged to the Hand, and the Hand was a league of powerful sorcerers on Morred's Isle, or on Roke; and the man Otter or Tern came from there, though originally from Havnor; and they held him in great respect, although he was only a finder. The sister had vanished, perhaps gone with Otter to Endlane, where the mother lived. Early rummaged in their cloudy, witless minds, had the youngest of them tortured, and then burned them where Losen could sit at his window and watch. The King needed some diversions.

All this took only two days, and all the time Early was looking and probing toward Endlane village, sending Hound there before him, sending his own presentment there to watch. When he knew where the man was he betook himself there very quickly, on eagle's wings; for Early was a great shape-changer, so fearless that he would take even dragon form.

He knew it was well to use caution with this man. Otter had defeated Tinaral, and there was this matter of Roke. There was some strength in him or with him. Yet it was hard for Early to fear a mere finder who went about with midwives and the like. He could not bring himself to sneak and skulk. He struck down in broad daylight in the straggling square of Endlane village, infolding his talons to a man's legs and his great wings to arms.

A child ran bawling to its mammy. No one else was about. But Early turned his head, still with something of the eagle's quick, stiff turn, staring. Wizard knows wizard, and he knew which house his prey was in. He walked to it and flung the door open.

A slight, brown man sitting at the table looked up at him.

Early raised his hand to lay the binding spell on him. His hand was stayed, held immobile half lifted at his side.

This was a contest, then, a foe worth fighting! Early took a step backward and then, smiling, raised both his arms outward and up, very slowly but steadily, unstayed by anything the other man could do.

The house vanished. No walls, no roof, nobody. Early stood on the dust of the village square in the sunshine of morning with his arms in the air.

It was only illusion, of course, but it checked him a moment in his spell, and then he had to undo the illusion, bringing back the door frame around him, the walls and roof beams, the gleam of light on crockery, the hearth stones, the table. But nobody sat at the table. His enemy was gone.

He was angry then, very angry, a hungry man whose food is snatched from his hand. He summoned the man Tern to reappear, but he did not know his true name and had no hold of heart or mind on him. The summons went unanswered.

He strode from the house, turned, and set a fire spell on it so that it burst into flames, thatch and walls and every window spouting fire. Women ran out of it screaming. They had been hiding no doubt in the back room; he paid them no attention. "Hound," he thought. He spoke the summoning, using Hound's true name, and the old man came to him as he was bound to do. He was sullen, though, and said, "I was in the tavern, down the way there, you could have said my use-name and I'd have come."

Early looked at him once. Hound's mouth snapped shut and stayed shut.

"Speak when I let you," the wizard said. "Where is the man?"

Hound nodded northeastwards.

"What's there?"

Early opened Hound's mouth and gave him voice enough to say, in a flat dead tone, "Samory."

"What form is he in?"

"Otter," said the flat voice.

Early laughed. "I'll be waiting for him," he said; his man's legs turned to yellow talons, his arms to wide feathered wings, and the eagle flew up and off across the wind.

Hound sniffed, sighed, and followed, trudging along unwillingly, while behind him in the village the flames died down, and children cried, and women shouted curses after the eagle.

The danger in trying to do good is that the mind comes to confuse the intent of goodness with the act of doing things well.

That is not what the otter was thinking as it swam fast down the Yennava. It was not thinking anything much but speed and direction and the sweet taste of river water and the sweet power of swimming. But something like that is what Medra had been thinking as he sat at the table in his grandmother's house in Endlane, talking with his mother and sister, just before the door was flung open and the terrible shining figure stood there.

Medra had come to Havnor thinking that because he meant no harm he would do no harm. He had done irreparable harm. Men and women and children had died because he was there. They had died in torment, burned alive. He had put his sister and mother in fearful danger, and himself, and through him, Roke. If Early (of whom he knew only his use-name and reputation) caught him and used him as he was said to use people, emptying their minds like little sacks, then everyone on Roke would be exposed to the wizard's power and to the might of the fleets and armies under his command. Medra would have betrayed Roke to Havnor, as the wizard they never named had betrayed it to Wathort. Maybe that man, too, had thought he could do no harm.

Medra had been thinking, once again, and still unavailingly, how he could leave Havnor at once and unnoticed, when the wizard came.

Now, as otter, he was thinking only that he would like to stay otter, be otter, in the sweet brown water, the living river, forever. There is no death for an otter, only life to the end. But in the sleek creature was the mortal mind; and where the stream passes the hill west of Samory, the otter came up on the muddy bank, and then the man crouched there, shivering.

Where to now? Why had he come here?

He had not thought. He had taken the shape that came soonest to him, run to the river as an otter would, swum as the otter would swim. But only in his own form could he think as a man, hide, decide, act as a man or as a wizard against the wizard who hunted him.

He knew he was no match for Early. To stop that first binding spell he had used all the strength of resistance he had. The illusion and the shape-change were all the tricks he had to play. If he faced the wizard again he would be destroyed. And Roke with him. Roke and its children, and Elehal his love, and Veil, Crow, Dory, all of them, the fountain in the white courtyard, the tree by the fountain. Only the Grove would stand. Only the green hill, silent, immovable. He heard Elehal say to him, *Havnor lies between us.* He heard her say, *All the true powers, all the old powers, at root are one.*

He looked up. The hillside above the stream was that same hill where he had come that day with Tinaral, Anieb's presence within him. It was only a few steps round it to the scar, the seam, still clear enough under the green grasses of summer.

"Mother," he said, on his knees there, "Mother, open to me."

He laid his hands on the seam of earth, but there was no power in them.

"Let me in, mother," he whispered in the tongue that was as old as the hill. The ground shivered a little and opened.

He heard an eagle scream. He got to his feet. He leapt into the dark.

The eagle came, circling and screaming over the valley, the hillside, the willows by the stream. It circled, searching and searching, and flew back as it had come.

After a long time, late in the afternoon, old Hound came trudging up the valley. He stopped now and then and sniffed. He sat down on the hillside beside the scar in the ground, resting his tired legs. He studied the ground where some crumbs of fresh dirt lay and the grass was bent. He stroked the bent grass to straighten it. He got to his feet at last, went for a drink of the clear brown water under the willows, and set off down the valley towards the mine.

Medra woke in pain, in darkness. For a long time that was all there was. The pain came and went, the darkness remained. Once it lightened a little into a twilight in which he could dimly see. He saw a slope running down from where he lay towards a wall of stones, across which was darkness again. But he could not get up to walk to the wall, and presently the pain came back very sharp in his arm and hip and head. Then the darkness came around him, and then nothing.

Thirst: and with it pain. Thirst, and the sound of water running.

He tried to remember how to make light. Anieb said to him, plaintively, "Can't you make the light?" But he could not. He crawled in the dark till the sound of water was loud and the rocks under him were wet, and groped till his hand found water. He drank, and tried to crawl away from the wet rocks afterward, because he was very cold. One arm hurt and had no strength in it.

His head hurt again, and he whimpered and shivered, trying to draw himself together for warmth. There was no warmth and no light.

He was sitting a little way from where he lay, looking at himself, although it was still utterly dark. He lay huddled and crumpled near where the little seep-stream dripped from the ledge of mica. Not far away lay another huddled heap, rotted red silk, long hair, bones. Beyond it the cavern stretched away. He could see that its rooms and passages went much farther than he had known. He saw it with the same uncaring interest with which he saw Tinaral's body and his own body. He felt a mild regret. It was only fair that he should die here with the man he had killed. It was right. Nothing was wrong. But something in him ached, not the sharp body pain, a long ache, lifelong.

"Anieb," he said.

Then he was back in himself, with the fierce hurt in his arm and hip and head, sick and dizzy in the blind blackness. When he moved, he whimpered; but he sat up. I have to live, he thought. I have to remember how to live. How to make light. I have to remember. I have to remember the shadows of the leaves.

How far does the forest go?

As far as the mind goes.

He looked up into the darkness. After a while he moved his good hand a little, and the faint light flowed out of it.

The roof of the cavern was far above him. The trickle of water dripping from the mica ledge glittered in short dashes in the werelight.

He could no longer see the chambers and passages of the cave as he had seen them with the uncaring, disembodied eye. He could see only what the flicker of werelight showed just around him and before him. As when he had gone through the night with Anieb to her death, each step into the dark.

He got to his knees, and thought then to whisper, "Thank you, mother." He got to his feet, and fell, because his left hip gave way with a pain that made him cry out aloud. After a while he tried again, and stood up. Then he started forward.

It took him a long time to cross the cavern. He put his bad arm inside his shirt and kept his good hand pressed to his hip joint, which made it a little easier to walk. The walls narrowed gradually to a passage. Here the roof was much lower, just above his head. Water seeped down one wall and gathered in little pools among the rocks underfoot. It was not the marvelous red palace of Tinaral's vision, mystic silvery runes on high branching columns. It was only the earth, only dirt, rock, water. The air was cool and still. Away from the dripping of the stream it was silent. Outside the gleam of werelight it was dark.

Medra bowed his head, standing there. "Anieb," he said, "can you come back this far? I don't know the way." He waited a while. He saw darkness, heard silence. Slow and halting, he entered the passage.

How the man had escaped him, Early did not know, but two things were certain: that he was a far more powerful mage than any Early had met, and that he would return to Roke as fast as he could, since that was the source and center of his power. There was no use trying to get there before him; he had the lead. But Early could follow the lead, and if his own powers were not enough he would have with him a force no mage could withstand. Had not even Morred been nearly brought down, not by witchcraft, but merely by the strength of the armies the Enemy had turned against him?

"Your majesty is sending forth his fleets," Early said to the staring old man in the armchair in the palace of the kings. "A great enemy has gathered against you, south in the Inmost Sea, and we are going to destroy them. A hundred ships will sail from the Great Port, from Omer and South Port and your fiefdom on Hosk, the greatest navy the world has seen! I shall lead them. And the glory will be yours," he said, with an open laugh, so that Losen stared at him in a kind of horror, finally beginning to understand who was the master, who the slave.

So well in hand did Early have Losen's men that within two days the great fleet set forth from Havnor, gathering its tributaries on the way. Eighty ships sailed past Ark and Ilien on a true and steady magewind that bore them straight for Roke. Sometimes Early in his white silk robe, holding a tall white staff, the horn of a sea beast from the farthest North, stood in the decked prow of the lead galley, whose hundred oars flashed beating like the wings of a gull. Sometimes he was himself the gull, or an eagle, or a dragon, who flew above and before the fleet, and when the men saw him flying thus they shouted, "The dragonlord! the dragonlord!"

They came ashore in Ilien for water and food. Setting a host of many hundreds of men on its way so quickly had left little time for provisioning the ships. They overran the towns along the west shore of Ilien, taking what they wanted, and did the same on Vissti and Kamery, looting what they could and burning what they left. Then the great fleet turned west, heading for the one harbor of Roke Island, the Bay of Thwil. Early knew of the harbor from the maps in Havnor, and knew there was a high hill above it. As they came nearer, he took dragon form and soared up high above his ships, leading them, gazing into the west for the sight of that hill.

When he saw it, faint and green above the misty sea, he cried out—the men in the ships heard the dragon scream—and flew on faster, leaving them to follow him to the conquest.

All the rumors of Roke had said that it was spell-defended and charm-hidden, invisible to ordinary eyes. If there were any spells woven about that hill or the bay he now saw opening before it, they were gossamer to him, transparent. Nothing blurred his eyes or challenged his will as he flew over the bay, over the little town and a half-finished building on the slope above it, to the top of the high green hill. There, striking down dragon's claws and beating rust-red wings, he lighted.

He stood in his own form. He had not made the change himself. He stood alert, uncertain.

The wind blew, the long grass nodded in the wind. Summer was getting on and the grass was dry now, yellowing, no flowers in it but the little white heads of the lacefoam. A woman came walking up the hill towards him through the long grass. She followed no path, and walked easily, without haste.

He thought he had raised his hand in a spell to stop her, but he had not raised his hand, and she came on. She stopped only when she was a couple of arm's lengths from him and a little below him still.

"Tell me your name," she said, and he said, "Teriel."

"Why did you come here, Teriel?"

"To destroy you."

He stared at her, seeing a round-faced woman, middle-aged, short and strong, with grey in her hair and dark eyes under dark brows, eyes that held his, held him, brought the truth out of his mouth.

"Destroy us? Destroy this hill? The trees there?" She looked down to a grove of trees not far from the hill. "Maybe Segoy who made them could unmake them. Maybe the earth will destroy herself. Maybe she'll destroy herself through our hands, in the end. But not through yours. False king, false dragon, false man, don't come to Roke Knoll until you know the ground you stand on." She made one gesture of her hand, downward to the earth.

Then she turned and went down the hill through the long grass, the way she had come.

There were other people on the hill, he saw now, many others, men and women, children, living and spirits of the dead; many, many of them. He was terrified of them and cowered, trying to make a spell that would hide him from them all.

But he made no spell. He had no magic left in him. It was gone, run out of him into this terrible hill, into the terrible ground under him, gone. He was no wizard, only a man like the others, powerless.

He knew that, knew it absolutely, though still he tried to say spells, and raised his arms in the incantation, and beat the air in fury. Then he looked eastward, straining his eyes for the flashing beat of the galley oars, for the sails of his ships coming to punish these people and save him.

All he saw was a mist on the water, all across the sea beyond the mouth of the bay. As he watched it thickened and darkened, creeping out over the slow waves.

Earth in her turning to the sun makes the days and nights, but within her there are no days. Medra walked through the night. He was very lame, and could not always keep up the werelight. When it failed he had to stop and sit down and sleep. The sleep was never death, as he thought it was. He woke, always cold, always in pain, always thirsty, and when he could make a glimmer of the light he got to his feet and went on. He never saw Anieb but he knew she was there. He followed her. Sometimes there were great rooms. Sometimes there were pools of motionless water. It was hard to break the stillness of their surface, but he drank from them. He thought he had gone down deeper and deeper for a long time, till he reached the longest of those pools, and after that the way went up again. Sometimes now Anieb followed him. He could say her name, though she did not answer. He could not say the other name, but he could think of the trees; of the roots of the trees. This was the kingdom of the roots of the trees. How far does the forest go? As far as forests go. As long as the lives, as deep as the roots of the trees. As long as leaves cast shadows. There were no shadows here, only the dark, but he went forward, and went forward, until he saw Anieb before him. He saw the flash of her eyes, the cloud of her curling hair. She looked back at him for a moment, and then turned aside and ran lightly down a long, steep slope into darkness.

Where he stood it was not wholly dark. The air moved against his face. Far ahead, dim, small, there was a light that was not werelight. He went forward. He had been crawling for a long time now, dragging the right leg, which would not bear his weight. He went forward. He smelled the wind of evening and saw the sky of evening through the branches and leaves of trees. An arched oak root formed the mouth of the cave, no bigger than a man or a badger needed to crawl through. He crawled through. He lay there under the root of the tree, seeing the light fade and a star or two come out among the leaves.

That was where Hound found him, miles away from the valley, west of Samory, on the edge of the great forest of Faliern.

"Got you," the old man said, looking down at the muddy, lax body. He added, "Too late," regretfully. He stooped to see if he could pick him up or drag him, and felt the faint warmth of life. "You're tough," he said. "Here, wake up. Come on. Otter, wake up."

He recognised Hound, though he could not sit up and could barely speak. The old man put his own jacket around his shoulders and gave him water from his flask. Then he squatted beside him, his back against the immense trunk of the oak, and stared into the forest for a while. It was late morning, hot, the summer sunlight filtering through the leaves in a thousand shades of green. A squirrel scolded, far up in the oak, and a jay replied. Hound scratched his neck and sighed.

"The wizard's off on the wrong track, as usual," he said at last. "Said you'd gone to Roke Island and he'd catch you there. I said nothing."

He looked at the man he knew only as Otter.

"You went in there, that hole, with the old wizard, didn't you? Did you find him?"

Medra nodded.

"Hmn," Hound went, a short, grunting laugh. "You find what you look for, don't you? Like me." He saw that his companion was in distress, and said, "I'll get you out of here. Fetch a carter from the village down there, when I've got my breath. Listen. Don't fret. I haven't hunted you all these years to give you to Early. The way I gave you to Gelluk. I was sorry for that. I thought about it. What I said to you about men of a craft sticking together. And who we work for. Couldn't see that I had much choice about that. But having done you a disfavor, I thought if I came across you again I'd do you a favor, if I could. As one finder to the other, see?"

Otter's breath was coming hard. Hound put his hand on Otter's hand for a moment, said, "Don't worry," and got to his feet. "Rest easy," he said.

He found a carter who would carry them down to Endlane. Otter's mother and sister were living with cousins while they re-built their burned house as best they could. They welcomed him with disbelieving joy. Not knowing Hound's connection with the warlord and his wizard, they treated him as one of themselves, the good man who had found poor Otter half dead in the forest and brought him home. A wise man, said Otter's mother Rose, surely a wise man. Nothing was too good for such a man.

Otter was slow to recover, to heal. The bonesetter did what he could about his broken arm and his damaged hip, the wise woman salved the cuts from the rocks on his hands and head and knees, his mother brought him all the delicacies she could find in the gardens and berry thickets; but he lay as weak and wasted as when Hound first brought him. There was no heart in him, the wise woman of Endlane said. It was somewhere else, being eaten up with worry or fear or shame.

"So where is it?" Hound said.

Otter, after a long silence, said, "Roke Island."

"Where old Early went with the great fleet. I see. Friends there. Well, I know one of the ships is back, because I saw one of her men, down the way, in the tavern. I'll go ask about. Find out if they got to Roke and what happened there. What I can tell you is that it seems old Early is late coming home. Hmn, hmn," he went, pleased with his joke. "Late coming home," he repeated, and got up. He looked at Otter, who was not much to look at. "Rest easy," he said, and went off.

He was gone several days. When he returned, riding in a horse-drawn cart, he had such a look about him that Otter's sister hurried in to tell him, "Hound's won a battle or a fortune! He's riding behind a city horse, in a city cart, like a prince!"

Hound came in on her heels. "Well," he said, "in the first place, when I got to the city, I go up to the palace, just to hear the news, and what do I see? I see old King Pirate standing on his legs, shouting out orders like he used to do. Standing up! Hasn't stood for years. Shouting orders! And some of 'em did what he said, and some of 'em didn't. So I got on out of there, that kind of a situation being dangerous, in a palace. Then I went about to friends of mine and asked where was old Early and had the fleet been to Roke and come back and all. Early, they said, nobody knew about

Early. Not a sign of him nor from him. Maybe I could find him, they said, joking me, hmn. They know I love him. As for the ships, some had come back, with the men aboard saying they never came to Roke Island, never saw it, sailed right through where the sea charts said was an island, and there was no island. Then there were some men from one of the great galleys. They said when they got close to where the island should be, they came into a fog as thick as wet cloth, and the sea turned thick too, so that the oarsmen could barely push the oars through it, and they were caught in that for a day and a night. When they got out, there wasn't another ship of all the fleet on the sea, and the slaves were near rebelling, so the master brought her home as quick as he could. Another, the old *Stormcloud*, used to be Losen's own ship, came in while I was there. I talked to some men off her. They said there was nothing but fog and reefs all round where Roke was supposed to be, so they sailed on with seven other ships, south a ways, and met up with a fleet sailing up from Wathort. Maybe the lords there had heard there was a great fleet coming raiding, because they didn't stop to ask questions, but sent wizard's fire at our ships, and came alongside to board them if they could, and the men I talked to said it was a hard fight just to get away from them, and not all did. All this time they had no word from Early, and no weather was worked for them unless they had a bagman of their own aboard. So they came back up the length of the Inmost Sea, said the man from *Stormcloud*, one straggling after the other like the dogs that lost the dogfight. Now, do you like the news I bring you?"

Otter had been struggling with tears; he hid his face. "Yes," he said, "thanks."

"Thought you might. As for King Losen," Hound said, "who knows." He sniffed and sighed. "If I was him I'd retire," he said. "I think I'll do that myself."

Otter had got control of his face and voice. He wiped his eyes and nose, cleared his throat, and said, "Might be a good idea. Come to Roke. Safer."

"Seems to be a hard place to find," Hound said.

"I can find it," said Otter.

IV. Medra

There was an old man by our door
Who opened it to rich or poor;
Many came there both small and great,
But few could pass through Medra's Gate.
*   So runs the water away, away,*
*   So runs the water away.*

HOUND STAYED IN ENDLANE. He could make a living as a finder there, and he liked the tavern, and Otter's mother's hospitality.

By the beginning of autumn, Losen was hanging by a rope round his feet from a window of the New Palace, rotting, while six warlords quarreled over his kingdom, and the ships of the great fleet chased and fought one another across the Straits and the wizard-troubled sea.

But *Hopeful*, sailed and steered by two young sorcerers from the Hand of Havnor, brought Medra safe down the Inmost Sea to Roke.

Ember was on the dock to meet him. Lame and very thin, he came to her and took her hands, but he could not lift his face to hers. He said, "I have too many deaths on my heart, Elehal."

"Come with me to the Grove," she said.

They went there together and stayed till the winter came. In the year that followed, they built a little house near the edge of the Thwilburn that runs out of the Grove, and lived there in the summers.

They worked and taught in the Great House. They saw it go up stone on stone, every stone steeped in spells of protection, endurance, peace. They saw the Rule of Roke established, though never so firmly as they might wish, and always against opposition; for mages came from other islands and rose up from among the students of the school, women and men of power, knowledge, and pride, sworn by the Rule to work together and for the good of all, but each seeing a different way to do it.

Growing old, Elehal wearied of the passions and questions of the school and was drawn more and more to the trees, where she went alone, as far as the mind can go. Medra walked there too, but not so far as she, for he was lame.

After she died, he lived a while alone in the small house near the Grove.

One day in autumn he came back to the school. He went in by the garden door, which gives on the path through the fields to Roke Knoll. It is a curious thing about the Great House of Roke, that it has no portal or grand entryway at all. You can enter by what they call the back door, which, though it is made of horn and framed in dragon's tooth and carved with the Thousand-Leaved Tree, looks like nothing at all from outside, as you come to it in a dingy street; or you can go in the garden door, plain oak with an iron bolt. But there is no front door.

He came through the halls and stone corridors to the inmost place, the marble-paved courtyard of the fountain, where the tree Elehal had planted now stood tall, its berries reddening.

Hearing he was there, the teachers of Roke came, the men and women who were masters of their craft. Medra had been the Master Finder, until he went to the Grove. A young woman now taught that art, as he had taught it to her.

"I've been thinking," he said. "There are eight of you. Nine's a better number. Count me as a master again, if you will."

"What will you do, Master Tern?" asked the Summoner, a grey-haired mage from Ilien.

"I'll keep the door," Medra said. "Being lame, I won't go far from it. Being old, I'll know what to say to those who come. Being a finder, I'll find out if they belong here."

"That would spare us much trouble and some danger," said the young Finder.

"How will you do it?" the Summoner asked.

"I'll ask them their name," Medra said. He smiled. "If they'll tell me, they can come in. And when they think they've learned everything, they can go out again. If they can tell me my name."

So it was. For the rest of his life, Medra kept the doors of the Great House on Roke. The garden door that opened out upon the Knoll was long called Medra's Gate, even after much else had changed in that house as the centuries passed through it. And still the ninth Master of Roke is the Doorkeeper.

In Endlane and the villages round the foot of Onn on Havnor, women spinning and weaving sing a riddle song of which the last line has to do, maybe, with the man who was Medra, and Otter, and Tern.

> *Three things were that will not be:*
> *Soléa's bright isle above the wave,*
> *A dragon swimming in the sea,*
> *A seabird flying in the grave.*

Darkrose and Diamond

A BOAT SONG FROM WEST HAVNOR

Where my love is going
There will I go.
Where his boat is rowing
I will row.

We will laugh together,
Together we will cry.
If he lives I will live,
If he dies I die.

Where my love is going
There will I go.
Where his boat is rowing
I will row.

IN THE WEST OF HAVNOR, among hills forested with oak and chestnut, is the town of Glade. A while ago, the rich man of that town was a merchant called Golden. Golden owned the mill that cut the oak boards for the ships they built in Havnor South Port and Havnor Great Port; he owned the biggest chestnut groves; he owned the carts and hired the carters that carried the timber and the chestnuts over the hills to be sold. He did very well from trees, and when his son was born, the mother said, "We could call him Chestnut, or Oak, maybe?" But the father said, "Diamond," diamond being in his estimation the one thing more precious than gold.

So little Diamond grew up in the finest house in Glade, a fat, bright-eyed baby, a ruddy, cheerful boy. He had a sweet singing voice, a true ear, and a love of music, so that his mother, Tuly, called him Songsparrow and Skylark, among other loving names, for she never really did like "Diamond." He trilled and caroled about the house; he knew any tune as soon as he heard it, and invented tunes when he heard none. His mother had the wise woman Tangle teach him *The Creation of Éa* and *The Deed of the Young King,* and at Sunreturn when he was eleven years old he sang *The Winter Carol* for the Lord of the Western Land, who was visiting his domain in the hills above Glade. The Lord and his Lady praised the boy's singing and gave him a tiny gold box with a diamond set in the lid, which seemed a kind and pretty gift to Diamond and his mother. But Golden was a bit impatient with the singing and the trinkets. "There are more important things for you to do, son," he said. "And greater prizes to be earned."

Diamond thought his father meant the business—the loggers, the sawyers, the sawmill, the chestnut groves, the pickers, the carters, the carts—all that work and talk and planning, those complicated, adult matters. He never felt that it had much to do with him, so how was he to have as much to do with it as his father expected? Maybe he'd find out when he grew up.

But in fact Golden wasn't thinking only about the business. He had observed something about his son that made him not exactly set his eyes higher than the business, but glance above it from time to time, and then shut his eyes.

At first he thought Diamond had a knack such as many children had and then lost, a stray spark of magery. When he was a little boy, Golden himself had been able to make his own shadow shine and sparkle. His family had praised him for the trick and made him show it off to visitors; and then when he was seven or eight he lost the hang of it and never could do it again.

When he saw Diamond come down the stairs without touching the stairs, he thought his eyes had deceived him; but a few days later, he saw the child float up the stairs, just a finger gliding along the oaken banister. "Can you do that coming down?" Golden asked, and Diamond said, "Oh, yes, like this," and sailed back down smooth as a cloud on the south wind.

"How did you learn to do that?"

"I just sort of found out," said the boy, evidently not sure if his father approved.

Golden did not praise the boy, not wanting to make him self-conscious or vain about what might be a passing, childish gift, like his sweet treble voice. There was too much fuss already made over that.

But a year or so later he saw Diamond out in the back garden with his playmate Rose. The children were squatting on their haunches, heads close together, laughing. Something intense or uncanny about them made him pause at the window on the stairs landing and watch them. A thing between them was leaping up and down, a frog? a toad? a big cricket? He went out into the garden and came up near them, moving so quietly, though he was a big man, that they in their absorption did not hear him. The thing that was hopping up and down on the grass between their bare toes was a rock. When Diamond raised his hand the rock jumped up in the air, and when he shook his hand a little the rock hovered in the air, and when he flipped his fingers downward it fell to earth.

"Now you," Diamond said to Rose, and she started to do what he had done, but the rock only twitched a little. "Oh," she whispered, "there's your dad."

"That's very clever," Golden said.

"Di thought it up," Rose said.

Golden did not like the child. She was both outspoken and defensive, both rash and timid. She was a girl, and a year younger than Diamond, and a witch's daughter. He wished his son would play with boys his own age, his own sort, from the respectable families of Glade. Tuly insisted on calling the witch "the wise woman," but a witch was a witch and her daughter was no fit companion for Diamond. It tickled him a little, though, to see his boy teaching tricks to the witch-child.

"What else can you do, Diamond?" he asked.

"Play the flute," Diamond said promptly, and took out of his pocket the little fife his mother had given him for his twelfth birthday. He put it to his lips, his fingers danced, and he played a sweet, familiar tune from the western coast, "Where My Love Is Going."

"Very nice," said the father. "But anybody can play the fife, you know."

Diamond glanced at Rose. The girl turned her head away, looking down.

"I learned it really quickly," Diamond said.

Golden grunted, unimpressed.

"It can do it by itself," Diamond said, and held out the fife away from his lips. His fingers danced on the stops, and the fife played a short jig. It hit several false notes and squealed on the last high note. "I haven't got it right yet," Diamond said, vexed and embarrassed.

"Pretty good, pretty good," his father said. "Keep practicing." And he went on. He was not sure what he ought to have said. He did not want to encourage the boy to spend any more time on music, or with this girl; he spent too much already, and neither of them would help him get anywhere in life. But this gift, this undeniable gift—the rock hovering, the unblown fife— Well, it would be wrong to make too much of it, but probably it should not be discouraged.

In Golden's understanding, money was power, but not the only power. There were two others, one equal, one greater. There was birth. When the Lord of the Western Land came to his domain near Glade, Golden was glad to show him fealty. The Lord was born to govern and to keep the peace, as Golden was born to deal with commerce and wealth, each in his place; and each, noble or common, if he served well and honestly, deserved honor and respect. But there were also lesser lords whom Golden could buy and sell, lend to or let beg, men born noble who deserved neither fealty nor honor. Power of birth and power of money were contingent, and must be earned lest they be lost.

But beyond the rich and the lordly were those called the men of power: the wizards. Their power, though little exercised, was absolute. In their hands lay the fate of the long-kingless kingdom of the Archipelago.

If Diamond had been born to that kind of power, if that was his gift, then all Golden's dreams and plans of training him in the business, and having him help in expanding the carting route to a regular trade with South Port, and buying up the chestnut forests above Reche—all such plans dwindled into trifles. Might Diamond go (as his mother's uncle had gone) to the School of

Wizards on Roke Island? Might he (as that uncle had done) gain glory for his family and dominion over lord and commoner, becoming a mage in the Court of the Lords Regent in the Great Port of Havnor? Golden all but floated up the stairs himself, borne on such visions.

But he said nothing to the boy and nothing to the boy's mother. He was a consciously close-mouthed man, distrustful of visions until they could be made acts; and she, though a dutiful, loving wife and mother and housekeeper, already made too much of Diamond's talents and accomplishments. Also, like all women, she was inclined to babble and gossip, and indiscriminate in her friendships. The girl Rose hung about with Diamond because Tuly encouraged Rose's mother, the witch Tangle, to visit, consulting her every time Diamond had a hangnail, and telling her more than she or anyone ought to know about Golden's household. His business was none of the witch's business. On the other hand, Tangle might be able to tell him if his son in fact showed promise, had a talent for magery... but he flinched away from the thought of asking her, asking a witch's opinion on anything, least of all a judgment on his son.

He resolved to wait and watch. Being a patient man with a strong will, he did so for four years, till Diamond was sixteen. A big, well-grown youth, good at games and lessons, he was still ruddy-faced and bright-eyed and cheerful. He had taken it hard when his voice changed, the sweet treble going all untuned and hoarse. Golden had hoped that that was the end of his singing, but the boy went on wandering about with itinerant musicians, ballad singers and such, learning all their trash. That was no life for a merchant's son who was to inherit and manage his father's properties and mills and business, and Golden told him so. "Singing time is over, son," he said. "You must think about being a man."

Diamond had been given his true name at the springs of the

Amia in the hills above Glade. The wizard Hemlock, who had known his great-uncle the mage, came up from South Port to name him. And Hemlock was invited to his nameday party the year after, a big party, beer and food for all, and new clothes, a shirt or skirt or shift for every child, which was an old custom in the West of Havnor, and dancing on the village green in the warm autumn evening. Diamond had many friends, all the boys his age in town and all the girls too. The young people danced, and some of them had a bit too much beer, but nobody misbehaved very badly, and it was a merry and memorable night. The next morning Golden told his son again that he must think about being a man.

"I have thought some about it," said the boy, in his husky voice.

"And?"

"Well, I," said Diamond, and stuck.

"I'd always counted on your going into the family business," Golden said. His tone was neutral, and Diamond said nothing. "Have you had any ideas of what you want to do?"

"Sometimes."

"Did you talk at all to Master Hemlock?"

Diamond hesitated and said, "No." He looked a question at his father.

"I talked to him last night," Golden said. "He said to me that there are certain natural gifts which it's not only difficult but actually wrong, harmful, to suppress."

The light had come back into Diamond's dark eyes.

"The master said that such gifts or capacities, untrained, are not only wasted, but may be dangerous. The art must be learned, and practiced, he said."

Diamond's face shone.

"But, he said, it must be learned and practiced for its own sake."

Diamond nodded eagerly.

"If it's a real gift, an unusual capacity, that's even more true. A witch with her love potions can't do much harm, but even a village sorcerer, he said, must take care, for if the art is used for base ends, it becomes weak and noxious . . . Of course, even a sorcerer gets paid. And wizards, as you know, live with lords, and have what they wish."

Diamond was listening intently, frowning a little.

"So, to be blunt about it, if you have this gift, Diamond, it's of no use, directly, to our business. It has to be cultivated on its own terms, and kept under control—learned and mastered. Only then, he said, can your teachers begin to tell you what to do with it, what good it will do you. Or others," he added conscientiously.

There was a long pause.

"I told him," Golden said, "that I had seen you, with a turn of your hand and a single word, change a wooden carving of a bird into a bird that flew up and sang. I've seen you make a light glow in thin air. You didn't know I was watching. I've watched and said nothing for a long time. I didn't want to make too much of mere childish play. But I believe you have a gift, perhaps a great gift. When I told Master Hemlock what I'd seen you do, he agreed with me. He said that you may go study with him in South Port for a year, or perhaps longer."

"Study with Master Hemlock?" said Diamond, his voice up half an octave.

"If you wish."

"I, I, I never thought about it. Can I think about it? For a while—a day?"

"Of course," Golden said, pleased with his son's caution. He had thought Diamond might leap at the offer, which would have been natural, perhaps, but painful to the father, the owl who had—perhaps—hatched out an eagle.

For Golden looked on the art magic with genuine humility as

something quite beyond him—not a mere toy, such as music or tale telling, but a practical business of immense potential, which his business could never quite equal. And he was also, though he wouldn't have put it that way, afraid of wizards. A bit contemptuous of sorcerers, with their sleights and illusions and gibblegabble, but afraid of wizards.

"Does Mother know?" Diamond asked.

"She will when the time comes. She has no part to play in your decision, Diamond. Women know nothing of these matters and have nothing to do with them. You must make your choice alone, as a man. Do you understand that?" Golden was earnest, seeing his chance to begin to wean the lad from his mother. She as a woman would cling, but he as a man must learn to let go. And Diamond nodded sturdily enough to satisfy his father, though he had a thoughtful look.

"Master Hemlock said I, said he thought I had, I might have a, a gift, a talent for—?"

Golden reassured him that the wizard had actually said so, though of course what kind of gift remained to be seen. The boy's modesty was a great relief to him. He had half-consciously dreaded that Diamond would triumph over him, asserting his power right away—that mysterious, dangerous, incalculable power against which Golden's wealth and mastery and dignity shrank to impotence.

"Thank you, Father," the boy said. Golden embraced him and left, well pleased with him.

Their meeting place was in the sallows, the willow thickets down by the Amia as it ran below the smithy. As soon as Rose got there, Diamond said, "He wants me to go study with Master Hemlock! What am I going to do?"

"Study with the wizard?"

"He thinks I have this huge great talent. For magic."

"Who does?"

"Father does. He saw some of the stuff we were practicing. But he says Hemlock says I should come study with him because it might be dangerous not to. Oh," and Diamond beat his head with his hands.

"But you do have a talent."

He groaned and scoured his scalp with his knuckles. He was sitting on the dirt in their old play place, a kind of bower deep in the willows, where they could hear the stream running over the stones nearby and the clang-clang of the smithy further off. The girl sat down facing him.

"Look at all the stuff you can do," she said. "You couldn't do any of it if you didn't have a gift."

"A little gift," Diamond said indistinctly. "Enough for tricks."

"How do you know that?"

Rose was very dark-skinned, with a cloud of crinkled hair, a thin mouth, an intent, serious face. Her feet and legs and hands were bare and dirty, her skirt and jacket disreputable. Her dirty toes and fingers were delicate and elegant, and a necklace of amethysts gleamed under the torn, buttonless jacket. Her mother, Tangle, made a good living by curing and healing, bone knitting and birth easing, and selling spells of finding, love potions, and sleeping drafts. She could afford to dress herself and her daughter in new clothes, buy shoes, and keep clean, but it didn't occur to her to do so. Nor was housekeeping one of her interests. She and Rose lived mostly on boiled chicken and fried eggs, as she was often paid in poultry. The yard of their two-room house was a wilderness of cats and hens. She liked cats, toads, and jewels. The amethyst necklace had been payment for the safe delivery of a son to Golden's head forester. Tangle herself wore armfuls of bracelets and bangles that flashed and crashed when she flicked out an impatient spell. At times she wore a kitten on her shoulder. She was not an attentive mother. Rose had demanded, at seven years old, "Why did you have me if you didn't want me?"

"How can you deliver babies properly if you haven't had one?" said her mother.

"So I was practice," Rose snarled.

"Everything is practice," Tangle said. She was never ill-natured. She seldom thought to do anything much for her daughter, but never hurt her, never scolded her, and gave her whatever she asked for, dinner, a toad of her own, the amethyst necklace, lessons in witchcraft. She would have provided new clothes if Rose had asked for them, but she never did. Rose had looked after herself from an early age; and this was one of the reasons Diamond loved her. With her, he knew what freedom was. Without her, he could attain it only when he was hearing and singing and playing music.

"I do have a gift," he said now, rubbing his temples and pulling his hair.

"Stop destroying your head," Rose told him.

"I know Tarry thinks I do."

"Of course you do! What does it matter what Tarry thinks? You already play the harp about nine times better than he ever did."

This was another of the reasons Diamond loved her.

"Are there any wizard musicians?" he asked, looking up.

She pondered. "I don't know."

"I don't either. Morred and Elfarran sang to each other, and he was a mage. I think there's a Master Chanter on Roke, that teaches the lays and the histories. But I never heard of a wizard being a musician."

"I don't see why one couldn't be." She never saw why something could not be. Another reason he loved her.

"It always seemed to me they're sort of alike," he said, "magic and music. Spells and tunes. For one thing, you have to get them just exactly right."

"Practice," Rose said, rather sourly. "I know." She flicked a pebble at Diamond. It turned into a butterfly in midair. He flicked a butterfly back at her, and the two flitted and flickered a moment before they fell back to earth as pebbles. Diamond and Rose had worked out several such variations on the old stone-hopping trick.

"You ought to go, Di," she said. "Just to find out."

"I know."

"What if you got to be a wizard! Oh! Think of the stuff you could teach me! Shape-changing— We could be anything. Horses! Bears!"

"Moles," Diamond said. "Honestly, I feel like hiding underground. I always thought Father was going to make me learn his kind of stuff, after I got my name. But all this year he's kept sort of holding off. I guess he had this in mind all along. But what if I go down there and I'm not any better at being a wizard than I am at bookkeeping? Why can't I do what I know I *can* do?"

"Well, why can't you do it all? The magic and the music, anyhow? You can always hire a bookkeeper."

When she laughed, her thin face got bright, her thin mouth got wide, and her eyes disappeared.

"Oh, Darkrose," Diamond said, "I love you."

"Of course you do. You'd better. I'll witch you if you don't."

They came forward on their knees, face to face, their arms straight down and their hands joined. They kissed each other all over their faces. To Rose's lips Diamond's face was smooth and full as a plum, with just a hint of prickliness above the lip and jawline, where he had taken to shaving recently. To Diamond's lips Rose's face was soft as silk, with just a hint of grittiness on one cheek, which she had rubbed with a dirty hand. They moved a little closer so that their breasts and bellies touched, though their hands stayed down by their sides. They went on kissing.

"Darkrose," he breathed in her ear, his secret name for her.

She said nothing, but breathed very warm in his ear, and he moaned. His hands clenched hers. He drew back a little. She drew back.

They sat back on their ankles.

"Oh Di," she said, "it will be awful when you go."

"I won't go," he said. "Anywhere. Ever."

But of course he went down to Havnor South Port, in one of his father's carts driven by one of his father's carters, along with Master Hemlock. As a rule, people do what wizards advise them to do. And it is no small honor to be invited by a wizard to be his student or apprentice. Hemlock, who had won his staff on Roke, was used to having boys come to him begging to be tested and, if they had the gift for it, taught. He was a little curious about this boy whose cheerful good manners hid some reluctance or self-doubt. It was the father's idea, not the boy's, that he was gifted. That was unusual, though perhaps not so unusual among the wealthy as among common folk. At any rate he came with a very good prenticing fee paid beforehand in gold and ivory. If he had the makings of a wizard Hemlock would train him, and if he had, as Hemlock suspected, a mere childish flair, then he'd be sent home with what remained of his fee. Hemlock was an honest, upright, humorless, scholarly wizard with little interest in feelings or ideas. His gift was for names. "The art begins and ends in naming," he said, which indeed is true, although there may be a good deal between the beginning and the end.

So Diamond, instead of learning spells and illusions and transformations and all such gaudy tricks, as Hemlock called them, sat in a narrow room at the back of the wizard's narrow house on a narrow back street of the old city, memorising long, long lists of words, words of power in the Language of the Making. Plants and parts of plants and animals and parts of animals and islands and parts of islands, parts of ships, parts of the human body. The words never made sense, never made sentences, only lists. Long, long lists.

His mind wandered. "Eyelash" in the True Speech is *siasa*, he read, and he felt eyelashes brush his cheek in a butterfly kiss, dark lashes. He looked up startled and did not know what had touched him. Later when he tried to repeat the word, he stood dumb.

"Memory, memory," Hemlock said. "Talent's no good without memory!" He was not harsh, but he was unyielding. Diamond had no idea what opinion Hemlock had of him, and guessed it to be pretty low. The wizard sometimes had him come with him to his work, mostly laying spells of safety on ships and houses, purifying wells, and sitting on the councils of the city, seldom speaking but always listening. Another wizard, not Roke-trained but with the healer's gift, looked after the sick and dying of South Port. Hemlock was glad to let him do so. His own pleasure was in studying and, as far as Diamond could see, doing no magic at all. "Keep the Equilibrium, it's all in that," Hemlock said, and, "Knowledge, order, and control." Those words he said so often that they made a tune in Diamond's head and sang themselves over and over: knowledge, or-der, and contro———l . . .

When Diamond put the lists of names to tunes he made up, he learned them much faster; but then the tune would come as part of the name, and he would sing out so clearly—for his voice had re-established itself as a strong, dark tenor—that Hemlock winced. Hemlock's was a very silent house.

Mostly the pupil was supposed to be with the master, or studying the lists of names in the room where the lore-books and word-books were, or asleep. Hemlock was a stickler for early abed and early afoot. But now and then Diamond had an hour or two free. He always went down to the docks and sat on a pier side or a water stair and thought about Darkrose. As soon as he was out of the house and away from Master Hemlock, he began to think about Darkrose, and went on thinking about her and very little else. It surprised him a little. He thought he ought to be home-sick, to think about his mother. He did think about his mother quite often, and often was homesick, lying on his cot in his bare and narrow little room after a scanty supper of cold pea por-ridge—for this wizard, at least, did not live in such luxury as Golden had imagined. Diamond never thought about Darkrose, nights. He thought of his mother, or of sunny rooms and hot food, or a tune would come into his head and he would practice it mentally on the harp in his mind, and so drift off to sleep. Darkrose would come to his mind only when he was down at the docks, staring out at the water of the harbor, the piers, the fishing boats, only when he was outdoors and away from Hemlock and his house.

So he cherished his free hours as if they were actual meetings with her. He had always loved her, but had not understood that he loved her beyond anyone and anything. When he was with her, even when he was down on the docks thinking of her, he was alive. He never felt entirely alive in Master Hemlock's house and presence. He felt a little dead. Not dead, but a little dead.

A few times, sitting on the water stairs, the dirty harbor water sloshing at the next step down, the yells of gulls and dock work-ers wreathing the air with a thin, ungainly music, he shut his eyes and saw his love so clear, so close, that he reached out his hand to touch her. If he reached out his hand in his mind only, as when he played the mental harp, then indeed he touched her. He felt her hand in his, and her cheek, warm-cool, silken-gritty, lay against his mouth. In his mind he spoke to her, and in his mind she answered, her voice, her husky voice saying his name, "Diamond . . ."

But as he went back up the streets of South Port he lost her. He swore to keep her with him, to think of her, to think of her that night, but she faded away. By the time he opened the door of Master Hemlock's house he was reciting lists of names, or wondering what would be for dinner, for he was hungry most of the time. Not till he could take an hour and run back down to the docks could he think of her.

So he came to feel that those hours were true meetings with her, and he lived for them, without knowing what he lived for until his feet were on the cobbles, and his eyes on the harbor and the far line of the sea. Then he remembered what was worth remembering.

The winter passed by, and the cold early spring, and with the warm late spring came a letter from his mother, brought by a carter. Diamond read it and took it to Master Hemlock, saying, "My mother wonders if I might spend a month at home this summer."

"Probably not," the wizard said, and then, appearing to notice Diamond, put down his pen and said, "Young man, I must ask you if you wish to continue studying with me."

Diamond had no idea what to say. The idea of its being up to him had not occurred to him. "Do you think I ought to?" he asked at last.

"Probably not," the wizard said.

Diamond expected to feel relieved, released, but found he felt rejected, ashamed.

"I'm sorry," he said, with enough dignity that Hemlock glanced up at him.

"You could go to Roke," the wizard said.

"To Roke?"

The boy's drop-jawed stare irritated Hemlock, though he knew it shouldn't. Wizards are used to overweening confidence in the young of their kind. They expect modesty to come later, if at all. "I said Roke." Hemlock's tone said he was unused to having to repeat himself. And then, because this boy, this soft-headed, spoiled, moony boy had endeared himself to Hemlock by his uncomplaining patience, he took pity on him and said, "You should either go to Roke or find a wizard to teach you what you need. Of course you need what I can teach you. You need the names. The art begins and ends in naming. But that's not your gift. You have a poor memory for words. You must train it diligently. However, it's clear that you do have capacities, and that they need cultivation and discipline, which another man can give you better than I can." So does modesty breed modesty, sometimes, even in unlikely places. "If you were to go to Roke, I'd send a letter with you drawing you to the particular attention of the Master Summoner."

"Ah," said Diamond, floored. The Summoner's art is perhaps the most arcane and dangerous of all the arts of magic.

"Perhaps I am wrong," said Hemlock in his dry, flat voice. "Your gift may be for Pattern. Or perhaps it's an ordinary gift for shaping and transformation. I'm not certain."

"But you are—I do actually—"

"Oh yes. You are uncommonly slow, young man, to recognise your own capacities." It was spoken harshly, and Diamond stiffened up a bit.

"I thought my gift was for music," he said.

Hemlock dismissed that with a flick of his hand. "I am talking of the True Art," he said. "Now I will be frank with you. I advise you to write your parents—I shall write them too—informing them of your decision to go to the school on Roke, if that is what you decide; or to the Great Port, if the Mage Restive will take you on, as I think he will, with my recommendation. But I advise against visiting home. The entanglement of family, friends, and so on is precisely what you need to be free of. Now, and henceforth."

"Do wizards have no family?"

Hemlock was glad to see a bit of fire in the boy. "They are one another's family," he said.

"And no friends?"

"They may be friends. Did I say it was an easy life?" A pause. Hemlock looked directly at Diamond. "There was a girl," he said.

Diamond met his gaze for a moment, looked down, and said nothing.

"Your father told me. A witch's daughter, a childhood play-mate. He believed that you had taught her spells."

"She taught me."

Hemlock nodded. "That is quite understandable, among children. And quite impossible now. Do you understand that?"

"No," Diamond said.

"Sit down," said Hemlock. After a moment Diamond took the stiff, high-backed chair facing him.

"I can protect you here, and have done so. On Roke, of course, you'll be perfectly safe. The very walls, there ... But if you go home, you must be willing to protect yourself. It's a difficult thing for a young man, very difficult—a test of a will that has not yet been steeled, a mind that has not yet seen its true goal. I very strongly advise that you not take that risk. Write your parents, and go to the Great Port, or to Roke. Half your year's fee, which I'll return to you, will see to your first expenses."

Diamond sat upright and still. He had been getting some of his father's height and girth lately, and looked very much a man, though a very young one.

"What did you mean, Master Hemlock, in saying that you had protected me here?"

"Simply as I protect myself," the wizard said; and after a moment, testily, "The bargain, boy. The power we give for our power. The lesser state of being we forgo. Surely you know that every true man of power is celibate."

There was a pause, and Diamond said, "So you saw to it . . . that I . . ."

"Of course. It was my responsibility as your teacher."

Diamond nodded. He said, "Thank you." Presently he stood up. "Excuse me, Master," he said. "I have to think."

"Where are you going?"

"Down to the waterfront."

"Better stay here."

"I can't think, here."

Hemlock might have known then what he was up against; but having told the boy he would not be his master any longer, he could not in conscience command him. "You have a true gift, Essiri," he said, using the name he had given the boy in the springs of the Amia, a word that in the Old Speech means Willow. "I don't entirely understand it. I think you don't understand it at all. Take care! To misuse a gift, or to refuse to use it, may cause great loss, great harm."

Diamond nodded, suffering, contrite, unrebellious, unmovable.

"Go on," the wizard said, and Diamond went.

Later Hemlock knew he should never have let the boy leave the house. He had underestimated Diamond's willpower, or the strength of the spell the girl had laid on him. Their conversation was in the morning; Hemlock went back to the ancient cantrip he was annotating; it was not till supper time that he thought about his pupil, and not until he had eaten supper alone that he admitted that Diamond had run away.

Hemlock was loath to practice any of the lesser arts of magic. He did not put out a finding spell, as any sorcerer might have done. Nor did he call to Diamond in any way. He was angry; perhaps he was hurt. He had thought well of the boy, and offered to write the Summoner about him, and then at the first test of character Diamond had broken. "Glass," the wizard muttered. At least this weakness proved he was not dangerous. Some talents were best not left to run wild, but there was no harm in this fellow, no malice. No ambition. "No spine," said Hemlock to the silence of the house. "Let him crawl home to his mother."

Still it rankled him that Diamond had let him down flat, without a word of thanks or apology. So much for good manners, he thought.

As she blew out the lamp and got into bed, the witch's daughter heard an owl calling, the little, liquid hu-hu-hu-hu that made people call them laughing owls. She heard it with a mournful heart. That had been their signal, summer nights, when they sneaked out to meet in the willow grove down on the banks of the Amia, when everybody else was sleeping. She would not think of him at night. Back in the winter she had sent to him night after night. She had learned her mother's spell of sending, and knew that it was a true spell. She had sent him her touch, her voice saying his name, again and again. She had met a wall of air and silence. She touched nothing. He had walled her out. He would not hear.

Several times, all of a sudden, in the daytime, there had been a moment when she had known him close in mind and could touch him if she reached out. But at night she knew only his blank absence, his refusal of her. She had stopped trying to reach him months ago, but her heart was still very sore.

"Hu-hu-hu," said the owl, under her window, and then it said, "Darkrose!" Startled from her misery, she leapt out of bed and opened the shutters.

"Come on out," whispered Diamond, a shadow in the starlight.

"Mother's not home. Come in!" She met him at the door.

They held each other tight, hard, silent for a long time. To Diamond it was as if he held his future, his own life, his whole life, in his arms.

At last she moved, and kissed his cheek, and whispered, "I missed you, I missed you, I missed you. How long can you stay?"

"As long as I like."

She kept his hand and led him in. He was always a little reluctant to enter the witch's house, a pungent, disorderly place thick with the mysteries of women and witchcraft, very different from his own clean comfortable home, even more different from the cold austerity of the wizard's house. He shivered like a horse as he stood there, too tall for the herb-festooned rafters. He was very highly strung, and worn out, having walked forty miles in sixteen hours without food.

"Where's your mother?" he asked in a whisper.

"Sitting with old Ferny. She died this afternoon, Mother will be there all night. But how did you get here?"

"Walked."

"The wizard let you visit home?"

"I ran away."

"Ran away! Why?"

"To keep you."

He looked at her, that vivid, fierce, dark face in its rough cloud of hair. She wore only her shift, and he saw the infinitely delicate, tender rise of her breasts. He drew her to him again, but though she hugged him she drew away again, frowning.

"Keep me?" she repeated. "You didn't seem to worry about losing me all winter. What made you come back now?"

"He wanted me to go to Roke."

"To Roke?" She stared. "To Roke, Di? Then you really do have the gift—you could be a sorcerer?"

To find her on Hemlock's side was a blow.

"Sorcerers are nothing to him. He means I could be a wizard. Do magery. Not just witchcraft."

"Oh I see," Rose said after a moment. "But I don't see why you ran away."

They had let go of each other's hands.

"Don't you understand?" he said, exasperated with her for not understanding, because he had not understood. "A wizard can't have anything to do with women. With witches. With all that."

"Oh, I know. It's beneath them."

"It's not just beneath them—"

"Oh, but it is. I'll bet you had to unlearn every spell I taught you. Didn't you?"

"It isn't the same kind of thing."

"No. It isn't the High Art. It isn't the True Speech. A wizard mustn't soil his lips with common words. 'Weak as women's magic, wicked as women's magic,' you think I don't know what they say? So, why did you come back here?"

"To see you!"

"What for?"

"What do you think?"

"You never sent to me, you never let me send to you, all the time you were gone. I was just supposed to wait until you got tired of playing wizard. Well, I got tired of waiting." Her voice was nearly inaudible, a rough whisper.

"Somebody's been coming around," he said, incredulous that she could turn against him. "Who's been after you?"

"None of your business if there is! You go off, you turn your back on me. Wizards can't have anything to do with what I do, what my mother does. Well, I don't want anything to do with what you do, either, ever. So go!"

Starving, frustrated, misunderstood, Diamond reached out to

hold her again, to make her body understand his body, repeating that first, deep embrace that had held all the years of their lives in it. He found himself standing two feet back, his hands stinging and his ears ringing and his eyes dazzled. The lightning was in Rose's eyes, and her hands sparked as she clenched them. "Never do that again," she whispered.

"Never fear," Diamond said, turned on his heel, and strode out. A string of dried sage caught on his head and trailed after him.

He spent the night in their old place in the sallows. Maybe he hoped she would come, but she did not come, and he soon slept in sheer weariness. He woke in the first, cold light. He sat up and thought. He looked at life in that cold light. It was a different matter from what he had believed it. He went down to the stream in which he had been named. He drank, washed his hands and face, made himself look as decent as he could, and went up through the town to the fine house at the high end, his father's house.

After the first outcries and embraces, the servants and his mother sat him right down to breakfast. So it was with warm food in his belly and a certain chill courage in his heart that he faced his father, who had been out before breakfast seeing off a string of timber carts to the Great Port.

"Well, son!" They touched cheeks. "So Master Hemlock gave you a vacation?"

"No, sir. I left."

Golden stared, then filled his plate and sat down. "Left," he said.

"Yes, sir. I decided that I don't want to be a wizard."

"Hmf," said Golden, chewing. "Left of your own accord? Entirely? With the Master's permission?"

"Of my own accord entirely, without his permission."

Golden chewed very slowly, his eyes on the table. Diamond had seen his father look like this when a forester reported an infestation in the chestnut groves, and when he found a mule dealer had cheated him.

"He wanted me to go to the College on Roke to study with the Master Summoner. He was going to send me there. I decided not to go."

After a while Golden asked, still looking at the table, "Why?"

"It isn't the life I want."

Another pause. Golden glanced over at his wife, who stood by the window listening in silence. Then he looked at his son. Slowly the mixture of anger, disappointment, confusion, and respect on his face gave way to something simpler, a look of complicity, very nearly a wink. "I see," he said. "And what did you decide you want?"

A pause. "This," Diamond said. His voice was level. He looked neither at his father nor his mother.

"Hah!" said Golden. "Well! I will say I'm glad of it, son." He ate a small pork pie in one mouthful. "Being a wizard, going to Roke, all that, it never seemed real, not exactly. And with you off there, I didn't know what all this was for, to tell you the truth. All my business. If you're here, it adds up, you see. It adds up. Well! But listen here, did you just run off from the wizard? Did he know you were going?"

"No. I'll write him," Diamond said, in his new, level voice.

"He won't be angry? They say wizards have short tempers. Full of pride."

"He's angry," Diamond said, "but he won't do anything."

So it proved. Indeed, to Golden's amazement, Master Hemlock sent back a scrupulous two-fifths of the prenticing fee. With the packet, which was delivered by one of Golden's carters who had taken a load of spars down to South Port, was a note for

Diamond. It said, "True art requires a single heart." The direction on the outside was the Hardic rune for willow. The note was signed with Hemlock's rune, which had two meanings: the hemlock tree, and suffering.

Diamond sat in his own sunny room upstairs, on his comfortable bed, hearing his mother singing as she went about the house. He held the wizard's letter and reread the message and the two runes many times. The cold and sluggish mind that had been born in him that morning down in the sallows accepted the lesson. No magic. Never again. He had never given his heart to it. It had been a game to him, a game to play with Darkrose. Even the names of the True Speech that he had learned in the wizard's house, though he knew the beauty and the power that lay in them, he could let go, let slip, forget. That was not his language.

He could speak his language only with her. And he had lost her, let her go. The double heart has no true speech. From now on he could talk only the language of duty: getting and spending, outlay and income, the profit and the loss.

And beyond that, nothing. There had been illusions, little spells, pebbles that turned to butterflies, wooden birds that flew on living wings for a minute or two. There had never been a choice, really. There was only one way for him to go.

Golden was immensely happy and quite unconscious of it. "Old man's got his jewel back," said the carter to the forester. "Sweet as new butter, he is." Golden, unaware of being sweet, thought only how sweet life was. He had bought the Reche grove, at a very stiff price to be sure, but at least old Lowbough of Easthill hadn't got it, and now he and Diamond could develop it as it ought to be developed. In among the chestnuts there were a lot of pines, which could be felled and sold for masts and spars and small lumber, and replanted with chestnut seedlings. It would in time be a pure stand like the Big Grove, the heart of his chestnut kingdom. In time, of course. Oak and chestnut don't shoot up overnight like alder and willow. But there was time. There was time, now. The boy was barely seventeen, and he himself just forty-five. In his prime. He had been feeling old, but that was nonsense. He was in his prime. The oldest trees, past bearing, ought to come out with the pines. Some good wood for furniture could be salvaged from them.

"Well, well, well," he said to his wife, frequently, "all rosy again, eh? Got the apple of your eye back home, eh? No more moping, eh?"

And Tuly smiled and stroked his hand.

Once instead of smiling and agreeing, she said, "It's lovely to have him back, but," and Golden stopped hearing. Mothers were born to worry about their children, and women were born never to be content. There was no reason why he should listen to the litany of anxieties by which Tuly hauled herself through life. Of course she thought a merchant's life wasn't good enough for the boy. She'd have thought being King in Havnor wasn't good enough for him.

"When he gets himself a girl," Golden said, in answer to whatever it was she had been saying, "he'll be all squared away. Living with the wizards, you know, the way they are, it set him back a bit. Don't worry about Diamond. He'll know what he wants when he sees it!"

"I hope so," said Tuly.

"At least he's not seeing the witch's girl," said Golden. "That's done with." Later on it occurred to him that neither was his wife seeing the witch any more. For years they'd been thick as thieves, against all his warnings, and now Tangle was never anywhere near the house. Women's friendships never lasted. He teased her about it. Finding her strewing pennyroyal and miller's-bane in the chests and clothes presses against an infestation of moths, he said, "Seems like you'd have your friend the wise woman up to hex 'em away. Or aren't you friends any more?"

"No," his wife said in her soft, level voice, "we aren't."

"And a good thing too!" Golden said roundly. "What's become of that daughter of hers, then? Went off with a juggler, I heard?"

"A musician," Tuly said. "Last summer."

"A nameday party," said Golden. "Time for a bit of play, a bit of music and dancing, boy. Nineteen years old. Celebrate it!"

"I'll be going to Easthill with Sul's mules."

"No, no, no. Sul can handle it. Stay home and have your party. You've been working hard. We'll hire a band. Who's the best in the country? Tarry and his lot?"

"Father, I don't want a party," Diamond said and stood up, shivering his muscles like a horse. He was bigger than Golden now, and when he moved abruptly it was startling. "I'll go to East-hill," he said, and left the room.

"What's that all about?" Golden said to his wife, a rhetorical question. She looked at him and said nothing, a non-rhetorical answer.

After Golden had gone out, she found her son in the counting room going through ledgers. She looked at the pages. Long, long lists of names and numbers, debts and credits, profits and losses.

"Di," she said, and he looked up. His face was still round and a bit peachy, though the bones were heavier and the eyes were melancholy.

"I didn't mean to hurt Father's feelings," he said.

"If he wants a party, he'll have it," she said. Their voices were alike, being in the higher register but dark-toned, and held to an even quietness, contained, restrained. She perched on a stool beside his at the high desk.

"I can't," he said, and stopped, and went on, "I really don't want to have any dancing."

"He's matchmaking," Tuly said, dry, fond.

"I don't care about that."

"I know you don't."

"The problem is . . ."

"The problem is the music," his mother said at last.

He nodded.

"My son, there is no reason," she said, suddenly passionate, "there is *no* reason why you should give up everything you love!"

He took her hand and kissed it as they sat side by side.

"Things don't mix," he said. "They ought to, but they don't. I found that out. When I left the wizard. I thought I could be everything. You know—do magic, play music, be Father's son, love Rose . . . It doesn't work that way. Things don't mix."

"They do, they do," Tuly said. "Everything is hooked together, tangled up!"

"Maybe things are, for women. But I . . . I can't be double-hearted."

"Double-hearted? You? You gave up wizardry because you knew that if you didn't, you'd betray it."

He took the word with a visible shock, but did not deny it.

"But why," she demanded, "why did you give up music?"

"I have to have a single heart. I can't play the harp while I'm bargaining with a mule breeder. I can't make ballads while I'm fig-uring what we have to pay the pickers to keep 'em from hiring out to Lowbough!" His voice shook a little now, a vibrato, and his eyes were not sad, but angry.

"So you put a spell on yourself," she said, "just as that wizard put one on you. A spell to keep you safe. To keep you with the mule breeders, and the nut pickers, and these." She struck the ledger full of lists of names and figures, a flicking, dismissive tap. "A spell of silence," she said.

After a long time the young man said, "What else can I do?"

"I don't know, my dear. I do want you to be safe. I do love to see your father happy and proud of you. But I can't bear to see you unhappy, without pride! I don't know. Maybe you're right. Maybe for a man it's only one thing ever. But I miss hearing you sing."

She was in tears. They hugged, and she stroked his thick, shining hair and apologised for being cruel, and he hugged her again and said she was the kindest mother in the world, and so she went off. But as she left she turned back a moment and said, "Let him have the party, Di. Let yourself have it."

"I will," he said, to comfort her.

Golden ordered the beer and food and fireworks, but Diamond saw to hiring the musicians.

"Of course I'll bring my band," Tarry said, "fat chance I'd miss it! You'll have every tootler in the west of the world here for one of your dad's parties."

"You can tell 'em you're the band that's getting paid."

"Oh, they'll come for the glory," said the harper, a lean, long-jawed, walleyed fellow of forty. "Maybe you'll have a go with us yourself, then? You had a hand for it, before you took to making money. And the voice not bad, if you'd worked on it."

"I doubt it," Diamond said.

"That girl you liked, witch's Rose, she's running about with Labby, I hear. No doubt they'll come by."

"I'll see you then," said Diamond, looking big and handsome and indifferent, and walked off.

"Too high and mighty these days to stop and talk," said Tarry, "though I taught him all he knows of harping. But what's that to a rich man?"

Tarry's malice had left Diamond's nerves raw, and the thought of the party weighed on him till he lost his appetite. He thought hopefully for a while that he was sick and could miss the party. But the day came, and he was there. Not so evidently, so eminently, so flamboyantly there as his father, but present, smiling, dancing. All his childhood friends were there too, half of them married by now to the other half, it seemed, but there was still plenty of flirting going on, and several pretty girls were always near him. He drank a good deal of Gadge Brewer's excellent beer, and found he could endure the music if he was dancing to it and talking and laughing while he danced. So he danced with all the pretty girls in turn, and then again with whichever one turned up again, which all of them did.

It was Golden's grandest party yet, with a dancing floor built on the town green down the way from Golden's house, and a tent for the old folks to eat and drink and gossip in, and new clothes for the children, and jugglers and puppeteers, some of them hired and some of them coming by to pick up whatever they could in the way of coppers and free beer. Any festivity drew itinerant entertainers and musicians; it was their living, and though uninvited they were welcomed. A tale singer with a droning voice and a droning bagpipe was singing *The Deed of the Dragonlord* to a group of people under the big oak on the hilltop. When Tarry's band of harp, fife, viol, and drum took time off for a breather and a swig, a new group hopped up onto the dance floor. "Hey, there's Labby's band!" cried the pretty girl nearest Diamond. "Come on, they're the best!"

Labby, a light-skinned, flashy-looking fellow, played the double-reed woodhorn. With him were a violist, a tabor player, and Rose, who played fife. Their first tune was a stampy, fast and brilliant, too fast for some of the dancers. Diamond and his partner stayed in, and people cheered and clapped them when they finished the dance, sweating and panting. "Beer!" Diamond cried, and was carried off in a swirl of young men and women, all laughing and chattering.

He heard behind him the next tune start up, the viol alone, strong and sad as a tenor voice: "Where My Love Is Going."

He drank a mug of beer down in one draft, and the girls with him watched the muscles in his strong throat as he swallowed, and they laughed and chattered, and he shivered all over like a cart horse stung by flies. He said, "Oh! I can't—!" He bolted off into the dusk beyond the lanterns hanging around the brewer's booth. "Where's he going?" said one, and another, "He'll be back," and they laughed and chattered.

The tune ended. "Darkrose," he said, behind her in the dark. She turned her head and looked at him. Their heads were on a level, she sitting cross-legged up on the dance platform, he kneeling on the grass.

"Come to the sallows," he said.

She said nothing. Labby, glancing at her, set his woodhorn to his lips. The drummer struck a triple beat on his tabor, and they were off into a sailor's jig.

When she looked around again Diamond was gone.

Tarry came back with his band in an hour or so, ungrateful for the respite and much the worse for beer. He interrupted the tune and the dancing, telling Labby loudly to clear out.

"Ah, pick your nose, harp picker," Labby said, and Tarry took offense, and people took sides, and while the dispute was at its brief height, Rose put her fife in her pocket and slipped away.

Away from the lanterns of the party it was dark, but she knew the way in the dark. He was there. The willows had grown, these two years. There was only a little space to sit among the green shoots and the long, falling leaves.

The music started up, distant, blurred by wind and the murmur of the river running.

"What did you want, Diamond?"

"To talk."

They were only voices and shadows to each other.

"So," she said.

"I wanted to ask you to go away with me," he said.

"When?"

"Then. When we quarreled. I said it all wrong. I thought . . ." A long pause. "I thought I could go on running away. With you. And play music. Make a living. Together. I meant to say that."

"You didn't say it."

"I know. I said everything wrong. I did everything wrong. I betrayed everything. The magic. And the music. And you."

"I'm all right," she said.

"Are you?"

"I'm not really good on the fife, but I'm good enough. What you didn't teach me, I can fill in with a spell, if I have to. And the band, they're all right. Labby isn't as bad as he looks. Nobody fools with me. We make a pretty good living. Winters, I go stay with Mother and help her out. So I'm all right. What about you, Di?"

"All wrong."

She started to say something, and did not say it.

"I guess we were children," he said. "Now . . ."

"What's changed?"

"I made the wrong choice."

"Once?" she said. "Or twice?"

"Twice."

"Third time's the charm."

Neither spoke for a while. She could just make out the bulk of him in the leafy shadows. "You're bigger than you were," she said. "Can you still make a light, Di? I want to see you."

He shook his head.

"That was the one thing you could do that I never could. And you never could teach me."

"I didn't know what I was doing," he said. "Sometimes it worked, sometimes it didn't."

"And the wizard in South Port didn't teach you how to make it work?"

"He only taught me names."

"Why can't you do it now?"

"I gave it up, Darkrose. I had to either do it and nothing else, or not do it. You have to have a single heart."

"I don't see why," she said. "My mother can cure a fever and ease a childbirth and find a lost ring, maybe that's nothing compared to what the wizards and the dragonlords can do, but it's not nothing, all the same. And she didn't give up anything for it. Having me didn't stop her. She had me so that she could *learn* how to do it! Just because I learned how to play music from you, did I have to give up saying spells? I can bring a fever down now too. Why should you have to stop doing one thing so you can do the other?"

"My father," he began, and stopped, and gave a kind of laugh. "They don't go together," he said. "The money and the music."

"The father and the witch-girl," said Darkrose.

Again there was silence between them. The leaves of the willows stirred.

"Would you come back to me?" he said. "Would you go with me, live with me, marry me, Darkrose?"

"Not in your father's house, Di."

"Anywhere. Run away."

"But you can't have me without the music."

"Or the music without you."

"I would," she said.

"Does Labby want a harper?"

She hesitated; she laughed. "If he wants a fife player," she said.

"I haven't practiced ever since I left, Darkrose," he said. "But the music was always in my head, and you..." She reached out her hands to him. They knelt facing, the willow leaves moving across their hair. They kissed each other, timidly at first.

In the years after Diamond left home, Golden made more money than he had ever done before. All his deals were profitable. It was as if good fortune stuck to him and he could not shake it off. He grew immensely wealthy.

He did not forgive his son. It would have made a happy ending, but he would not have it. To leave so, without a word, on his nameday night, to go off with the witch-girl, leaving all the honest work undone, to be a vagrant musician, a harper twanging and singing and grinning for pennies—there was nothing but shame and pain and anger in it for Golden. So he had his tragedy.

Tuly shared it with him for a long time, since she could see her son only by lying to her husband, which she found hard to do. She wept to think of Diamond hungry, sleeping hard. Cold nights of autumn were a misery to her. But as time went on and she heard him spoken of as Diamond the sweet singer of the West of Havnor, Diamond who had harped and sung to the great lords in the Tower of the Sword, her heart grew lighter. And once, when Golden was down at South Port, she and Tangle took a donkey cart and drove over to Easthill, where they heard Diamond sing the *Lay of the Lost Queen*, while Rose sat with them, and Little Tuly sat on Tuly's knee. And if not a happy ending, that was a true joy, which may be enough to ask for, after all.

The Bones
of the Earth

IT WAS RAINING AGAIN, and the wizard of Re Albi was sorely tempted to make a weather spell, just a little, small spell, to send the rain on round the mountain. His bones ached. They ached for the sun to come out and shine through his flesh and dry them out. Of course he could say a pain spell, but all that would do was hide the ache for a while. There was no cure for what ailed him. Old bones need the sun. The wizard stood still in the doorway of his house, between the dark room and the rain-streaked open air, preventing himself from making a spell, and angry at himself for preventing himself and for having to be prevented.

He never swore—men of power do not swear, it is not safe—but he cleared his throat with a coughing growl, like a bear. A moment later a thunderclap rolled off the hidden upper slopes of Gont Mountain, echoing round from north to south, dying away in the cloud-filled forests.

A good sign, thunder, Dulse thought. It would stop raining soon. He pulled up his hood and went out into the rain to feed the chickens.

He checked the henhouse, finding three eggs. Red Bucca was

setting. Her eggs were about due to hatch. The mites were bothering her, and she looked scruffy and jaded. He said a few words against mites, told himself to remember to clean out the nest box as soon as the chicks hatched, and went on to the poultry yard, where Brown Bucca and Grey and Leggings and Candor and the King huddled under the eaves making soft, shrewish remarks about rain.

"It'll stop by midday," the wizard told the chickens. He fed them and squelched back to the house with three warm eggs. When he was a child he had liked to walk in mud. He remembered enjoying the cool of it rising between his toes. He still liked to go barefoot, but no longer enjoyed mud; it was sticky stuff, and he disliked stooping to clean his feet before going into the house. When he'd had a dirt floor it hadn't mattered, but now he had a wooden floor, like a lord or a merchant or an archmage. To keep the cold and damp out of his bones. Not his own notion. Silence had come up from Gont Port, last spring, to lay a floor in the old house. They had had one of their arguments about it. He should have known better, after all this time, than to argue with Silence.

"I've walked on dirt for seventy-five years," Dulse had said. "A few more won't kill me!"

To which Silence of course made no reply, letting him hear what he had said and feel its foolishness thoroughly.

"Dirt's easier to keep clean," he said, knowing the struggle already lost. It was true that all you had to do with a good hard-packed clay floor was sweep it and now and then sprinkle it to keep the dust down. But it sounded silly all the same.

"Who's to lay this floor?" he said, now merely querulous.

Silence nodded, meaning himself.

The boy was in fact a workman of the first order, carpenter, cabinetmaker, stonelayer, roofer; he had proved that when he lived up here as Dulse's student, and his life with the rich folk of

Gont Port had not softened his hands. He brought the boards from Sixth's mill in Re Albi, driving Gammer's ox team; he laid the floor and polished it the next day, while the old wizard was up at Bog Lake gathering simples. When Dulse came home there it was, shining like a dark lake itself. "Have to wash my feet every time I come in," he grumbled. He walked in gingerly. The wood was so smooth it seemed soft to the bare sole. "Satin," he said. "You didn't do all that in one day without a spell or two. A village hut with a palace floor. Well, it'll be a sight, come winter, to see the fire shine in that! Or do I have to get me a carpet now? A fleecefell, on a golden warp?"

Silence smiled. He was pleased with himself.

He had turned up on Dulse's doorstep a few years ago. Well, no, twenty years ago it must be, or twenty-five. A while ago now. He had been truly a boy then, long-legged, rough-haired, soft-faced. A set mouth, clear eyes. "What do you want?" the wizard had asked, knowing what he wanted, what they all wanted, and keeping his eyes from those clear eyes. He was a good teacher, the best on Gont, he knew that. But he was tired of teaching, didn't want another prentice underfoot. And he sensed danger.

"To learn," the boy whispered.

"Go to Roke," the wizard said. The boy wore shoes and a good leather vest. He could afford or earn ship's passage to the school.

"I've been there."

At that Dulse looked him over again. No cloak, no staff.

"Failed? Sent away? Ran away?"

The boy shook his head at each question. He shut his eyes; his mouth was already shut. He stood there, intensely gathered, suffering: drew breath: looked straight into the wizard's eyes.

"My mastery is here, on Gont," he said, still speaking hardly above a whisper. "My master is Heleth."

At that the wizard whose true name was Heleth stood as still as he did, looking back at him, till the boy's gaze dropped.

In silence Dulse sought the boy's name, and saw two things: a fir cone, and the rune of the Closed Mouth. Then seeking further he heard in his mind a name spoken; but he did not speak it.

"I'm tired of teaching and talking," he said. "I need silence. Is that enough for you?"

The boy nodded once.

"Then to me you are Silence," the wizard said. "You can sleep in the nook under the west window. There's an old pallet in the woodhouse. Air it. Don't bring mice in with it." And he stalked off towards the Overfell, angry with the boy for coming and with himself for giving in; but it was not anger that made his heart pound. Striding along—he could stride, then—with the sea wind pushing at him always from the left and the early sunlight on the sea out past the vast shadow of the mountain, he thought of the Mages of Roke, the masters of the art magic, the professors of mystery and power. "He was too much for 'em, was he? And he'll be too much for me," he thought, and smiled. He was a peaceful man, but he did not mind a bit of danger.

He stopped then and felt the dirt under his feet. He was barefoot, as usual. When he was a student on Roke, he had worn shoes. But he had come back home to Gont, to Re Albi, with his wizard's staff, and kicked his shoes off. He stood still and felt the dust and rock of the cliff-top path under his feet, and the cliffs under that, and the roots of the island in the dark under that. In the dark under the waters all islands touched and were one. So his teacher Ard had said, and so his teachers on Roke had said. But this was his island, his rock, his dirt. His wizardry grew out of it. "My mastery is here," the boy had said, but it went deeper than mastery. That, perhaps, was something Dulse could teach him: what went deeper than mastery. What he had learned here, on Gont, before he ever went to Roke.

And the boy must have a staff. Why had Nemmerle let him leave Roke without one, empty-handed as a prentice or a witch? Power like that shouldn't go wandering about unchanneled and unsignaled.

My teacher had no staff, Dulse thought, and at the same moment thought, The boy wants his staff from me. Gontish oak, from the hands of a Gontish wizard. Well, if he earns it I'll make him one. If he can keep his mouth closed. And I'll leave him my lore-books. If he can clean out a henhouse, and understand the Glosses of Danemer, and keep his mouth closed.

The new student cleaned out the henhouse and hoed the bean patch, learned the meaning of the Glosses of Danemer and the Arcana of the Enlades, and kept his mouth closed. He listened. He heard what Dulse said; sometimes he heard what Dulse thought. He did what Dulse wanted and what Dulse did not know he wanted. His gift was far beyond Dulse's guidance, yet he had been right to come to Re Albi, and they both knew it.

Dulse thought sometimes in those years about sons and fathers. He had quarreled with his own father, a sorcerer-prospector, over his choice of Ard as his teacher. His father had shouted that a student of Ard's was no son of his, had nursed his rage, died unforgiving.

Dulse had seen young men weep for joy at the birth of a first son. He had seen poor men pay witches a year's earnings for the promise of a healthy boy, and a rich man touch his gold-bedizened baby's face and whisper, adoring, "My immortality!" He had seen men beat their sons, bully and humiliate them, spite and thwart them, hating the death they saw in them. He had seen the answering hatred in the sons' eyes, the threat, the pitiless contempt. And seeing it, Dulse knew why he had never sought reconciliation with his father.

He had seen a father and son work together from daybreak to sundown, the old man guiding a blind ox, the middle-aged man driving the iron-bladed plough, never a word spoken. As they started home the old man laid his hand a moment on the son's shoulder.

He had always remembered that. He remembered it now, when he looked across the hearth, winter evenings, at the dark face bent above a lore-book or a shirt that needed mending. The eyes cast down, the mouth closed, the spirit listening.

"Once in his lifetime, if he's lucky, a wizard finds somebody he can talk to." Nemmerle had said that to Dulse a night or two before Dulse left Roke, a year or two before Nemmerle was chosen Archmage. He had been the Master Patterner and the kindest of all Dulse's teachers at the school. "I think, if you stayed, Heleth, we could talk."

Dulse had been unable to answer at all for a while. Then, stammering, guilty at his ingratitude and incredulous at his obstinacy—"Master, I would stay, but my work is on Gont. I wish it was here, with you—"

"It's a rare gift, to know where you need to be, before you've been to all the places you don't need to be. Well, send me a student now and then. Roke needs Gontish wizardry. I think we're leaving things out, here, things worth knowing..."

Dulse had sent students on to the school, three or four of them, nice lads with a gift for this or that; but the one Nemmerle waited for had come and gone of his own will, and what they had thought of him on Roke Dulse did not know. And Silence, of course, did not say. It was evident that he had learned there in two or three years what some boys learned in six or seven and many never learned at all. To him it had been mere groundwork.

"Why didn't you come to me first?" Dulse had demanded. "And then go to Roke, to put a polish on it?"

"I didn't want to waste your time."

"Did Nemmerle know you were coming to work with me?"

Silence shook his head.

"If you'd deigned to tell him your intentions, he might have sent a message to me."

Silence looked stricken. "Was he your friend?"

Dulse paused. "He was my master. Would have been my friend, perhaps, if I'd stayed on Roke. Have wizards friends? No more than they have wives, or sons, I suppose . . . Once he said to me that in our trade it's a lucky man who finds someone to talk to . . . Keep that in mind. If you're lucky, one day you'll have to open your mouth."

Silence bowed his rough, thoughtful head.

"If it hasn't rusted shut," Dulse added.

"If you ask me to, I'll talk," the young man said, so earnest, so willing to deny his whole nature at Dulse's request that the wizard had to laugh.

"I asked you not to," he said. "And it's not my need I spoke of. I talk enough for two. Never mind. You'll know what to say when the time comes. That's the art, eh? What to say, and when to say it. And the rest is silence."

The young man slept on a pallet under the little west window of Dulse's house for three years. He learned wizardry, fed the chickens, milked the cow. He suggested, once, that Dulse keep goats. He had not said anything for a week or so, a cold, wet week of autumn. He said, "You might keep some goats."

Dulse had the big lore-book open on the table. He had been

trying to reweave one of the Acastan Spells, much broken and made powerless by the Emanations of Fundaur centuries ago. He had just begun to get a sense of the missing word that might fill one of the gaps, he almost had it, and—"You might keep some goats," Silence said.

Dulse considered himself a wordy, impatient man with a short temper. The necessity of not swearing had been a burden to him in his youth, and for thirty years the imbecility of prentices, clients, cows, and chickens had tried him sorely. Prentices and clients were afraid of his tongue, though cows and chickens paid no attention to his outbursts. He had never been angry at Silence before. There was a very long pause.

"What for?"

Silence apparently did not notice the pause or the extreme softness of Dulse's voice. "Milk, cheese, roast kid, company," he said.

"Have you ever kept goats?" Dulse asked, in the same soft, polite voice.

Silence shook his head.

He was in fact a town boy, born in Gont Port. He had said nothing about himself, but Dulse had asked around a bit. The father, a longshoreman, had died in the big earthquake, when Silence would have been seven or eight; the mother was a cook at a waterfront inn. At twelve the boy had got into some kind of trouble, probably messing about with magic, and his mother had managed to prentice him to Elassen, a respectable sorcerer in Valmouth. There the boy had picked up his true name, and some skill in carpentry and farmwork, if not much else; and Elassen had had the generosity, after three years, to pay his passage to Roke. That was all Dulse knew about him.

"I dislike goat cheese," Dulse said.

Silence nodded, acceptant as always.

From time to time in the years since then, Dulse remembered

how he hadn't lost his temper when Silence asked about keeping goats; and each time the memory gave him a quiet satisfaction, like that of finishing the last bite of a perfectly ripe pear.

After spending the next several days trying to recapture the missing word, he had set Silence to studying the Acastan Spells. Together they finally worked it out, a long toil. "Like ploughing with a blind ox," Dulse said.

Not long after that he gave Silence the staff he had made for him of Gontish oak.

And the Lord of Gont Port had tried once again to get Dulse to come down to do what needed doing in Gont Port, and Dulse had sent Silence down instead, and there he had stayed.

And Dulse was standing on his own doorstep, three eggs in his hand and the rain running cold down his back.

How long had he been standing here? Why was he standing here? He had been thinking about mud, about the floor, about Silence. Had he been out walking on the path above the Overfell? No, that was years ago, years ago, in the sunlight. It was raining. He had fed the chickens, and come back to the house with three eggs, they were still warm in his hand, silky brown lukewarm eggs, and the sound of thunder was still in his mind, the vibration of thunder was in his bones, in his feet. Thunder?

No. There had been a thunderclap, a while ago. This was not thunder. He had had this queer feeling and had not recognised it, back—when? long ago, back before all the days and years he had been thinking of. When, when had it been?—before the earthquake. Just before the earthquake. Just before a half mile of the coast at Essary slumped into the sea, and people died crushed in the ruins of their villages, and a great wave swamped the wharfs at Gont Port.

He stepped down from the doorstep onto the dirt so that he could feel the ground with the nerves of his soles, but the mud slimed and fouled any messages the dirt had for him. He set the eggs down on the doorstep, sat down beside them, cleaned his feet with rainwater from the pot by the step, wiped them dry with the rag that hung on the handle of the pot, rinsed and wrung out the rag and hung it on the handle of the pot, picked up the eggs, stood up slowly, and went into his house.

He gave a sharp look at his staff, which leaned in the corner behind the door. He put the eggs in the larder, ate an apple quickly because he was hungry, and took up his staff. It was yew, bound at the foot with copper, worn to satin at the grip. Nemmerle had given it to him.

"Stand!" he said to it in its language, and let go of it. It stood as if he had driven it into a socket.

"To the root," he said impatiently, in the Language of the Making. "To the root!"

He watched the staff that stood on the shining floor. In a little while he saw it quiver very slightly, a shiver, a tremble.

"Ah, ah, ah," said the old wizard.

"What should I do?" he said aloud after a while.

The staff swayed, was still, shivered again.

"Enough of that, my dear," Dulse said, laying his hand on it. "Come now. No wonder I kept thinking about Silence. I should send for him . . . send to him . . . No. What did Ard say? Find the center, find the center. That's the question to ask. That's what to do . . ." As he muttered on to himself, routing out his heavy cloak, setting water to boil on the small fire he had lighted earlier, he wondered if he had always talked to himself, if he had talked all the time when Silence lived with him. No. It had become a habit after Silence left, he thought, with the bit of his mind that went on thinking the ordinary thoughts of life, while the rest of it made preparations for terror and destruction.

He hard-boiled the three new eggs and one already in the larder and put them into a pouch along with four apples and a bladder of resinated wine, in case he had to stay out all night. He shrugged arthritically into his heavy cloak, took up his staff, told the fire to go out, and left.

He no longer kept a cow. He stood looking into the poultry yard, considering. The fox had been visiting the orchard lately. But the chickens would have to forage if he stayed away. They must take their chances, like everyone else. He opened their gate a little. Though the rain was no more than a misty drizzle now, they stayed hunched up under the henhouse eaves, disconsolate. The King had not crowed once this morning.

"Have you anything to tell me?" Dulse asked them.

Brown Bucca, his favorite, shook herself and said her name a few times. The others said nothing.

"Well, take care. I saw the fox on the full-moon night," Dulse said, and went on his way.

As he walked he thought; he thought hard; he recalled. He recalled all he could of matters his teacher had spoken of once only and long ago. Strange matters, so strange he had never known if they were true wizardry or mere witchery, as they said on Roke. Matters he certainly had never heard about on Roke, nor had he ever spoken about them there, maybe fearing the Masters would despise him for taking such things seriously, maybe knowing they would not understand them, because they were Gontish matters, truths of Gont. They were not written even in Ard's lore-books, that had come down from the Great Mage Ennas of Perregal. They were all word of mouth. They were home truths.

"If you need to read the Mountain," his teacher had told him, "go to the Dark Pond at the top of Semere's cow pasture. You can see the ways from there. You need to find the center. See where to go in."

"Go in?" the boy Dulse had whispered.

"What could you do from outside?"

Dulse was silent for a long time, and then said, "How?"

"Thus." And Ard's long arms stretched out and upward in the invocation of what Dulse would know later was a great spell of Transforming. Ard spoke the words of the spell awry, as teachers of wizardry must do lest the spell operate. Dulse knew the trick of hearing them aright and remembering them. When Ard was done, Dulse had repeated the words in his mind in silence, half-sketching the strange, awkward gestures that were part of them. All at once his hand stopped.

"But you can't undo this!" he said aloud.

Ard nodded. "It is irrevocable."

Dulse knew no transformation that was irrevocable, no spell that could not be unsaid, except the Word of Unbinding, which is spoken only once.

"But why—?"

"At need," Ard said.

Dulse knew better than to ask for explanation. The need to speak such a spell could not come often; the chance of his ever having to use it was very slight. He let the terrible spell sink down in his mind and be hidden and layered over with a thousand useful or beautiful or enlightening mageries and charms, all the lore and rules of Roke, all the wisdom of the books Ard had bequeathed him. Crude, monstrous, useless, it lay in the dark of his mind for sixty years, like the cornerstone of an earlier, forgotten house down in the cellar of a mansion full of lights and treasures and children.

The rain had ceased, though mist still hid the peak and shreds of cloud drifted through the high forests. Though not a tireless walker like Silence, who would have spent his life wandering in the forests of Gont Mountain if he could, Dulse had been born in Re Albi and knew the roads and ways around it as part of himself. He took the shortcut at Rissi's well and came out before midday on Semere's high pasture, a level step on the mountainside. A mile below it, all in sunlight now, the farm buildings stood in the lee of a hill across which a flock of sheep moved like a cloud-shadow. Gont Port and its bay were hidden under the steep, knotted hills that stood inland above the city.

Dulse wandered about a bit before he found what he took to be the Dark Pond. It was small, half mud and reeds, with one vague, boggy path to the water, and no tracks on that but goat hoofs. The water was dark, though it lay out under the bright sky and far above the peat soils. Dulse followed the goat tracks, growling when his foot slipped in the mud and he wrenched his ankle to keep from falling. At the brink of the water he stood still. He stooped to rub his ankle. He listened.

It was absolutely silent.

No wind. No birdcall. No distant lowing or bleating or call of voice. As if all the island had gone still. Not a fly buzzed.

He looked at the dark water. It reflected nothing.

Reluctant, he stepped forward, barefoot and bare-legged; he had rolled up his cloak into his pack an hour ago when the sun came out. Reeds brushed his legs. The mud was soft and sucking under his feet, full of tangling reed-roots. He made no noise as he moved slowly out into the pool, and the circles of ripples from his movement were slight and small. It was shallow for a long way. Then his cautious foot felt no bottom, and he paused.

The water shivered. He felt it first on his thighs, a lapping like the tickling touch of fur; then he saw it, the trembling of the surface all over the pond. Not the round ripples he made, which had already died away, but a ruffling, a roughening, a shudder, again, and again.

"Where?" he whispered, and then said the word aloud in the language all things understand that have no other language.

There was the silence. Then a fish leapt from the black, shaking water, a white-grey fish the length of his hand, and as it leapt it cried out in a small, clear voice, in that same language, "Yaved!"

The old wizard stood there. He recollected all he knew of the names of Gont, brought all its slopes and cliffs and ravines into his mind, and in a minute he saw where Yaved was. It was the place where the ridges parted, just inland from Gont Port, deep in the knot of hills above the city. It was the place of the fault. An earthquake centered there could shake the city down, bring avalanche and tidal wave, close the cliffs of the bay together like hands clapping. Dulse shivered, shuddered all over like the water of the pool.

He turned and made for the shore, hasty, careless where he set his feet and not caring if he broke the silence by splashing and breathing hard. He slogged back up the path through the reeds till he reached dry ground and coarse grass, and heard the buzz of midges and crickets. He sat down then on the ground, hard, for his legs were shaking.

"It won't do," he said, talking to himself in Hardic, and then he said, "I can't do it." Then he said, "I can't do it by myself."

He was so distraught that when he made up his mind to call Silence he could not think of the opening of the spell, which he had known for sixty years; then when he thought he had it, he began to speak a Summoning instead, and the spell had begun to work before he realised what he was doing and stopped and undid it word by word.

He pulled up some grass and rubbed at the slimy mud on his feet and legs. It was not dry yet, and only smeared about on his skin. "I hate mud," he whispered. Then he snapped his jaws and stopped trying to clean his legs. "Dirt, dirt," he said, gently patting the ground he sat on. Then, very slow, very careful, he began to speak the spell of calling.

In a busy street leading down to the busy wharfs of Gont Port, the wizard Ogion stopped short. The ship's captain beside him walked on several steps and turned to see Ogion talking to the air.

"But I will come, master!" he said. And then after a pause, "How soon?" And after a longer pause, he told the air something in a language the ship's captain did not understand, and made a gesture that darkened the air about him for an instant.

"Captain," he said, "I'm sorry, I must wait to spell your sails. An earthquake is near. I must warn the city. Do you tell them down there, every ship that can sail make for the open sea. Clear out past the Armed Cliffs! Good luck to you." And he turned and ran back up the street, a tall, strong man with rough greying hair, running now like a stag.

Gont Port lies at the inner end of a long narrow bay between steep shores. Its entrance from the sea is between two great headlands, the Gates of the Port, the Armed Cliffs, not a hundred feet apart. The people of Gont Port are safe from sea-pirates. But their safety is their danger: the long bay follows a fault in the earth, and jaws that have opened may shut.

When he had done what he could to warn the city, and seen all the gate guards and port guards doing what they could to keep the few roads out from becoming choked and murderous with panicky people, Ogion shut himself into a room in the signal tower of the Port, locked the door, for everybody wanted him at once, and sent a sending to the Dark Pond in Semere's cow pasture up on the Mountain.

His old master was sitting in the grass near the pond, eating an apple. Bits of eggshell flecked the ground near his legs, which were caked with drying mud. When he looked up and saw Ogion's sending he smiled a wide, sweet smile. But he looked old. He had never looked so old. Ogion had not seen him for over a year, having been busy; he was always busy in Gont Port, doing the business of the lords and people, never a chance to walk in the forests on the mountainside or to come sit with Heleth in the little house at Re Albi and listen and be still. Heleth was an old man, near eighty now; and he was frightened. He smiled with joy to see Ogion, but he was frightened.

"I think what we have to do," he said without preamble, "is try to hold the fault from slipping much. You at the Gates and me at the inner end, in the Mountain. Working together, you know. We might be able to. I can feel it building up, can you?"

Ogion shook his head. He let his sending sit down in the grass near Heleth, though it did not bend the stems of the grass where it stepped or sat. "I've done nothing but set the city in a panic and send the ships out of the bay," he said. "What is it you feel? How do you feel it?"

They were technical questions, mage to mage. Heleth hesitated before answering.

"I learned about this from Ard," he said, and paused again.

He had never told Ogion anything about his first teacher, a sorcerer of no fame even in Gont, and perhaps of ill fame. Ogion knew only that Ard had never gone to Roke, had been trained on Perregal, and that some mystery or shame darkened the name. Though he was talkative, for a wizard, Heleth was silent as a stone about some things. And so Ogion, who respected silence, had never asked him about his teacher.

"It's not Roke magic," the old man said. His voice was dry, a little forced. "Nothing against the balance, though. Nothing sticky."

That had always been his word for evil doings, spells for gain, curses, black magic: "sticky stuff."

After a while, searching for words, he went on: "Dirt. Rocks. It's a dirty magic. Old. Very old. As old as Gont Island."

"The Old Powers?" Ogion murmured.

Heleth said, "I'm not sure."

"Will it control the earth itself?"

"More a matter of getting in with it, I think. Inside." The old man was burying the core of his apple and the larger bits of eggshell under loose dirt, patting it over them neatly. "Of course I know the words, but I'll have to learn what to do as I go. That's the trouble with the big spells, isn't it? You learn what you're doing while you do it. No chance to practice." He looked up. "Ah— there! You feel that?"

Ogion shook his head.

"Straining," Heleth said, his hand still absently, gently patting the dirt as one might pat a scared cow. "Quite soon now, I think. Can you hold the Gates open, my dear?"

"Tell me what you'll be doing—"

But Heleth was shaking his head: "No," he said. "No time. Not your kind of thing." He was more and more distracted by whatever it was he sensed in the earth or air, and through him Ogion too felt that gathering, intolerable tension.

They sat unspeaking. The crisis passed. Heleth relaxed a little and even smiled. "Very old stuff," he said, "what I'll be doing. I wish now I'd thought about it more. Passed it on to you. But it seemed a bit crude. Heavy-handed . . . She didn't say where she'd learned it. Here, of course . . . There are different kinds of knowledge, after all."

"She?"

"Ard. My teacher." Heleth looked up, his face unreadable, its expression possibly sly. "You didn't know that? No, I suppose I never mentioned it. I wonder what difference it made to her wizardry, her being a woman. Or to mine, my being a man . . . What matters, it seems to me, is whose house we live in. And who we let enter the house. This kind of thing— There! There again—"

His sudden tension and immobility, the strained face and

inward look, were like those of a woman in labor when her womb contracts. That was Ogion's thought, even as he asked, "What did you mean, 'in the Mountain'?"

The spasm passed; Heleth answered, "Inside it. There at Yaved." He pointed to the knotted hills below them. "I'll go in, try to keep things from sliding around, eh? I'll find out how when I'm doing it, no doubt. I think you should be getting back to yourself. Things are tightening up." He stopped again, looking as if he were in intense pain, hunched and clenched. He struggled to stand up. Unthinking, Ogion held out his hand to help him.

"No use," said the old wizard, grinning, "you're only wind and sunlight. Now I'm going to be dirt and stone. You'd best go on. Farewell, Aihal. Keep the—keep the mouth open, for once, eh?"

Ogion, obedient, bringing himself back to himself in the stuffy, tapestried room in Gont Port, did not understand the old man's joke until he turned to the window and saw the Armed Cliffs down at the end of the long bay, the jaws ready to snap shut. "I will," he said, and set to it.

"What I have to do, you see," the old wizard said, still talking to Silence because it was a comfort to talk to him even if he was no longer there, "is get into the mountain, right inside. But not the way a sorcerer-prospector does, not just slipping about between things and looking and tasting. Deeper. All the way in. Not the veins, but the bones. So," and standing there alone in the high pasture, in the noon light, Heleth opened his arms wide in the gesture of invocation that opens all the greater spells; and he spoke.

Nothing happened as he said the words Ard had taught him, his old witch-teacher with her bitter mouth and her long, lean arms, the words spoken awry then, spoken truly now.

Nothing happened, and he had time to regret the sunlight

and the sea wind, and to doubt the spell, and to doubt himself, before the earth rose up around him, dry, warm, and dark.

In there he knew he should hurry, that the bones of the earth ached to move, and that he must become them to guide them, but he could not hurry. There was on him the bewilderment of any transformation. He had in his day been fox, and bull, and dragonfly, and knew what it was to change being. But this was different, this slow enlargement. I am vastening, he thought.

He reached out towards Yaved, towards the ache, the suffering. As he came closer to it he felt a great strength flow into him from the west, as if Silence had taken him by the hand after all. Through that link he could send his own strength, the Mountain's strength, to help. I didn't tell him I wasn't coming back, he thought, his last words in Hardic, his last grief, for he was in the bones of the mountain now. He knew the arteries of fire, and the beat of the great heart. He knew what to do. It was in no tongue of man that he said, "Be quiet, be easy. There now, there. Hold fast. So, there. We can be easy."

And he was easy, he was still, he held fast, rock in rock and earth in earth in the fiery dark of the mountain.

It was their mage Ogion whom the people saw stand alone on the roof of the signal tower on the wharf, when the streets ran up and down in waves, the cobbles bursting out of them, and walls of clay brick puffed into dust, and the Armed Cliffs leaned together, groaning. It was Ogion they saw, his hands held out before him, straining, parting: and the cliffs parted with them, and stood straight, unmoved. The city shuddered and stood still. It was Ogion who stopped the earthquake. They saw it, they said it.

"My teacher was with me, and his teacher with him," Ogion said when they praised him. "I could hold the Gate open because he held the Mountain still." They praised his modesty and did not listen to him. Listening is a rare gift, and men will have their heroes.

When the city was in order again, and the ships had all come back, and the walls were being rebuilt, Ogion escaped from praise and went up into the hills above Gont Port. He found the queer little valley called Trimmer's Dell, the true name of which in the Language of the Making was Yaved, as Ogion's true name was Aihal. He walked about there all one day, as if seeking something. In the evening he lay down on the ground and talked to it. "You should have told me. I could have said goodbye," he said. He wept then, and his tears fell on the dry dirt among the grass stems and made little spots of mud, little sticky spots.

He slept there on the ground, with no pallet or blanket between him and the dirt. At sunrise he got up and walked by the high road over to Re Albi. He did not go into the village, but past it to the house that stood alone north of the other houses at the beginning of the Overfell. The door stood open.

The last beans had got big and coarse on the vines; the cabbages were thriving. Three hens came clucking and pecking around the dusty dooryard, a red, a brown, a white; a grey hen was setting her clutch in the henhouse. There were no chicks, and no sign of the cock, the King, Heleth had called him. The king is dead, Ogion thought. Maybe a chick is hatching even now to take his place. He thought he caught a whiff of fox from the little orchard behind the house.

He swept out the dust and leaves that had blown in the open doorway across the floor of polished wood. He set Heleth's mattress and blanket in the sun to air. "I'll stay here a while," he thought. "It's a good house." After a while he thought, "I might keep some goats."

On the High Marsh

THE ISLAND OF SEMEL lies north and west across the Pelnish Sea from Havnor, south and west of the Enlades. Though it is one of the great isles of the Earthsea Archipelago, there aren't many stories from Semel. Enlad has its glorious history, and Havnor its wealth, and Paln its ill repute, but Semel has only cattle and sheep, forests and little towns, and the great silent volcano called Andanden standing over all.

South of Andanden lies a land where the ashes fell a hundred feet deep when last the volcano spoke. Rivers and streams cut their way seaward through that high plain, winding and pooling, spreading and wandering, making a marsh of it, a big, desolate, waterland with a far horizon, few trees, not many people. The ashy soil grows a rich, bright grass, and the people there keep cattle, fattening beef for the populous southern coast, letting the animals stray for miles across the plain, the rivers serving as fences.

As mountains will, Andanden makes the weather. It gathers clouds around it. The summer is short, the winter long, out on the high marsh.

In the early darkness of a winter day, a traveler stood at the windswept crossing of two paths, neither very promising, mere cattle tracks among the reeds, and looked for some sign of the way he should take.

As he came down the last slope of the mountain, he had seen houses here and there out in the marshlands, a village not far away. He had thought he was on the way to the village, but had taken a wrong turning somewhere. Tall reeds rose up close beside the paths, so that if a light shone anywhere he could not see it. Water chuckled softly somewhere near his feet. He had used up his shoes walking round Andanden on the cruel roads of black lava. The soles were worn right through, and his feet ached with the icy damp of the marsh paths.

It grew darker quickly. A haze was coming up from the south, blotting out the sky. Only above the huge, dim bulk of the mountain did stars burn clearly. Wind whistled in the reeds, soft, dismal.

The traveler stood at the crossway and whistled back at the reeds.

Something moved on one of the tracks, something big, dark, in the darkness.

"Are you there, my dear?" said the traveler. He spoke in the Old Speech, the Language of the Making. "Come along, then, Ulla," he said, and the heifer came a step or two towards him, towards her name, while he walked to meet her. He made out the big head more by touch than sight, stroking the silken dip between her eyes, scratching her forehead at the roots of the nubbin horns. "Beautiful, you are beautiful," he told her, breathing her grassy breath, leaning against her large warmth. "Will you lead me, dear Ulla? Will you lead me where I need to go?"

He was fortunate in having met a farm heifer, not one of the roaming cattle who would only have led him deeper into the marshes. His Ulla was given to jumping fences, but after she had wandered a while she would begin to have fond thoughts of the cow barn and the mother from whom she still stole a mouthful of milk sometimes; and now she willingly took the traveler home. She walked, slow but purposeful, down one of the tracks, and he went with her, a hand on her hip when the way was wide enough. When she waded a knee-deep stream, he held on to her tail. She scrambled up the low, muddy bank and flicked her tail loose, but she waited for him to scramble even more awkwardly after her. Then she plodded gently on. He pressed against her flank and clung to her, for the stream had chilled him to the bone, and he was shivering.

"Moo," said his guide, softly, and he saw the dim, small square of yellow light just a little to his left.

"Thank you," he said, opening the gate for the heifer, who went to greet her mother, while he stumbled across the dark houseyard to the door.

It would be Berry at the door, though why he knocked she didn't know. "Come in, you fool!" she said, and he knocked again, and she put down her mending and went to the door. "Can you be drunk already?" she said, and then saw him.

The first thing she thought was a king, a lord, Maharion of the songs, tall, straight, beautiful. The next thing she thought was a beggar, a lost man, in dirty clothes, hugging himself with shivering arms.

He said, "I lost my way. Have I come to the village?" His voice was hoarse and harsh, a beggar's voice, but not a beggar's accent.

"It's a half mile on," said Gift.

"Is there an inn?"

"Not till you'd come to Oraby, a ten-twelve miles on south." She considered only briefly. "If you need a room for the night, I have one. Or San might, if you're going to the village."

"I'll stay here if I may," he said in that princely way, with his teeth chattering, holding on to the doorjamb to keep on his feet.

"Take your shoes off," she said, "they're soaking. Come in then." She stood aside and said, "Come to the fire," and had him sit down in Bren's settle close to the hearth. "Stir the fire up a bit," she said. "Will you have a bit of soup? It's still hot."

"Thank you, mistress," he muttered, crouching at the fire. She brought him a bowl of broth. He drank from it eagerly yet warily, as if long unaccustomed to hot soup.

"You came over the mountain?"

He nodded.

"Whatever for?"

"To come here," he said. He was beginning to tremble less. His bare feet were a sad sight, bruised, swollen, sodden. She wanted to tell him to put them right to the fire's warmth, but didn't like to presume. Whatever he was, he wasn't a beggar by choice.

"Not many come here to the High Marsh," she said. "Peddlers and such. But not in winter."

He finished his soup, and she took the bowl. She sat down in her place, the stool by the oil lamp to the right of the hearth, and took up her mending. "Get warm through, and then I'll show you your bed," she said. "There's no fire in that room. Did you meet weather, up on the mountain? They say there's been snow."

"Some flurries," he said. She got a good look at him now in the light of lamp and fire. He was not a young man, thin, not as tall as she had thought. It was a fine face, but there was some-thing wrong, something amiss. He looks ruined, she thought, a ruined man.

"Why would you come to the Marsh?" she asked. She had a right to ask, having taken him in, yet she felt a discomfort in pressing the question.

"I was told there's a murrain among the cattle here." Now that he wasn't all locked up with cold his voice was beautiful. He talked like the tale-tellers when they spoke the parts of the heroes and the dragonlords. Maybe he was a teller or a singer? But no; the murrain, he had said.

"There is."

"I may be able to help the beasts."

"You're a curer?"

He nodded.

"Then you'll be more than welcome. The plague is terrible among the cattle. And getting worse."

He said nothing. She could see the warmth coming into him, untying him.

"Put your feet up to the fire," she said abruptly. "I have some old shoes of my husband's." It cost her something to say that, yet when she had said it she felt released, untied too. What was she keeping Bren's shoes for, anyhow? They were too small for Berry and too big for her. She'd given away his clothes, but kept the shoes, she didn't know what for. For this fellow, it would seem. Things came round if you could wait for them, she thought. "I'll set 'em out for you," she said. "Yours are perished."

He glanced at her. His dark eyes were large, deep, opaque like a horse's eyes, unreadable.

"He's dead," she said, "two years. The marsh fever. You have to watch out for that, here. The water. I live with my brother. He's in the village, at the tavern. We keep a dairy. I make cheese. Our herd's been all right," and she made the sign to avert evil. "I keep 'em close in. Out on the ranges, the murrain's very bad. Maybe the cold weather'll put an end to it."

"More likely to kill the beasts that sicken with it," the man said. He sounded a bit sleepy.

"I'm called Gift," she said. "My brother's Berry."

"Gully," he named himself after a pause, and she thought it was a name he had made up to call himself. It did not fit him. Nothing about him fit together, made a whole. Yet she felt no distrust of him. She was easy with him. He meant no harm to her. She thought there was kindness in him, the way he spoke of the animals. He would have a way with them, she thought. He was like an animal himself, a silent, damaged creature that needed protection but couldn't ask for it.

"Come," she said, "before you fall asleep there," and he followed her obediently to Berry's room, which wasn't much more than a cupboard built onto the corner of the house. Her room was behind the chimney. Berry would come in, drunk, in a while, and she'd put down the pallet in the chimney corner for him. Let the traveler have a good bed for a night. Maybe he'd leave a copper or two with her when he went on. There was a terrible shortage of coppers in her household these days.

He woke, as he always did, in his room in the Great House. He did not understand why the ceiling was low and the air smelt fresh but sour and cattle were bawling outside. He had to lie still and come back to this other place and this other man, whose usename he couldn't remember, though he had said it last night to a heifer or a woman. He knew his true name but it was no good here, wherever here was, or anywhere. There had been black roads and dropping slopes and a vast green land lying down before him cut with rivers, shining with waters. A cold wind blowing. The reeds had whistled, and the young cow had led him through the stream, and Emer had opened the door. He had known her name as soon as he saw her. But he must use some other name. He must not call her by her name. He must remember what name he had told her to call him. He must not be Irioth, though he was Irioth. Maybe in time he would be another man. No; that was wrong; he must be this man. This man's legs ached and his feet hurt. But it was a good bed, a feather bed, warm, and he need not get out of it yet. He drowsed a while, drifting away from Irioth.

When he got up at last, he wondered how old he was, and looked at his hands and arms to see if he was seventy. He still looked forty, though he felt seventy and moved like it, wincing. He got his clothes on, foul as they were from days and days of travel. There was a pair of shoes under the chair, worn but good, strong shoes, and a pair of knit wool stockings to go with them. He put the stockings on his battered feet and limped into the kitchen. Emer stood at the big sink, straining something heavy in a cloth.

"Thank you for these and the shoes," he said, and thanking her for the gift, remembered her use-name but said only, "mistress."

"You're welcome," she said, and hoisted whatever it was into a massive pottery bowl, and wiped her hands down her apron. He knew nothing at all about women. He had not lived where women were since he was ten years old. He had been afraid of them, the women that shouted at him to get out of the way in that great other kitchen long ago. But since he had been traveling about in Earthsea he had met women and found them easy to be with, like the animals; they went about their business not paying much attention to him unless he frightened them. He tried not to do that. He had no wish or reason to frighten them. They were not men.

"Would you like some fresh curds? It makes a good break-fast." She was eyeing him, but not for long, and not meeting his eyes. Like an animal, like a cat, she was, sizing him up but not challenging. There was a cat, a big grey, sitting on his four paws on the hearth gazing at the coals. Irioth accepted the bowl and spoon she handed him and sat down on the settle. The cat jumped up beside him and purred.

"Look at that," said the woman. "He's not friendly with most folk."

"It's the curds."

"He knows a curer, maybe."

It was peaceful here with the woman and the cat. He had come to a good house.

"It's cold out," she said. "Ice on the trough this morning. Will you be going on, this day?"

There was a pause. He forgot that he had to answer in words. "I'd stay if I might," he said. "I'd stay here."

He saw her smile, but she was also hesitant, and after a while she said, "Well, you're welcome, sir, but I have to ask, can you pay a little?"

"Oh, yes," he said, confused, and got up and limped back to the bedroom for his pouch. He brought her a piece of money, a little Enladian crownpiece of gold.

"Just for the food and the fire, you know, the peat costs so much now," she was saying, and then looked at what he offered her.

"Oh, sir," she said, and he knew he had done wrong.

"There's nobody in the village could change that," she said. She looked up into his face for a moment. "The whole village together couldn't change that!" she said, and laughed. It was all right, then, though the word "change" rang and rang in his head.

"It hasn't been changed," he said, but he knew that was not what she meant. "I'm sorry," he said. "If I stayed a month, if I stayed the winter, would that use it up? I should have a place to stay, while I work with the beasts."

"Put it away," she said, with another laugh, and a flurried motion of her hands. "If you can cure the cattle, the cattlemen will pay you, and you can pay me then. Call that surety, if you like. But put it away, sir! It makes me dizzy to look at it. —Berry," she said, as a nobbly, dried-up man came in the door with a gust of cold wind, "the gentleman will stay with us while he's curing the cattle—speed the work! He's given us surety of payment. So you'll sleep in the chimney corner, and him in the room. This is my brother Berry, sir."

Berry ducked his head and muttered. His eyes were dull. It seemed to Irioth that the man had been poisoned. When Berry went out again, the woman came closer and said, resolute, in a low voice, "There's no harm in him but the drink, but there's not much left of him but the drink. It's eaten up most of his mind, and most of what we have. So, do you see, put up your money where he won't see it, if you don't mind, sir. He won't come looking for it. But if he saw it, he'd take it. He often doesn't know what he's doing, do you see."

"Yes," Irioth said. "I understand. You are a kind woman." She was talking about him, about his not knowing what he was doing. She was forgiving him. "A kind sister," he said. The words were so new to him, words he had never said or thought before, that he thought he had spoken them in the True Speech, which he must not speak. But she only shrugged, with a frowning smile.

"Times I could shake his fool head off," she said, and went back to her work.

He had not known how tired he was until he came to haven. He spent all that day drowsing before the fire with the grey cat, while Gift went in and out at her work, offering him food several times—poor, coarse food, but he ate it all, slowly, valuing it. Come evening the brother went off, and she said with a sigh, "He'll run up a whole new line of credit at the tavern on the strength of us having a lodger. Not that it's your fault."

"Oh, yes," Irioth said. "It was my fault." But she forgave; and the grey cat was pressed up against his thigh, dreaming. The cat's dreams came into his mind, in the low fields where he spoke with the animals, the dusky places. The cat leapt there, and then there was milk, and the deep soft thrilling. There was no fault, only the great innocence. No need for words. They would not find him here. He was not here to find. There was no need to speak any name. There was nobody but her, and the cat dreaming, and the fire flickering. He had come over the dead mountain on black roads, but here the streams ran slow among the pastures.

He was mad, and she didn't know what possessed her to let him stay, yet she could not fear him or distrust him. What did it matter if he was mad? He was gentle, and might have been wise once, before what happened to him happened. And he wasn't so mad as all that. Mad in patches, mad at moments. Nothing in him was whole, not even his madness. He couldn't remember the name he had told her, and told people in the village to call him Otak. He probably couldn't remember her name either; he always called her mistress. But maybe that was his courtesy. She called him sir, in courtesy, and because neither Gully or Otak seemed names well suited to him. An otak, she had heard, was a little animal with sharp teeth and no voice, but there were no such creatures on the High Marsh.

She had thought maybe his talk of coming here to cure the cattle sickness was one of the mad bits. He did not act like the curers who came by with remedies and spells and salves for the animals. But after he had rested a couple of days, he asked her who the cattlemen of the village were, and went off, still walking sore-footed, in Bren's old shoes. It made her heart turn in her, seeing that.

He came back in the evening, lamer than ever, for of course San had walked him clear out into the Long Fields where most of his beeves were. Nobody had horses but Alder, and they were for his cowboys. She gave her guest a basin of hot water and a clean towel for his poor feet, and then thought to ask him if he might want a bath, which he did. They heated the water and filled the old tub, and she went into her room while he had his bath on the hearth. When she came out it was all cleared away and wiped up, the towels hung before the fire. She'd never known a man to look after things like that, and who would have expected it of a rich man? Wouldn't he have servants, where he came from? But he was no more trouble than the cat. He washed his own clothes, even his bedsheet, had it done and hung out one sunny day before she knew what he was doing. "You needn't do that, sir, I'll do your things with mine," she said.

"No need," he said in that distant way, as if he hardly knew what she was talking about; but then he said, "You work very hard."

"Who doesn't? I like the cheese making. There's an interest to it. And I'm strong. All I fear is getting old, when I can't lift the buckets and the molds." She showed him her round, muscular arm, making a fist and smiling. "Pretty good for fifty years old!" she said. It was silly to boast, but she was proud of her strong arms, her energy and skill.

"Speed the work," he said gravely.

He had a way with her cows that was wonderful. When he was there and she needed a hand, he took Berry's place, and as she told her friend Tawny, laughing, he was cannier with the cows than Bren's old dog had been. "He talks to 'em, and I'll swear they consider what he says. And that heifer follows him about like a puppy." Whatever he was doing out on the ranges with the beeves, the cattlemen were coming to think well of him. Of course they would grab at any promise of help. Half San's herd was dead. Alder would not say how many head he had lost. The bodies of cattle were everywhere. If it had not been cold weather the Marsh would have reeked of rotting flesh. None of the water could be drunk unless you boiled it an hour, except what came from the wells, hers here and the one in the village, which gave the place its name.

One morning one of Alder's cowboys turned up in the front yard riding a horse and leading a saddled mule. "Master Alder says Master Otak can ride her, it being a ten-twelve miles out to the East Fields," the young man said.

Her guest came out of the house. It was a bright, misty morning, the marshes hidden by gleaming vapors. Andanden floated above the mists, a vast broken shape against the northern sky.

The curer said nothing to the cowboy but went straight to the mule, or hinny, rather, being out of San's big jenny by Alder's white horse. She was a whitey roan, young, with a pretty face. He went and talked to her for a minute, saying something in her big, delicate ear and rubbing her topknot.

"He does that," the cowboy said to Gift. "Talks at 'em." He was amused, disdainful. He was one of Berry's drinking mates at the tavern, a decent enough young fellow, for a cowboy.

"Is he curing the cattle?" she asked.

"Well, he can't lift the murrain all at once. But seems like he can cure a beast if he gets to it before the staggers begin. And those not struck yet, he says he can keep it off 'em. So the master's sending him all about the range to do what can be done. It's too late for many."

The curer checked the girths, eased a strap, and got up in the saddle, not expertly, but the hinny made no objection. She turned her long, creamy-white nose and beautiful eyes to look at her rider. He smiled. Gift had never seen him smile.

"Shall we go?" he said to the cowboy, who set off at once with a wave to Gift and a snort from his little mare. The curer followed. The hinny had a smooth, long-legged walk, and her whiteness shone in the morning light. Gift thought it was like seeing a prince ride off, like something out of a tale, the mounted figures that walked through bright mist across the vague dun of the winter fields, and faded into the light, and were gone.

It was hard work out in the pastures. "Who doesn't do hard work?" Emer had asked, showing her round, strong arms, her hard, red hands. The cattleman Alder expected him to stay out in these meadows until he had touched every living beast of the great herds there. Alder had sent two cowboys along. They made a camp of sorts, with a groundcloth and a half tent. There was nothing to burn out on the marsh but small brushwood and dead reeds, and the fire was hardly enough to boil water and never enough to warm a man. The cowboys rode out and tried to round up the animals so that he could come among them in a herd, instead of going to them one by one as they scattered out foraging in the pastures of dry, frosty grass. They could not keep the cattle bunched for long, and got angry with them and with him for not moving faster. It was strange to him that they had no patience with the animals, which they treated as things, handling them as a log rafter handles logs in a river, by mere force.

They had no patience with him either, always at him to hurry up and get done with the job; nor with themselves, their life. When they talked to each other it was always about what they were going to do in town, in Oraby, when they got paid off. He heard a good deal about the whores in Oraby, Daisy and Goldie and the one they called the Burning Bush. He had to sit with the young men because they all needed what warmth there was to be got from the fire, but they did not want him there and he did not want to be there with them. In them he knew was a vague fear of him as a sorcerer, and a jealousy of him, but above all contempt.

He was old, other, not one of them. Fear and jealousy he knew and shrank from, and contempt he remembered. He was glad he was not one of them, that they did not want to talk to him. He was afraid of doing wrong to them.

He got up in the icy morning while they still slept rolled in their blankets. He knew where the cattle were nearby, and went to them. The sickness was very familiar to him now. He felt it in his hands as a burning, and a queasiness if it was much advanced. Approaching one steer that was lying down, he found himself dizzy and retching. He came no closer, but said words that might ease the dying, and went on.

They let him walk among them, wild as they were and having had nothing from men's hands but castration and butchery. He had a pleasure in their trust in him, a pride in it. He should not, but he did. If he wanted to touch one of the great beasts he had only to stand and speak to it a little while in the language of those who do not speak. "Ulla," he said, naming them. "Ellu. Ellua." They stood, big, indifferent; sometimes one looked at him for a long time. Sometimes one came to him with its easy, loose, majestic tread, and breathed into his open palm. All those that came to him he could cure. He laid his hands on them, on the stiff-haired, hot flanks and neck, and sent the healing into his hands with the words of power spoken over and over. After a while the beast would give a shake, or toss its head a bit, or step on. And he would drop his hands and stand there, drained and blank, for a while. Then there would be another one, big, curious, shyly bold, muddy-coated, with the sickness in it like a prickling, a tingling, a hotness in his hands, a dizziness. "Ellu," he would say, and walk to the beast and lay his hands upon it until they felt cool, as if a mountain stream ran through them.

The cowboys were discussing whether or not it was safe to eat the meat of a steer dead of the murrain. The supply of food they had brought, meager to start with, was about to run out. Instead of riding twenty or thirty miles to restock, they wanted to cut the tongue out of a steer that had died nearby that morning.

He had forced them to boil any water they used. Now he said, "If you eat that meat, in a year you'll begin to get dizzy. You'll end with the blind staggers and die as they do."

They cursed and sneered, but believed him. He had no idea if what he said was true. It had seemed true as he said it. Perhaps he wanted to spite them. Perhaps he wanted to get rid of them.

"Ride back," he said. "Leave me here. There's enough food for one man for three or four days more. The hinny will bring me back."

They needed no persuasion. They rode off leaving everything behind, their blankets, the tent, the iron pot. "How do we get all that back to the village?" he asked the hinny. She looked after the two ponies and said what hinnies say. "Aaawww!" she said. She would miss the ponies.

"We have to finish the work here," he told her, and she looked at him mildly. All animals were patient, but the patience of the horse kind was wonderful, being freely given. Dogs were loyal, but there was more of obedience in it. Dogs were hierarchs, dividing the world into lords and commoners. Horses were all lords. They agreed to collude. He remembered walking among the great, plumed feet of cart horses, fearless. The comfort of their breath on his head. A long time ago. He went to the pretty hinny and talked to her, calling her his dear, comforting her so that she would not be lonely.

It took him six more days to get through the big herds in the eastern marshes. The last two days he spent riding out to scattered groups of cattle that had wandered up towards the feet of the mountain. Many of them were not infected yet, and he could protect them. The hinny carried him bareback and made the going easy. But there was nothing left for him to eat. When he rode back to the village he was light-headed and weak-kneed. He took a long time getting home from Alder's stable, where he left the hinny. Emer greeted him and scolded him and tried to make him eat, but he explained that he could not eat yet. "As I stayed there in the sickness, in the sick fields, I felt sick. After a while I'll be able to eat again," he explained.

"You're crazy," she said, very angry. It was a sweet anger. Why could not more anger be sweet?

"At least have a bath!" she said.

He knew what he smelled like, and thanked her.

"What's Alder paying you for all this?" she demanded while the water was heating. She was still indignant, speaking more bluntly even than usual.

"I don't know," he said.

She stopped and stared at him.

"You didn't set a price?"

"Set a price?" he flashed out. Then he remembered who he was not, and spoke humbly. "No. I didn't."

"Of all the innocence," Gift said, hissing the word. "He'll skin you." She dumped a kettleful of steaming water into the bath. "He has ivory," she said. "Tell him ivory it has to be. Out there ten days starving in the cold to cure his beasts! San's got nothing but copper, but Alder can pay you in ivory. I'm sorry if I'm meddling in your business. Sir." She flung out the door with two buckets, going to the pump. She would not use the stream water for anything at all, these days. She was wise, and kind. Why had he lived so long among those who were not kind?

"We'll have to see," said Alder, the next day, "if my beasts are cured. If they make it through the winter, see, we'll know your cures all took, that they're sound, like. Not that I doubt it, but fair's fair, right? You wouldn't ask me to pay you what I have in

mind to pay you, would you now, if the cure didn't take and the
beasts died after all. Avert the chance! But I wouldn't ask you to
wait all that time unpaid, neither. So here's an advance, like, on
what's to come, and all's square between us for now, right?"

The coppers weren't decently in a bag, even. Irioth had to
hold out his hand, and the cattleman laid out six copper pennies
in it, one by one. "Now then! That's fair and square!" he said, ex-
pansive. "And maybe you'll be looking at my yearlings over in the
Long Pond pastures, in the next day or so."

"No," Irioth said. "San's herd was going down fast when I left.
I'm needed there."

"Oh, no, you're not, Master Otak. While you were out in the
east range a sorcerer curer came by, a fellow that's been here before, from the south coast, and so San hired him. You work for me
and you'll be paid well. Better than copper, maybe, if the beasts
fare well!"

Irioth did not say yes, or no, or thanks, but went off unspeaking. The cattleman looked after him and spat. "Avert," he said.

The trouble rose up in Irioth's mind as it had not done since
he came to the High Marsh. He struggled against it. A man of
power had come to heal the cattle, another man of power. But a
sorcerer, Alder had said. Not a wizard, not a mage. Only a curer,
a cattle healer. I do not need to fear him. I do not need to fear his
power. I do not need his power. I must see him, to be sure, to be
certain. If he does what I do here there is no harm. We can work
together. If I do what he does here. If he uses only sorcery and
means no harm. As I do.

He walked down the straggling street of Purewells to San's
house, which was about midway, opposite the tavern. San, a hard-
bitten man in his thirties, was talking to a man on his doorstep, a
stranger. When they saw Irioth they looked uneasy. San went
into his house and the stranger followed.

Irioth came up onto the doorstep. He did not go in, but spoke in the open door. "Master San, it's about the cattle you have there between the rivers. I can go to them today." He did not know why he said this. It was not what he had meant to say.

"Ah," San said, coming to the door, and hemmed a bit. "No need, Master Otak. This here is Master Sunbright, come up to deal with the murrain. He's cured beasts for me before, the hoof rot and all. Being as how you have all one man can do with Alder's beeves, you see . . ."

The sorcerer came out from behind San. His name was Ayeth. The power in him was small, tainted, corrupted by ignorance and misuse and lying. But the jealousy in him was like a stinging fire. "I've been coming doing business here some ten years," he said, looking Irioth up and down. "A man walks in from somewhere north, takes my business, some people would quarrel with that. A quarrel of sorcerers is a bad thing. If you're a sorcerer, a man of power, that is. I am. As the good people here well know."

Irioth tried to say he did not want a quarrel. He tried to say that there was work for two. He tried to say he would not take the man's work from him. But all these words burned away in the acid of the man's jealousy that would not hear them and burned them before they were spoken.

Ayeth's stare grew more insolent as he watched Irioth stammer. He began to say something to San, but Irioth spoke.

"You have—" he said—"you have to go. Back." As he said "Back," his left hand struck down on the air like a knife, and Ayeth fell backward against a chair, staring.

He was only a little sorcerer, a cheating healer with a few sorry spells. Or so he seemed. What if he was cheating, hiding his power, a rival hiding his power? A jealous rival. He must be stopped, he must be bound, named, called. Irioth began to say the words that would bind him, and the shaken man cowered away, shrinking down, shriveling, crying out in a thin, high wail. It is wrong, wrong, I am doing the wrong, I am the ill, Irioth thought. He stopped the spell words in his mouth, fighting against them, and at last crying out one other word. Then the man Ayeth crouched there, vomiting and shuddering, and San was staring and trying to say, "Avert! Avert!" And no harm was done. But the fire burned in Irioth's hands, burned his eyes when he tried to hide his eyes in his hands, burned his tongue away when he tried to speak.

For a long time nobody would touch him. He had fallen down in a fit in San's doorway. He lay there now like a dead man. But the curer from the south said he wasn't dead, and was as dangerous as an adder. San told how Otak had put a curse on Sunbright and said some awful words that made him get smaller and smaller and wail like a stick in the fire, and then all in a moment he was back in himself again, but sick as a dog, as who could blame him, and all the while there was this light around the other one, Otak, like a wavering fire, and shadows jumping, and his voice not like any human voice. A terrible thing.

Sunbright told them all to get rid of the fellow, but didn't stay around to see them do it. He went back down the south road as soon as he'd gulped a pint of beer at the tavern, telling them there was no room for two sorcerers in one village and he'd be back, maybe, when that man, or whatever he was, had gone.

Nobody would touch him. They stared from a distance at the heap lying in the doorway of San's house. San's wife wept aloud up and down the street. "Bad cess! Bad cess!" she cried. "Oh, my babe will be born dead, I know it!"

Berry went and fetched his sister, after he had heard Sunbright's tale at the tavern, and San's version of it, and several other versions already current. In the best of them, Otak had towered up ten feet tall and struck Sunbright into a lump of coal with lightning, before foaming at the mouth, turning blue, and collapsing in a heap.

Gift hurried to the village. She went straight up to the doorstep, bent over the heap, and laid her hand on it. Everybody gasped and muttered, "Avert! Avert!" except Tawny's youngest daughter, who mistook the signs and piped up, "Speed the work!"

The heap moved, and roused up slowly. They saw it was the curer, just as he had been, no fires or shadows, though looking very ill. "Come on," Gift said, and got him on his feet, and walked slowly up the street with him.

The villagers shook their heads. Gift was a brave woman, but there was such a thing as being too brave. Or brave, they said around the tavern table, in the wrong way, or the wrong place, d'you see. Nobody should ought to meddle with sorcery that ain't born to it. Nor with sorcerers. You forget that. They seem the same as other folk. But they ain't like other folk. Seems there's no harm in a curer. Heal the foot rot, clear a caked udder. That's all fine. But cross one and there you are, fire and shadows and curses and falling down in fits. Uncanny. Always was uncanny, that one. Where'd he come from, anyhow? Answer me that.

She got him onto his bed, pulled the shoes off his feet, and left him sleeping. Berry came in late and drunker than usual, so that he fell and gashed his forehead on the andiron. Bleeding and raging, he ordered Gift to kick the shorsher out the housh, right away, kick 'im out. Then he vomited into the ashes and fell asleep on the hearth. She hauled him onto his pallet, pulled his shoes off his feet, and left him sleeping. She went to look at the other one. He looked feverish, and she put her hand on his forehead. He opened his eyes, looking straight into hers without expression. "Emer," he said, and closed his eyes again.

She backed away from him, terrified.

In her bed, in the dark, she lay and thought: He knew the wizard who named me. Or I said my name. Maybe I said it out loud in my sleep. Or somebody told him. But nobody knows it. Nobody ever knew my name but the wizard, and my mother. And they're dead, they're dead . . . I said it in my sleep . . .

But she knew better.

She stood with the little oil lamp in her hand, and the light of it shone red between her fingers and golden on her face. He said her name. She gave him sleep.

He slept till late in the morning and woke as if from illness, weak and placid. She was unable to be afraid of him. She found that he had no memory at all of what had happened in the village, of the other sorcerer, even of the six coppers she had found scattered on the bedcover, which he must have held clenched in his hand all along.

"No doubt that's what Alder gave you," she said. "The flint!"

"I said I'd see to his beasts at . . . at the pasture between the rivers, was it?" he said, getting anxious, the hunted look coming back into him, and he got up from the settle.

"Sit down," she said. He sat down, but he sat fretting.

"How can you cure when you're sick?" she said.

"How else?" he said.

But he quieted down again presently, stroking the grey cat.

Her brother came in. "Come on out," he said to her as soon as he saw the curer dozing on the settle. She stepped outside with him.

"Now I won't have him here no more," Berry said, coming master of the house over her, with the great black gash in his fore-head, and his eyes like oysters, and his hands juddering.

"Where'll you go?" she said.

"It's him has to go."

"It's my house. Bren's house. He stays. Go or stay, it's up to you."

"It's up to me too if he stays or goes, and he goes. You haven't got all the sayso. All the people say he ought to go. He's not canny."

"Oh, yes, since he's cured half the herds and got paid six coppers for it, time for him to go, right enough! I'll have him here as long as I choose, and that's the end of it."

"They won't buy our milk and cheese," Berry whined.

"Who says that?"

"San's wife. All the women."

"Then I'll carry the cheeses to Oraby," she said, "and sell 'em there. In the name of honor, brother, go wash out that cut, and change your shirt. You stink of the pothouse." And she went back into the house. "Oh, dear," she said, and burst into tears.

"What's the matter, Emer?" said the curer, turning his thin face and strange eyes to her.

"Oh, it's no good, I know it's no good. Nothing's any good with a drunkard," she said. She wiped her eyes with her apron. "Was that what broke you," she said, "the drink?"

"No," he said, taking no offense, perhaps not understanding.

"Of course it wasn't. I beg your pardon," she said.

"Maybe he drinks to try to be another man," he said. "To alter, to change . . ."

"He drinks because he drinks," she said. "With some, that's all it is. I'll be in the dairy, now. I'll lock the house door. There's . . . there's been strangers about. You rest yourself. It's bitter out." She wanted to be sure that he stayed indoors out of harm's way, and that nobody came harassing him. Later on she would go into the village, have a word with some of the sensible people, and put a stop to this rubbishy talk, if she could.

When she did so, Alder's wife Tawny and several other people agreed with her that a squabble between sorcerers over work was nothing new and nothing to take on about. But San and his wife and the tavern crew wouldn't let it rest, it being the only thing of interest to talk about for the rest of the winter, except the cattle dying. "Besides," Tawny said, "my man's never averse to paying copper where he thought he might have to pay ivory."

"Are the cattle he touched keeping afoot, then?"

"So far as we can see, they are. And no new sickenings."

"He's a true sorcerer, Tawny," Gift said, very earnest. "I know it."

"That's the trouble, love," said Tawny. "And you know it! This is no place for a man like that. Whoever he is is none of our business, but why did he come here, is what you have to ask."

"To cure the beasts," Gift said.

Sunbright had not been gone three days when a new stranger appeared in town: a man riding up the south road on a good horse and asking at the tavern for lodging. They sent him to San's house, but San's wife screeched when she heard there was a stranger at the door, crying that if San let another witch-man in the door her baby would be born dead twice over. Her screaming could be heard for several houses up and down the street, and a crowd, that is, ten or eleven people, gathered between San's house and the tavern.

"Well, that won't do," said the stranger pleasantly. "I can't be bringing on a birth untimely. Is there maybe a room above the tavern?"

"Send him on out to the dairy," said one of Alder's cowboys. "Gift's taking whatever comes." There was some sniggering and shushing.

"Back that way," said the taverner.

"Thanks," said the traveler, and led his horse along the way they pointed.

"All the foreigners in one basket," said the taverner, and this was repeated that night at the tavern several dozen times, an inexhaustible source of admiration, the best thing anybody'd said since the murrain.

Gift was in the dairy, having finished the evening milking. She was straining the milk and setting out the pans. "Mistress," said a voice at the door, and she thought it was the curer and said, "Just a minute while I finish this," and then turning saw a stranger and nearly dropped the pan. "Oh, you startled me!" she said. "What can I do for you, then?"

"I'm looking for a bed for the night."

"No, I'm sorry, there's my lodger, and my brother, and me. Maybe San, in the village—"

"They sent me here. They said, 'All the foreigners in one basket.'" The stranger was in his thirties, with a blunt face and a pleasant look, dressed plain, though the cob that stood behind him was a good horse. "Put me up in the cow barn, mistress, it'll do fine. It's my horse needs a good bed; he's tired. I'll sleep in the barn and be off in the morning. Cows are a pleasure to sleep with on a cold night. I'll be glad to pay you, mistress, if two coppers would suit, and my name's Hawk."

"I'm Gift," she said, a bit flustered, but liking the fellow. "All right, then, Master Hawk. Put your horse up and see to him. There's the pump, there's plenty of hay. Come on in the house after. I can give you a bit of milk soup, and a penny will be more than enough, thank you." She didn't feel like calling him sir, as she always did the curer. This one had nothing of that lordly way about him. She hadn't seen a king when she first saw him, as with the other one.

When she finished in the dairy and went to the house, the new fellow, Hawk, was squatting on the hearth, skillfully making up the fire. The curer was in his room asleep. She looked in, and closed the door.

"He's not too well," she said, speaking low. "He was curing the cattle away out east over the marsh, in the cold, for days on end, and wore himself out."

As she went about her work in the kitchen, Hawk lent her a hand now and then in the most natural way, so that she began to wonder if men from foreign parts were all so much handier about the house than the men of the Marsh. He was easy to talk with, and she told him about the curer, since there was nothing much to say about herself.

"They'll use a sorcerer and then ill-mouth him for his usefulness," she said. "It's not just."

"But he scared 'em, somehow, did he?"

"I guess he did. Another curer came up this way, a fellow that's been by here before. Doesn't amount to much that I can see. He did no good to my cow with the caked bag, two years ago. And his balm's just pig fat, I'd swear. Well, so, he says to Otak, you're taking my business. And maybe Otak says the same back. And they lose their tempers, and they did some black spells, maybe. I guess Otak did. But he did no harm to the man at all, but fell down in a swoon himself. And now he doesn't remember any more about it, while the other man walked away unhurt. And they say every beast he touched is standing yet, and hale. Ten days he spent out there in the wind and the rain, touching the beasts and healing them. And you know what the cattleman gave him? Six pennies! Can you wonder he was a little rageous? But I don't say . . ." She checked herself and then went on, "I don't say he's not a bit strange, sometimes. The way witches and sorcerers are, I guess. Maybe they have to be, dealing with such powers and evils as they do. But he is a true man, and kind."

"Mistress," said Hawk, "may I tell you a story?"

"Oh, are you a teller? Oh, why didn't you say so to begin with! Is that what you are then? I wondered, it being winter and all, and you being on the roads. But with that horse, I thought you must be a merchant. Can you tell me a story? It would be the joy of my life, and the longer the better! But drink your soup first, and let me sit down to hear..."

"I'm not truly a teller, mistress," he said with his pleasant smile, "but I do have a story for you." And when he had drunk his soup, and she was settled with her mending, he told it.

"In the Inmost Sea, on the Isle of the Wise, on Roke Island, where all magery is taught, there are nine Masters," he began.

She closed her eyes in bliss and listened.

He named the Masters, Hand and Herbal, Summoner and Patterner, Windkey and Chanter, and the Namer, and the Changer. "The Changer's and the Summoner's are very perilous arts," he said. "Changing, or transformation, you maybe know of, mistress. Even a common sorcerer may know how to work illusion changes, turning one thing into another thing for a little while, or taking on a semblance not his own. Have you seen that?"

"Heard of it," she whispered.

"And sometimes witches and sorcerers will say that they've summoned the dead to speak through them. Maybe a child the parents are grieving for. In the witch's hut, in the darkness, they hear it cry, or laugh..."

She nodded.

"Those are spells of illusion only, of seeming. But there are true changes, and true summonings. And these may be true temptations to the wizard! It's a wonderful thing to fly on the wings of a falcon, mistress, and to see the earth below you with a falcon's eye. And summoning, which is naming truly, is a great power. To know the true name is to have power, as you know, mistress. And the summoner's art goes straight to that. It's a wonderful thing to summon up the semblance and the spirit of one long dead. To see the beauty of Elfarran in the orchards of Soléa, as Morred saw it when the world was young..."

His voice had become very soft, very dark.

"Well, to my story. Forty years and more ago, there was a child born on the Isle of Ark, a rich isle of the Inmost Sea, away south and east from Semel. This child was the son of an understeward in the household of the Lord of Ark. Not a poor man's son, but not a child of much account. And the parents died young. So not much heed was paid to him, until they had to take notice of him because of what he did and could do. He was an uncanny brat, as they say. He had powers. He could light a fire or douse it with a word. He could make pots and pans fly through the air. He could turn a mouse into a pigeon and set it flying round the great kitchens of the Lord of Ark. And if he was crossed, or frightened, then he did harm. He turned a kettle of boiling water over a cook who had mistreated him."

"Mercy," whispered Gift. She had not sewn a stitch since he began.

"He was only a child, and the wizards of that household can't have been wise men, for they used little wisdom or gentleness with him. Maybe they were afraid of him. They bound his hands and gagged his mouth to keep him from making spells. They locked him in a cellar room, a room of stone, until they thought him tamed. Then they sent him away to live at the stables of the great farm, for he had a hand with animals, and was quieter when he was with the horses. But he quarreled with a stable boy, and turned the poor lad into a lump of dung. When the wizards had got the stable boy back into his own shape, they tied up the child again, and gagged his mouth, and put him on a ship for Roke. They thought maybe the Masters there could tame him."

"Poor child," she murmured.

"Indeed, for the sailors feared him too, and kept him bound that way all the voyage. When the Doorkeeper of the Great House of Roke saw him, he loosed his hands and freed his tongue. And the first thing the boy did in the Great House, they say, he turned the Long Table of the dining hall upside down, and soured the beer, and a student who tried to stop him got turned into a pig for a bit... But the boy had met his match in the Masters.

"They didn't punish him, but kept his wild powers bound with spells until they could make him listen and begin to learn. It took them a long time. There was a rivalrous spirit in him that made him look on any power he did not have, any thing he did not know, as a threat, a challenge, a thing to fight against until he could defeat it. There are many boys like that. I was one. But I was lucky. I learned my lesson young.

"Well, this boy did learn at last to tame his anger and control his power. And a very great power it was. Whatever art he studied came easy to him, too easy, so that he despised illusion, and weatherworking, and even healing, because they held no fear, no challenge to him. He saw no virtue in himself for his mastery of them. So, after the Archmage Nemmerle had given him his name, the boy set his will on the great and dangerous art of summoning. And he studied with the Master of that art for a long time.

"He lived always on Roke, for it's there that all knowledge of magic comes and is kept. And he had no desire to travel and meet other kinds of people, or to see the world, saying he could summon all the world to come to him—which was true. Maybe that's where the danger of that art lies.

"Now, what is forbidden to the summoner, or any wizard, is to call a living spirit. We can call to them, yes. We can send to them a voice or a presentment, a seeming, of ourself. But we do not summon them, in spirit or in flesh, to come to us. Only the dead may we summon. Only the shadows. You can see why this must be. To summon a living man is to have entire power over him, body and mind. No one, no matter how strong or wise or great, can rightly own and use another.

"But the spirit of rivalry worked in the boy as he grew to be a man. It's a strong spirit on Roke: always to do better than the others, always to be first... The art becomes a contest, a game. The end becomes a means to an end less than itself... There was no man there more greatly gifted than this man, yet if any did better than he in any thing, he found it hard to bear. It frightened him, it galled him.

"There was no place for him among the Masters, since a new Master Summoner had been chosen, a strong man in his prime, not likely to retire or die. Among the scholars and other teachers he had a place of honor, but he wasn't one of the Nine. He'd been passed over. Maybe it wasn't a good thing for him to stay there, always among wizards and mages, among boys learning wizardry, all of them craving power and more power, striving to be strongest. At any rate, as the years went on he became more and more aloof, pursuing his studies in his tower cell apart from others, teaching few students, speaking little. The Summoner would send gifted students to him, but many of the boys there scarcely knew of him. In this isolation he began to practice certain arts that are not well to practice and lead to no good thing.

"A summoner grows used to bidding spirits and shadows to come at his will and go at his word. Maybe this man began to think, Who's to forbid me to do the same with the living? Why have I the power if I cannot use it? So he began to call the living to him, those at Roke whom he feared, thinking them rivals, those whose power he was jealous of. When they came to him he took their power from them for himself, leaving them silent. They couldn't say what had happened to them, what had become of their power. They didn't know.

"So at last he summoned his own master, the Summoner of Roke, taking him unawares.

"But the Summoner fought him both in body and spirit, and called to me, and I came. Together we fought against the will that would destroy us."

Night had come. Gift's lamp had flickered out. Only the red glow of the fire shone on Hawk's face. It was not the face she had thought it. It was worn, and hard, and scarred all down one side. The hawk's face, she thought. She held still, listening.

"This is not a teller's tale, mistress. This is not a story you will ever hear anyone else tell.

"I was new at the business of being Archmage then. And younger than the man we fought, and maybe not afraid enough of him. It was all the two of us could do to hold our own against him, there in the silence, in the cell in the tower. Nobody else knew what was going on. We fought. A long time we fought. And then it was over. He broke. Like a stick breaking. He was broken. But he fled away. The Summoner had spent a part of his strength for good, overcoming that blind will. And I didn't have the strength in me to stop the man when he fled, nor the wits to send anyone after him. And not a shred of power left in me to follow him with. So he got away from Roke. Clean gone.

"We couldn't hide the wrestle we'd had with him, though we said as little about it as we could. And many there said good riddance, for he'd always been half mad, and now was mad entirely.

"But after the Summoner and I got over the bruises on our souls, as you might say, and the great stupidity of mind that follows such a struggle, we began to think that it wasn't a good thing to have a man of very great power, a mage, wandering about

Earthsea not in his right mind, and maybe full of shame and rage and vengefulness.

"We could find no trace of him. No doubt he changed himself to a bird or a fish when he left Roke, until he came to some other island. And a wizard can hide himself from all finding spells. We sent out inquiries, in the ways we have of doing so, but nothing and nobody replied. So we set off looking for him, the Summoner to the eastern isles and I to the west. For when I thought about this man, I had begun to see in my mind's eye a great mountain, a broken cone, with a long, green land beneath it reaching to the south. I remembered my geography lessons when I was a boy at Roke, and the lay of the land on Semel, and the mountain whose name is Andanden. So I came to the High Marsh. I think I came the right way."

There was a silence. The fire whispered.

"Should I speak to him?" Gift asked in a steady voice.

"No need," said the man like a falcon. "I will." And he said, "Irioth."

She looked at the door of the bedroom. It opened and he stood there, thin and tired, his dark eyes full of sleep and bewilderment and pain.

"Ged," he said. He bowed his head. After a while he looked up and asked, "Will you take my name from me?"

"Why should I do that?"

"It means only hurt. Hate, pride, greed."

"I'll take those names from you, Irioth, but not your own."

"I didn't understand," Irioth said, "about the others. That they are other. We are all other. We must be. I was wrong."

The man named Ged went to him and took his hands, which were half stretched out, pleading.

"You went wrong. You've come back. But you're tired, Irioth, and the way's hard when you go alone. Come home with me."

Irioth's head drooped as if in utter weariness. All tension and passion had gone out of his body. But he looked up, not at Ged but at Gift, silent in the hearth corner.

"I have work here," he said.

Ged too looked at her.

"He does," she said. "He heals the cattle."

"They show me what I should do," Irioth said, "and who I am. They know my name. But they never say it."

After a while Ged gently drew the older man to him and held him in his arms. He said something quietly to him and let him go. Irioth drew a deep breath.

"I'm no good there, you see, Ged," he said. "I am, here. If they'll let me do the work." He looked again at Gift, and Ged did also. She looked at them both.

"What say you, Emer?" asked the one like a falcon.

"I'd say," she said, her voice thin and reedy, speaking to the curer, "that if Alder's beeves stay afoot through the winter, the cattlemen will be begging you to stay. Though they may not love you."

"Nobody loves a sorcerer," said the Archmage. "Well, Irioth! Did I come all this way for you in the dead of winter, and must go back alone?"

"Tell them—tell them I was wrong," Irioth said. "Tell them I did wrong. Tell Thorion—" He halted, confused.

"I'll tell him that the changes in a man's life may be beyond all the arts we know, and all our wisdom," said the Archmage. He looked at Emer again. "May he stay here, mistress? Is that your wish as well as his?"

"He's ten times the use and company to me my brother is," she said. "And a kind true man, as I told you. Sir."

"Very well, then. Irioth, my dear companion, teacher, rival, friend, farewell. Emer, brave woman, my honor and thanks to you. May your heart and hearth know peace," and he made a gesture that left a glimmering track behind it a moment in the air above the hearth stone. "Now I'm off to the cow barn," he said, and he was.

The door closed. It was silent except for the whisper of the fire.

"Come to the fire," she said. Irioth came and sat down on the settle.

"Was that the Archmage? Truly?"

He nodded.

"The Archmage of the world," she said. "In my cow barn. He should have my bed—"

"He won't," said Irioth.

She knew he was right.

"Your name is beautiful, Irioth," she said after a while. "I never knew my husband's true name. Nor he mine. I won't speak yours again. But I like to know it, since you know mine."

"Your name is beautiful, Emer," he said. "I will speak it when you tell me to."

Dragonfly

I. Iria

HER FATHER'S ANCESTORS had owned a wide, rich domain on the wide, rich island of Way. Claiming no title or court privilege in the days of the kings, through all the dark years after Maharion fell they held their land and people with firm hands, putting their gains back into the land, upholding some sort of justice, and fighting off petty tyrants. As order and peace returned to the Archipelago under the sway of the wise men of Roke, for a while yet the family and their farms and villages prospered. That prosperity and the beauty of the meadows and upland pastures and oak-crowned hills made the domain a byword, so that people said "as fat as a cow of Iria," or "as lucky as an Irian." The masters and many tenants of the domain added its name to their own, calling themselves Irian. But though the farmers and shepherds went on from season to season and year to year and generation to generation as steady and regenerative as the oaks, the family that owned the land altered and declined with time and chance.

A quarrel between brothers over their inheritance divided them. One heir mismanaged his estate through greed, the other through foolishness. One had a daughter who married a merchant and tried to run her estate from the city, the other had a son whose sons quarreled again, redividing the divided land. By the time the girl called Dragonfly was born, the domain of Iria, though still one of the loveliest regions of hill and field and meadow in all Earthsea, was a battleground of feuds and litigations. Farmlands went to weeds, farmsteads went unroofed, milking sheds stood unused, and shepherds followed their flocks over the mountain to better pastures. The old house that had been the center of the domain was half in ruins on its hill among the oaks.

Its owner was one of four men who called themselves Master of Iria. The other three called him Master of Old Iria. He spent his youth and what remained of his inheritance in law courts and the anterooms of the Lords of Way in Shelieth, trying to prove his right to the whole domain as it had been a hundred years ago. He came back unsuccessful and embittered and spent his age drinking the hard red wine from his last vineyard and walking his boundaries with a troop of ill-treated, underfed dogs to keep interlopers off his land.

He had married while he was in Shelieth, a woman no one at Iria knew anything about, for she came from some other island, it was said, somewhere in the west; and she never came to Iria, for she died in childbirth there in the city.

When he came home he had a three-year-old daughter with him. He turned her over to the housekeeper and forgot about her. When he was drunk sometimes he remembered her. If he could find her, he made her stand by his chair or sit on his knees and listen to all the wrongs that had been done to him and to the house of Iria. He cursed and cried and drank and made her drink too, pledging to honor her inheritance and be true to Iria. She swallowed the mouthful of wine, but she hated the curses and pledges and tears, and the slobbered caresses that followed them.

She would escape, as soon as she could, if she could, and go down to the dogs and horses and cattle. She swore to them that she would be loyal to her mother, whom nobody knew or honored or was true to, except herself.

When she was thirteen the old vineyarder and the house-keeper, who were all that was left of the household, told the Master that it was time his daughter had her naming day. They asked if they should send for the sorcerer over at Westpool, or would their own village witch do. The Master of Iria fell into a screaming rage. "A village witch? A hex-hag to give Irian's daughter her true name? Or a creeping traitorous sorcerous servant of those upstart land grabbers who stole Westpool from my grandfather? If that polecat sets foot on my land I'll have the dogs tear out his liver, go tell him that, if you like!" And so on. Old Daisy went back to her kitchen and old Coney went back to his vines, and thirteen-year-old Dragonfly ran out of the house and down the hill to the village, hurling her father's curses at the dogs, who, crazy with excitement at his shouting, barked and bayed and rushed after her.

"Get back, you black-hearted bitch!" she yelled. "Home, you crawling traitor!" And the dogs fell silent and went sidling back to the house with their tails down.

Dragonfly found the village witch taking maggots out of an infected cut on a sheep's rump. The witch's use-name was Rose, like a great many women of Way and other islands of the Hardic Archipelago. People who have a secret name that holds their power the way a diamond holds light may well like their public name to be ordinary, common, like other people's names.

Rose was muttering a rote spell, but it was her hands and her little short sharp knife that did most of the work. The ewe bore the digging knife patiently, her opaque, amber, slotted eyes gazing into silence; only she stamped her small left front foot now and then, and sighed.

Dragonfly peered close at Rose's work. Rose brought out a maggot, dropped it, spat on it, and probed again. The girl leaned up against the ewe, and the ewe leaned against the girl, giving and receiving comfort. Rose extracted, dropped, and spat on the last maggot, and said, "Just hand me that bucket now." She bathed the sore with salt water. The ewe sighed deeply and suddenly walked out of the yard, heading for home. She had had enough of medicine. "Bucky!" Rose shouted. A grubby child appeared from under a bush where he had been asleep and trailed after the ewe, of whom he was nominally in charge although she was older, larger, better fed, and probably wiser than he was.

"They said you should give me my name," said Dragonfly. "Father fell to raging. So that's that."

The witch said nothing. She knew the girl was right. Once the Master of Iria said he would or would not allow a thing, he never changed his mind, priding himself on his intransigence, since in his view only weak men said a thing and then unsaid it.

"Why can't I give myself my own true name?" Dragonfly asked, while Rose washed the knife and her hands in the salt water.

"Can't be done."

"Why not? Why does it have to be a witch or a sorcerer? What do you *do*?"

"Well," Rose said, and dumped out the salt water on the bare dirt of the small front yard of her house, which, like most witches' houses, stood somewhat apart from the village. "Well," she said, straightening up and looking about vaguely as if for an answer, or a ewe, or a towel. "You have to know something about the power, see," she said at last, and looked at Dragonfly with one eye. Her other eye looked a little off to the side. Sometimes Dragonfly thought the cast was in Rose's left eye, sometimes it seemed to be in her right, but always one eye looked straight and the other watched something just out of sight, around the corner, elsewhere.

"Which power?"

"The one," Rose said. As suddenly as the ewe had walked off, she went into her house. Dragonfly followed her, but only to the door. Nobody entered a witch's house uninvited.

"You said I had it," the girl said into the reeking gloom of the one-roomed hut.

"I said you have a strength in you, a great one," the witch said from the darkness. "And you know it too. What you are to do I don't know, nor do you. That's to find. But there's no such power as to name yourself."

"Why not? What's more yourself than your own true name?"

A long silence.

The witch emerged with a soapstone drop spindle and a ball of greasy wool. She sat down on the bench beside her door and set the spindle turning. She had spun a yard of grey-brown yarn before she answered.

"My name's myself. True. But what's a name, then? It's what another calls me. If there was no other, only me, what would I want a name for?"

"But," said Dragonfly and stopped, caught by the argument. After a while she said, "So a name has to be a gift?"

Rose nodded.

"Give me my name, Rose," the girl said.

"Your dad says not."

"I say to."

"He's the master here."

"He can keep me poor and stupid and worthless, but he can't keep me nameless!"

The witch sighed, like the ewe, uneasy and constrained.

"Tonight," Dragonfly said. "At our spring, under Iria Hill. What he doesn't know won't hurt him." Her voice was half coaxing, half savage.

"You ought to have your proper nameday, your feast and dancing, like any young 'un," the witch said. "It's at daybreak a name should be given. And then there ought to be music and feasting and all. A party. Not sneaking about at night and no one knowing..."

"I'll know. How do you know what name to say, Rose? Does the water tell you?"

The witch shook her iron-grey head once. "I can't tell you." Her "can't" did not mean "won't." Dragonfly waited. "It's the power, like I said. It comes just so." Rose stopped her spinning and looked up with one eye at a cloud in the west; the other looked a little northward of the sky. "You're there in the water, together, you and the child. You take away the child-name. People may go on using that name for a use-name, but it's not her name, nor ever was. So now she's not a child, and she has no name. So then you wait. In the water there. You open your mind up, like. Like opening the doors of a house to the wind. So it comes. Your tongue speaks it, the name. Your breath makes it. You give it to that child, the breath, the name. You can't think of it. You let it come to you. It must come through you and the water to her it belongs to. That's the power, the way it works. It's all like that. It's not a thing you do. You have to know how to let it do. That's all the mastery."

"Mages can do more than that," the girl said after a while.

"Nobody can do more than that," said Rose.

Dragonfly rolled her head round on her neck, stretching till the vertebrae cracked, restlessly stretching out her long arms and legs. "Will you?" she said.

After some time, Rose nodded once.

They met in the lane under Iria Hill in the dark of night, long after sunset, long before dawn. Rose made a dim glow of were-light so that they could find their way through the marshy ground around the spring without falling in a sinkhole among the reeds. In the cold darkness under a few stars and the black curve of the hill, they stripped and waded into the shallow water, their feet sinking deep in velvet mud. The witch touched the girl's hand, saying, "I take your name, child. You are no child. You have no name."

It was utterly still.

In a whisper the witch said, "Woman, be named. You are Irian."

For a moment longer they held still; then the night wind blew across their naked shoulders, and shivering, they waded out, dried themselves as well as they could, struggled barefoot and wretched through the sharp-edged reeds and tangling roots, and found their way back to the lane. And there Dragonfly spoke in a ragged, raging whisper: "How could you name me that!"

The witch said nothing.

"It isn't right. It isn't my true name! I thought my name would make me be me. But this makes it worse. You got it wrong. You're only a witch. You did it wrong. It's *his* name. He can have it. He's so proud of it, his stupid domain, his stupid grandfather. I don't want it. I won't have it. It isn't me. I still don't know who I am. I'm not Irian!" She fell silent abruptly, having spoken the name.

The witch still said nothing. They walked along in the darkness side by side. At last, in a placating, frightened voice, Rose said, "It came so . . ."

"If you ever tell it to anyone I'll kill you," Dragonfly said.

At that, the witch stopped walking. She hissed in her throat like a cat. "*Tell* anyone?"

Dragonfly stopped too. She said after a moment, "I'm sorry. But I feel like—I feel like you betrayed me."

"I spoke your true name. It's not what I thought it would be. And I don't feel easy about it. As if I'd left something unfinished. But it is your name. If it betrays you, then that's the truth of it." Rose hesitated and then spoke less angrily, more coldly: "If you want the power to betray me, Irian, I'll give you that. My name is Etaudis."

The wind had come up again. They were both shivering, their teeth chattering. They stood face to face in the black lane, hardly able to see where the other was. Dragonfly put out her groping hand and met the witch's hand. They put their arms round each other in a fierce, long embrace. Then they hurried on, the witch to her hut near the village, the heiress of Iria up the hill to her ruinous house, where all the dogs, who had let her go without much fuss, received her back with a clamor and racket of barking that woke everybody for a half mile round except the master, sodden drunk by his cold hearth.

II. Ivory

THE MASTER OF IRIA of Westpool, Birch, didn't own the old house, but he did own the central and richest lands of the old domain. His father, more interested in vines and orchards than in quarrels with his relatives, had left Birch a thriving property. Birch hired men to manage the farms and wineries and cooperage and cartage and all, while he enjoyed his wealth. He married the timid daughter of the younger brother of the Lord of Wayfirth, and took infinite pleasure in thinking that his daughters were of noble blood.

The fashion of the time among the nobility was to have a wizard in their service, a genuine wizard with a staff and a grey cloak, trained on the Isle of the Wise; and so the Master of Iria of Westpool got himself a wizard from Roke. He was surprised how easy it was to get one, if you paid the price.

The young man, called Ivory, did not actually have his staff and cloak yet; he explained that he was to be made wizard when he went back to Roke. The Masters had sent him out in the world to gain experience, for all the classes in the school cannot give a man the experience he needs to be a wizard. Birch looked a little dubious at this, and Ivory reassured him that his training on Roke had equipped him with every kind of magic that could be needed in Iria of Westpool on Way. To prove it, he made it seem that a herd of deer ran through the dining hall, followed by a flight of swans, who marvelously soared in through the south wall and out through the north wall; and lastly a fountain in a silver basin sprang up in the center of the table, and when the master and his family cautiously imitated their wizard and filled their cups from it and tasted it, it was a sweet golden wine. "Wine of the Andrades," said the young man with a modest, complacent smile. By then the wife and daughters were entirely won over. And Birch thought the young man was worth his fee, although his own silent preference was for the dry red Fanian of his own vineyards, which got you drunk if you drank enough, while this yellow stuff was just honeywater.

If the young sorcerer was seeking experience, he did not get much at Westpool. Whenever Birch had guests from Kembermouth or from neighboring domains, the herd of deer, the swans, and the fountain of golden wine made their appearance. He also worked up some very pretty fireworks for warm spring evenings. But if the managers of the orchards and vineyards came to the master to ask if his wizard might put a spell of increase on the pears this year or maybe charm the black rot off the Fanian vines on the south hill, Birch said, "A wizard of Roke doesn't lower himself to such stuff. Go tell the village sorcerer to earn his keep!" And when the youngest daughter came down with a wasting cough, Birch's wife dared not trouble the wise young man about it, but sent humbly to Rose of Old Iria, asking her to come in by the back door and maybe make a poultice or sing a chant to bring the girl back to health.

Ivory never noticed that the girl was ailing, nor the pear trees, nor the vines. He kept himself to himself, as a man of craft and learning should. He spent his days riding about the countryside on the pretty black mare that his employer had given him for his use when he made it clear that he had not come from Roke to trudge about on foot in the mud and dust of country byways.

On his rides he sometimes passed an old house on a hill among great oaks. Once he turned off the village lane up the hill, but a pack of scrawny, evil-mouthed dogs came pelting and bellowing down at him. The mare was afraid of dogs and liable to buck and bolt, so after that he kept his distance. But he had an eye for beauty, and liked to look at the old house dreaming away in the dappled light of the early summer afternoons.

He asked Birch about the place. "That's Iria," Birch said— "Old Iria, I mean to say. I own that house by rights. But after a century of feuds and fights over it, my granddad let the place go to settle the quarrel. Though the master there would still be quarreling with me if he didn't keep too drunk to talk. Haven't seen the old man for years. He had a daughter, I think."

"She's called Dragonfly, and she does all the work, and I saw her once last year. She's tall, and as beautiful as a flowering tree," said the youngest daughter, Rose, who was busy crowding a lifetime of keen observation into the fourteen years that were all she was going to have for it. She broke off, coughing. Her mother shot an anguished, yearning glance at the wizard. Surely he would hear that cough, this time? He smiled at young Rose, and the mother's heart lifted. Surely he wouldn't smile so if Rose's cough was anything serious?

"Nothing to do with us, that lot at the old place," Birch said, displeased. The tactful Ivory asked no more. But he wanted to see the girl as beautiful as a flowering tree. He rode past Old Iria regularly. He tried stopping in the village at the foot of the hill to ask questions, but there was nowhere to stop and nobody would answer questions. A walleyed witch took one look at him and scuttled into her hut. If he went up to the house he would have to face the pack of hellhounds and probably a drunk old man. But it was worth the chance, he thought; he was bored out of his wits with the dull life at Westpool, and was never slow to take a risk. He rode up the hill till the dogs were yelling around him in a frenzy snapping at the mare's legs. She plunged and lashed out her hoofs at them, and he kept her from bolting only by a staying spell and all the strength in his arms. The dogs were leaping and snapping at his own legs now, and he was about to let the mare have her head when somebody came among the dogs shouting curses and beating them back with a strap. When he got the lathered, gasping mare to stand still, he saw the girl as beautiful as a flowering tree. She was very tall, very sweaty, with big hands and feet and mouth and nose and eyes, and a head of wild dusty hair. She was yelling, "Down! Back to the house, you carrion, you vile sons of bitches!" to the whining, cowering dogs.

Ivory clapped his hand to his right leg. A dog's tooth had ripped his breeches at the calf, and a trickle of blood came through.

"Is she hurt?" the woman said. "Oh, the traitorous vermin!" She was stroking down the mare's right foreleg. Her hands came away covered with blood-streaked horse sweat. "There, there," she said. "The brave girl, the brave heart." The mare put her head down and shivered all over with relief. "What did you keep her standing there in the middle of the dogs for?" the woman demanded furiously. She was kneeling at the horse's leg, looking up at Ivory. He was looking down at her from horseback, yet he felt short; he felt small.

She did not wait for an answer. "I'll walk her up," she said, standing, and put out her hand for the reins. Ivory saw that he was supposed to dismount. He did so, asking, "Is it very bad?" and peering at the horse's leg, seeing only bright, bloody foam.

"Come on then, my love," the young woman said, not to him. The mare followed her trustfully. They set off up the rough path round the hillside to an old stone and brick stableyard, empty of horses, inhabited only by nesting swallows that swooped about over the roofs calling their quick gossip.

"Keep her quiet," said the young woman, and left him holding the mare's reins in this deserted place. She returned after some time lugging a heavy bucket, and set to sponging off the mare's leg. "Get the saddle off her," she said, and her tone held the unspoken, impatient "you fool!" Ivory obeyed, half annoyed by this crude giantess and half intrigued. She did not put him in mind of a flowering tree at all, but she was in fact beautiful, in a large, fierce way. The mare submitted to her absolutely. When she said, "Move your foot!" the mare moved her foot. The woman wiped her down all over, put the saddle blanket back on her, and made sure she was standing in the sun. "She'll be all right," she said. "There's a gash, but if you'll wash it with warm salt water four or five times a day, it'll heal clean. I'm sorry." She said the last honestly, though grudgingly, as if she still wondered how he could have let his mare stand there to be assaulted, and she looked straight at him for the first time. Her eyes were clear orange-brown, like dark topaz or amber. They were strange eyes, right on a level with his own.

"I'm sorry too," he said, trying to speak carelessly, lightly.

"She's Irian of Westpool's mare. You're the wizard, then?"

He bowed. "Ivory, of Havnor Great Port, at your service. May I—"

She interrupted. "I thought you were from Roke."

"I am," he said, his composure regained.

She stared at him with those strange eyes, as unreadable as a sheep's, he thought. Then she burst out: "You lived there? You studied there? Do you know the Archmage?"

"Yes," he said with a smile. Then he winced and stooped to press his hand against his shin for a moment.

"Are you hurt too?"

"It's nothing," he said. In fact, rather to his annoyance, the cut had stopped bleeding.

The woman's gaze returned to his face.

"What is it—what is it like—on Roke?"

Ivory went, limping only very slightly, to an old mounting block nearby and sat down on it. He stretched his leg, nursing the torn place, and looked up at the woman. "It would take a long time to tell you what Roke is like," he said. "But it would be my pleasure."

"The man's a wizard, or nearly," said Rose the witch, "a Roke wizard! You must not ask him questions!" She was more than scandalized, she was frightened.

"He doesn't mind," Dragonfly reassured her. "Only he hardly ever really answers."

"Of course not!"

"Why of course not?"

"Because he's a wizard! Because you're a woman, with no art, no knowledge, no learning!"

"You could have taught me! You never would!"

Rose dismissed all she had taught or could teach with a flick of the fingers.

"Well, so I have to learn from him," said Dragonfly.

"Wizards don't teach women. You're besotted."

"You and Broom trade spells."

"Broom's a village sorcerer. This man is a wise man. He learned the High Arts at the Great House on Roke!"

"He told me what it's like," Dragonfly said. "You walk up through the town, Thwil Town. There's a door opening on the street, but it's shut. It looks like an ordinary door."

The witch listened, unable to resist the lure of secrets revealed and the contagion of passionate desire.

"And a man comes when you knock, an ordinary looking man. And he gives you a test. You have to say a certain word, a password, before he'll let you in. If you don't know it, you can never go in. But if he lets you in, then from inside you see that the door is entirely different—it's made out of horn, with a tree carved on it, and the frame is made out of a tooth, one tooth of a dragon that lived long, long before Erreth-Akbe, before Morred, before there were people in Earthsea. There were only dragons, to begin with. They found the tooth on Mount Onn, in Havnor, at the center of the world. And the leaves of the tree are carved so thin that the light shines through them, but the door's so strong that if the Doorkeeper shuts it no spell could ever open it. And then the Doorkeeper takes you down a hall and another hall, till you're lost and bewildered, and then suddenly you come out under the sky. In the Court of the Fountain, in the very deepest inside of the Great House. And that's where the Archmage would be, if he was there . . ."

"Go on," the witch murmured.

"That's all he really told me, yet," said Dragonfly, coming back to the mild, overcast spring day and the infinite familiarity of the village lane, Rose's front yard, her own seven milch ewes grazing on Iria Hill, the bronze crowns of the oaks. "He's very careful how he talks about the Masters."

Rose nodded.

"But he told me about some of the students."

"No harm in that, I suppose."

"I don't know," Dragonfly said. "To hear about the Great House is wonderful, but I thought the people there would be—I don't know. Of course they're mostly just boys when they go there. But I thought they'd be . . ." She gazed off at the sheep on the hill, her face troubled. "Some of them are really bad and stupid," she said in a low voice. "They get into the school because they're rich. And they study there just to get richer. Or to get power."

"Well, of course they do," said Rose, "that's what they're there for!"

"But power—like you told me about—that isn't the same as making people do what you want, or pay you—"

"Isn't it?"

"No!"

"If a word can heal, a word can wound," the witch said. "If a hand can kill, a hand can cure. It's a poor cart that goes only one direction."

"But on Roke, they learn to use power well, not for harm, not for gain."

"Everything's for gain some way, I'd say. People have to live. But what do I know? I make my living doing what I know how to do. But I don't meddle with the great arts, the perilous crafts, like summoning the dead," and Rose made the hand sign to avert the danger spoken of.

"Everything's perilous," Dragonfly said, gazing now through the sheep, the hill, the trees, into still depths, a colorless, vast emptiness like the clear sky before sunrise.

Rose watched her. She knew she did not know who Irian was or what she might be. A big, strong, awkward, ignorant, innocent, angry woman, yes. But ever since Irian was a child Rose had seen something more in her, something beyond what she was. And when Irian looked away from the world like that, she seemed to enter that place or time or being beyond herself, utterly beyond Rose's knowledge. Then Rose feared her, and feared for her.

"You take care," the witch said, grim. "Everything's perilous, right enough, and meddling with wizards most of all."

Through love, respect, and trust, Dragonfly would never disregard a warning from Rose; but she was unable to see Ivory as perilous. She didn't understand him, but the idea of fearing him, him personally, was not one she could keep in mind. She tried to be respectful, but it was impossible. She thought he was clever and quite handsome, but she didn't think much about him, except for what he could tell her. He knew what she wanted to know and little by little he told it to her, and then it was not really what she had wanted to know, but she wanted to know more. He was patient with her, and she was grateful to him for his patience, knowing he was much quicker than she. Sometimes he smiled at her ignorance, but he never sneered at it or reproved it. Like the witch, he liked to answer a question with a question; but the answers to Rose's questions were always something she'd always known, while the answers to his questions were things she had never imagined and found startling, unwelcome, even painful, altering her beliefs.

Day by day, as they talked in the old stableyard of Iria, where they had fallen into the habit of meeting, she asked him and he told her more, though reluctantly, always partially; he shielded his

Masters, she thought, trying to defend the bright image of Roke, until one day he gave in to her insistence and spoke freely at last.

"There are good men there," he said. "Great and wise the Archmage certainly was. But he's gone. And the Masters... Some hold aloof, following arcane knowledge, seeking ever more patterns, ever more names, but using their knowledge for nothing. Others hide their ambition under the grey cloak of wisdom. Roke is no longer where power is in Earthsea. That's the Court in Havnor, now. Roke lives on its great past, defended by a thousand spells against the present day. And inside those spell-walls, what is there? Quarreling ambitions, fear of anything new, fear of young men who challenge the power of the old. And at the center, nothing. An empty courtyard. The Archmage will never return."

"How do you know?" she whispered.

He looked stern. "The dragon bore him away."

"You saw it? You saw that?" She clenched her hands, imagining that flight, not even hearing his reply.

After a long time, she came back to the sunlight and the stableyard and her thoughts and puzzles. "But even if he's gone," she said, "surely some of the Masters are truly wise?"

When he looked up and spoke it was with reluctance, with a hint of a melancholy smile. "All the mystery and wisdom of the Masters, when it's out in the daylight, doesn't amount to so much, you know. Tricks of the trade—wonderful illusions. But people don't want to know that. They want the illusions, the mysteries. Who can blame them? There's so little in life that's beautiful or worthy."

As if to illustrate what he was saying, he had picked up a bit of brick from the broken pavement, and tossed it up in the air, and as he spoke it fluttered about their heads on delicate blue wings, a butterfly. He put out his finger and the butterfly lighted on it. He shook his finger and the butterfly fell to the ground, a fragment of brick.

"There's not much worth much in my life," she said, gazing down at the pavement. "All I know how to do is run the farm, and try to stand up and speak truth. But if I thought it was all tricks and lies even on Roke, I'd hate those men for fooling me, fooling us all. It can't be lies. Not all of it. The Archmage did go into the labyrinth among the Hoary Men and come back with the Ring of Peace. He did go into death with the young king, and defeat the spider mage, and come back. We know that on the word of the King himself. Even here, the harpers came to sing that song, and a teller came to tell it."

Ivory nodded. "But the Archmage lost all his power in the land of death. Maybe all magery was weakened then."

"Rose's spells work as well as ever," she said stoutly.

Ivory smiled. He said nothing, but she saw how petty the doings of a village witch appeared to him, who had seen great deeds and powers. She sighed and spoke from her heart—"Oh, if only I wasn't a woman!"

He smiled again. "You're a beautiful woman," he said, but plainly, not in the flattering way he had used with her at first, before she showed him she hated it. "Why would you be a man?"

"So I could go to Roke! And see, and learn! Why, why is it only men can go there?"

"So it was ordained by the first Archmage, centuries ago," said Ivory. "But . . . I too have wondered."

"You have?"

"Often. Seeing only boys and men, day after day, in the Great House and all the precincts of the school. Knowing that the townswomen are spell-bound from so much as setting foot on the fields about Roke Knoll. Once in years, perhaps, some great lady is allowed to come briefly into the outer courts . . . Why is it so? Are all women incapable of understanding? Or is it that the Masters fear them, fear to be corrupted— No, but fear that to admit women might change the rule they cling to—the purity of that rule—"

"Women can live chaste as well as men can," Dragonfly said bluntly. She knew she was blunt and coarse where he was delicate and subtle, but she did not know any other way to be.

"Of course," he said, his smile growing brilliant. "But witches aren't always chaste, are they?... Maybe that's what the Masters are afraid of. Maybe celibacy isn't as necessary as the Rule of Roke teaches. Maybe it's not a way of keeping the power pure, but of keeping the power to themselves. Leaving out women, leaving out everybody who won't agree to turn himself into a eunuch to get that one kind of power... Who knows? A she-mage! Now that would change everything, all the rules!"

She could see his mind dance ahead of hers, taking up and playing with ideas, transforming them as he had transformed brick into butterfly. She could not dance with him, she could not play with him, but she watched him in wonder.

"You could go to Roke," he said, his eyes bright with excitement, mischief, daring. Meeting her almost pleading, incredulous silence, he insisted—"You could. A woman you are, but there are ways to change your seeming. You have the heart, the courage, the will of a man. You could enter the Great House. I know it."

"And what would I do there?"

"What all the students do. Live alone in a stone cell and learn to be wise! It might not be what you dream it to be, but that, too, you'd learn."

"I couldn't. They'd know. I couldn't even get in. There's the Doorkeeper, you said. I don't know the word to say to him."

"The password, yes. But I can teach it to you."

"You can? Is it allowed?"

"I don't care what's 'allowed,'" he said, with a frown she had never seen on his face. "The Archmage himself said, *Rules are made to be broken.* Injustice makes the rules, and courage breaks them. I have the courage, if you do!"

She looked at him. She could not speak. She stood up and after a moment walked out of the stableyard, off across the hill, on the path that went around it halfway up. One of the dogs, her favorite, a big, ugly, heavy-headed hound, followed her. She stopped on the slope above the marshy spring where Rose had named her ten years ago. She stood there. The dog sat down beside her and looked up at her face. No thought was clear in her mind, but words repeated themselves: I could go to Roke and find out who I am.

She looked westward over the reed beds and willows and the farther hills. The whole western sky was empty, clear. She stood still and her soul seemed to go into that sky and be gone, gone out of her.

There was a little noise, the soft clip-clop of the black mare's hoofs, coming along the lane. Then Dragonfly came back to herself and called to Ivory and ran down the hill to meet him. "I will go," she said.

He had not planned or intended any such adventure, but crazy as it was, it suited him better the more he thought about it. The prospect of spending the long grey winter at Westpool sank his spirits like a stone. There was nothing here for him except the girl Dragonfly, who had come to fill his thoughts. Her massive, innocent strength had defeated him absolutely so far, but he did what she pleased in order to have her do at last what he pleased, and the game, he thought, was worth playing. If she ran away with him, the game was as good as won. As for the joke of it, the notion of actually getting her into the school on Roke disguised as a man, there was little chance of pulling it off, but it pleased him as a gesture of disrespect to all the piety and pomposity of the Masters and their toadies. And if somehow it succeeded, if he could actually get a woman through that door, even for a moment, what a sweet revenge it would be!

Money was a problem. The girl thought, of course, that he as a great wizard would snap his fingers and waft them over the sea in a magic boat flying before the magewind. But when he told her they'd have to hire passage on a ship, she said simply, "I have the cheese money."

He treasured her rustic sayings of that kind. Sometimes she frightened him, and he resented it. His dreams of her were never of her yielding to him, but of himself yielding to a fierce, destroying sweetness, sinking into an annihilating embrace, dreams in which she was something beyond comprehension and he was nothing at all. He woke from those dreams shaken and shamed. In daylight, when he saw her big, dirty hands, when she talked like a yokel, a simpleton, he regained his superiority. He only wished there were someone to repeat her sayings to, one of his old friends in the Great Port who would find them amusing. "I have the cheese money," he repeated to himself, riding back to Westpool, and laughed. "I do indeed," he said aloud. The black mare flicked her ear.

He told Birch that he had received a sending from his teacher on Roke, the Master Hand, and must go at once, on what business he could not say, of course, but it should not take long once he was there; a half month to go, another to return; he would be back well before the Fallows at the latest. He must ask Master Birch to provide him an advance on his salary to pay for ship passage and lodging, since a wizard of Roke should not take advantage of people's willingness to give him whatever he needed, but pay his way like an ordinary man. As Birch agreed with this, he had to give Ivory a purse for his journey, the first real money he had had in his pocket for years: ten ivory counters carved with the Otter of Shelieth on one side and the Rune of Peace on the other in honor of King Lebannen. "Hello, little namesakes," he told them when he was alone with them. "You and the cheese money will get along nicely."

He told Dragonfly very little of his plans, largely because he made few, trusting to chance and his own wits, which seldom let him down if he was given a fair chance to use them. The girl asked almost no questions. "Will I go as a man all the way?" was one.

"Yes," he said, "but only disguised. I won't put a semblance spell on you till we're on Roke Island."

"I thought it would be a spell of change," she said.

"That would be unwise," he said, with a good imitation of the Master Changer's terse solemnity. "If need be, I'll do it, of course. But you'll find wizards very sparing of the great spells. For good reason."

"The Equilibrium," she said, accepting all he said in its simplest sense, as always.

"And perhaps because such arts have not the power they once had," he said. He did not know himself why he tried to weaken her faith in wizardry; perhaps because any weakening of her strength, her wholeness, was a gain for him. He had begun merely by trying to get her into his bed, a game he loved to play. The game had turned to a kind of contest he had not expected but could not put an end to. He was determined now not to win her, but to defeat her. He could not let her defeat him. He must prove to her and himself that his dreams were meaningless.

Quite early on, impatient with wooing her massive physical indifference, he had worked up a charm, a sorcerer's seduction spell of which he was contemptuous even as he made it, though he knew it was effective. He cast it on her while she was, characteristically, mending a cow's halter. The result had not been the melting eagerness it had produced in girls he had used it on in Havnor and Thwil. Dragonfly had gradually become silent and sullen. She ceased asking her endless questions about Roke and did not answer when he spoke. When he very tentatively approached her, taking her hand, she struck him away with a blow to the head that left him dizzy. He saw her stand up and stride out of the stableyard without a word, the ugly hound she favored trotting after her. The hound looked back at him with a grin.

She took the path to the old house. When his ears stopped ringing he stole after her, hoping the charm was working and that this was only her particularly uncouth way of leading him at last to her bed. Nearing the house, he heard crockery breaking. The father, the drunkard, came wobbling out looking scared and confused, followed by Dragonfly's loud, harsh voice—"Out of the house, you drunken, crawling traitor! You foul, shameless lecher!"

"She took my cup away," the Master of Iria said to the stranger, whining like a puppy, while his dogs yammered around him. "She broke it."

Ivory departed. He did not return for two days. On the third day he rode experimentally past Old Iria, and she came striding down to meet him. "I'm sorry, Ivory," she said, looking up at him with her smoky orange eyes. "I don't know what came over me the other day. I was angry. But not at you. I beg your pardon."

He forgave her gracefully. He did not try a love charm on her again.

Soon, he thought now, he would not need one. He would have real power over her. He had finally seen how to get it. She had given it into his hands. Her strength and her willpower were tremendous, but fortunately she was stupid, and he was not.

Birch was sending a carter down to Kembermouth with six barrels of ten-year-old Fanian ordered by the wine merchant there. He was glad to send his wizard along as bodyguard, for the wine was valuable, and though the young king was putting things to rights as fast as he could, there were still gangs of robbers on the roads. So Ivory left Westpool on the big wagon pulled by four big cart horses, jolting slowly along, his legs dangling. Down by Jackass Hill an uncouth figure rose up from the wayside and asked the carter for a lift. "I don't know you," the carter said, lifting his whip to warn the stranger off, but Ivory came round the wagon and said, "Let the lad ride, my good man. He'll do no harm while I'm with you."

"Keep an eye on him then, master," said the carter.

"I will," said Ivory, with a wink at Dragonfly. She, well disguised in dirt and a farmhand's old smock and leggings and a loathsome felt hat, did not wink back. She played her part even while they sat side by side dangling their legs over the tailgate, with six great halftuns of wine jolting between them and the drowsy carter, and the drowsy summer hills and fields slipping slowly, slowly past. Ivory tried to tease her, but she only shook her head. Maybe she was scared by this wild scheme, now she was embarked on it. There was no telling. She was solemnly, heavily silent. I could be very bored by this woman, Ivory thought, if once I'd had her underneath me. That thought stirred him almost unbearably, but when he looked back at her, his desire died away before her massive, actual presence.

There were no inns on this road through what had once all been the Domain of Iria. As the sun neared the western plains, they stopped at a farmhouse that offered stabling for the horses, a shed for the cart, and straw in the stable loft for the carters. The loft was dark and stuffy and the straw musty. Ivory felt no lust at all, though Dragonfly lay not three feet from him. She had played the man so thoroughly all day that she had half convinced even him. Maybe she'll fool the old men after all! he thought. He grinned at the thought, and slept.

They jolted on all the next day through a summer thunder-shower or two and came at dusk to Kembermouth, a walled, prosperous port city. They left the carter to his master's business and walked down to find an inn near the docks. Dragonfly looked about at the sights of the city in a silence that might have been awe or disapproval or mere stolidity. "This is a nice little town," Ivory said, "but the only city in the world is Havnor."

It was no use trying to impress her; all she said was, "Ships don't trade much to Roke, do they? Will it take a long time to find one to take us, do you think?"

"Not if I carry a staff," he said.

She stopped looking about and strode along in thought for a while. She was beautiful in movement, bold and graceful, her head carried high.

"You mean they'll oblige a wizard? But you aren't a wizard."

"That's a formality. We senior sorcerers may carry a staff when we're on Roke's business. Which I am."

"Taking *me* there?"

"Bringing them a student—yes. A student of great gifts!"

She asked no more questions. She never argued; it was one of her virtues.

That night, over supper at the waterfront inn, she asked with unusual timidity in her voice, "Do I have great gifts?"

"In my judgment, you do," he said.

She pondered—conversation with her was often a slow business—and said, "Rose always said I had power, but she didn't know what kind. And I . . . I know I do, but I don't know what it is."

"You're going to Roke to find out," he said, raising his glass to her. After a moment she raised hers and smiled at him, a smile so tender and radiant that he said spontaneously, "And may what you find be all you seek!"

"If I do, it will be thanks to you," she said. In that moment he loved her for her true heart, and would have foresworn any thought of her but as his companion in a bold adventure, a gallant joke.

They had to share a room at the crowded inn with two other travelers, but Ivory's thoughts were perfectly chaste, though he laughed at himself a little for it.

Next morning he picked a sprig of an herb from the kitchen garden of the inn and spelled it into the semblance of a fine staff, copper-shod and his own height exactly. "What is the wood?" Dragonfly asked, fascinated, when she saw it, and when he answered with a laugh, "Rosemary," she laughed too.

They set off along the wharves, asking for a ship bound south that might take a wizard and his prentice to the Isle of the Wise, and soon enough they found a heavy trader bound for Wathort, whose master would carry the wizard for goodwill and the prentice for half price. Even half price was half the cheese money; but they would have the luxury of a cabin, for *Sea Otter* was a decked, two-masted ship.

As they were talking with her master a wagon drew up on the dock and began to unload six familiar halftun barrels. "That's ours," Ivory said, and the ship's master said, "Bound for Hort Town," and Dragonfly said softly, "From Iria."

She glanced back at the land then. It was the only time he ever saw her look back.

The ship's weatherworker came aboard just before they sailed, no Roke wizard but a weatherbeaten fellow in a worn sea cloak. Ivory flourished his staff a little in greeting him. The sorcerer looked him up and down and said, "One man works weather on this ship. If it's not me, I'm off."

"I'm a mere passenger, Master Bagman. I gladly leave the winds in your hands."

The sorcerer looked at Dragonfly, who stood straight as a tree and said nothing.

"Good," he said, and that was the last word he spoke to Ivory.

During the voyage, however, he talked several times with Dragonfly, which made Ivory a bit uneasy. Her ignorance and trustfulness could endanger her and therefore him. What did she and the bagman talk about? he asked, and she answered, "What is to become of us."

He stared.

"Of all of us. Of Way and Felkway, and Havnor, and Wathort, and Roke. All the people of the islands. He says that when King Lebannen was to be crowned, last autumn, he sent to Gont for the old Archmage to come crown him, and he wouldn't come. And there was no new Archmage. So the King put on his crown himself. And some say that's wrong, and he doesn't rightly hold the throne. But others say the King himself is the new Archmage. But he isn't a wizard, only a king. So others say the dark years will come again, when there was no rule of justice, and wizardry was used for evil ends."

After a pause Ivory said, "That old weatherworker says all this?"

"It's common talk, I think," said Dragonfly, with her grave simplicity.

The weatherworker knew his trade, at least. *Sea Otter* sped south; they met summer squalls and choppy seas, but never a storm or a troublesome wind. They put off and took on cargo at ports on the north shore of O, at Ilien, Leng, Kamery, and O Port, and then headed west to carry the passengers to Roke. And facing the west Ivory felt a little hollow at the pit of his stomach, for he knew all too well how Roke was guarded. He knew neither he nor the weatherworker could do anything at all to turn the Roke wind if it blew against them. And if it did, Dragonfly would ask why? why did it blow against them?

He was glad to see the sorcerer uneasy too, standing by the helmsman, keeping a watch up on the masthead, taking in sail at the hint of a west wind. But the wind held steady from the north. A thunder squall came pelting on that wind, and Ivory went down to the cabin, but Dragonfly stayed up on deck. She was afraid of the water, she had told him. She could not swim; she said, "Drowning must be a horrible thing— Not to breathe the air—" She had shuddered at the thought. It was the only fear she had ever shown of anything. But she disliked the low, cramped cabin, and had stayed on deck every day and slept there on the warm nights. Ivory had not tried to coax her into the cabin. He knew now that coaxing was no good. To have her he must master her; and that he would do, if only they could come to Roke.

He came up on deck again. It was clearing, and as the sun set, the clouds broke all across the west, showing a golden sky behind the high dark curve of a hill.

Ivory looked at that hill with a kind of longing hatred.

"That's Roke Knoll, lad," the weatherworker said to Dragon-fly, who stood beside him at the rail. "We're coming into Thwil Bay now. Where there's no wind but the wind they want."

By the time they were well into the bay and had let down the anchor it was dark, and Ivory said to the ship's master, "I'll go ashore in the morning."

Down in their tiny cabin Dragonfly sat waiting for him, solemn as ever but her eyes blazing with excitement. "We'll go ashore in the morning," he repeated to her, and she nodded, acceptant.

She said, "Do I look all right?"

He sat down on his narrow bunk and looked at her sitting on her narrow bunk; they could not face each other directly, as there was no room for their knees. At O Port she had bought herself a decent shirt and breeches, at his suggestion, so as to look a more probable candidate for the school. Her face was windburnt and scrubbed clean. Her hair was braided and the braid clubbed, like Ivory's. She had got her hands clean too, and they lay flat on her thighs, long strong hands, like a man's.

"You don't look like a man," he said. Her face fell. "Not to me. You'll never look like a man to me. But don't worry. You will to them."

She nodded, with an anxious face.

"The first test is the great test, Dragonfly," he said. Every night as he lay alone in this cabin he had planned this conversation. "To enter the Great House. To go through that door."

"I've been thinking about it," she said, hurried and earnest. "Couldn't I just tell them who I am? With you there to vouch for me—to say even if I am a woman, I have some gift—and I'd promise to take the vow and make the spell of celibacy, and live apart if they wanted me to—"

He was shaking his head all through her speech. "No, no, no, no. Hopeless. Useless. Fatal!"

"Even if you—"

"Even if I argued for you. They won't listen. The Rule of Roke forbids women to be taught any high art, any word of the Language of the Making. It's always been so. They will not listen. So they must be shown! And we'll show them, you and I. We'll teach them. You must have courage, Dragonfly. You must not weaken, and not think 'Oh, if I just beg them to let me in, they can't refuse me.' They can, and will. And if you reveal yourself, they will punish you. And me." He put a ponderous emphasis on the last word, and inwardly murmured, "Avert."

She gazed at him from her unreadable eyes, and finally asked, "What must I do?"

"Do you trust me, Dragonfly?"

"Yes."

"Will you trust me entirely, wholly—knowing that the risk I take for you is greater even than your risk in this venture?"

"Yes."

"Then you must tell me the word you will speak to the Doorkeeper."

She stared. "But I thought you'd tell it to me—the password."

"The password he will ask you for is your true name."

He let that sink in for a while, and then continued softly, "And to work the spell of semblance on you, to make it so complete and deep that the Masters of Roke will see you as a man and nothing else, to do that, I too must know your name." He paused again. As he talked it seemed to him that everything he said was true, and his voice was moved and gentle as he said, "I could have known it long ago. But I chose not to use those arts. I wanted you to trust me enough to tell me your name yourself."

She was looking down at her hands, clasped now on her knees. In the faint reddish glow of the cabin lantern her lashes cast very delicate, long shadows on her cheeks. She looked up, straight at him. "My name is Irian," she said.

He smiled. She did not smile.

He said nothing. In fact he was at a loss. If he had known it would be this easy, he could have had her name and with it the power to make her do whatever he wanted, days ago, weeks ago, with a mere pretense at this crazy scheme—without giving up his salary and his precarious respectability, without this sea voyage, without having to go all the way to Roke for it! For he saw the whole plan now was folly. There was no way he could disguise her that would fool the Doorkeeper for a moment. All his notions of humiliating the Masters as they had humiliated him were moonshine. Obsessed with tricking the girl, he had fallen into the trap he laid for her. Bitterly he recognised that he was always believing his own lies, caught in nets he had elaborately woven. Having once made a fool of himself on Roke, he had come back to do it all over again. A great, desolate anger swelled up in him. There was no good, no good in anything.

"What's wrong?" she asked. The gentleness of her deep, husky voice unmanned him, and he hid his face in his hands, fighting against the shame of tears.

She put her hand on his knee. It was the first time she had ever touched him. He endured it, the warmth and weight of her touch that he had wasted so much time wanting.

He wanted to hurt her, to shock her out of her terrible, ignorant kindness, but what he said when he finally spoke was "I only wanted to make love to you."

"You did?"

"Did you think I was one of their eunuchs? That I'd castrate myself with spells so I could be holy? Why do you think I don't have a staff? Why do you think I'm not at the school? Did you believe everything I said?"

"Yes," she said. "I'm sorry." Her hand was still on his knee. She said, "We can make love if you want."

He sat up, sat still.

"What are you?" he said to her at last.

"I don't know. It's why I wanted to come to Roke. To find out."

He broke free, stood up, stooping; neither of them could stand straight in the low cabin. Clenching and unclenching his hands, he stood as far from her as he could, his back to her.

"You won't find out. It's all lies, shams. Old men playing games with words. I wouldn't play their games, so I left. Do you know what I did?" He turned, showing his teeth in a rictus of triumph. "I got a girl, a town girl, to come to my room. My cell. My little stone celibate cell. It had a window looking out on a back street. No spells—you can't make spells with all their magic going on. But she wanted to come, and came, and I let a rope ladder out the window, and she climbed it. And we were at it when the old men came in! I showed 'em! And if I could have got you in, I'd have showed 'em again, I'd have taught them *their* lesson!"

"Well, I'll try," she said.

He stared.

"Not for the same reasons as you," she said, "but I still want to. And we came all this way. And you know my name."

It was true. He knew her name: Irian. It was like a coal of fire, a burning ember in his mind. His thought could not hold it. His knowledge could not use it. His tongue could not say it.

She looked up at him, her sharp, strong face softened by the shadowy lantern light. "If it was only to make love you brought me here, Ivory," she said, "we can do that. If you still want to."

Wordless at first, he simply shook his head. After a while he was able to laugh. "I think we've gone on past . . . that possibility . . ."

She looked at him without regret, or reproach, or shame.

"Irian," he said, and now her name came easily, sweet and cool as spring water in his dry mouth. "Irian, here's what you must do to enter the Great House . . ."

III. Azver

He left her at the corner of the street, a narrow, dull, somehow sly-looking street that slanted up between featureless walls to a wooden door in a higher wall. He had put his spell on her, and she looked like a man, though she did not feel like one. She and Ivory took each other in their arms, because after all they had been friends, companions, and he had done all this for her.

"Courage!" he said, and let her go. She walked up the street and stood before the door. She looked back then, but he was gone.

She knocked.

After a while she heard the latch rattle. The door opened. A middle-aged man stood there. "What can I do for you?" he said. He did not smile, but his voice was pleasant.

"You can let me into the Great House, sir."

"Do you know the way in?" His almond-shaped eyes were attentive, yet seemed to look at her from miles or years away.

"This is the way in, sir."

"Do you know whose name you must tell me before I let you in?"

"My own, sir. It is Irian."

"Is it?" he said.

That gave her pause. She stood silent. "It's the name the witch Rose of my village on Way gave me, in the spring under Iria Hill," she said at last, standing up and speaking truth.

The Doorkeeper looked at her for what seemed a long time. "Then it is your name," he said. "But maybe not all your name. I think you have another."

"I don't know it, sir."

After another long time she said, "Maybe I can learn it here, sir."

The Doorkeeper bowed his head a little. A very faint smile made crescent curves in his cheeks. He stood aside. "Come in, daughter," he said.

She stepped across the threshold of the Great House.

Ivory's spell of semblance dropped away like a cobweb. She was and looked herself.

She followed the Doorkeeper down a stone passageway. Only at the end of it did she think to turn back to see the light shine through the thousand leaves of the tree carved in the high door in its bone-white frame.

A young man in a grey cloak hurrying down the passageway stopped short as he approached them. He stared at Irian; then with a brief nod he went on. She looked back at him. He was looking back at her.

A globe of misty, greenish fire drifted swiftly down the corridor at eye level, apparently pursuing the young man. The Doorkeeper waved his hand at it, and it avoided him. Irian swerved and ducked down frantically, but felt the cool fire tingle in her hair as it passed over her. The Doorkeeper glanced round, and now his smile was wider. Though he said nothing, she felt he was aware of her, concerned for her. She stood up and followed him.

He stopped before an oak door. Instead of knocking he sketched a little sign or rune on it with the top of his staff, a light staff of some greyish wood. The door opened as a resonant voice behind it said, "Come in!"

"Wait here a little, if you please, Irian," the Doorkeeper said, and went into the room, leaving the door wide open behind him. She could see bookshelves and books, a table piled with more books and ink pots and writings, two or three boys seated at the table, and the grey-haired, stocky man the Doorkeeper spoke to. She saw the man's face change, saw his eyes shift to her in a brief, startled gaze, saw him question the Doorkeeper, low-voiced, intense.

They both came to her. "The Master Changer of Roke: Irian of Way," said the Doorkeeper.

The Changer stared openly at her. He was not as tall as she was. He stared at the Doorkeeper, and then at her again.

"Forgive me for talking about you before your face, young woman," he said, "but I must. Master Doorkeeper, you know I'd never question your judgment, but the Rule is clear. I have to ask what moved you to break it and let her come in."

"She asked to," said the Doorkeeper.

"But—" The Changer paused.

"When did a woman last ask to enter the school?"

"They know the Rule doesn't allow them."

"Did you know that, Irian?" the Doorkeeper asked her, and she said, "Yes, sir."

"So what brought you here?" the Changer asked, stern, but not hiding his curiosity.

"Master Ivory said I could pass for a man. Though I thought I should say who I was. I will be as celibate as anyone, sir."

Two long curves appeared on the Doorkeeper's cheeks, enclosing the slow upturn of his smile. The Changer's face remained stern, but he blinked, and after a little thought said, "I'm sure—yes—It was definitely the better plan to be honest. What Master did you speak of?"

"Ivory," said the Doorkeeper. "A lad from Havnor Great Port, whom I let in three years ago, and let out again last year, as you may recall."

"Ivory! That fellow that studied with the Hand?— Is he here?" the Changer demanded of Irian, wrathily. She stood straight and said nothing.

"Not in the school," the Doorkeeper said, smiling.

"He fooled you, young woman. Made a fool of you by trying to make fools of us."

"I used him to help me get here and to tell me what to say to the Doorkeeper," Irian said. "I'm not here to fool anybody, but to learn what I need to know."

"I've often wondered why I let that boy in," said the Doorkeeper. "Now I begin to understand."

At that the Changer looked at him, and after pondering said soberly, "Doorkeeper, what have you in mind?"

"I think Irian of Way may have come to us seeking not only what she needs to know, but also what we need to know." The

Doorkeeper's tone was equally sober, and his smile was gone. "I think this may be a matter for talk among the nine of us."

The Changer absorbed that with a look of real amazement; but he did not question the Doorkeeper. He said only, "But not among the students."

The Doorkeeper shook his head, agreeing.

"She can lodge in the town," the Changer said, with some relief.

"While we talk behind her back?"

"You won't bring her into the Council Room?" the Changer said in disbelief.

"The Archmage brought the boy Arren there."

"But— But Arren was King Lebannen—"

"And who is Irian?"

The Changer stood silent, and then he said quietly, with respect, "My friend, what is it you think to do, to learn? What is she, that you ask this for her?"

"Who are we," said the Doorkeeper, "that we refuse her without knowing what she is?"

"A woman," said the Master Summoner.

Irian had waited some hours in the Doorkeeper's chamber, a low, light, bare room with a window seat at a small-paned window looking out on the kitchen gardens of the Great House— handsome, well-kept gardens, long rows and beds of vegetables, greens, and herbs, with berry canes and fruit trees beyond. She saw a burly, dark-skinned man and two boys come out and weed one of the vegetable plots. It eased her mind to watch their careful work. She wished she could help them at it. The waiting and the strangeness were very difficult. Once the Doorkeeper came in, bringing her a mug of water and a plate with cold meat and bread and scallions, and she ate because he told her to eat, but chewing and swallowing were hard work. The gardeners went away and there was nothing to watch out the window but the cabbages growing and the sparrows hopping, and now and then a hawk far up in the sky, and the wind moving softly in the tops of tall trees, on beyond the gardens.

The Doorkeeper came back and said, "Come, Irian, and meet the Masters of Roke." Her heart began to go at a cart-horse gallop. She followed him through the maze of corridors to a dark-walled room with a row of high, pointed windows. A group of men stood there. Every one of them turned to look at her as she came into the room.

"Irian of Way, my lords," said the Doorkeeper. They were all silent. He motioned her to come farther into the room. "The Master Changer you have met," he said to her. He named all the others, but she could not take in their names and masteries, except that the Master Herbal was the one she had supposed to be a gardener, and the youngest of them, a tall man with a stern, beautiful face that seemed carved out of dark stone, was the Master Summoner. It was he who spoke when the Doorkeeper was done. "A woman," he said.

The Doorkeeper nodded once, mild as ever.

"This is what you brought the Nine together for? This and no more?"

"This and no more," said the Doorkeeper.

"Dragons have been seen flying above the Inmost Sea. Roke has no archmage, and the islands no true-crowned king. There is real work to do," the Summoner said, and his voice too was like stone, cold and heavy. "When will we do it?"

There was an uncomfortable silence, as the Doorkeeper did not speak. At last a slight, bright-eyed man who wore a red tunic under his grey wizard's cloak said, "Do you bring this woman into the House as a student, Master Doorkeeper?"

"If I did, it would be up to you all to approve or disapprove," said he.

"Do you?" asked the man in the red tunic, smiling a little.

"Master Hand," said the Doorkeeper, "she asked to enter as a student, and I saw no reason to deny her."

"Every reason," said the Summoner.

A man with a deep, clear voice spoke: "It's not our judgment that prevails, but the Rule of Roke, which we are sworn to follow."

"I doubt the Doorkeeper would defy it lightly," said one whom Irian had not noticed till he spoke, though he was a big man, white-haired, rawboned, and crag-faced. Unlike the others, he looked at her as he spoke. "I am Kurremkarmerruk," he said to her. "As the Master Namer here, I make free with names, my own included. Who named you, Irian?"

"The witch Rose of our village, lord," she answered, standing straight, though her voice came out high-pitched and rough.

"Is she misnamed?" the Doorkeeper asked the Namer.

Kurremkarmerruk shook his head. "No. But . . ."

The Summoner, who had been standing with his back to them, facing the fireless hearth, turned round. "The names witches give each other are not our concern here," he said. "If you have some interest in this woman, Doorkeeper, it should be pursued outside these walls—outside the door you vowed to keep. She has no place here nor ever will. She can bring only confusion, dissension, and further weakness among us. I will speak no longer and say nothing else in her presence. The only answer to conscious error is silence."

"Silence is not enough, my lord," said one who had not spoken before. To Irian's eyes he was very strange-looking, having pale reddish skin, long pale hair, and narrow eyes the color of ice. His speech was also strange, stiff and somehow deformed. "Silence is the answer to everything, and to nothing," he said.

The Summoner lifted his noble, dark face and looked across the room at the pale man, but did not speak. Without a word or gesture he turned away again and left the room. As he walked slowly past Irian, she shrank back from him. It was as if a grave had opened, a winter grave, cold, wet, dark. Her breath stuck in her throat. She gasped a little for air. When she recovered herself, she saw the Changer and the pale man both watching her intently.

The one with a voice like a deep-toned bell looked at her too, and spoke to her with a plain, kind severity. "As I see it, the man who brought you here meant to do harm, but you do not. Yet being here, Irian, you do us and yourself harm. Everything not in its own place does harm. A note sung, however well sung, wrecks the tune it isn't part of. Women teach women. Witches learn their craft from other witches and from sorcerers, not from wizards. What we teach here is in a language not for women's tongues. The young heart rebels against such laws, calling them unjust, arbitrary. But they are true laws, founded not on what we want, but on what is. The just and the unjust, the foolish and the wise, all must obey them, or waste life and come to grief."

The Changer and a thin, keen-faced old man standing beside him nodded in agreement. The Master Hand said, "Irian, I am sorry. Ivory was my pupil. If I taught him badly, I did worse in sending him away. I thought him insignificant, and so harmless. But he lied to you and beguiled you. You must not feel shame. The fault was his and mine."

"I am not ashamed," Irian said. She looked at them all. She felt that she should thank them for their courtesy but the words would not come. She nodded stiffly to them, turned round, and strode out of the room.

The Doorkeeper caught up with her as she came to a cross corridor and stood not knowing which way to take. "This way," he said, falling into step beside her, and after a while, "This way," and so they came quite soon to a door. It was not made of horn and ivory. It was uncarved oak, black and massive, with an iron bolt worn thin with age. "This is the garden door," the mage said, unbolting it. "Medra's Gate, they used to call it. I keep both doors." He opened it. The brightness of the day dazzled Irian's eyes. When she could see clearly she saw a path leading from the door through the gardens and the fields beyond them; on past the fields were the high trees, and the swell of Roke Knoll was off to the right. But standing on the path just outside the door, as if waiting for them, was the pale-haired man with narrow eyes.

"Patterner," said the Doorkeeper, not at all surprised.

"Where do you send this lady?" said the Patterner in his strange speech.

"Nowhere," said the Doorkeeper. "I let her out as I let her in, at her desire."

"Will you come with me?" the Patterner said to Irian.

She looked at him and at the Doorkeeper and said nothing.

"I don't live in this House. In any house," the Patterner said. "I live there. The Grove. —Ah," he said, turning suddenly. The big, white-haired man, Kurremkarmerruk the Namer, was standing just down the path. He had not been standing there until the other mage said "Ah." Irian stared from one to the other in blank bewilderment.

"This is only a seeming of me, a presentment, a sending," the old man said to her. "I don't live here either. Miles off." He gestured northward. "You might come there when you're done with the Patterner here. I'd like to learn more about your name." He nodded to the other two mages and was not there. A bumblebee buzzed heavily through the air where he had been.

Irian looked down at the ground. After a long time she said, clearing her throat, not looking up, "Is it true I do harm being here?"

"I don't know," said the Doorkeeper.

"In the Grove is no harm," said the Patterner. "Come on. There is an old house, a hut. Old, dirty. You don't care, eh? Stay a while. You can see." And he set off down the path between the parsley and the bush beans. She looked at the Doorkeeper; he smiled a little. She followed the pale-haired man.

They walked a half mile or so. The round-topped knoll rose up full in the western sun on their right. Behind them the school sprawled grey and many-roofed on its lower hill. The grove of trees towered before them now. She saw oak and willow, chestnut and ash, and tall evergreens. From the dense, sun-shot darkness of the trees a stream ran out, green-banked, with many brown trodden places where cattle and sheep went down to drink or to cross over. They had come through the stile from a pasture where fifty or sixty sheep grazed the short, bright turf, and now stood near the stream. "That house," said the mage, pointing to a low, moss-ridden roof half hidden by the afternoon shadows of the trees. "Stay tonight. You will?"

He asked her to stay, he did not tell her to. All she could do was nod.

"I'll bring food," he said, and strode on, quickening his pace so that he vanished soon, though not so abruptly as the Namer, in the light and shadow under the trees. Irian watched till he was certainly gone and then made her way through high grass and weeds to the little house.

It looked very old. It had been rebuilt and rebuilt again, but not for a long time. Nor had anyone lived in it for a long time, from the still, lonesome air of it. Yet it had a pleasant air, as if those who had slept there slept peacefully. As for decrepit walls, mice, dust, cobwebs, and scant furniture, all that was quite home-like to Irian. She found a bald broom and swept out the mouse droppings. She unrolled her blanket on the plank bed. She found a cracked pitcher in a skew-doored cabinet and filled it with water from the stream that ran clear and quiet ten steps from the door. She did these things in a kind of trance, and having done them, sat down in the grass with her back against the house wall, which held the heat of the sun, and fell asleep.

When she woke, the Master Patterner was sitting nearby, and a basket was on the grass between them.

"Hungry? Eat," he said.

"I'll eat later, sir. Thank you," said Irian.

"I am hungry now," said the mage. He took a hard-boiled egg from the basket, cracked, shelled, and ate it.

"They call this the Otter's House," he said. "Very old. As old as the Great House. Everything is old, here. We are old—the Masters."

"You're not very," Irian said. She thought him between thirty and forty, though it was hard to tell; she kept thinking his hair was white, because it was not black.

"But I came far. Miles can be years. I am Kargish, from Karego. You know?"

"The Hoary Men!" said Irian, staring openly at him. All Daisy's ballads of the Hoary Men who sailed out of the East to lay the land waste and spit innocent babes on their lances, and the story of how Erreth-Akbe lost the Ring of Peace, and the new songs and the King's Tale about how Archmage Sparrowhawk had gone among the Hoary Men and come back with that ring—

"Hoary?" said the Patterner.

"Frosty. White," she said, looking away, embarrassed.

"Ah." Presently he said, "The Master Summoner is not old." And she got a sidelong look from those narrow, ice-colored eyes.

She said nothing.

"I think you feared him."

She nodded.

When she said nothing, and some time had passed, he said, "In the shadow of these trees is no harm. Only truth."

"When he passed me," she said in a low voice, "I saw a grave."

"Ah," said the Patterner.

He had made a little heap of bits of eggshell on the ground by his knee. He arranged the white fragments into a curve, then closed it into a circle. "Yes," he said, studying his eggshells; then, scratching up the earth a bit, he neatly and delicately buried them. He dusted off his hands. Again his glance flicked to Irian and away.

"You have been a witch, Irian?"

"No."

"But you have some knowledge."

"No. I don't. Rose wouldn't teach me. She said she didn't dare. Because I had power but she didn't know what it was."

"Your Rose is a wise flower," said the mage, unsmiling.

"But I know I have something to do. Something to be. That's why I wanted to come here. To find out. On the Isle of the Wise."

She was getting used to his strange face now and was able to read it. She thought that he looked sad. His way of speaking was harsh, quick, dry, peaceable. "The men of the Isle are not always wise, eh?" he said. "Maybe the Doorkeeper." He looked at her now, not glancing but squarely, his eyes catching and holding hers. "But there. In the wood. Under the trees. There is the old wisdom. Never old. I can't teach you. I can take you into the Grove." After a minute he stood up. "Yes?"

"Yes," she said uncertainly.

"The house is all right?"

"Yes—"

"Tomorrow," he said, and strode off.

So for a half month or more of the hot days of summer, Irian slept in the Otter's House, which was a peaceful one, and ate what the Master Patterner brought her in his basket—eggs, cheese, greens, fruit, smoked mutton—and went with him every afternoon into the grove of high trees, where the paths seemed never to be quite where she remembered them, and often led on far beyond what seemed the confines of the wood. They walked there in silence, and spoke seldom when they rested. The mage was a quiet man. Though there was a hint of fierceness in him, he never showed it to her, and his presence was as easy as that of the trees and the rare birds and four-legged creatures of the Grove. As he had said, he did not try to teach her. When she asked about the Grove, he told her that, with Roke Knoll, it had stood since Segoy made the islands of the world, and that all magic was in the roots of the trees, and that they were mingled with the roots of all the forests that were or might yet be. "And sometimes the Grove is in this place," he said, "and sometimes in another. But it is always."

She had never seen where he lived. He slept wherever he chose to, she imagined, in these warm summer nights. She asked him where the food they ate came from. What the school did not supply for itself, he said, the farmers round about provided, considering themselves well recompensed by the protections the Masters set on their flocks and fields and orchards. That made sense to her. On Way, the phrase "a wizard without his porridge" meant something unprecedented, unheard-of. But she was no wizard, and so, wanting to earn her porridge, she did her best to repair the Otter's House, borrowing tools from a farmer and buying nails and plaster in Thwil Town, for she still had half the cheese money.

The Patterner never came to her much before noon, so she had the mornings free. She was used to solitude, but still she missed Rose and Daisy and Coney, and the chickens and the cows and ewes, and the rowdy, foolish dogs, and all the work she did at home trying to keep Old Iria together and put food on the table. So she worked away unhurriedly every morning till she saw the mage come out from the trees with his sunlight-colored hair shining in the sunlight.

Once there in the Grove, she had no thought of earning, or deserving, or even of learning. To be there was enough, was all.

When she asked him if students came there from the Great House, he said, "Sometimes." Another time he said, "My words are nothing. Hear the leaves." That was all he said that could be called teaching. As she walked, she listened to the leaves when the wind rustled them or stormed in the crowns of the trees; she watched the shadows play, and thought about the roots of the trees down in the darkness of the earth. She was utterly content to be there. Yet always, without discontent or ugency, she felt that she was waiting. And that silent expectancy was deepest and clearest when she came out of the shelter of the woods and saw the open sky.

Once, when they had gone a long way and the trees, dark evergreens she did not know, stood very high about them, she heard a call—a horn blowing, a cry?—remote, on the very edge of hearing. She stood still, listening towards the west. The mage walked on, turning only when he realised she had stopped.

"I heard—" she said, and could not say what she had heard.

He listened. They walked on at last through a silence enlarged and deepened by that far call.

She never went into the Grove without him, and it was many days before he left her alone within it. But one hot afternoon when they came to a glade among a stand of oaks, he said, "I will come back here, eh?" and walked off with his quick, silent step, lost almost at once in the dappled, shifting depths of the forest.

She had no wish to explore for herself. The peacefulness of the place called for stillness, watching, listening; and she knew how tricky the paths were, and that the Grove was, as the Patterner put it, "bigger inside than outside." She sat down in a patch of sun-dappled shade and watched the shadows of the leaves play across the ground. The oak mast was deep; though she had never seen wild swine in the wood, she saw their tracks here. For a moment she caught the scent of a fox. Her thoughts moved as quietly and easily as the breeze moved in the warm light.

Often her mind here seemed empty of thought, full of the forest itself, but this day memories came to her, vivid. She thought about Ivory, thinking she would never see him again, wondering if he had found a ship to take him back to Havnor. He had told her he'd never go back to Westpool; the only place for him was the Great Port, the King's City, and for all he cared the island of Way could sink in the sea as deep as Soléa. But she thought with love of the roads and fields of Way. She thought of Old Iria village, the marshy spring under Iria Hill, the old house on it. She thought about Daisy singing ballads in the kitchen, winter evenings, beating out the time with her wooden clogs; and old Coney in the vineyards with his razor-edge knife, showing her how to prune the vine "right down to the life in it;" and Rose, her Etaudis, whispering charms to ease the pain in a child's broken arm. I have known wise people, she thought. Her mind flinched away from remembering her father, but the motion of the leaves and shadows drew it on. She saw him drunk, shouting. She felt his prying, tremulous hands on her. She saw him weeping, sick, shamed; and grief rose up through her body and dissolved, like an ache that melts away in a long stretch of the arms. He was less to her than the mother she had not known.

She stretched, feeling the ease of her body in the warmth, and her mind drifted back to Ivory. She had had no one in her life to desire. When the young wizard first came riding by so slim and arrogant, she wished she could want him; but she didn't and couldn't, and so she had thought him spell-protected. Rose had explained to her how wizards' spells worked "so that it never enters your head nor theirs, see, because it would take from their power, they say." But Ivory, poor Ivory, had been all too unprotected. If anybody was under a spell of chastity it must have been herself, for charming and handsome as he was she had never been able to feel a thing for him but liking, and her only lust had been to learn what he could teach her.

She considered herself, sitting in the deep silence of the Grove. No bird sang; the breeze was down; the leaves hung still. Am I ensorcelled? Am I a sterile thing, not whole, not a woman? she asked herself, looking at her strong bare arms, the soft swell of her breasts in the shadow under the throat of her shirt.

She looked up and saw the Hoary Man come out of a dark aisle of great oaks and come towards her across the glade.

He stopped in front of her. She felt herself blush, her face and throat burning, dizzy, her ears ringing. She sought words, anything to say, to turn his attention away from her, and could find nothing at all. He sat down near her. She looked down, as if studying the skeleton of a last-year's leaf by her hand.

What do I want? she asked herself, and the answer came not in words but throughout her whole body and soul: the fire, a greater fire than that, the flight, the flight burning—

She came back into herself, into the still air under the trees. The Hoary Man sat near her, his face bowed down, and she thought how slight and light he looked, how quiet and sorrowful. There was nothing to fear. There was no harm.

He looked over at her.

"Irian," he said, "do you hear the leaves?"

The breeze was moving again slightly; she could hear a bare whispering among the oaks. "A little," she said.

"Do you hear the words?"

"No."

She asked nothing and he said no more. Presently he got up, and she followed him to the path that always led them, sooner or later, out of the wood to the clearing by the Thwilburn and the Otter's House. When they came there, it was late afternoon. He went down to the stream and knelt to drink from it where it left the wood, above all the crossings. She did the same. Then sitting in the cool, long grass of the bank, he began to speak.

"My people, the Kargs, they worship gods. Twin gods, brothers. And the king there is also a god. But before the gods and after, always, are the streams. Caves, stones, hills. Trees. The earth. The darkness of the earth."

"The Old Powers," Irian said.

He nodded. "There, women know the Old Powers. Here too, witches. And the knowledge is bad—eh?"

When he added that little questioning "eh?" or "neh?" to the end of what had seemed a statement it always took her by surprise. She said nothing.

"Dark is bad," said the Patterner. "Eh?"

Irian drew a deep breath and looked at him eye to eye as they sat there. "Only in dark the light," she said.

"Ah," he said. He looked away so that she could not see his expression.

"I should go," she said. "I can walk in the Grove, but not live there. It isn't my—my place. And the Master Chanter said I did harm by being here."

"We all do harm by being," said the Patterner.

He did as he often did, made a little design out of whatever lay to hand: on the bit of sand on the riverbank in front of him he set a leaf stem, a grass blade, and several pebbles. He studied them and rearranged them. "Now I must speak of harm," he said.

After a long pause he went on. "You know that a dragon

brought back our Lord Sparrowhawk, with the young king, from the shores of death. Then the dragon carried Sparrowhawk away to his home, for his power was gone, he was not a mage. So presently the Masters of Roke met to choose a new archmage, here, in the Grove, as always. But not as always.

"Before the dragon came, the Summoner too had returned from death, where he can go, where his art can take him. He had seen our lord and the young king there, in that country across the wall of stones. He said they would not come back. He said Lord Sparrowhawk had told him to come back to us, to life, to bear that word. So we grieved for our lord.

"But then came the dragon, Kalessin, bearing him living.

"The Summoner was among us when we stood on Roke Knoll and saw the Archmage kneel to King Lebannen. Then, as the dragon bore our friend away, the Summoner fell down.

"He lay as if dead, cold, his heart not beating, yet he breathed. The Herbal used all his art, but could not rouse him. 'He is dead,' he said. 'The breath will not leave him, but he is dead.' So we mourned him. Then, because there was dismay among us, and all my patterns spoke of change and danger, we met to choose a new warden of Roke, an archmage to guide us. And in our council we set the young king in the Summoner's place. To us it seemed right that he should sit among us. Only the Changer spoke against it at first, and then agreed.

"But we met, we sat, and we could not choose. We said this and said that, but no name was spoken. And then I . . ." He paused a while. "There came on me what my people call the *eduevanu*, the other breath. Words came to me and I spoke them. I said, *Hama Gondun!*— And Kurremkarmerruk told them this in Hardic: 'A woman on Gont.' But when I came back to my own wits, I could not tell them what that meant. And so we parted with no archmage chosen.

"The king left soon after, and the Master Windkey went with him. Before the king was to be crowned, they went to Gont and sought our lord Sparrowhawk, to find what that meant, 'a woman on Gont.' Eh? But they did not see him, only my countrywoman Tenar of the Ring. She said she was not the woman they sought. And they found no one, nothing. So Lebannen judged it to be a prophecy yet to be fulfilled. And in Havnor he set his crown on his own head.

"The Herbal, and I too, judged the Summoner dead. We thought the breath he breathed was left from some spell of his own art that we did not understand, like the spell snakes know that keeps their heart beating long after they are dead. Though it seemed terrible to bury a breathing body, yet he was cold, and his blood did not run, and no soul was in him. That was more terrible. So we made ready to bury him. And then, as he lay beside his grave, his eyes opened. He moved, and spoke. He said, 'I have summoned myself again into life, to do what must be done.'"

The Patterner's voice had grown rougher. He suddenly brushed the little design of pebbles apart with the palm of his hand.

"So when the Windkey returned from the king's crowning, we were nine again. But divided. For the Summoner said we must meet again and choose an archmage. The king had had no place among us, he said. And 'a woman on Gont,' whoever she may be, has no place among the men on Roke. Eh? The Windkey, the Chanter, the Changer, the Hand, say he is right. And as King Lebannen is a man returned from death, fulfilling that prophecy, they say so will the archmage be a man returned from death."

"But—" Irian said, and stopped.

After a while the Patterner said, "That art, summoning, you know, is terrible. It is always danger. Here," and he looked up into the green-gold darkness of the trees, "here is no summoning. No bringing back across the wall. No wall."

His face was a warrior's face, but when he looked into the trees it was softened, yearning.

"So," he said, "now he makes you his reason for our meeting. But I will not go to the Great House. I will not be summoned."

"He won't come here?"

"I think he will not walk in the Grove. Nor on Roke Knoll. On the Knoll, what is, is so."

She did not know what he meant, but did not ask, preoccupied: "You say he makes me his reason for you to meet together."

"Yes. To send away one woman, it takes nine mages." He very seldom smiled, and when he did it was quick and fierce. "We are to meet to uphold the Rule of Roke. And so to choose an archmage."

"If I went away—" She saw him shake his head. "I could go to the Namer—"

"You are safer here."

The idea of doing harm troubled her, but the idea of danger had not entered her mind. She found it inconceivable. "I'll be all right," she said. "So the Namer, and you—and the Doorkeeper?—"

"—do not wish Thorion to be archmage. Also the Master Herbal, though he digs and says little."

He saw Irian staring at him in amazement. "Thorion the Summoner speaks his true name," he said. "He died, eh?"

She knew that King Lebannen used his true name openly. He too had returned from death. Yet that the Summoner should do so continued to shock and disturb her as she thought about it.

"And the ... the students?"

"Divided also."

She thought about the school, where she had been so briefly. From here, under the eaves of the Grove, she saw it as stone walls enclosing one kind of being and keeping out all others, like a pen, a cage. How could any of them keep their balance in a place like that?

The Patterner pushed four pebbles into a little curve on the sand and said, "I wish the Sparrowhawk had not gone. I wish I could read what the shadows write. But all I can hear the leaves say is Change, change... Everything will change but them." He looked up into the trees again with that yearning look. The sun was setting. He stood up, bade her goodnight gently, and walked away, entering under the trees.

She sat on a while by the Thwilburn. She was troubled by what he had told her and by her thoughts and feelings in the Grove, and troubled that any thought or feeling could have troubled her there. She went to the house, set out her supper of smoked meat and bread and summer lettuce, and ate it without tasting it. She roamed restlessly back down the stream bank to the water. It was very still and warm in the late dusk, only the largest stars burning through a milky overcast. She slipped off her sandals and put her feet in the water. It was cool, but veins of sun warmth ran through it. She slid out of her clothes, the man's breeches and shirt that were all she had, and slipped naked into the water, feeling the push and stir of the current all along her body. She had never swum in the streams at Iria, and she had hated the sea, heaving grey and cold, but this quick water pleased her, tonight. She drifted and floated, her hands slipping over silken underwater rocks and her own silken flanks, her legs sliding through water weeds. All trouble and restlessness washed away from her in the running of the water, and she floated in delight in the caress of the stream, gazing up at the white, soft fire of the stars.

A chill ran through her. The water ran cold. Gathering herself together, her limbs still soft and loose, she looked up and saw on the bank above her the black figure of a man.

She stood straight up, naked, in the water.

"Get away!" she shouted. "Get away, you traitor, you foul lecher, or I'll cut the liver out of you!" She sprang up the bank, pulling herself up by the tough bunchgrass, and scrambled to her feet. No one was there. She stood afire, shaking with rage. She leapt back down the bank, found her clothes, and pulled them on, still swearing aloud—"You coward wizard! You traitorous son of a bitch!"

"Irian?"

"He was here!" she cried. "That foul heart, that Thorion!" She strode to meet the Patterner as he came into the starlight by the house. "I was bathing in the stream, and he stood there watching me!"

"A sending—only a seeming of him. It could not hurt you, Irian."

"A sending with eyes, a seeming with seeing! May he be—" She stopped, at a loss suddenly for the word. She felt sick. She shuddered, and swallowed the cold spittle that welled in her mouth.

The Patterner came forward and took her hands in his. His hands were warm, and she felt so mortally cold that she came close up against him for the warmth of his body. They stood so for a while, her face turned from him but their hands joined and their bodies pressed close. At last she broke free, straightening herself, pushing back her lank wet hair. "Thank you," she said. "I was cold."

"I know."

"I'm never cold," she said. "It was him."

"I tell you, Irian, he cannot come here, he cannot harm you here."

"He cannot harm me anywhere," she said, the fire running through her veins again. "If he tries to, I'll destroy him."

"Ah," said the Patterner.

She looked at him in the starlight, and said, "Tell me your name— Not your true name— Only a name I can call you. When I think of you."

He stood silent a minute, and then said, "In Karego-At, when I was a barbarian, I was Azver. In Hardic, that is a banner of war."

"Azver," she said. "Thank you."

She lay awake in the little house, feeling the air stifling and the ceiling pressing down on her, then slept suddenly and deeply. She woke as suddenly when the east was just getting light. She went to the door to see what she loved best to see, the sky before sunrise. Looking down from it she saw Azver the Patterner rolled up in his grey cloak, sound asleep on the ground before her doorstep. She withdrew noiselessly into the house. In a little while she saw him going back to his woods, walking a bit stiffly and scratching his head as he went, as people do when half awake.

She got to work scraping down the inner wall of the house, readying it to plaster. Just as the first sunlight struck in the window, there was a knock at her open door. Outside was the man she had thought was a gardener, the Master Herbal, looking solid and stolid, like a brown ox, beside the gaunt, grim-faced old Namer.

She came to the door and muttered some kind of greeting. They daunted her, these Masters of Roke; and also their presence meant that the peaceful time was over, the days of walking in the silent summer forest with the Patterner. That had come to an end last night. She knew it, but she did not want to know it.

"The Patterner sent for us," said the Master Herbal. He looked uncomfortable. Noticing a clump of weeds under the window, he said, "That's velver. Somebody from Havnor planted it here. Didn't know there was any on the island." He examined it attentively, and put some seed pods into his pouch.

Irian was studying the Namer covertly but equally attentively, trying to see if she could tell if he was what he had called a sending or was there in flesh and blood. Nothing about him appeared insubstantial, but she thought he was not there, and when he stepped into the slanting sunlight and cast no shadow, she knew it.

"Is it a long way from where you live, sir?" she asked.

He nodded. "Left myself halfway," he said. He looked up; the Patterner was coming towards them, wide awake now.

He greeted them and asked, "The Doorkeeper will come?"

"Said he thought he'd better keep the doors," said the Herbal. He closed his many-pocketed pouch carefully and looked around at the others. "But I don't know if he can keep a lid on the ant hill."

"What's up?" said Kurremkarmerruk. "I've been reading about dragons. Not paying attention to ants. But all the boys I had studying at the Tower left."

"Summoned," said the Herbal, drily.

"So?" said the Namer, more drily.

"I can tell you only how it seems to me," the Herbal said, reluctant, uncomfortable.

"Do that," the old mage said.

The Herbal still hesitated. "This lady is not of our council," he said at last.

"She is of mine," said Azver.

"She came to this place at this time," the Namer said. "And to this place, at this time, no one comes by chance. All any of us knows is how it seems to us. There are names behind names, my Lord Healer."

The dark-eyed mage bowed his head at that, and said, "Very well," evidently with relief at accepting their judgment over his own. "Thorion has been much with the other Masters, and with the young men. Secret meetings, inner circles. Rumors, whispers.

The younger students are frightened, and several have asked me or the Doorkeeper if they may go—leave Roke. And we'd let them go. But there's no ship in port, and none has come into Thwil Bay since the one that brought you, lady, and sailed again next day for Wathort. The Windkey keeps the Roke wind against all. If the king himself should come, he could not land on Roke."

"Until the wind changes, eh?" said the Patterner.

"Thorion says Lebannen is not truly king, since no archmage crowned him."

"Nonsense! Not history!" said the old Namer. "The first archmage came centuries after the last king. Roke ruled in the kings' stead."

"Ah," said the Patterner. "Hard for the housekeeper to give up the keys when the owner comes home. Eh?"

"The Ring of Peace is healed," said the Herbal, in his patient, troubled voice, "the prophecy is fulfilled, the son of Morred is crowned, and yet we have no peace. Where have we gone wrong? Why can we not find the balance?"

"What does Thorion intend?" asked the Namer.

"To bring Lebannen here," said the Herbal. "The young men talk of 'the true crown.' A second coronation, here. By the Archmage Thorion."

"Avert!" Irian blurted out, making the sign to prevent word from becoming deed. None of the men smiled, and the Herbal belatedly made the same gesture.

"How does he hold them all?" the Namer said. "Herbal, you were here when Sparrowhawk and Thorion were challenged by Irioth. His gift was as great as Thorion's, I think. He used it to use men, to control them wholly. Is that what Thorion does?"

"I don't know," the Herbal said. "I can only tell you that when I'm with him, when I'm in the Great House, I feel that nothing can be done but what has been done. That nothing will change. Nothing will grow. That no matter what cures I use, the sickness will end in death." He looked around at them all like a hurt ox. "And I think it is true. There is no way to regain the Equilibrium but by holding still. We have gone too far. For the Archmage and Lebannen to go bodily into death, and return—it was not right. They broke a law that must not be broken. It was to restore the law that Thorion returned."

"What, to send them back into death?" the Namer said, and the Patterner, "Who is to say what is the law?"

"There is a wall," the Herbal said.

"That wall is not as deep-rooted as my trees," said the Patterner.

"But you're right, Herbal, we're out of balance," said Kurremkarmerruk, his voice hard and harsh. "When and where did we begin to go too far? What have we forgotten, turned our back on, overlooked?"

Irian looked from one to the other.

"When the balance is wrong, holding still is not good. It must get more wrong," said the Patterner. "Until—" He made a quick gesture of reversal with his open hands, down going up and up down.

"What's more wrong than to summon oneself back from death?" said the Namer.

"Thorion was the best of us all—a brave heart, a noble mind." The Herbal spoke almost in anger. "Sparrowhawk loved him. So did we all."

"Conscience caught him," said the Namer. "Conscience told him he alone could set things right. To do it, he denied his death. So he denies life."

"And who shall stand against him?" said the Patterner. "I can only hide in my woods."

"And I in my tower," said the Namer. "And you, Herbal, and the Doorkeeper, are in the trap, in the Great House. The walls we built to keep all evil out. Or in, as the case may be."

"We are four against him," said the Patterner.

"They are five against us," said the Herbal.

"Has it come to this," the Namer said, "that we stand at the edge of the forest Segoy planted and talk of how to destroy one another?"

"Yes," said the Patterner. "What goes too long unchanged destroys itself. The forest is forever because it dies and dies and so lives. I will not let this dead hand touch me. Or touch the king who brought us hope. A promise was made, made through me. I spoke it—'A woman on Gont.' I will not see that word forgotten."

"Then should we go to Gont?" said the Herbal, caught in Azver's passion. "Sparrowhawk is there."

"Tenar of the Ring is there," said Azver.

"Maybe our hope is there," said the Namer.

They stood silent, uncertain, trying to cherish hope.

Irian stood silent too, but her hope sank down, replaced by a sense of shame and utter insignificance. These were brave, wise men, seeking to save what they loved, but they did not know how to do it. And she had no share in their wisdom, no part in their decisions. She drew away from them, and they did not notice. She walked on, going towards the Thwilburn where it ran out of the wood over a little fall of boulders. The water was bright in the morning sunlight and made a happy noise. She wanted to cry, but she had never been good at crying. She stood and watched the water, and her shame turned slowly into anger.

She came back towards the three men, and said, "Azver."

He turned to her, startled, and came forward a little.

"Why did you break your Rule for me? Was it fair to me, who can never be what you are?"

Azver frowned. "The Doorkeeper admitted you because you asked," he said. "I brought you to the Grove because the leaves of the trees spoke your name to me before you ever came here. *Irian*, they said, *Irian*. Why you came I don't know, but not by chance. The Summoner too knows that."

"Maybe I came to destroy him."

He looked at her and said nothing.

"Maybe I came to destroy Roke."

His pale eyes blazed then. "Try!"

A long shudder went through her as she stood facing him. She felt herself larger than he was, larger than she was, enormously larger. She could reach out one finger and destroy him. He stood there in his small, brave, brief humanity, his mortality, defenseless. She drew a long, long breath. She stepped back from him.

The sense of huge strength was draining out of her. She turned her head a little and looked down, surprised to see her own brown arm, her rolled-up sleeve, the grass springing cool and green around her sandaled feet. She looked back at the Patterner and he still seemed a fragile being. She pitied and honored him. She wanted to warn him of the peril he was in. But no words came to her at all. She turned round and went back to the stream bank by the little falls. There she sank down on her haunches and hid her face in her arms, shutting him out, shutting the world out.

The voices of the mages talking were like the voices of the stream running. The stream said its words and they said theirs, but none of them were the right words.

IV. Irian

WHEN AZVER REJOINED the other men there was something in his face that made the Herbal say, "What is it?"

"I don't know," he answered. "Maybe we should not leave Roke."

"Probably we can't," said the Herbal. "If the Windkey locks the winds against us..."

"I'm going back to where I am," Kurremkarmerruk said abruptly. "I don't like leaving myself about like an old shoe. I'll be here with you this evening." And he was gone.

"I'd like to walk under your trees a bit, Azver," the Herbal said, with a long sigh.

"Go on, Deyala. I'll stay here." The Herbal went off. Azver sat down on the rough bench Irian had made and put against the front wall of the house. He looked upstream at her, crouching motionless on the bank. Sheep in the field between them and the Great House blatted softly. The morning sun was getting hot.

His father had named him Banner of War. He had come west, leaving all he knew behind him. He had learned his true name from the trees of the Immanent Grove, and become the Patterner of Roke. All this year the patterns of the shadows and the branches and the roots, all the silent language of his forest, had spoken of destruction, of transgression, of all things changed. Now it was upon them, he knew. It had come with her.

She was in his charge, in his care, he had known that when he saw her. Though she came to destroy Roke, as she had said, he must serve her. He did so willingly. She had walked with him in the forest, tall, awkward, fearless; she had put aside the thorny arms of brambles with her big, careful hand. Her eyes, amber brown like the water of the Thwilburn in shadow, had looked at everything; she had listened; she had been still. He wanted to protect her and knew he could not. He had given her a little warmth when she was cold. He had nothing else to give her. Where she must go she would go. She did not understand danger. She had no wisdom but her innocence, no armor but her anger. Who are you, Irian? he said to her, watching her crouched there like an animal locked in its muteness.

The Herbal came back from the woods and sat with him a while, not speaking. In the middle of the day he went back to the Great House, agreeing to return with the Doorkeeper in the morning. They would ask all the other Masters to meet with them in the Grove. "But *he* won't come," Deyala said, and Azver nodded.

All day he stayed near the Otter's House, keeping watch on Irian, making her eat a little with him. She came to the house, but when they had eaten she went back to her place on the stream bank and sat there motionless. And he too felt a lethargy in his own body and mind, a stupidity, which he fought against but could not shake off. He thought of the Summoner's eyes, and then it was he that felt cold, cold through, though he was sitting in the full heat of the summer's day. We are ruled by the dead, he thought. The thought would not leave him.

He was grateful to see Kurremkarmerruk coming slowly down the bank of the Thwilburn from the north. The old man waded through the stream barefoot, holding his shoes in one hand and his tall staff in the other, snarling when he missed his footing on the rocks. He sat down on the near bank to dry his feet and put his shoes back on. "When I go back to the Tower," he said, "I'll ride. Hire a carter, buy a mule. I'm old, Azver."

"Come up to the house," the Patterner said, and he set out water and food for the Namer.

"Where's the girl?"

"Asleep." Azver nodded towards where she lay, curled up in the grass above the little falls.

The heat of the day was beginning to lessen and the shadows of the Grove lay across the grass, though the Otter's House was still in sunlight. Kurremkarmerruk sat on the bench with his back against the house wall, and Azver on the doorstep.

"We've come to the end of it," the old man said out of silence.

Azver nodded, in silence.

"What brought you here, Azver?" the Namer asked. "I've often thought of asking you. A long, long way to come. And you have no wizards in the Kargish lands."

"No. But we have the things wizardry is made of. Water, stones, trees, words . . ."

"But not the words of the Making."

"No. Nor dragons."

"Never?"

"Only in old tales from the farthest east, from the desert of Hur-at-Hur. Before the gods were. Before men were. Before men were men, they were dragons."

"Now that is interesting," said the old scholar, sitting up straighter. "I told you I've been reading about dragons. You know these rumors of them flying over the Inmost Sea as far east as Gont. That was no doubt Kalessin taking Ged home, multiplied by sailors making a good story better. But a boy here swore to me that his whole village had seen dragons flying, this spring, west of Mount Onn. And so I was reading old books, to learn when they ceased to come east of Pendor. And in an old Pelnish scroll, I came on your story, or something like it. That men and dragons were all one kind, but they quarreled. Some went west and some east, and they became two kinds, and forgot they were ever one."

"We went farthest east," Azver said. "But do you know what the leader of an army is, in my tongue?"

"*Edran*," said the Namer promptly, and laughed. "Drake. Dragon . . ."

After a while he said, "I could chase an etymology on the brink of doom . . . But I think, Azver, that that's where we are. We won't defeat him."

"He has the advantage," Azver said, very dry.

"He does. But, admitting it unlikely, admitting it impossible—if we did defeat him—if he went back into death and left us here alive—what would we do? What comes next?"

After a long time, Azver said, "I have no idea."

"Your leaves and shadows tell you nothing?"

"Change, change," said the Patterner. "Transformation."

He looked up suddenly. The sheep, who had been grouped near the stile, were scurrying off, and someone was coming along the path from the Great House.

"A group of young men," said the Herbal, breathless, as he came to them. "Thorion's army. Coming here. To take the girl. To send her away." He stood and drew breath. "The Doorkeeper was speaking with them when I left. I think—"

"Here he is," said Azver, and the Doorkeeper was there, his smooth, yellow-brown face tranquil as ever.

"I told them," he said, "that if they went out Medra's Gate this day, they'd never go back through it into a house they knew. Some of them were for turning back, then. But the Windkey and the Chanter urged them on. They'll be along soon."

They could hear men's voices in the fields east of the Grove.

Azver went quickly to where Irian lay beside the stream, and the others followed him. She roused up and got to her feet, looking dull and dazed. They were standing around her, a kind of guard, when the group of thirty or more men came past the little house and approached them. They were mostly older students; there were five or six wizard's staffs among the crowd, and the Master Windkey led them. His thin, keen old face looked strained and weary, but he greeted the four mages courteously by their titles.

They greeted him, and Azver took the word— "Come into

the Grove, Master Windkey," he said, "and we will wait there for the others of the Nine."

"First we must settle the matter that divides us," said the Windkey.

"That is a stony matter," said the Namer.

"The woman with you defies the Rule of Roke," the Windkey said. "She must leave. A boat is waiting at the dock to take her, and the wind, I can tell you, will stand fair for Way."

"I have no doubt of that, my lord," said Azver, "but I doubt she will go."

"My Lord Patterner, will you defy our Rule and our community, that has been one so long, upholding order against the forces of ruin? Will it be you, of all men, who break the pattern?"

"It is not glass, to break," Azver said. "It is breath, it is fire."

It cost him a great effort to speak.

"It does not know death," he said, but he spoke in his own language, and they did not understand him. He drew closer to Irian. He felt the warmth of her body. She stood staring, in that animal silence, as if she did not understand any of them.

"Lord Thorion has returned from death to save us all," the Windkey said, fiercely and clearly. "He will be Archmage. Under his rule Roke will be as it was. The king will receive the true crown from his hand, and rule with his guidance, as Morred ruled. No witches will defile sacred ground. No dragons will threaten the Inmost Sea. There will be order, safety, and peace."

None of the four mages with Irian answered him. In the silence, the men with him murmured, and a voice among them said, "Let us have the witch."

"No," Azver said, but could say nothing else. He held his staff of willow, but it was only wood in his hand.

Of the four of them, only the Doorkeeper moved and spoke. He took a step forward, looking from one young man to the next and the next. He said, "You trusted me, giving me your names. Will you trust me now?"

"My lord," said one of them with a fine, dark face and a wizard's oaken staff, "we do trust you, and therefore ask you to let the witch go, and peace return."

Irian stepped forward before the Doorkeeper could answer.

"I am not a witch," she said. Her voice sounded high, metallic, after the men's deep voices. "I have no art. No knowledge. I came to learn."

"We do not teach women here," said the Windkey. "You know that."

"I know nothing," Irian said. She took another step forward, facing the mage directly. "Tell me who I am."

"Learn your place, woman," the mage said with cold passion.

"My place," she said, slowly, the words dragging—"my place is on the hill. Where things are what they are. Tell the dead man I will meet him there."

The Windkey stood silent. The group of men muttered, angry, and some of them moved forward. Azver came between her and them, her words releasing him from the paralysis of mind and body that had held him. "Tell Thorion we will meet him on Roke Knoll," he said. "When he comes, we will be there. Now come with me," he said to Irian.

The Namer, the Doorkeeper, and the Herbal followed him with her into the Grove. There was a path for them. But when some of the young men started after them, there was no path.

"Come back," the Windkey said to the young men.

They turned back, uncertain. The low sun was still bright on the fields and the roofs of the Great House, but inside the wood it was all shadows.

"Witchery," they said, "sacrilege, defilement."

"Best come away," said the Master Windkey, his face set and

somber, his keen eyes troubled. He set off back to the school, and they straggled after him, arguing and debating in frustration and anger.

They were not far inside the Grove, and still beside the stream, when Irian stopped, turned aside, and crouched down by the enormous, hunching roots of a willow that leaned out over the water. The four mages stood on the path.

"She spoke with the other breath," Azver said.

The Namer nodded.

"So we must follow her?" the Herbal asked.

This time the Doorkeeper nodded. He smiled faintly and said, "So it would seem."

"Very well," said the Herbal, with his patient, troubled look; and he went aside a little, and knelt to look at some small plant or fungus on the forest floor.

Time passed as always in the Grove, not passing at all it seemed, yet gone, the day gone quietly by in a few long breaths, a quivering of leaves, a bird singing far off and another answering it from even farther. Irian stood up slowly. She did not speak, but looked down the path, and then walked down it. The four men followed her.

They came out into the calm, open evening air. The west still held some brightness as they crossed the Thwilburn and walked across the fields to Roke Knoll, which stood up before them in a high dark curve against the sky.

"They're coming," the Doorkeeper said. Men were coming through the gardens and up the path from the Great House, the five mages, many students. Leading them was Thorion the Summoner, tall in his grey cloak, carrying his tall staff of bone-white wood, about which a faint gleam of werelight hovered.

Where the two paths met and joined to wind up to the

heights of the Knoll, Thorion stopped and stood waiting for them. Irian strode forward to face him.

"Irian of Way," the Summoner said in his deep, clear voice, "that there may be peace and order, and for the sake of the balance of all things, I bid you now leave this island. We cannot give you what you ask, and for that we ask your forgiveness. But if you seek to stay here you forfeit forgiveness, and must learn what follows on transgression."

She stood up, almost as tall as he, and as straight. She said nothing for a minute and then spoke out in a high, harsh voice. "Come up onto the hill, Thorion," she said.

She left him standing at the waymeet, on level ground, and walked up the hill path for a little way, a few strides. She turned and looked back down at him. "What keeps you from the hill?" she said.

The air was darkening around them. The west was only a dull red line, the eastern sky was shadowy above the sea.

The Summoner looked up at Irian. Slowly he raised his arms and the white staff in the invocation of a spell, speaking in the tongue that all the wizards and mages of Roke had learned, the language of their art, the Language of the Making: "Irian, by your name I summon you and bind you to obey me!"

She hesitated, seeming for a moment to yield, to come to him, and then cried out, "I am not only Irian!"

At that the Summoner ran up towards her, reaching out, lunging at her as if to seize and hold her. They were both on the hill now. She towered above him impossibly, fire breaking forth between them, a flare of red flame in the dusk air, a gleam of red-gold scales, of vast wings—then that was gone, and there was nothing there but the woman standing on the hill path and the tall man bowing down before her, bowing slowly down to earth, and lying on it.

Of them all it was the Herbal, the healer, who was the first to move. He went up the path and knelt down by Thorion. "My lord," he said, "my friend."

Under the huddle of the grey cloak his hands found only a huddle of clothes and dry bones and a broken staff.

"This is better, Thorion," he said, but he was weeping.

The old Namer came forward and said to the woman on the hill, "Who are you?"

"I do not know my other name," she said. She spoke as he had spoken, as she had spoken to the Summoner, in the Language of the Making, the tongue the dragons speak.

She turned away and began to walk on up the hill.

"Irian," said Azver the Patterner, "will you come back to us?"

She halted and let him come up to her. "I will, if you call me," she said.

She reached out and touched his hand. He drew his breath sharply.

"Where will you go?" he said.

"To those who will give me my name. In fire, not water. My people."

"In the west," he said.

She said, "Beyond the west."

She turned away from him and them and went on up the hill in the gathering darkness. As she went farther from them they saw her, all of them, the great gold-mailed flanks, the spiked, coiling tail, the talons, the breath that was bright fire. On the crest of the knoll she paused a while, her long head turning to look slowly round the Isle of Roke, gazing longest at the Grove, only a blur of darkness in darkness now. Then with a rattle like the shaking of sheets of brass the wide, vaned wings opened and the dragon sprang up into the air, circled Roke Knoll once, and flew.

A curl of fire, a wisp of smoke drifted down through the dark air.

Azver the Patterner stood with his left hand holding his right hand, which her touch had burnt. He looked down at the men, who stood silent at the foot of the hill, staring after the dragon. "Well, my friends," he said, "what now?"

Only the Doorkeeper answered. He said, "I think we should go to our house, and open its doors."

A Description
of Earthsea

Peoples and Languages

People

The Hardic Lands

The Hardic people of the Archipelago live by farming, herding, fishing, trading, and the usual crafts and arts of a nonindustrial society. Their population is stable and has never overcrowded the limited habitable land available to them. Famine is unknown and poverty seldom acute.

Small islands and villages are generally governed by a more or less democratic council or Parley, headed, or represented in dealings with other groups, by an elected Isleman or Islewoman. In the Reaches there is often no government other than the Isle Parley and the Town Parleys. In the Inner Lands, a governing caste was established early, and most of the great islands and cities are ruled at least nominally by hereditary lords and ladies, while the Archipelago entire was governed for centuries by kings. Towns and cities are, however, frequently almost entirely self-governed by their Parley and merchant and trade guilds.

The great guilds, since their network covers all the Inner Lands, answer to no overlord or authority except the King in Havnor.

Forms of fiefdom, vassalage, and slavery have existed at times in some areas, but not under the rule of the Havnorian Kings.

The existence of magic as a recognised, effective power wielded by certain individuals, but not by all, shapes and influences all the institutions of the Hardic peoples, so that, much as ordinary life in the Archipelago seems to resemble that of nonindustrial peoples elsewhere, there are almost immeasurable differences. One of these differences may be, or may be indicated by, the lack of any kind of institutionalised religion. Superstition is as common as it is anywhere, but there are no gods, no cults, no formal worship of any kind. Ritual occurs only in traditional offerings at the sites of the Old Powers, in the great, universally celebrated annual festivals such as Sunreturn and the Long Dance, in the speaking and singing of the traditional songs and epics at these festivals, and, perhaps, in the performance of spells of magic.

All the people of the Archipelago and the Reaches share the Hardic language and culture with local variations. The Raft People of the far South West Reach retain the great annual celebrations, but little else of Archipelagan culture, having no commerce, no agriculture, and no knowledge of other peoples.

Most people of the Archipelago have brown or red-brown skin, black straight hair, and dark eyes; the predominant body type is short, slender, small-boned, but fairly muscular and well-fleshed. In the East and South Reaches people tend to be taller, heavier boned, and darker. Many Southerners have very dark brown skin. Most Archipelagan men have little or no facial hair.

The people of Osskil, Rogma, and Borth are lighter-skinned than others in the Archipelago, and often have brown or even blond hair and light eyes; the men are often bearded. Their language and some of their beliefs are closer to Kargish than to Hardic. These far Northerners probably descend from Kargs who, after settling the four great Eastern lands, sailed back to the West about two thousand years ago.

THE KARGAD LANDS

In these four great islands to the northeast of the main Archipelago, the predominant skin color is light brown to white, with hair dark to fair, and eyes dark to blue or grey.

Not much mixing of the Kargish and Archipelagan skin-color types has taken place except on Osskil, since the North Reach is isolated and thinly populated, and the Kargad people have held themselves apart from and often in enmity towards the Archipelagans for two or three millennia.

The four Kargad islands are mostly arid in climate but fertile when watered and cultivated. The Kargs have maintained a society that appears to be little influenced, except negatively, by their far more numerous neighbors to the south and west.

Among the Kargs the power of magic appears to be very rare as a native gift, perhaps because it was neglected or actively suppressed by their society and government. Except as an evil to be dreaded and shunned, magic plays no recognised part in their society. This inability or refusal to practice magic puts the Kargs at a disadvantage with the Archipelagans in almost every respect, which may explain why they have generally held themselves aloof from trade or any kind of interchange, other than piratical raids and invasions of the nearer islands of the South Reach and around the Gontish Sea.

DRAGONS

Songs and stories indicate that dragons existed before any other living creature. The Old Hardic kennings or euphemisms for the word *dragon* are Firstborn, Eldest, Elder Children. (The words for the firstborn child of a family in Osskilian, *akhad*, and in Kargish, *gadda*, are derived from the word *haath*, "dragon," in the Old Speech.)

Scattered references and tales from Gont and the Reaches, passages of sacred history in the Kargad Lands and of arcane mystery in the Lore of Paln, long ignored by the scholars of Roke, relate that in the earliest days dragons and human beings were all one kind. Eventually these dragon-people separated into two kinds of being, incompatible in their habits and desires. Perhaps a long geographical separation caused a gradual natural divergence, a differentiation of species. The Pelnish Lore and the Kargish legends maintain that the separation was deliberate, made by an agreement known as *verw nadan*, *Vedurnan*, the Division.

These legends are best preserved in Hur-at-Hur, the easternmost of the Kargad Lands, where dragons have degenerated into animals without high intelligence. Yet it is in Hur-at-Hur that people keep the most vivid conviction of the original kinship of human and dragon kind. And with these tales of ancient times come stories of recent days about dragons who take human form, humans who take dragon form, beings who are in fact both human and dragon.

However the Division came about, from the beginning of historical time human beings have lived in the main Archipelago and the Kargad Lands east of it, while the dragons kept to the westernmost isles—and beyond. People have puzzled at their choosing the empty sea for their domain, since dragons are "creatures of wind and fire," who drown if plunged under the sea. But they have no need to touch down either on water or on earth; they live on the wing, aloft in air, sunlight, starlight. The only use a dragon has for the ground is some kind of rocky place where it can lay its eggs and rear the drakelets. The small, barren islets of the farthest West Reach suffice for this.

The Creation of Éa contains no clear references to an original unity and eventual separation of dragons and humans, but this may be because the poem in its presumed original form, in the Language of the Making, dated back to a time before the separation. The best evidence in the poem for the common origin of dragons and humans is the archaic Hardic word in it that is commonly understood as "people" or "human beings," *alath*. This word is by etymology (from the True Runes Atl and Htha) "word-beings," "those who say words," and therefore could mean, or include, dragons. Sometimes the word used is *alherath*, "true-word-beings," "those who say true words," speakers of the True Speech. This could mean human wizards, or dragons, or both. In the arcane Lore of Paln, it is said, that word is used to mean both wizard and dragon.

Dragons are born knowing the True Speech, or, as Ged put it, "the dragon and the speech of the dragon are one." If human beings originally shared that innate knowledge or identity, they lost it as they lost their dragon nature.

LANGUAGES

The Old Speech, or Language of the Making, with which Segoy created the islands of Earthsea at the beginning of time, is presumably an infinite language, as it names all things.

This language is innate to dragons, not to humans, as said above. There are exceptions. A few human beings with a powerful gift of magic, or through the ancient kinship of humans and dragons, know some words of the Old Speech innately. But the very great majority of people must learn the Old Speech. Hardic practitioners of the art magic learn it from their teachers. Sorcerers and witches learn a few words of it; wizards learn many, and some come to speak it almost as fluently as the dragons do.

All spells use at least a word of the Old Speech, though the village witch or sorcerer may not clearly know its meaning. Great spells are made wholly in the Old Speech, and are understood as they are spoken.

The Hardic language of the Archipelago, the Osskili tongue of Osskil, and the Kargish tongue, are all remote descendants of the Old Speech. None of these languages serves for the making of spells of magic.

The people of the Archipelago speak Hardic. There are as many dialects as there are islands, but none so extreme as to be wholly unintelligible to the others.

Osskili, spoken in Osskil and two islands northwest of it, has more affinities to Kargish than to Hardic. Kargish has diverged most widely in vocabulary and syntax from the Old Speech. Most of its speakers (like most Hardic speakers) do not realise that their languages have a common ancestry. Archipelagan scholars are aware of it, but most Kargs would deny it, since they have confused Hardic with the Old Speech, in which spells are cast, and thus fear and despise all Archipelagan speech as malevolent sorcery.

WRITING

Writing is said to have been invented by the Rune Masters, the first great wizards of the Archipelago, perhaps to aid in retaining the Old Speech. The dragons have no writing.

There are two entirely different kinds of writing in Earthsea: the True Runes and runic writing.

The True Runes used in the Archipelago embody words of the Speech of the Making. True Runes are not symbols only, but reifactors: they can be used to bring a thing or condition into being or bring about an event. To write such a rune is to act. The power of the action varies with the circumstances. Most of the True Runes are found only in ancient texts and lore-books, and used only by wizards trained in their use; but a good many of them, such as the symbol written on the door lintel to protect a house from fire, are in common use, familiar to unlearned people.

Long after the invention of the True Runes, a related but nonmagical runic writing was developed for the Hardic language. This writing does not affect reality any more than any writing does; that is to say, indirectly, but considerably.

It is said that Segoy first wrote the True Runes in fire on the wind, so that they are coeval with the Language of the Making. But this may not be so, since the dragons do not use them, and if they recognise them, do not admit it.

Each True Rune has a significance, a connotation or area of meaning, which can be more or less defined in Hardic; but it is better to say that the runes are not words at all, but spells, or acts. Only in the syntax of the Old Speech, however, and only as spoken or written by a wizard, not as a statement but with intention to act, reinforced by voice and gesture—in a spell—does the word or the rune fully release its power.

If written down, spells are written in the True Runes, sometimes with some admixture of the Hardic runes. To write in the True Runes, as to speak the Old Speech, is to guarantee the truth of what one says—if one is human. Human beings cannot lie in that language. Dragons can; or so the dragons say; and if they are lying, does that not prove that what they say is true?

The spoken name of a True Rune may be the word it signifies in the Old Speech, or it may be one of the connotations of the rune translated into Hardic. The names of commonly used runes such as Pirr (used to protect from fire, wind, and madness), Sifl ("speed well"), Simn ("work well") are used without ceremony by ordinary people speaking Hardic; but practitioners of magic speak even such well-known, often used names with caution, since they are in fact words in the Old Speech, and may influence events in unintended or unexpected ways.

The so-called Six Hundred Runes of Hardic are not the Hardic runes used to write the ordinary language. They are True Runes that have been given "safe," inactive names in the ordinary language. Their true names in the Old Speech must be memorised in silence. The ambitious student of wizardry will go on to learn the "Further Runes," the "Runes of Éa," and many others. If the Old Speech is endless, so are the runes.

Ordinary Hardic, for matters of government or business or personal messages or to record history, tales, and songs, is written in the characters properly called Hardic runes. Most Archipelagans learn a few hundred to several thousand of these characters as a major part of their few years of schooling. Spoken or written, Hardic is useless for casting spells.

LITERATURE AND THE SOURCES OF HISTORY

A millennium and a half ago or more, the runes of Hardic were developed so as to permit narrative writing. From that time on, *The Creation* of Éa, *The Winter Carol*, the Deeds, the Lays, and the Songs, all of which began as sung or spoken texts, were written down and preserved as texts. They continue to exist in both forms. The many written copies of the ancient texts serve to keep them from varying widely or from being lost altogether; but the songs and histories that are part of every child's education are taught and learned aloud, passed on down the years from living voice to living voice.

Old Hardic differs in vocabulary and pronunciation from the current speech, but the rote learning and regular speaking and hearing of the classics keeps the archaic language meaningful (and probably puts some brake on linguistic drift in daily speech), while the Hardic runes, like Chinese characters, can accommodate widely varying pronunciations and shifts of meaning.

Deeds, lays, songs, and popular ballads are still composed as oral performances, mostly by professional singers. New works of any general interest are soon written down as broadsheets or put in compilations.

Whether performed or read silently, all such poems and songs are consciously valued for their content, not for their literary qualities, which range from high to nil. Loose regular meter, alliteration, stylised phrasing, and structuring by repetition are the principal poetic devices. Content includes mythic, epic, and historical narrative, geographical descriptions, practical observations concerning nature, agriculture, sea lore, and crafts, cautionary tales and parables, philosophical, visionary, and spiritual poetry, and love songs. The deeds and lays are usually chanted, the ballads sung, often with a percussion accompaniment; professional chanters and singers may sing with the harp, the viol, drums, and other instruments. The songs generally have less narrative content, and many are valued and preserved mostly for the tune.

Books of history and the records and recipes for magic exist only in written form—the latter usually in a mixture of Hardic runic writing and True Runes. Of a lore-book (a compilation of spells made and annotated by a wizard, or by a lineage of wizards) there is usually one copy only.

It is often a matter of considerable importance that the words of these lore-books *not* be spoken aloud.

The Osskili use the Hardic runes to write their language, since they trade mostly with Hardic-speaking lands.

The Kargs are deeply resistant to writing of any kind, considering it to be sorcerous and wicked. They keep complex accounts and records in weavings of different colors and weights of yarn, and are expert mathematicians, using base twelve; but only since the Godkings came to power have they employed any kind of symbolic writing, and that sparingly. Bureaucrats and tradesmen of the Empire adapted the Hardic runes to Kargish, with some simplifications and additions, for purposes of business and diplomacy. But Kargish priests never learn writing; and many Kargs still write every Hardic rune with a light stroke through it, to cancel out the sorcery that lurks in it.

History

Note on dates: Many islands have their own local count of years. The most widely used dating system in the Archipelago, which stems from the Havnorian Tale, *makes the year Morred took the throne the first year of history. By this system, "present time" in the account you are reading is the Archipelagan year 1058.*

THE BEGINNINGS

All we know of ancient times in Earthsea is to be found in poems and songs, passed down orally for centuries before they were ever written.

The Creation of Éa, the oldest and most sacred poem, is at least two thousand years old in the Hardic language; its original version may have existed millennia before that. Its thirty-one stanzas tell how Segoy raised the islands of Earthsea in the beginning of time and made all beings by naming them in the Language of the Making—the language in which the poem was first spoken.

The ocean, however, is older than the islands; so say the songs.

> *Before bright Éa was, before Segoy*
> *bade the islands be,*
> *the wind of dawn blew on the sea . . .*

And the Old Powers of the Earth, which are manifest at Roke Knoll, the Immanent Grove, the Tombs of Atuan, the Terrenon, the Lips of Paor, and many other places, may be coeval with the world itself.

It may be that Segoy is or was one of the Old Powers of the Earth. It may be that Segoy is a name for the Earth itself. Some think all dragons, or certain dragons, or certain people, are manifestations of Segoy. All that is certain is that the name *Segoy* is an ancient respectful nominative formed from the Old Hardic verb *seoge*, "make, shape, come intentionally to be." From the same root comes the noun *esege*, "creative force, breath, poetry."

The Creation of Éa is the foundation of education in the Archipelago. By the age of six or seven, all children have heard the poem and most have begun to memorise it. An adult who doesn't know it by heart, so as to be able to speak or sing it with others and teach it to children, is considered grossly ignorant. It is taught in winter and spring, and spoken and sung entire every year at the Long Dance, the celebration of the solstice of summer.

A quotation from it stands at the head of *A Wizard of Earthsea*:

> *Only in silence the word,*
> *only in dark the light,*
> *only in dying life:*
> *bright the hawk's flight*
> *on the empty sky.*

The beginning of the first stanza is quoted in *Tehanu*:

> *The making from the unmaking,*
> *the ending from the beginning,*
> *who shall know surely?*
> *What we know is the doorway between them*

> *that we enter departing.*
> *Among all beings ever returning,*
> *the eldest, the Doorkeeper, Segoy . . .*

and the last line of the first stanza:

> *Then from the foam bright Éa broke.*

History of the Archipelago

The Kings of Enlad

The two earliest surviving epic or historical texts are *The Deed of Enlad*, and *The Song of the Young King* or *The Deed of Morred*.

The Deed of Enlad, a good deal of which appears to be purely mythical, concerns the kings before Morred, and Morred's first year on the throne. The capital city of these rulers was Berila, on the island of Enlad.

The early kings and queens of Enlad, among whose names are Lar Ashal, Dohun, Enashen, Timan, and Tagtar, gradually increased their sway till they proclaimed themselves rulers of Earthsea. Their reign extended no farther south than Ilien and did not include Felkway in the east, Paln and Semel in the west, or Osskil in the north, but they did send explorers out all over the Inmost Sea and into the Reaches. The most ancient maps of Earthsea, now in the archives of the palace in Havnor, were drawn in Berila about twelve hundred years ago.

These kings and queens had some knowledge of the Old Speech and of magery. Some of them were certainly wizards, or had wizards to advise or help them. But magic in *The Deed of Enlad* is an erratic force, not to be relied on. Morred was the first man, and the first king, to be called Mage.

Morred

The Song of the Young King, sung annually at Sunreturn, the festival of the winter solstice, tells the story of Morred, called the Mage-King, the

White Enchanter, and the Young King. Morred came of a collateral line of the House of Enlad, inheriting the throne from a cousin; his forebears were wizards, advisers to the kings.

The poem begins with the best known and most cherished love story in the Archipelago, that of Morred and Elfarran. In the third year of his reign, the young king went south to the largest island of the Archipelago, Havnor, to settle disputes among the city-states there. Returning in his "oarless longship," he came to the island Soléa and there saw Elfarran, the Islewoman or Lady of Soléa, "in the orchards in the spring." He did not continue on to Enlad, but stayed with Elfarran. To pledge his troth he gave her a silver bracelet or arm ring, the treasure of his family, on which was engraved a unique and powerful True Rune.

Morred and Elfarran married, and the poem describes their reign as a brief golden age, the foundation and touchstone of ethic and governance thereafter.

Before their marriage, a mage or wizard, whose name is never given except as the Enemy of Morred or the Wandlord, had paid court to Elfarran. Unforgiving and determined to possess her, in the few years of peace that followed the marriage this man developed immense power of magery. After five years he came forth and announced, in the words of the poem,

> If Elfarran be not my own, I will unsay Segoy's word,
> I will unmake the islands, the white waves will whelm all.

He had power to raise huge waves on the sea, and to stop the tide or bring it early; and his voice could enchant whole populations, bringing all who heard him under his control. So he turned Morred's people against him. Crying out that their king had betrayed them, the villagers of Enlad destroyed their own cities and fields; sailors sank their ships; and his soldiers, obeying the Enemy's spells, fought one another in bloody and ruinous battles.

While Morred sought to free his people from these spells and to confront his enemy, Elfarran returned with their year-old child to her native island, Soléa, where her own powers would be strongest. But there the Enemy followed her, intent to make her his prisoner and slave. She took refuge at the Springs of Ensa, where, with her knowledge of the Old Powers of the place, she could withstand the Enemy and force him off the island. "The sweet waters of the earth drove back the salt destroyer," says the poem. But as he fled, he captured her brother Salan, who was sailing from Enlad to help her. Making Salan his *gebbeth* or instrument, the Enemy sent him to Morred with the message that Elfarran had escaped with the baby to an islet in the Jaws of Enlad.

Trusting the messenger, Morred entered the trap. He barely escaped with his life. The Enemy pursued him from the east to the west of Enlad in a trail of ruin. On the Plains of Enlad, meeting the companions who had stayed loyal to him, most of them sailors who had brought their ships to Enlad to aid him, Morred turned and gave battle. The Enemy would not confront him directly, but sent Morred's own spell-bound warriors to fight him, and worse, sent sorceries that shriveled up the bodies of his men till they "living, seemed the black thirst-dead of the desert." To spare his people, Morred withdrew.

As he left the battlefield it began to rain, and he saw his enemy's true name written in raindrops in the dust.

Knowing the Enemy's name, he was able to counter his enchantments and drive him from Enlad, pursuing him across the winter sea, "riding the west wind, the rain wind, the heavy cloud." Each had met his match, and in their final confrontation, somewhere in the Sea of Éa, both perished.

In the rage of his agony the Enemy raised up a great wave and sent it speeding to overwhelm the island of Soléa. Elfarran knew this, as she knew the moment of Morred's death. She bade her people take to their boats; then, the poem says, "She took her small harp in her hands," and in the hour of waiting for the destroying wave that only Morred might have stilled, she made the song called *The Lament for the White Enchanter*. The island was drowned beneath the sea, and Elfarran with it. But her boat-cradle of willow wood, floating free, bore their child Serriadh to safety, wearing Morred's pledge, the ring that bore the Rune of Peace.

On maps of the Archipelago, the island Soléa is signified by a white space or a whirlpool.

After Morred, seven more kings and queens ruled from Enlad, and the realm increased steadily in size and prosperity.

THE KINGS OF HAVNOR

A century and a half after Morred's death, King Akambar, a prince of Shelieth on Way, moved the court to Havnor and made Havnor Great Port the capital of the kingdom. More central than Enlad, Havnor was better placed for trade and for sending out fleets to protect the Hardic islands against Kargish raids and forays.

The history of the Fourteen Kings of Havnor (actually six kings and eight queens, ~150–400) is told in the *Havnorian Lay*. Tracing descent both through the male and the female lines, and intermarrying with various noble houses of the Archipelago, the royal house embraced five principalities: the House of Enlad, the oldest, tracing direct descent from Morred and Serriadh; the Houses of Shelieth, Éa, and Havnor; and lastly the House of Ilien. Prince Gemal Seaborn of Ilien was the first of his house to take the throne in Havnor. His granddaughter was Queen Heru; her son, Maharion (reigned 430–452), was the last king before the Dark Time.

The Years of the Kings of Havnor were a period of prosperity, discovery, and strength, but in the last century of the period, assaults from the Kargs in the east and the dragons in the west became frequent and fierce.

Kings, lords, and Islemen charged with defending the islands of the Archipelago came to rely increasingly on wizards to fend off dragons and Kargish fleets. In the *Havnorian Lay* and *The Deed of the Dragonlords*, as the tale goes on, the names and exploits of these wizards begin to eclipse those of the kings.

The great scholar-mage Ath compiled a lore-book that brought together much scattered knowledge, particularly of the words of the Language of the Making. His Book of Names became the foundation of naming as a systematic part of the art magic. Ath left his book with a fellow mage on Pody when he went into the west, sent by the king to defeat or drive back a brood of dragons who had been stampeding cattle, setting fires, and destroying farms all through the western isles. Somewhere west of Ensmer, Ath confronted the great dragon Orm. Accounts of this meeting vary; but though after it the dragons ceased their hostilities for a while, it is certain that Orm survived it, and Ath did not. His book, lost for centuries, is now in the Isolate Tower on Roke.

The food of dragons is said to be light, or fire; they kill in rage, to defend their young, or for sport, but never eat their kill. Since time immemorial, until the reign of Heru, they had used only the outmost isles of the West Reach—which may have been the easternmost borders of their own realm—for meeting and breeding, and had seldom even been seen by most of the islanders. Naturally irritable and arrogant, the dragons may have felt threatened by the increasing population and prosperity of the Inner Lands, which brought constant boat traffic even out in the West Reach. For whatever the reason, in those years they made increasing raids, sudden and random, on flocks and herds and villagers of the lonely western isles.

A tale of the *Vedurnan* or Division, known in Hur-at-Hur, says:

> *Men chose the yoke,*
> *dragons the wing.*
> *Men to own,*
> *dragons no thing.*

That is, human beings chose to have possessions and dragons chose not to. But, as there are ascetics among humans, some dragons are greedy for shining things, gold, jewels; one was Yevaud, who sometimes came among people in human form, and who made the rich Isle of Pendor into a dragon nursery, until driven back into the west by Ged. But the marauding dragons of the *Lay* and the songs seem to have been moved not so much by greed as by anger, a sense of having been cheated, betrayed.

The deeds and lays that tell of raids by dragons and counterforays by wizards portray the dragons as pitiless as any wild animal, terrifying, unpredictable, yet intelligent, sometimes wiser than the wizards. Though they speak the True Speech, they are endlessly devious. Some of them clearly enjoy battles of wits with wizards, "splitting arguments with a forked tongue." Like human beings, all but the greatest of them conceal their true names. In the lay *Hasa's Voyage*, the dragons appear as formidable but feeling beings, whose anger at the invading human fleet is justified by their love of their own desolate domain. They address the hero:

> Sail home to the houses of the sunrise, Hasa.
> Leave to our wings the long winds of the west,
> leave us the air-sea, the unknown, the utmost...

MAHARION AND ERRETH-AKBE

Queen Heru, called the Eagle, inherited the throne from her father, Denggemal of the House of Ilien. Her consort Aiman was of the House of Morred. When she had ruled thirty years she gave the crown to their son Maharion.

Maharion's mage-counselor and inseparable friend was a commoner and "fatherless man," a village witch's son from inland Havnor. The most beloved hero of the Archipelago, his story is told in *The Deed of Erreth-Akbe*, which bards sing at the Long Dance of midsummer.

Erreth-Akbe's gifts in magic became apparent when he was still a boy. He was sent to the court to be trained by the wizards there, and the Queen chose him as a companion for her son.

Maharion and Erreth-Akbe became "heart's brothers." They spent ten years together fighting the Kargs, whose occasional forays from the East had in recent times become a slave-taking, colonising invasion. Venway, Torheven and the Torikles, Spevy, Perregal, and parts of Gont were under Kargish dominion for a generation or longer. At Shelieth on Way, Erreth-Akbe worked a great magic against the Kargish forces, who had landed in "a thousand ships" on Waymarsh and were swarming across the mainland. Using an invocation of the Old Powers called the Waterlore (perhaps the same that Elfarran had used on Soléa against the Enemy), he turned the waters of the Fountains of Shelieth—sacred springs and pools in the gardens of the Lords of Way—into a flood that swept the invaders back to the seacoast, where Maharion's army awaited them. No ship of the fleet returned to Karego-At.

Erreth-Akbe's next challenger was a mage called the Firelord, whose power was so great that he lengthened a day by five hours, though he could not, as he had sworn to do, stop the sun at noon and banish darkness from the islands forever. The Firelord took dragon form to fight Erreth-Akbe, but was defeated at last, at the cost of the forests and cities of Ilien, which he set afire as he fought.

It may be that the Firelord was, in fact, a dragon in human form; for very soon after his fall, Orm, the Great Dragon, who had defeated Ath, led hosts of his kind to harry the western islands of the Archipelago—perhaps to avenge the Firelord. These fiery flights caused great terror, and hundreds of boats carried people fleeing from Paln and Semel to the Inner Islands; but the dragons were not doing as much damage as the Kargs, and Maharion judged the urgent danger lay in the east. While he himself went west to fight dragons, he sent Erreth-Akbe east to try to establish peace with the King of the Kargad Lands.

Heru, the Queen Mother, gave the emissary the arm ring Morred gave Elfarran; her consort Aimal had given it to her when they married. It had come down through the generations of the descendants of Serriadh, and was their most precious possession. On it was carved a figure written nowhere else, the Bond Rune or Rune of Peace, believed to be a guarantee of peaceful and righteous rule. "Let the Kargish king wear Morred's ring," the Queen Mother said. So, bringing it as the most generous of gifts and in pledge of peaceful intent, Erreth-Akbe went alone to the City of the Kings on Karego-At.

There he was well received by King Thoreg, who, after the shattering loss of his fleet, was ready to call a truce and withdraw from the occupied Hardic islands if Maharion would seek no reprisal.

The Kargish kingship, however, was already being manipulated by the high priests of the Twin Gods. Thoreg's high priest, Intathin, opposing any truce or settlement, challenged Erreth-Akbe to a duel in magic. Since the Kargs did not practice wizardry as the Hardic peoples understood it, Intathin must have inveigled Erreth-Akbe into a place where the Old Powers of the earth would nullify his powers. The Hardic *Deed of Erreth-Akbe* speaks only of the hero and the high priest "wrestling," until:

> *the weakness of the old darkness came into Erreth-Akbe's limbs,*
> *the silence of the mother darkness into his mind.*
> *Long he lay, forgetful of bright fame and brotherhood,*
> *long, and on his breast lay the rune-ring broken.*

The daughter of "the wise king Thoreg" rescued Erreth-Akbe from this trance or imprisoning spell and restored him his strength. He gave her the half of the Ring of Peace that remained to him. (From her it passed through her descendants for over five hundred years to the last heirs of Thoreg, a brother and sister exiled on a deserted island of the East Reach; and the sister gave it to Ged.) Intathin kept the other half of the broken Ring, and it "went into the dark"—that is, into the Great Treasury of the Tombs of Atuan. (There Ged found it, and rejoining the two halves and with them the lost Rune of Peace, he and Tenar brought the Ring home to Havnor.)

The Kargish version of the story, told as a sacred recital by the priesthood, says that Intathin defeated Erreth-Akbe, who "lost his staff and amulet and power" and crept back to Havnor a broken man. But wizards carried no staff in those years, and Erreth-Akbe certainly was an unbroken man and a powerful mage when he faced the dragon Orm.

King Maharion sought peace and never found it. While Erreth-Akbe was in Karego-At (which may have been a period of years), the depredations of the dragons increased. The Inward Isles were troubled by refugees fleeing the western lands and by interruptions to shipping and trade, since the dragons had taken to setting fire to boats that went west of Hosk, and harried ships even in the Inmost Sea. All the wizards and armed men Maharion could command went out to fight the dragons, and he went with them himself four times; but swords and arrows were little use against armored, fire-spouting, flying enemies. Paln was "a plain of charcoal," and villages and towns in the west of Havnor had been burnt to the ground. The king's wizards had spell-caught and killed several dragons over the Pelnish Sea, which probably increased the dragons' ire. Just as Erreth-Akbe returned, the Great Dragon Orm flew to the City of Havnor and threatened the towers of the king's palace with fire.

Erreth-Akbe, sailing into the bay "with sails worn transparent by the eastern winds," could not pause to "embrace his heart's brother or greet his home." Taking dragon form himself, he flew to battle with Orm over Mount Onn. "Flame and fire in the midnight air" could be seen from the palace in Havnor. They flew north, Erreth-Akbe in pursuit. Over the sea near Taon, Orm turned again and this time wounded the mage so that he had to come down to earth and take his own form. He came, with the dragon now following him, to the Old Island, Éa, the first land Segoy raised from the sea. On that sacred and powerful soil, he and Orm met. Ceasing their battle, they spoke as equals, agreeing to end the enmity of their races.

Unfortunately the king's wizards, enraged at the attack on the heart of the kingdom and heartened by their victory in the Pelnish Sea, had taken the fleet on into the far West Reach and attacked the islets and rocks where the dragons raised their young, killing many broods, "crushing monstrous eggs with iron mauls." Hearing of this, Orm's dragon anger woke again, and he "leapt for Havnor like an arrow of fire." (Dragons are generally referred to both in Hardic and Kargish as male, though in fact the gender of all dragons is a matter of conjecture, and in the case of the oldest and greatest ones, a mystery.)

Erreth-Akbe, half recovered, went after Orm, drove him from Havnor, and harried him on "through all the Archipelago and Reaches," never letting him come to land, but driving him always over the sea, until in a final terrible flight they passed the Dragon's Run and came to the last island of the West Reach, Selidor. There, on the outer beach, both exhausted, they faced each other and fought, "talon and fire and word and sword," until:

> *their blood ran mingled, making the sand red.*
> *Their breath ceased. Their bodies by the loud sea*
> *lay entangled. They entered death's land together.*

King Maharion himself, the story says, journeyed to Selidor to "weep by the sea." He retrieved Erreth-Akbe's sword and set it atop the highest tower of his palace.

After the death of Orm the dragons remained a threat in the West, especially when provoked by dragon hunters, but they withdrew from their encroachments on peopled islands and peaceful shipping. Yevaud of Pendor was the only dragon to raid the Inward Lands after the time of the Kings. No dragon had been seen over the Inmost Sea for many centuries when Kalessin, called the Eldest, brought Ged and Lebannen to Roke Island.

Maharion died a few years after Erreth-Akbe, having seen no peace established, and much unrest and dissent within his kingdom. It was widely said that since the Ring of Peace was lost there could be no true king of Earthsea. Mortally wounded in battle against the rebel lord Gehis of the Havens, Maharion spoke a prophecy: *"He shall inherit my throne who has crossed the dark land living and come to the far shores of the day."*

THE DARK TIME, THE HAND, AND ROKE SCHOOL

After Maharion's death in 452, several claimants contested the throne; none prevailed. Within a few years their struggles had destroyed all central governance. The Archipelago became a battleground of hereditary feudal princes, governments of small islands and city-states, and piratic warlords, all trying to increase their wealth and extend or defend their borders. Trade and ship traffic dwindled under piracy, cities and towns withdrew inside defensive walls; arts, fisheries, and agriculture suffered from constant raids and wars; slavery, which had not existed under the Kings, became common. Magic was the primary weapon in forays and battles. Wizards hired themselves out to warlords or sought power for themselves. Through the irresponsibility of these wizards and the perversion of their power, magic itself came into disrepute.

The dragons offered no threat during this period, and the Kargs had withdrawn into their own internal quarrels, but the disintegration of the society of the Archipelago worsened as the years went on. Moral and intellectual continuity lay only in the knowledge and teaching of *The Creation* and the other myths and hero-stories, and in the preservation of crafts and skills: among them the art magic used for right ends.

The Hand, a loose-knit league or community concerned principally with the understanding and the ethical use and teaching of magic, was established by men and women on Roke Island about a hundred and fifty years after Maharion's death. Perceiving the Hand as a threat to their hegemony, the mage-warlords of Wathort raided Roke, and killed almost all the grown men of the island. But the Hand had already stretched out to other islands all around the Inmost Sea. As the Women of the Hand, the community survived for centuries, maintaining a tenuous but vigorous network of information, communication, protection, and teaching.

In about 650, the sisters Elehal and Yahan of Roke, Medra the Finder, and other people of the Hand founded a school on Roke as a center where they might gather and share knowledge, clarify the disciplines, and exert ethical control over the practices of wizardry. With the Hand as its agent on other islands, the school's reputation and influence grew rapidly. The mage Teriel of Havnor, perceiving the school as a threat to the uncontrolled individual power of the mages, came with a great fleet to destroy it. He was destroyed, and his fleet scattered.

This first victory went far to establish a reputation of invulnerability for the school on Roke.

Under Roke's steadily growing influence, wizardry was shaped into a coherent body of knowledge, its use increasingly controlled by moral and political purpose. Wizards trained at the school went to other islands of the Archipelago to work against warlords, pirates, and feuding nobles, preventing raids and forays, imposing penalties and settlements, enforcing boundaries, and protecting individuals, farms, towns, cities, and shipping, until social order was re-established. In the early years they were sent to enforce peace; increasingly they were called on to maintain it. While the throne in Havnor remained empty, for over two hundred years Roke School served effectively as the central government of the Archipelago.

The power of the Archmage of Roke was in many respects that of a king. Ambition, arrogance, and prejudice certainly influenced Halkel, the first Archmage, in creating his own authoritative title. Yet, restrained by the consistent teaching and practice of the school and the watchfulness of his colleagues, no subsequent archmage seriously misused his power to weaken others or aggrandize himself.

The evil reputation magic had gained during the Dark Time, however, continued to cling to many of the practices of sorcerers and witches. Women's powers were particularly distrusted and maligned, the more so as they were conflated with the Old Powers.

Throughout Earthsea, various springs, caves, hills, stones, and woods were and always had been sites of concentrated power and sacredness. All were locally feared or venerated; some were known far and wide.

Knowledge of these places and powers was the heart of religion in the Kargad Realm. In the Archipelago, the lore of the Old Powers was still part of the profound, common basis of thought and reverence. On all the islands, the arts mostly practiced by witches, such as midwifery, healing, animal husbandry, dousing, mining and metallurgy, planting and growing spells, love spells, and so on, often invoked or drew upon the Old Powers. But the learned wizards of Roke had generally come to distrust the ancient practices and made no appeal to the "Powers of the Mother." Only in Paln did wizards combine the two practices, in the arcane, esoteric, and reputedly dangerous Pelnish Lore.

Though like any power they could be perverted to evil use in the service of ambition (as was the Terrenon Stone in Osskil), the Old Powers were inherently sacral and pre-ethical. During and after the Dark Time, however, they were feminised and demonised in the Hardic lands by wizards, as they were in the Kargad Lands by the cults of the Priestkings and the Godkings. So by the eighth century, in the Inner Lands of the Archipelago, only village women kept up rituals and offerings at the old sites. They were despised or abused for doing so. Wizards kept clear of such places. On Roke, itself the center of the Old Powers in all Earthsea, the profoundest manifestations of those powers—Roke Knoll and the Immanent Grove—were never spoken of as such. Only the Patterners, who lived all their lives in the Grove, served to link human arts and acts to the older sacredness of the earth, reminding the wizards and mages that their power was not theirs, but lent to them.

HISTORY OF THE KARGAD LANDS

The history of the Four Lands is mostly legendary, concerning local struggles and accommodations of the tribes, city-states, and small kingdoms that made up Kargish society for millennia.

Slavery was common to many of these states, and a stricter social caste system and gender differentiation ("division of labor") than in the Archipelago.

Religion was a unifying element even among the most warlike tribes. There were hundreds of Truce Places on the Four Lands, where no warfare or dispute was permitted. Kargish religion was a domestic and community worship of the Old Powers, the chthonic or gaean forces manifest as spirits of place. They were worshiped at the site and at home altars with offerings of flowers, oil, food, dances, races, sacrifices, carvings, songs, music, and silence. Worship was both casual and ritual, private and communal. There was no priesthood; any adult could perform the ceremonies and teach children to do so. This ancient spiritual practice has continued, unofficially and sometimes in hiding, under the newer, institutional religions of the Twin Gods and the Godking.

Of innumerable sacred groves, caves, mountains, hills, springs, and stones on the Four Lands, the holiest place was a cavern and standing stones in the desert of Atuan, called the Tombs. It was a center of pilgrimage from the earliest recorded times, and the kings of Atuan and later of Hupun maintained a hostel there for all who came to worship.

Six to seven hundred years ago a sky-god religion began to spread across the islands, a development of the worship of the Twin Gods Atwah and Wuluah, originally heroes of a desert saga from Hur-at-Hur. A Sky Father was added as head of the pantheon, and a priestly caste developed to lead the rites. Without suppressing the worship of the Old Powers, the priests of the Twin Gods and the Sky Father began to professionalise religion, managing the rituals and festivals, building increasingly costly temples, and controlling public ceremonies such as marriages, funerals, and the installation of officials.

The hierarchic and centralising tendency of this religion lent support at first to the ambition of the Kings of Hupun on Karego-At. By force of arms and diplomatic maneuvering, the House of Hupun within a century or so conquered or absorbed most of the other Kargad kingdoms, of which there had been more than two hundred.

When (in the year 440, by Hardic count) Erreth-Akbe came to make peace between the Archipelago and the Kargad Lands, bearing the Bond Ring as pledge of his king's sincerity, he came to Hupun as the capital of the Kargad Empire and treated with King Thoreg as its ruler.

But for some decades the kings of Hupun had been in conflict with the high priest and his followers in Awabath, the Holy City, fifty miles from Hupun. The priests of the Twin Gods were in the process of wresting power from the kings and making Awabath not only the religious but the political center of the country. Erreth-Akbe's visit seems to have coincided with the final shift of power from the kings to the priests. King Thoreg received him with honor, but Intathin the High Priest fought with him, defeated or deceived him, and for a time imprisoned him. The Ring that was to bond the two kingdoms was broken.

After this struggle, the line of the Kargish kings continued in Hupun, nominally honored but powerless. The Four Lands were governed from Awabath. The high priests of the Twin Gods became Priestkings.

In the year 840 of the Archipelagan count, one of the two Priest-kings poisoned the other and declared himself to be the incarnation of the Sky Father, the Godking, to be worshiped in the flesh. Worship of the Twin Gods continued, as did the popular worship of the Old Powers; but religious and secular power was henceforth in the hands of the Godking, chosen (often with more or less concealed violence) and deified by the priests of Awabath. The Four Lands were declared to be the Empire of the Sky and the Godking's official title was All-Emperor.

The last heirs of the House of Hupun were a boy and girl, Ensar and Anthil. Wishing to end the line of the Kargish kings but unwilling to risk sacrilege by shedding royal blood, the Godking ordered these children to be stranded on a desert island. Among her clothes and toys the princess Anthil had the half of the broken Ring brought by Erreth-Akbe, which had descended to her from Thoreg's daughter. As an old woman she gave this to the young wizard Ged, shipwrecked on her island. Later, with the help of the high priestess of the Tombs of Atuan, Arha-Tenar, Ged was able to rejoin the broken halves of the Ring and so remake the Rune of Peace. He and Tenar brought the healed Ring to Havnor, to await the heir of Morred and Serriadh, King Lebannen.

Magic

Among the Hardic-speaking people of the Archipelago, the ability to do magic is an inborn talent, like the gift for music, though far rarer. Most people lack it entirely. In a few people, perhaps one in a hundred, it is a latent, cultivable talent. In a very few people it is manifest without training.

The gift for magic is empowered mainly by the use of the True Speech, the Language of the Making, in which the name of a thing is the thing.

This speech, innate to dragons, can be learned by human beings. Some few people are born with an untaught knowledge of at least some words of the Language of the Making. The teaching of it is the heart of the teaching of magic.

The true name of a person is a word in the True Speech. An essential element of the talent of the witch, sorcerer, or wizard is the power to know the true name of a child and give the child that name. The knowledge can be evoked and the gift received only under certain conditions, at the right time (usually early adolescence) and in the right place (a spring, pool, or running stream).

Since the name of the person is the person, in the most literal and absolute sense, anyone who knows it has real power, power of life and death, over the person. Often a true name is never known to anybody but the giver and to the owner, who both keep it secret all their life. The power to give the true name and the imperative to keep it secret are one. True names have been betrayed, but never by the name giver.

Some people of great innate and trained power are able to find out the true name of another, or even to have it come to them unsought. Since such knowledge can be betrayed or misused, it is immensely dangerous. Ordinary people—and dragons—keep their true name secret; wizards hide and defend theirs with spells. Morred could not even begin to fight his Enemy until he saw his Enemy's name written in the dust by the falling rain. Ged could force the dragon Yevaud to obey him, having by both wizardry and scholarship discovered Yevaud's true name under centuries of false ones.

Magic was a wild talent before the time of Morred, who as both king and mage established intellectual and moral discipline for the art magic, gathering wizards to work together at the court for the general good and to study the ethical bases and constraints of their practice.

This harmony generally prevailed through the reign of Maharion. In the Dark Time, with no control over wizardly powers and widespread misuse of them, magic came into general disrepute.

THE SCHOOL ON ROKE

The school was founded in about 650, as described above. The Nine Masters or master-teachers of Roke were originally:

Windkey, master of the spells controlling weather
Hand, master of all illusions
Herbal, master of the arts of healing
Changer, master of the spells that transform matter and bodies
Summoner, master of the spells that call the spirits of the living and the dead
Namer, master of the knowledge of the True Speech
Patterner, dweller in the Immanent Grove, master of meaning and intent
Finder, master of the spells of finding, binding, and returning
Doorkeeper, master of the entering and leaving of the Great House

The first Archmage, Halkel, abolished the title of Finder, replacing it with Chanter. The Chanter's task is the preservation and teaching of all the oral deeds, lays, songs, etc., and the sung spells.

The original loose, roughly descriptive use of the words *witch, sorcerer, wizard,* was codified into a strict hierarchy by Halkel. Under his rules:

Witchery was restricted to women. All magic practiced by women was called "base craft," even when it included practices otherwise called "high arts," such as healing, chanting, changing, etc. Witches were to learn only from one another or from sorcerers. They were forbidden to enter Roke School, and Halkel discouraged wizards from teaching women anything at all. He specifically forbade the teaching of any word of the True Speech to women, and though this proscription was widely ignored, it led in the long run to a profound, long-lasting loss of knowledge and power among the women who practiced magic.

Sorcery was practiced by men—its only real distinction from witchery. Sorcerers trained one another, and had some knowledge of the True Speech. Sorcery included both base crafts as defined by Halkel (finding, mending, dowsing, animal healing, etc.) and some high arts (human healing, chanting, weatherworking). A student who showed a gift for sorcery and was sent to Roke for training would first study the high arts of sorcery, and if successful in them might pursue his training in the art magic, especially in naming, summoning, and patterning, and so become a wizard.

A *wizard*, as Halkel defined the term, was a man who received his staff from a teacher, himself a wizard, who had taken special responsibility for his training. It was usually the Archmage who gave a student his staff and made him wizard. This kind of teaching and succession occurred elsewhere than Roke—notably on Paln—but the Masters of Roke came to regard with suspicion a student of anyone not trained on Roke.

Mage remained an essentially undefined term: a wizard of great power.

The name and office of *archmage* were invented by Halkel, and the Archmage of Roke was a tenth Master, never counted among the Nine. A vital ethical and intellectual force, the archmage also exerted considerable political power. On the whole this power was used benevolently. Maintaining Roke as a strong centralising, normalising, pacific element in Archipelagan society, the archmages sent out sorcerers and wizards trained to understand the ethical practice of magic and to protect communities from drought, plague, invaders, dragons, and the unscrupulous use of their art.

Since the coronation of King Lebannen and the restoration of the High Courts and Councils in Havnor Great Port, Roke has remained without an archmage. It appears that this office, not originally part of the governance of the school or of the Archipelago, is no longer useful

or appropriate, and that Ged, whom many call the greatest of the archmages, may have been the last.

CELIBACY AND WIZARDRY

Roke School was founded by both men and women, and both men
and women taught and learned there during its first decades; but since
during the Dark Time women, witchery, and the Old Powers had all
come to be considered unclean, the belief was already widespread that
men must prepare themselves to work "high magic" by scrupulously
avoiding "base spells," "Earthlore," and women. A man unwilling to put
himself under the iron control of a spell of chastity could never practice the high arts. He could be no more than a common sorcerer. Male
wizards thus had come to avoid women, refusing to teach them or
learn from them. Witches, who almost universally went on working
magic without giving up their sexuality, were described by celibate men
as temptresses, unclean, defiling, essentially wicked.

When in 730 the first Archmage of Roke, Halkel of Way, excluded
women from the school, among his Nine Masters only the Patterner
and the Doorkeeper protested; they were overruled. For more than
three centuries, no woman taught or studied at the school on Roke.
During those centuries, wizardry was an honored art, conferring status
and power, while witchery was an unclean and ignorant superstition,
practiced by women, paid for by peasants.

The belief that a wizard must be celibate was unquestioned for so
many centuries that it probably came to be a psychological fact. Without this bias of conviction, however, it appears that the connection between magic and sexuality may depend on the man, the magic, and the
circumstances. There is no doubt that so great a mage as Morred was a
husband and father.

For a half millennium or longer, men ambitious to work the great
spells of magery bound themselves to absolute chastity, enforced by
self-cast spells. At the school on Roke, the students lived under this

spell of chastity from the time they entered the Great House and, if they became wizards, for the rest of their lives.

Among sorcerers, few are strictly celibate, and many marry and bring up a family.

Women who work magic may practice periods of celibacy as well as fasting and other disciplines believed to purify and concentrate power; but most witches lead active sexual lives, having more freedom than most village women and less need to fear abuse. Many pledge "witch-troth" with another witch or an ordinary woman. They do not often marry men, and if they do, they are likely to choose a sorcerer.

EARTHSEA

Hogen Land

Borth
Udrath
Rogmy

Miles

25 50 100   200   300

Osskil

Sorresk
Gut of Osskil
Osskil

Norst
The Gravels
Toop
The Enlades
Sea

Ebosskil

Hille

Mt Andanden
Semel
Taon
Sea of

Derhemen
Narveduen
Paln
Bishi
Ebishi
Besu

Havnor

Onon
Gmet
Faliern

Selidor
Lasso
Mt

Gate of
Selidor
Ully
Eppaln
South
Port

Risk
Usidero
The Pelnish Sea
Omer
Ar

The Dragons' Run
Ettil
Seppish
Toming
Hosk

Ingat
The Toringates
Ontuego
Low
Toming
The Inmost
Sea

Pendor
The
Nine
Isles
Drag-
gan
Roke

The West Reach
Kaltuel
Geath
Thwil
Town

Arrins
Serd

Near
Kaltuel
Faltuel
Pody
Horth

Simly
Ensmer
Wathort

Obb

Jessage
The Sand Isles

Lorbanery
Rood

Obehol

The South Reach
Toom

The Long Dune
Wellogy
Far
Sorr